NUMBER
10

Books by **CJ Daugherty**

Night School
Night School Legacy
Night School Fracture
Night School Resistance
Night School Endgame
Night School The Short Stories
The Secret Fire
The Secret City
Number 10
Codename Firefly

As **Christi Daugherty**

The Echo Killing
A Beautiful Corpse
Revolver Road

NUMBER 10

C J DAUGHERTY

**BEWARE THE
ENEMY WITHIN**

Published by Moonflower Publishing Ltd.
www.MoonflowerBooks.co.uk

1st Edition

ISBN: 978-1919618722

Moonflower Publishing Registered Office: 303 The Pillbox, 115 Coventry Road, London E2 6GG

MOONFLOWER

'It is better to light a candle
than curse the darkness.'

ELEANOR ROOSEVELT

'When you light a candle,
you also cast a shadow.'

URSULA LE GUIN

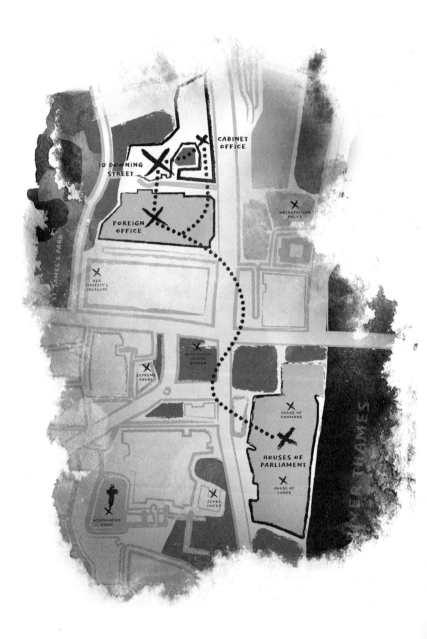

ONE

'Want to do some shots?'

Gray could barely hear Chloe's question above the bass thumping from the speakers.

It was nearly midnight and the Bijou nightclub was in full swing. Lights spun and collided around them – purple, blue, yellow, green – and then whirled away, dizzyingly. The effect was so blinding that she had to squint to see the small, glittering glasses Chloe held.

Taking one, Gray peered at the clear liquid inside.

'What happened to the punch?' she asked, nearly shouting to be heard over the music.

There'd been some fruity punch around earlier – a technicolor concoction of juice so tooth-achingly sweet it was hard to detect the alcohol in it.

'This's all I could get.' Chloe slurred her words slightly as she leaned closer so Gray could hear her.

She didn't have to explain. They were underage, which meant they had to rely on older clubbers to buy their drinks.

Raising the glass, Gray sniffed the contents, wrinkling her nose at the sharp, astringent smell. 'What is it?'

'Dunno. Vodka, maybe?' Chloe's shrug told her how little she cared. 'Everyone else is drinking it so it must be fine.'

'Are you doing shots?' The Bolino twins walked up, with Aidan in tow, grinning at the two girls. 'Down in one!'

They were all here for Aidan's birthday – his dad owned the Bijou, and had arranged for everyone to get in regardless of age, as long as they promised not to drink alcohol. It was one of the trendiest clubs in London right now for the younger set, so this was the party of the year. It seemed like half the school had lied to their parents and come here tonight. From the moment Gray had heard about it, the whole thing had seemed exciting and illicit. She and Chloe had spent a week deciding what to wear, settling on skin-tight minidresses in silver (Chloe) and blue (Gray), paired with terrifyingly high heels. Gray could hardly walk, but she thought she looked at least eighteen, if not older.

There was no way her mother would have given her permission, so she'd used the oldest trick in the book, saying that she was spending the night at Chloe's. Meanwhile, Chloe's mother thought they were at Aidan's.

The lies only made it more exciting. They'd both been on a high from the moment they'd arrived to find their classmates similarly buzzing. Earlier, they'd all sung happy birthday to Aidan and danced around him as he turned the same russet colour as his freckles.

Now, though, it was getting late. Gray was tired. She'd borrowed high heels from Chloe and her feet hurt. She was also starting to feel a bit queasy. Their plan for the night had not included food and right now she was regretting that.

Chloe had no such concerns. Holding up her shot glass, she shook it until the liquid sloshed. 'Come on, Gray,' she cajoled. 'We're here to have fun.'

'Yeah,' Tom Bolino said, nudging her. 'Don't be a buzz kill.'

'I *am* having fun,' Gray insisted. 'I just don't want to drink mystery booze and wake up to everyone saying, "Why on earth did she drink that? She didn't even know what it was. Now, she's in a coma. What an idiot."'

'This is the *Bijou*.' Chloe said it as if this fact were emphatic evidence of safety. 'It's something like vodka. It's not *toxic*.' She swung an arm to take in the room, crowded with sweating dancers, gyrating under the strobing lights. 'Everyone here isn't going to wake up in a coma.'

'My dad's club is safe,' Aidan agreed, taking unexpected offence.

Gray bit back an argument about how people get their drinks tampered with in nice places all the time. There was a lot she could have said but the music was too loud and nobody was in the mood to listen. So all she said was, 'I just don't think so.'

Chloe shrugged. 'Well, I'm not wasting this.' She raised her glass, smiling. 'To better grades. And wilder parties.'

The boys cheered as she downed the shot. She winced at the taste but as soon as she finished, she laughed, slamming the little glass down on the sticky table next to them.

'That was *awesome*.'

Closing her eyes, she began weaving to the music, which was so loud Gray could feel the beat of it in her chest. Chloe's glossy dark curls shimmered in the magenta lights, and her body moved sinuously.

Across the room, Gray saw a group of men nudge each other and point at her, hunger in their grins.

Standing abruptly, she angled herself until she blocked her friend from their view. Misunderstanding this move, Chloe beamed at her and gestured at the glass Gray had almost forgotten she was holding.

'Come on,' Chloe said, slurring her words slightly. 'I haven't died yet so it must be safe.'

The boys laughed.

'Yeah, come on Langtry. We're all still alive,' Tyler Bolino goaded. 'Don't be so boring.'

That stung. Gray never wanted to be boring. Her mother was boring. Her stepdad was boring. She was nothing like them.

"Fine," she said.

Just as she raised the glass though, Jake McIntyre walked out of the fog of fake smoke billowing across the dance floor. Gray froze, the glass hovering in front of her lips.

In jeans and a dark shirt, he looked as cool and bored as ever, surveying the room with an air of disapproval. He was too thin. Too arrogant. And so stuck on himself.

When his eyes found her, she saw his gaze flick to her shot glass. His left eyebrow lifted.

Heat rose Gray's face. Without thinking, she hastily lowered her drink. Instantly, she regretted it.

He was always doing this. Giving her superior looks. He was always looking for ways to make her feel like an idiot. He wasn't going to decide what she did tonight.

Defiantly, she turned to Chloe.

'To wild parties,' she said, and threw her head back to down the drink. The others cheered as she slammed the glass down on the table next to Chloe's.

It wasn't vodka. It had a strong liquorice flavour that made her stomach burn.

She coughed, her eyes streaming. Her throat felt like it was on fire. Before she could recover, the music changed. Chloe gave an excited scream. 'I love this song!'

Grabbing Gray's arm, she dragged her to the dance floor, where a hundred other bodies were already bouncing to the beat. Surrounded by laughing, gyrating young people, with the beat all around, Gray suddenly did want to dance, and she held Chloe's hand, laughing as they moved to the music. Tyler and Tom had followed them to the floor, and they all danced in a circle.

Out of the corner of her eye, Gray noticed Jake walk over and stand next to Aidan, who offered him one of the shot glasses. Jake shook his head. Shrugging, Aidan downed the shot and then ran out to dance. Jake stayed where he was, watching them with a frown.

Conscious of his gaze, Gray threw herself into dancing. The powdery fog rose around her. Her body felt light and lithe. She was part of the music. She whirled easily, soon oblivious to whether anyone was watching.

Chloe's face was damp with perspiration as she gyrated, singing the words of the song aloud. Closing her eyes, Gray raised her arms above her head, letting the music take her. Letting herself be free.

Ten minutes later, though, the music abandoned her. Her lips were dry, and her head was woozy. Her stomach didn't feel right.

'What's wrong?' Chloe shouted over the noise. 'You look weird.'

'Feel a bit sick,' Gray said and immediately wished she hadn't. Talking about it made it worse.

'Let's get some air.' Chloe grabbed her hand and led her across the bar.

Strands of hair clung unpleasantly to Gray's face as they made their way through the crowds, towards the exit. Her stomach lurched with every step.

Maddeningly, Chloe didn't seem queasy at all. She just looked worried.

It was quieter as they neared the door, and noticeably cooler. Wiping the sweat from her face, Gray took deep breaths, trying to steady her stomach. Her mouth felt Sahara dry.

'Need somethin' to drink,' she muttered.

She barely noticed when Chloe disappeared for a minute, returning with a bottle of beer that she shoved into Gray's hand. 'Drink this. You'll feel better.'

It didn't seem like great advice.

'I need water,' Gray insisted.

'The bartender wouldn't give me any. He said he only sold it in bottles and I couldn't buy anything because I'm underage. Tyler gave me this. He thought it would help.'

Gray wasn't going to drink any more alcohol. The cold bottle felt good against her overheated skin, though, and she held it up to her face, pressing the glass against her cheek.

'Gray.' Jake's northern accented voice was unmistakable.

She spun around to see him a few feet away, his expression dripping disapproval.

'What do you want?' she asked.

His brows furrowing, he glanced from the bottle in her hand back to her face. 'Maybe you should go easy on that. You don't look so great.'

This was insulting on multiple levels. But before Gray could think of a devastating reply, Chloe stepped between them, bristling.

'Why don't you mind your own business, Jake?' she asked. 'You're always messing with Gray. Giving her looks. It's so obvious you're jealous of her. It's ridiculous.'

Even in heels she was so tiny she had to stand on her toes to bring her face to the same level as his. She looked like a really angry butterfly. He gazed at her with cool, infuriating detachment.

'I'm just trying to help.'

Chloe, fuelled by alcohol and a determination to protect Gray, wasn't backing down.

'She doesn't need your help. You're always picking on her. Why don't you get over it?'

Jake's lips tightened, and he turned to Gray. 'Look,' he said steadily, 'I'm not trying to insult you or anything. But you don't want to get drunk here. There are too many people watching. Too many eyes.'

Maybe on a different night she would have taken this advice differently. Right now, it made her furious. He was so patronising.

Ignoring the churning in her stomach, she threw him an imperious look.

'Thanks for your concern. But I'm perfectly able to decide how much I want to drink.'

For a second, he held her gaze, and she thought he'd argue. But then, shaking his head, he walked away. As Gray watched, one hand on her unruly stomach, he paused at the coat check to retrieve his jacket, and then, without looking back, disappeared out of the wide glass door.

A cool autumnal breeze flowed in as he departed. It felt good against Gray's hot skin. When the door closed, the damp heat returned.

Gray's stomach flipped. She covered her mouth with her fingers.

'He's so arrogant.' Chloe was still fuming, but as soon as she saw Gray's face, her anger faded. 'Is it worse?'

15

Mutely, Gray nodded. 'Have to go home,' she said, thickly. 'Gonna be sick.'

She didn't trust herself to say more, and Chloe must have seen the seriousness of the situation in her face, because her only reply was, 'I'll get our coats.'

Gray leaned against the wall as Chloe ran to the cloakroom and handed over the small white ticket. A minute later she came rushing back, clutching their jackets, which they'd checked together at the beginning of the night, when everything was so exciting.

But Gray couldn't wait for her coat. She needed air. Now.

The bouncer stepped aside with a wary look as she bolted, her borrowed high heels skidding on the cement. Under the black and white awning with the illuminated word 'BIJOU' in magenta neon, she paused for a split second.

Then she took two steps to the right and vomited into the base of a giant potted palm tree.

'Gray!' Chloe ran to her.

'She can't be sick there,' the bouncer objected.

Pulling Gray's hair back, Chloe fired a glare at him over her shoulder. 'Leave her alone.'

The two of them argued across Gray's back as the sickness slowly subsided and Gray began to straighten, wiping her mouth with the back of her hand.

What happened next happened fast.

'Bloody hell, is that Gray Langtry?' A male voice came from a few feet away.

'That's her!' Another man responded.

A blinding series of flashes lit up the night. The *rat-a-tat-tat* of camera clicks came from everywhere, like weapons being fired at them.

Chloe gasped and stumbled back as voices barraged them.

'How are you feeling, Gray?' An adult male voice with an Essex accent taunted her. 'Bit tired and emotional?'

'Who's your friend? What's your name, sweet 'eart?'

'Had a bit too much to drink, love?'

Flash. Flash. Flash.

Blinded by the camera flashbulbs, Gray couldn't see the men, but she knew instantly who they were. *What* they were.

Her heart sank.

'Does your mother know you're drinking?' the first man asked. The others laughed.

'You're underage, young lady,' one of them said. 'I should take you over my knee.'

Through it all, the flashes lit up the night.

'Gray.' Chloe's voice sounded strange – high and nervous; her hand gripped Gray's fingers hard. 'What do we do?'

Desperate, Gray looked for escape. Behind them, the black-clad bouncer stood blocking the doorway, his arms crossed impassively. They couldn't go back in to their friends.

Behind the paparazzi, London's Park Lane was busy with late evening traffic.

Gray looked at Chloe.

'Run,' she said.

TWO

Clutching each other's hands, the two girls stumbled into the night.

Gray was still blinded by the flashes – through the spots swimming in front of her eyes, she saw four burly men clutching cameras. They stretched across the pavement, shoulder-to-shoulder, a human roadblock.

They were laughing, firing off shots like bullets.

Using her elbows, she slammed between them, pulling Chloe with her. It was like pushing past boulders.

The men kept laughing, but they gave way, letting the girls through.

Heads down, hands covering their faces, the two of them raced down the street in their heels. Behind them, Gray could hear the heavy thud of the men's footsteps as they followed, cameras flashing like tiny bomb blasts.

'Come on, Gray!' one of them shouted. 'Give us a smile.'

Neither of the girls felt like smiling.

Even in heels, they were faster than out-of-shape, middle-aged photographers, and gradually the voices faded in the distance.

The men were still laughing as they dropped behind.

'It doesn't matter,' one of them taunted. 'We got what we need.'

Finally, the noise of the city rose around them and Gray couldn't hear them anymore.

She kept running, hurtling down Park Lane, its trendy hotels and restaurants blurring at the side of her vision, until Chloe tripped on an uneven paving stone and fell to one knee, her hand slipping free of Gray's.

'Chloe!' Gray spun around, breathless and scared. 'Are you OK?'

Chloe didn't answer. She stayed on her hands and knees, their jackets pooled around her.

Gray knelt beside her. 'Are you hurt?'

'I'm fine.' When Chloe looked up, though, her cheeks were damp. Eyeliner was smudged under her eyes. She looked scared. 'Help me up? These heels…'

Gray pulled her to her feet with too much force and the two of them stumbled, clutching each other. A well-dressed couple walking by stared at them with open disapproval.

Feeling raw and exposed, Gray turned her face away.

She should have expected all of this. Bijou – popular with young royals and television celebrities – was often in the tabloids. Besides, this wasn't the first time Gray had been targeted by the paparazzi. Things had been pretty bad right after the election. Back then, photographers had showed up everywhere – outside her school, at the coffeeshop where the kids from her school went after class.

After a tabloid posted a picture of her walking into school with the headline, 'PM's Teen Rocks Uber Short Skirt' her mother had filed a formal press complaint. There'd been tense meetings with newspaper publishers and, for a while, they'd backed off. She'd believed the worst was over. She'd let her guard down.

The alcohol buzz had completely evaporated now. Gray felt clear-headed, tired and bone cold. Scooping her jacket off the pavement, she handed Chloe hers.

'We have to get going,' she said. 'They might follow us.'

'We can't run far in these heels.' Chloe's teeth chattered and she pulled the jacket tightly across her chest. She looked around desperately. 'We need a cab or something.'

But there were no free cabs. Gray pulled out her phone to check for an Uber, but there was a 15 minute wait. It was midnight on a Thursday night. All the central London pubs were emptying. Gray couldn't stand on a street corner a few blocks from Bijou waiting for the photographers to find them while she tried to flag down a cab.

A block away, a red double-decker bus rumbled up to a stop. The interior looked safe. And warm. She made an instant decision.

'Let's get on that bus,' she said, pointing. 'Then we'll figure it out.'

It was a relief to find the bus mostly empty. A young couple sat at the front, talking quietly in a language she didn't recognise. An older man sat a few rows away, staring out of the window.

Chloe swiped her bus pass. Gray, who didn't have one, stayed close to her and hoped no one would notice her.

A few men clustered near the front door eyed the girls. Several of them were clutching cans of beer.

NUMBER 10

'Alright, darlin'?' one of them said, and the others snickered.

Keeping her head down, Gray held firmly onto Chloe's arm until they found a seat near the back. Only when the bus pulled away from the stop, did she feel like she could breathe. Twisting around, she looked back towards the club. There was no sign of the photographers.

'Where are we going?' Chloe asked, frowning. She glanced out of the window as the bus turned down an unfamiliar street.

'I don't know.' Gray swallowed hard. 'I think I'd better call my mum.'

Chloe's eyes widened. 'Are you sure? She thinks you're at my place.'

'She's going to find out when she reads the papers tomorrow, anyway.' Gray glanced down the bus. The men were still staring at them. 'Besides, this isn't safe.'

Chloe followed her eyes and said, 'Yeah, call her. Those guys might recognise you.'

At least Gray had never put her bag down at the club. It still hung from her shoulder on a slim gold chain. There wasn't much in it – no keys were necessary where she lived. Just a lipstick and powder, a twenty-pound note, and her phone.

Her fingers were still too cold to work properly, and she fumbled as she dialled the number for the mobile nobody knew her mother had.

It rang twice, before her mother answered. 'Gray? What's wrong?'

At the sound of her voice, all of Gray's bravery fell away. Tears burned her eyes.

'I need help.' Her voice quivered. 'Chloe and I went to a party at Aidan's dad's club and these photographers showed up. They chased us down the street. It was really scary.'

To her mother's credit, she absorbed this unexpected avalanche of information quickly. 'Are they following you now?' she asked sharply. 'Where are you?'

'I'm with Chloe. We're on a bus going … somewhere.' Her voice broke, and she shielded her eyes with one hand, whispering, 'There are men staring at me. I just want to come home.'

'Don't you worry. I'm getting you out of there.' Her voice was crisp and efficient. Gray recognised this as her 'fixing things' tone. Usually it bugged her. Right now, it made her feel better.

Across the bus she heard one of the men say, 'Oh look. She's crying. I should give her a cuddle.'

They had to be at least thirty. Why were men so disgusting?

Her mother's voice pulled her back. 'Gray, I need to call security on my other line, but I'm right here. I'm not leaving you, OK? Don't hang up.'

'OK.'

Chloe looked at Gray questioningly.

'She's getting help.' Gray pointed at the window next to them. 'Try to figure out where we are.'

Obediently, Chloe leaned over to press her face against the glass, shielding her eyes with her hands.

A minute later, her mother was back on the line.

'I'm patching someone through who can help you, Gray. He needs to ask you a few questions. But I'm not going away. I'll be right here.'

A series of clicks followed, and then a deep male voice spoke. 'Gray? This is Raj Patel. I handle security for your mother. First, are you safe right now?'

He had the same northern accent as Jake and, although his words were urgent, there was something calming in his voice that made Gray's panic recede.

'We're safe,' she said. 'We caught a bus.'

'Which bus is it? Did you see the number?'

'It's the 704.'

'Good,' he said. 'Do you know where the bus is right now?'

Gray tapped Chloe's arm. 'Where are we?'

Chloe turned from the window and said, 'Culross Street.'

Gray relayed this to Raj, who said, 'Good. Now, I need you to sit tight. Try not to draw attention to yourself. But, and this is important – under no circumstances are you to get off that bus with anyone until you see a badge and hear them say my name. Am I clear?'

The seriousness in his voice was unmistakeable. He wasn't messing around. Panic flared in Gray's chest. Nothing like this had happened since her mother took office. She'd never needed to be rescued.

'Completely clear,' she told him.

'How much battery have you got on your phone?'

Gray turned it to check. 'Twenty per cent.'

'We need to save that in case something goes wrong,' he said. 'When I leave the line, I'm going to ask your mum to hang up, but I need you to keep your phone turned on.'

After a few more instructions, he left the conversation. When he'd gone Gray squeezed the phone tightly. She could hear her mother breathing.

'Mum,' she said softly, 'I'm sorry.'

'Don't worry about that right now,' her mother told her. 'Now, I have to hang up. Raj wants you to save your battery. But,

I want you to promise to call me if you need me. Phone battery or not.'

'OK.' Gray heard her own voice, small and frightened.

'And please, Gray,' her mother said, 'stay safe.'

After she'd hung up, Gray kept her head down, not meeting anyone's eyes. She and Chloe were talking in whispers, looking out of the window, when a man dropped into the seat in front of them and grinned at them wolfishly.

She recognised his thick brown hair and pale blue button-down shirt – he was the one who'd said he would 'cuddle' her. She repressed a shudder.

'I thought we should get to know each other.' He leaned forward, openly examining Chloe's figure. 'Since we're gonna be friends, like.'

From the front of the bus, the other men laughed and hooted.

'They can't resist,' one of them said, pounding another on the shoulder.

Gray wanted to tell him where he could go but she couldn't risk being recognised right now. She kept her gaze down and said nothing. Taking the lead, Chloe leaned forward. 'Look, can't you leave us alone? We're just going home.'

His mouth twisted. 'Why do you have to be like that, huh?' A new, ugly tone entered his voice. 'I'm just trying to be nice. Is that a crime? Why can't you be nice, too?'

Gray covered her mouth with one hand. She didn't know what to do. Things would get so much worse if he recognised her. But her actions only seemed to draw his attention.

'Hang on,' he said, eyes fixed on her. 'Don't I know you from somewhere?'

She could almost hear his drunken brain working. Trying to place her. She needed to get rid of him before he put the pieces together.

'You don't know her,' Chloe said, icily. 'By the way, she's sixteen years old. How old are you?'

For an instant, he looked startled. But he quickly recovered. 'Sixteen's old enough,' he said. 'It's legal.'

'You're disgusting.' Snatching Gray's phone from her hands, Chloe held it up. 'Anyway, we just called the police.'

'Oh, so that's how you're going to play it?' His lip curled. 'You think you're so pretty you can do whatever you want? I got news. Cops don't stop buses because pretty little girls get their knickers in a twist.'

Gray looked around for help but most of the other passengers were averting their faces from the drama. Only his friends were watching them, and baying with unpleasant laughter.

The man jabbed his finger at Gray. 'I know you're somebody. I seen your face before. You some model or something? Some singer? Is that why you think you're so hot you don't have to talk to people?'

Just out of his view, Chloe was gripping Gray's hand so tightly it hurt. Gray had begun to shake again – not from cold this time.

'I'm nobody,' she said, wishing it was true. 'I'm nobody.'

'Please, *please* leave us alone,' Chloe pleaded, still clinging to Gray. 'We just want to go home.'

'We just want to go home.' He made his voice high and mocking. 'You should try not being so arrogant. You're both up yourselves, you know that?'

He'd barely finished saying the words when a shriek of sirens filled the air. The driver braked so abruptly the vehicle swerved. Blue lights lit up the night.

'What the fu...' The man turned to see.

The other passengers murmured in concern, craning their necks to see what was going on.

Through the window Gray saw a motorcycle police officer pull in alongside the driver's window, motioning firmly for him to pull over.

The bus rolled to a stop.

Next to her, Gray heard Chloe whisper, 'Please, please, please...'

Everything grew quiet. The man who'd been harassing them was staring at the front of the bus, his mouth agape as the driver opened the door.

A man and a woman – both young and in dark suits – got in.

'Sorry to interrupt your journey,' the woman announced, with unexpected cheerfulness. She had blonde hair pulled back tightly and moved with athletic authority. 'Won't be a second.'

Her partner had been scanning the passengers as she spoke. He said something to her, and pointed to where Gray and Chloe were huddled at the back.

The two strode towards them. The woman reached them first.

'Gray, Chloe?'

They nodded hard.

The woman's gaze flicked to the man who was staring at her, open-mouthed. Gray saw her assess the situation in an instant. 'Is he bothering you?'

They both nodded again, harder.

Turning to him, the woman held out a small black wallet and flipped it open. A silver badge gleamed in the bright light.

'Get lost,' she told him. 'Or go to jail. Your choice.'

Scrambling to his feet, he bolted down the aisle to join his friends, who were no longer laughing.

The woman turned back to Gray.

She had dark blue eyes and an indomitable expression that said she wasn't someone to mess with.

'My name is Julia.' She pointed at the man. 'This is Ryan. Raj Patel sent us to get you. You're going home.'

THREE

Julia and Ryan hustled the girls out, Julia taking the lead, with Gray and Chloe close behind her. Ryan stayed a few steps back. The other passengers stared and whispered. Gray kept her face tilted down.

Outside, police motorcycles formed a loose circle around the bus, blue lights flashing.

The October night felt even colder now than it had earlier. Gray began to shiver again.

Ryan pointed to a dark four-door car. Julia was already opening the back door. Gray recognised it as the same make and model as all the government-issued cars she'd travelled in.

'This way,' he said.

Gray and Chloe didn't need any more of an invitation. They climbed into the back seat, grateful for the warmth. When she was settled, Gray leaned back against the headrest with a sigh of relief. Some of the tension left her shoulders. They were safe.

Julia took the driver's seat, and Ryan settled into the passenger side. While she started the engine, he picked up a radio. 'Unit C5,' he said. 'Firefly is secure.'

'Copy that, C5,' someone replied.

As soon as they pulled out onto the road, the motorcycles sped away, their blue lights flickering out one by one. Gray glanced back at the bus. In the glowing light, she could see the men near the front, watching them go with a look of slack-jawed puzzlement.

Julia met Gray's gaze in the narrow slice of rearview mirror. 'We're dropping Chloe off first. Then we'll take you home.'

Her brisk tone held no judgement, but Gray felt humiliated all the same. She knew the security team had better things to do than rescue her from drunks. She knew word would get around government about what had happened.

'Thanks,' she mumbled.

When the bodyguard's attention turned back to the front, Chloe leaned over to whisper, 'How mad will your mum be?'

Gray didn't sugarcoat it. 'I have a feeling that's my last party this year.'

After that, there didn't seem to be much to say. Her head had begun to thump, and her mouth was dry and sour. She stared out of the window in silence. Even at this hour, there were people everywhere. Walking, in cars, crossing the road, getting off buses. As she watched them go about their lives, it was hard to believe she had once been able to walk down the pavement like that without being recognised. Or chased. Or photographed. Or taunted.

That sort of anonymous life seemed like a hundred years ago.

It had been eight months.

When she'd got up that memorable Thursday morning, she'd been the child of a British politician – one of thousands. By eleven o'clock that night, she was the only daughter of a female prime minister.

That had been the end of everything. The end of coffee shops. The end of parties.

The end of normal.

Now, she lived her life in the back seats of four-door cars with blacked out windows, surrounded by security men in suits, too busy keeping her safe to speak to her. Everything she wanted to do was a problem. Hanging out with friends. Going shopping. Even walking to a pizza place was a huge issue.

Going to Aidan's party? That would be impossible, thanks for asking. Too hard to secure. Too many people.

So, she'd lied and sneaked around – anything to have some sort of normality. And now, that was going to be over too.

By the time the car stopped fifteen minutes later, Chloe was asleep with her head on Gray's shoulder. She shook her lightly to wake her up.

'Hey, we're here,' she said.

'Already?' Chloe mumbled, rubbing her eyes.

Ryan got out of the car and walked around to open her door.

As she unclipped her seatbelt, Chloe squeezed Gray's hands and said, 'I'll call you tomorrow.' She added, quietly, 'I hope your mum doesn't kill you.'

She got out, tugging her short skirt down as she thanked Ryan, before hurrying up the steps, her heels clicking on the stone.

They waited until she was inside, and then Julia started the engine again and they headed back to the main road. For the rest of the journey, Gray sat alone in the back seat, staring straight ahead, trying to decide how she was going to explain this to her mother.

Far too soon, the tall, spiked gates leading into Downing Street appeared in front of them. The police standing guard outside bristled with weaponry.

Rolling down her window, Julia showed her badge to an officer in black with a machine gun strapped across his chest. Glancing into the back seat, his eyes scanned her face without expression. Giving a curt nod, he stepped back and waved at the guard house behind him. The gate slid open with a shiver.

As the car passed onto the quiet, dark lane, Ryan pressed a button on his radio.

'Unit C5 at base,' he said. 'Firefly delivered.'

'Copy that,' the voice through the radio said. 'Good job, you two.'

At night, Downing Street looked like any other posh London street. Georgian townhouses lined one side, lit by old-fashioned cast iron lights. It looked perfectly ordinary.

But this was no ordinary road.

This was the most secure, monitored, and protected street in the country. The normal-looking front doors were a disguise. Behind them were huge office buildings, holding thousands of high-level government employees. Nothing here was what it seemed to be.

Julia stopped the car and cut the engine. Ryan got out and walked quickly to open Gray's door.

Popping off her seatbelt, Julia twisted around to look back at her. 'Home sweet home,' she said, cheerfully.

There was nothing sweet about it, but Gray wasn't about to get into that. 'Thank you very much for coming to get me,' she said. 'It was scarier than it looked.'

'I know,' Julia said, simply. 'And you're welcome.'

As she left the car, Gray felt drained, as if the night had taken all she had. She trudged towards the shiny black door with the number 10 mounted at the centre in gleaming, constantly polished, white. Gray still found it strange that there was no handle on the outside. No way to open the door if the people inside didn't want you.

But the door swung open before she could even think about knocking, as it always did. A guard wearing a Kevlar vest and white shirt sleeves stood back to let her pass into what looked much like a normal sitting room. Except that, behind him, two more guards sat at a small booth in front of a row of computer screens.

Their impassive faces betrayed no emotion as Gray trudged past, bedraggled and exhausted, longing for her bed.

'Good night, miss,' one of them said, as she headed down the corridor.

''Night,' she replied automatically.

The lights were always on downstairs so there was no need to flip a switch as she made her way across the black and white tiled floor, passing a grandfather clock and a heavy walnut cabinet with dozens of tiny cubbyholes. During the day, it held the mobile phones of everyone who visited the building. Right now, it was almost empty.

She followed the first corridor to the left, passing a grand, sweeping staircase without looking at it, and continuing on until she reached another, narrower set of stairs.

As she headed up, she kept her eyes on her feet. The white heels she'd borrowed from Chloe earlier that evening were dirty and battered. Everything she wore seemed tainted. It was hard to believe she'd been so happy earlier, in this dress.

On the landing, she walked down a shadowy corridor lit only by the dim glow of subtle wall sconces, and opened the first door she came to.

Her mother was still in her working-at-night clothes of neat black trousers and white blouse. As soon as Gray walked in, she ran to her.

'Oh, thank God.' She pulled her into a tight hug. 'You scared me to death.'

Despite the phone call earlier, this wasn't the greeting Gray had expected. The two of them had not been close lately and she was certain her actions tonight would have serious ramifications. But she welcomed the warmth. For a moment, she let herself be a normal daughter, hugging her mother back.

'Mum, I'm so sorry,' she whispered.

'I know.' Gripping her wrists firmly, her mother stepped back, her gaze sweeping her daughter's face. 'Raj told me you were fine, but I needed to see for myself.'

'Mum, I didn't know the photographers would be there. I don't know how they knew I'd be at the party…'

'They have ways of finding things out.' Gray's stepfather, Richard, walked in, holding a mug. 'They probably paid the bar staff – or one of your classmates – for information.'

Gray stiffened.

Of course, he was still up, too. He was always there whenever her mother had a moment free. Always getting between the two of them.

Handing her mother the steaming cup of tea, he told Gray, 'You must have had quite a scare.'

'Well,' she muttered, stepping back from the two of them, 'I'm fine.'

'What were you thinking, Gray?' her mother asked. 'Why would you go to that party without telling us? You said you were studying at Chloe's.'

Clearly, the moment of relief had passed. Now they could get straight to the anger she'd expected earlier.

'Chloe really wanted to go to Aidan's party. His dad owns the club, so I figured it would be safe. I thought we'd just be there an hour or so but…' Gray shrugged.

'But what?' Richard took a step towards her, inhaling sharply. 'Have you been drinking?'

'No.' She lied reflexively, without pausing to think about it. Then she remembered the photographers – the flashes of light as she threw up in the potted plant – and her shoulders slumped.

There was no point in lying. They'd find out soon enough anyway.

'Only a little,' she conceded.

'Oh, Gray.'

Seeing the disappointed look in her mother's eyes she insisted, 'Not much. There was some fruity punch. That was it.'

Her mother and Richard exchanged a look.

It was always like this. Ever since Richard had married her mother. They were a team. And Gray was on the outside.

'I'm not a child,' she reminded the two of them. 'I'm nearly seventeen years old. If I want to have a glass of punch at a party, I'm having it. Sue me.' She threw up her hands. 'I said I was sorry and I am. Thanks for helping me. I hope I didn't ruin your life. Now, I've got to get some sleep.'

Turning on her heel, she headed across the living room.

'Don't you dare walk out on me.'

Her mother's voice could make a room full of politicians freeze in their tracks but Gray didn't stop. A headache had begun hammering behind her eyes, and she felt exhausted.

Besides, she couldn't look at the two of them for one more minute and think about how badly she'd screwed up.

'I need to sleep,' she said, without turning back. 'Shout at me in the morning, OK?'

'This isn't over,' her mother said.

Gray gave a helpless shrug, and said, 'I know.'

FOUR

Through the open car window, Julia watched Gray trudge down the pavement, shoulders slumped, head down.

In her heels and that tiny dress, she'd clearly wanted to look older than she was. But the person she'd walked up to on the bus had been a scared kid.

'It took everything in me not to punch that guy,' she told her partner. 'No way did he think those girls were old enough for whatever he had in mind.'

Ryan shot her a sideways glance. 'I think it'll be a while before he tries something like that again.'

'He got off *lightly*.'

Hearing the heat in her voice, Ryan studied her curiously but asked no questions. Julia didn't offer any explanations. She was new on the security team, but he'd already gathered that she was prickly about personal questions.

He knew little about her aside from the fact that her background was military, and that she seemed tough, and driven. But driven by what?

Julia was still watching the kid, her expression thoughtful.

'I can't imagine being her,' she said. 'She can't go anywhere without being noticed. Harassed. It's got to be hard.'

Ryan made a dismissive sound. 'From what I hear, she's trouble. Partying hard. Evading her security team. Everyone says she's a handful.'

'Maybe she is.' Julia turned to face him. 'Can't say I blame her for it.'

Ryan's phone buzzed and he glanced at the screen. It was a message from Raj:

My office. Five minutes.

He glanced up at Julia. 'Boss wants to see us.'

She started the car.

They parked in a nondescript car park tucked away behind a grand government building. Julia dropped the keys off with the gate officer and followed Ryan through the door of a small brick building that overlooked the lush green expanse of St James's Park. From the top floor, if you stood on your toes, you could just make out the roof of Buckingham Palace. Despite the location, it was so ordinary in appearance that thousands of tourists walked by it every day without giving it a second glance.

That was typical of Talos Inc. It was one of the country's top security companies, providing discreet protection for billionaires, royalty and government officials.

Inside, the small lobby was brightly lit. An armed guard watched as, one at a time, Julia and Ryan pressed their fingertips against the small blue screens to open the bulletproof security gates.

Raj Patel, the owner and founder of the company, kept his office on the top floor. When Julia knocked, his familiar deep voice invited them in.

NUMBER 10

It wasn't a surprise to find him here at one in the morning. It was well known that he preferred to work nights.

He was at his desk, two laptops open in front of him. His office was spacious and sparsely decorated, with polished wood floors, and a large desk that he kept almost completely clear. One entire wall was covered in bookshelves, filled with large books and box files.

'Good. You're back.' He motioned to the two black leather chairs facing him. 'Take a seat.'

The security chief wasn't tall but he was sturdily built, with olive skin and dark hair and eyes. He was in his late 40s, although Julia had never spotted a single grey hair. His accent betrayed a childhood in the north of England.

She'd known him a long time. When she was a teenager, he'd worked at her school, but she'd lost touch with him after that.

When she'd turned nineteen, in defiance of her parents, she'd gone straight into the Army, specialising in Intelligence. When that ended, she hadn't known what to do with herself.

One day, though, Raj had called. 'I hear you're looking for work. I've a job you might like.'

She had no idea how he'd got hold of her number – or how he could possibly have known her situation. But she went to meet him, because she remembered him as a wise, thoughtful man who only worked with the best.

One week later, she was at a training camp, studying with the best security team in the country. After her training ended, she'd had her first job protecting a low-risk corporate executive. Last month, he'd given her a higher profile case involving a government official.

Tonight had been her biggest job yet. And it had gone perfectly.

Raj closed his laptops and studied them both across his desk.

'How'd it go?'

Before Julia could speak, Ryan answered for them both. 'Smooth. Bus driver gave us no problems. The girl was right where she said she'd be.'

Julia suppressed a flicker of irritation. This had been her first job with Ryan. She liked him okay, but found him a bit sure of himself.

'How is Firefly doing?' Raj glanced at Julia, as if he knew what she was thinking.

Firefly was Gray's security codename. Everyone in the residence at Number 10 had one.

'Scared,' she said, 'but fine.'

'Good.'

Raj never asked many questions after operations. He knew they'd file a written report by morning, and he expected it to be thorough.

'You worked well together tonight,' he told them. 'I'm going to keep you as a team for a while. I've got an assignment for you.' His expression was serious. 'We're hearing a lot of chatter through reliable channels about a new, Russia-backed organisation planning a targeted attack against the prime minister and her family. This threat is credible and very dangerous,' he continued. 'I will be personally involved in the prime minister's protection. I want the two of you to provide security for Firefly over the next few weeks as we look into this.'

Julia fought back a grin. This job did not get more important than providing security for the prime minister's family.

'Firefly is young and rebellious, and that makes her vulnerable to kidnapping,' Raj continued. 'After what happened tonight, we are enhancing her security.' He leaned forward, his gaze flicking between the two of them. 'We have to find a way to get through to her. To make her understand how dangerous the situation is, without scaring her to death. These threats against her and her mother are credible. The goal of this organisation is to create chaos. To make the government weak. Killing or taking the girl would accomplish that. They must not succeed.'

His words sent a prickle down Julia's spine. She'd never heard him sound more serious.

'They won't succeed,' she assured him. 'We won't let them.'

He gave her an approving look. 'That's what I wanted to hear. You are to be with her at all times when she's outside of Number 10. Accompanying her to school, and waiting there inside the building to bring her home after class. Making sure she doesn't slip away on her own again.' He glanced at Julia. 'You in particular, I think, could form a bond with her. She doesn't respond well to authority. You'll get more from her by building a friendship. Confide in her and earn her trust.'

Julia thought of the scared girl on the bus, huddled with her friend as if the night itself had become her enemy. She'd looked like she needed someone to talk to.

'I'll do my best,' she promised.

Raj turned to Ryan. 'Your experience will be invaluable on this job. Julia's new to the team and we're dealing with skilled Russian agents here. They'll know all our tricks. I expect you to anticipate theirs.'

Ryan raised his chin, his shoulders stiff. 'Count on it.'

'It should be an easy start,' Raj told them. 'Firefly won't be going anywhere except school and Number 10 for a while — her mother's going to be pretty cross about what happened tonight.

You can divide the duties as you want, but I want you both with her whenever she leaves the building.' From a file on his desk, Raj produced two plastic cards. 'These security passes give you access to Number 10 at any time, day or night.'

Julia glanced at hers. There was nothing on it except a thumbprint, a smart chip, and the word 'Talos'. But her heart leapt at the sight of it.

She was inside the highest echelon of government, working as security for the child of the prime minister. This was everything she'd dreamed of.

'Now, file your reports and then go home and get some rest,' Raj ordered, closing the folder. 'Be back in Number 10 by eight hundred hours to take her to school.'

As they stood, he added one last thing.

'Keep your eyes open, every day. This new group is very skilled. They will exploit any weakness in our security.' His face darkened. 'If they get their hands on her, she won't survive.'

FIVE

The paparazzi had been too late to make the early papers, but the internet never sleeps. By morning, the tabloid websites were filled with images of Gray and Chloe, looking panicked. And Gray, bent over that pot, puking her guts up.

'PM's Wildchild Daughter On Illegal Bender,' one headline gloated.

'Little Langtry On The Lash,' read another.

The worst one showed Gray staring wide-eyed into the lens, mascara ringing her blue eyes. That headline read: 'Does Your Mother Know You're Out?'

Gray scrolled through the images on her phone, her stomach churning.

She'd spent an uneasy night dreaming of flashing lights and mocking laughter. Sarcastic voices shouting, 'Look over 'ere, luv.' Her phone had buzzed just before 7 a.m. with a message from Chloe. All it said was:

I'm so sorry. Don't go online.

She lay in bed for a few minutes after that, but sleep was over. Besides, her head hurt and she needed food. She took a quick shower, her mind still on those hateful headlines. Everyone at school would see this. They would all know.

The family apartment inside Number 10 had an open-plan living area, with the family room, kitchen, and dining section all in one tastefully decorated space. When Gray walked down the hall to the kitchen a short while later, she could see her mother standing at the kitchen island in a dark blue designer skirt and blazer. Her highlighted hair was smoothly styled, curling under just behind her ears. Despite the late night they'd both had, she looked perfect. She rarely went to bed before midnight anyway, and always insisted five hours of sleep was plenty.

Her press secretary, Anna, stood beside her. They were both looking at something on her laptop. There was no sign of Richard, who usually left for work before seven.

'Dear God.' Her mother pressed her fingertips against her forehead. 'I don't understand how any of this is possible. They're acting like she killed someone.'

Anna shot Gray a cool look as she crossed the kitchen to the fridge. She'd handled the press the last time Gray had been in trouble. Normally, the two of them got along, but clearly she thought this time it was all Gray's fault.

She was smaller than the prime minister, with a soft Glaswegian accent and blonde hair that always looked like she'd just raked her fingers through it in despair.

'We need a response for all the calls we're getting,' she said. 'The phone's ringing off the hook. I'm getting calls from *Australia*.' Pulling a paper out of a folder, she said. 'I suggest something like this.'

She began to read aloud: 'Gray Langtry was at a party with school friends last night at the Bijou nightclub, with the permission of the club's owner. Feeling ill, she left, and was accosted by the press, who frightened and intimidated her. We'd like to remind you that Gray is sixteen years old, and deserves some degree of privacy.

Last night, aggressive photographers put Gray's life, and that of her friend, in danger. They were forced to flee on foot in an unfamiliar neighbourhood. This must not happen again.'

'Very good,' Gray's mother murmured, taking the page from her to read it again. 'This puts the responsibility on the press.' She tapped the paper. 'Add a line that says, 'If the press fail to respect my family's privacy, I will be forced to take stronger actions through the courts.'

Nodding, Anna spun the laptop around to face her and typed. 'That's great,' she murmured.

While they worked, Gray poured herself a glass of orange juice, got some bread out of the cupboard and dropped a slice in the toaster.

This was how it always went. She did something normal that all sixteen-year-olds did, the entire government freaked out, and then her mother and Anna crafted a response while essentially ignoring her.

Rinse and repeat.

'It's funny,' she said, with her back to the two women. 'Neither of you ever thinks to ask how I feel about being chased down the street by photographers.' She added sarcasm to her tone. 'Oh, hey, Gray. How do you like having your entire private life photographed by middle-aged men with huge cameras and a gross interest in your figure?' She looked up to glare at them. 'Not great. That's how I feel.'

The women exchanged a look.

'Right then. I'd better run.' Anna snapped the laptop shut. 'I think we can turn this into a positive. If we spin this right, the reporters will be talking about this instead of the problems with the immigration bill.' She stuffed the computer into the glossy bag at her feet. 'You could go up three points in the polls by Friday.'

Gray glowered at her. 'Glad I could help your careers.'

Anna headed for the door. Gray's mother turned to look at her, her expression icy.

'Enough, young lady. Stay right there. We need to talk.'

Seething, Gray stayed at the sink, waiting as her mother and Anna walked to the door and said hushed goodbyes.

The door shut with a restrained thud. Gray waited as her mother returned to the kitchen, her face already set in the professionally blank expression she used at work.

'Have a seat.' She pointed at the table. 'There are some things we need to discuss.'

There was no point in arguing. Gray did as she was told.

Across the room, her toast popped up with a cheerful click. Gray left it where it was.

'I don't know how many times I have to tell you that your actions have consequences,' her mother said.

'Anna just said you'll go up in the polls,' Gray reminded her. 'Isn't that all you care about?'

'No.' Her mother's voice was even. 'That's not all I care about. And you know that. I care about you.' She leaned forward, blue eyes searching Gray's face. 'You could have been hurt last night. You know the security situation in this country. And yet you take risks. You lie about where you are. You go out without protection. You put yourself in danger. You put *Chloe* in danger.'

At the mention of Chloe, Gray's head dropped between her shoulders, eyes fixed on her hands. She hated that her mother was right.

'Why?' Her mother pressed the point. 'Why would you do that?'

'I just want to be a normal person,' Gray said quietly. 'I went to a party. Everyone from my class was there. Why is that so hard to understand?'

'Gray…' Her mother looked weary. 'That's no excuse for lying to me.'

'I'm not trying to make excuses. I'm trying to tell you – I can't live like this.' Gray swung her arm at the small, elegantly-equipped apartment. A slight tremble edged her voice. 'I asked you not to run for prime minister until I was out of school. You ran anyway. It turned everything upside down. We moved out of our house. Suddenly I had to get permission seven days in advance to go to a *birthday party*. Did you ever consider that none of this would have happened if you'd cared at all about what I think?'

'That's not fair. I do care,' her mother insisted. 'You know the reasons. We've gone over and over it. Politicians don't get to choose when they become prime minister. It's a once-in-a-lifetime opportunity. When it was offered to me, I took it because I felt like I could do something good for my country. I didn't want to hurt you, but I had to take my chance. It might never happen again in my life.' She drew a breath. When she spoke again, she sounded calmer. 'I've tried to make this easier for you. But I know it's hard.'

Gray could both see the logic of what she said and also not lose sight of the fact that her own life mattered, too.

'You've made it *easier* for me by giving me a list of things I can't do anymore. I can't go out after school on my own. I can't go to parties with my friends. I can't make mistakes without ending up on the cover of a newspaper.' She dropped her head into her hands. 'I just… I'm sorry. I'm proud of you being prime minister. I just miss my old life.' Her voice was muffled by her fingers. 'I miss our old house.' She drew a shaky breath. 'I miss Dad.'

The room grew so quiet she could hear the faint sound of a door closing somewhere in the huge building that surrounded their tiny apartment.

Her parents had divorced three years ago. Her father, who worked for the Foreign Office, was often out of the country. Lately, his long absences had become harder for Gray to bear. He was never here to help when things got awful. Without his flat to escape to, she was trapped inside Number 10.

'Gray.' Her mother's voice softened. 'I haven't wanted to say anything because I know how you'll react. But, if I'm completely honest, I've wondered if you wouldn't be happier somewhere else.'

Gray lifted her head, instantly suspicious. 'Somewhere else? Where?'

'There's a school,' her mother said, hesitantly. 'A boarding school. Out of London. Quite a few MPs send their children there. It's very good. You'd be safe.'

Betrayal sliced Gray's heart with such a sharp blade that, for a moment, she couldn't catch her breath. 'You want to get *rid of me*?'

'Of course I don't want to get rid of you.' Her mother reached across the table for her hand. 'I'm just thinking about what's best for you. This school is good, Gray. They're used to difficult situations like this – protecting the children of powerful people. Raj Patel worked there in the past, and he recommends it highly. It's secure. You'd be safe.' She added the last line like she thought it would seal the deal. 'There are no paparazzi.'

Gray yanked her hand free, and shoved her chair back so abruptly its legs shrieked against the tiled floor.

'I'm sorry I'm such a "difficult situation" for you,' she said stiffly. 'I'm afraid I don't want to go to boarding school so you can spend more time with your career and your new husband. If you want to get rid of me, send me to my dad.'

It was a low blow, and her mother's face reddened. 'You know I wish your father was in the country more…'

Gray cut her off. 'Sure you do.' There was no point in continuing this argument. It always went the same way. 'I'm going to be late for school.'

Gray crossed from the open-plan kitchen with its gleaming appliances into the living room, and the short corridor leading to her bedroom.

'Gray.' Her mother's tone sharpened. '*Stop*.'

With sullen reluctance, Gray slowed her steps and looked back.

'This can't go on.' Her mother stood next to the table, her expression weary. 'I don't trust you right now. You lie all the time. You ignore my rules and do what you want. You put yourself in danger. I need you where I can keep an eye on you, for your own safety as much as anything else. You're grounded for three weeks.'

Gray opened her mouth to object, but her mother raised her hand in a gesture that shut off any discussion.

'I'm not debating this. I'm telling you how it is. Whenever you are not in school, I want you in this building. Your security detail has been enhanced. A permanent team is now assigned to you. They're waiting for you downstairs now.'

Gray glared at her. 'Is that all?'

Her mother didn't back down. 'I'm doing this to keep you safe.'

Gray gave her a disbelieving look. 'Awesome.'

She stormed to her room and slammed the door behind her.

In the privacy of her bedroom, Gray stood in front of the mirror for a long time. She was so angry and hurt, she barely recognised herself. She saw some other girl in a short blue dress and tights. That girl's dark hair hung over her shoulders in heavy waves. Her blue eyes were furious.

There'd been a time when she and her mother had been close. Right after the divorce, when they'd moved into a smaller house in South London. Gray had been twelve. She'd taken her father's absence hard. But her mother had been right there with her, making sure she had friends. Showing up for choir performances and cheering wildly. Buying cakes when they were supposed to bake them for the class and then working with Gray to repackage them so no one would know. And Gray had helped with her election work — going with her to events and small meetings. Helping to stuff envelopes when she was up for re-election.

That time had been hard but good, too, in a way. She'd grown closer to both her parents for a while. They'd got through those hard years that way.

And then Richard showed up. Her mother became prime minister. And everything was ruined.

Her phone buzzed angrily. Chloe had texted her about twenty times so far this morning.

'They're talking about you on Radio One.

You're famous!'

Gray started to put the phone away but paused. Hesitantly, she scrolled through her messages until she reached 'Dad'.

The last time he'd texted was two weeks ago.

'Just thinking of you, sweetheart,' he'd written that day. By then, he'd already been gone for months.

Tears burned her eyes.

'I miss you, Dad,' she whispered. Then she picked up her bookbag and headed out across the open-plan kitchen and living room, pausing only to snatch the slice of cold toast from the toaster to eat on the way to school.

Her footsteps sounded hollow as she walked slowly through the empty apartment. There was no sound from her mother's bedroom — she must have already gone to work.

'See you later, Gray,' she told herself ironically as she reached the door. 'Have a great day at school.'

SIX

As soon as she stepped out of the flat into the hallway, her home disappeared and the sounds of a busy office building rose around her. A phone rang somewhere, steady, unanswered. She could hear voices from downstairs.

Everyone who worked at Number 10 talked urgently – a constant panicked stream of words. It was as though they were all convinced someone would cut them off, right before they got to the good part.

At the foot of the stairs, she had to step out of the way of three men in suits, each carrying piles of folders.

'Good morning, Gray,' one of them said.

Gray had absolutely no idea who he was. She mumbled something and hurried down the corridor, weaving through a steady stream of incoming staff. When she reached the entrance hall, she angled towards the main exit with her head down.

A voice stopped her. 'Not that way.'

Julia was leaning against a wall near the door, her phone held loosely in one hand.

In the daylight, she looked even younger than she had the night before. Too young to be a bodyguard. Part of that might have been her clothes, though. The suit had been replaced with jeans, knee-high boots, and a loose black jumper. Her straight blonde hair hung nearly to her shoulders.

'Excuse me?'

'Don't go out that door.' Pushing herself off the wall, Julia strode to her. 'There are about a million photographers out there right now waiting to get a shot of you.'

'Oh, right,' Gray said, swallowing the panic that rose in her throat. 'So, where should I go instead?' She looked around. 'I'm supposed to have a new security team or something. But I don't know who.'

Julia tilted her head. 'Come with me.'

The two of them walked down a long hallway, threading through a crowd of workers. They hadn't gone far before Julia opened an unmarked door on the left, revealing a flight of stairs leading down.

'This way.'

The air coming up from the steps was cool and musty. The light flickered unsteadily.

If there was one thing Gray had learned during her brief time here, it was that Number 10 was a maze. There were many ways in and out. She'd used quite a few, but she'd never noticed this door before.

This staircase was old. The walls were scuffed; the paint was peeling in places. At the bottom, they entered another long, narrow corridor.

Gray looked around. There were no signs saying what the area was used for, or who, if anyone, worked down here, but Julia seemed to know her way. She moved so quickly Gray had to hurry to keep up.

'Where are we?' Gray asked.

Julia shot her a sideways glance. 'Shortcut.'

Gray didn't give up. 'I can see that. But where?'

Julia slowed down. When she spoke, her voice was low. 'These tunnels connect government buildings to each other. They are top secret. Most of the people who work in those buildings don't even know they're here. But they're handy.'

'What are they for?' Gray found she'd unconsciously lowered her voice nearly to a whisper.

'They've been used for different things,' Julia said. 'They were bomb shelters during the Blitz. They stored documents and valuables when the city was threatened. But mostly, they're just so important people can get around quickly.' She gave Gray a significant look. 'And without being seen.'

The air smelled stale – as if no fresh air ever made it down here. Periodically, the underground hallway intersected with other corridors. Some bore signs in an old-fashioned font, like old street signs. One said 'Foreign Office', with an arrow, pointing down a shadowy hallway.

They passed a series of doors with old-fashioned, frosted glass windows and blackened brass doorknobs. Each had an ornate number: B09 on one. B11 on the next. No lights were visible through the cloudy glass.

It was like looking into the past. Gray tried to see through the windows but could only make out shapes of what must have been furniture.

They walked for a while in silence before Julia spoke again. 'So, your mother explained the new plan to you?'

Gray frowned. 'What plan?'

'Your new security detail.'

'Oh, that. She just said it was happening.' Gray looked at the scuffed wall next to her. 'Mum doesn't really explain things.'

There was a pause, and then Julia said, 'Right. Well, I'm your new bodyguard. And I'll be working with Ryan, who you met last night. We'll be keeping you safe for the next few weeks.'

Gray didn't hide her surprise. Usually her guards were quietly disapproving men in suits who talked into their hidden microphones a lot and sighed when she was five seconds late.

'You're better than the usual blokes,' Gray told her.

A smile flitted across Julia's face. Instead of commenting though, she pointed ahead. 'We're here.'

'Here' turned out to be a small, white-washed room, where an armed guard in a bullet-proof vest stood stiffly in front of a plain desk.

Gray saw recognition in his eyes when he glanced at her. But he said nothing.

Julia held out her ID. The officer touched it against an electronic device at his elbow.

After reading what appeared on the screen, he opened the door behind him, revealing a stone staircase awash in daylight.

'Stay safe,' he told them.

Gray followed Julia out. At the top of the steps, she breathed in the cold city air and tried to get her bearings. They'd emerged in a small parking area, shielded on all sides by fences and high hedges. Behind them stood a nondescript stone building that didn't look like Number 10.

The door of a dark car swung open and Ryan stepped out.

Like Julia, he'd dressed differently today, in jeans and a dark grey pullover that made him look cooler and younger.

'So you're my new security detail,' Gray said, as she climbed into the back seat.

'Get used to us,' Julia said, getting into the passenger seat. 'We're your new best friends.'

During the journey, the two of them explained the situation to Gray.

'We're going to be with you whenever you leave Number 10.' Julia turned sideways to look at her. 'We won't actually go into classes with you, but we'll be in the school whenever you're in the school. If you go to a party, well…' She glanced at Ryan, who made a face. 'We'll talk about it.'

'Parties won't be a problem.' Gray turned to look at the city passing outside the window. The sharp, Gothic spires of Parliament disappeared slowly behind them. 'I'm grounded.'

'Mum's not thrilled about the headlines?' Julia guessed.

'You could say that.' Gray's tone was morose. 'You're my punishment. She wants me watched constantly so I don't accidentally have any fun.'

Julia and Ryan exchanged another look. They weren't smiling.

There was something in the air. Something they weren't telling her. Gray had felt it last night when she called her mother – the relief that preceded the anger. She'd felt it in the tunnels with Julia, and she could sense it again now. Something had changed overnight.

'What's going on?' she asked. 'There's something else, isn't there?'

Neither of the bodyguards replied.

'Seriously.' Gray leaned forward. 'I need to know what's happening. Is there some sort of danger?'

Julia turned to face her. 'Your mother really didn't tell you?'

Gray held up her hands. 'She never tells me anything. What's happened?'

'Nothing you need to worry about,' Ryan insisted gruffly, but Gray wasn't about to accept that. Her stomach had tightened – she couldn't say why but she could sense that something bad had happened.

'Is it my dad?' Her voice rose. 'Did something happen to my dad?'

A brief silence fell as they crawled through the south London traffic. Ryan shot Julia a warning look. But she obviously wasn't going to be told what to do, because she turned around abruptly. 'It's not about your dad. It's just… There have been some threats.'

'Julia.' Ryan's tone was sharp.

'She has a right to know,' Julia insisted. 'It's her life.'

Gray's brow creased. 'There are always threats.'

'Not like these,' Julia said. 'These are different.'

Gray had been given a security talk when they had first moved to Number 10, with her mother, Richard, and some guy from the Secret Service. They'd told her about hate groups, racist groups, religious groups, Nazi groups – all kinds of groups that could try to blow them up. At the end, though, the Secret Service guy had made it clear she shouldn't worry too much.

'Get on with your life,' he'd said. 'Your security is our job. We'll take care of you.'

For a while after that, she'd been anxious about some sort of attack. But nothing had happened, and months had gone by. After a while, security had become a routine hassle.

Now nervousness uncurled inside her chest. 'I don't understand. How are these threats different?'

'The government received credible threats from a new organisation,' Julia told her, ignoring the barbed looks Ryan shot her from behind the wheel. 'They are unusually specific.'

Gray swallowed hard. She almost didn't want to know more. But she had to. 'What's specific about them?'

Julia met her eyes. 'They say they want you, Gray. You and your mother. You're both targets.' She hesitated before adding, 'And they seem to know a lot about you.'

All at once, Gray understood her mother's reaction last night – her palpable relief that she was fine, when anger usually would have been her first response.

She knew about the threat. She'd known for some time. And she hadn't told Gray. Instead, a total stranger had given her the information she needed, while her mother treated her like a five year old.

It was so stupid. If she'd known things were that bad, Gray would never have gone to that party. There would have been no damning photographs – no creepy paparazzi photographing her throwing up. She wouldn't be grounded.

But she hadn't told her. She didn't trust her enough.

'Honestly,' she said, as the car began moving again. 'You've told me more in five minutes than my mother has in five months.'

Julia gave her a strange look. 'Don't be too hard on her. She's trying to protect you.'

Gray slid down further in her seat. 'Sure she is.'

After that, conversation faded. Ryan drove the rest of the way, stony-faced with disapproval.

When they pulled up in front of the school, Julia got out while the car was still coming to a stop.

Automatically, Gray reached for the door handle but Ryan motioned for her to stay where she was. 'Give her a second,' he said, eyes on his partner.

A moment later, Julia opened her door from the outside. 'All clear,' she said. 'Time to go soak up that learning.'

They walked into school in a line – Ryan in the lead, Gray in the middle, Julia behind her. The crowds of students gathered outside watched with undisguised interest as they powered through. Gray's cheeks burned.

'What's going on?' someone asked.

'It's that girl. The prime minister's kid,' someone replied. 'The one who got busted.'

She tried to block out the other voices as they made it through the gate and up the walk towards the modern school building.

It was mortifying. In the past, the security guards just let her out in front and she could blend in with the other students being dropped off by their parents. Now though, everyone was staring.

When they reached the administration offices, Julia and Gray stopped just inside the door, while Ryan walked over to the desk. Gray stared bleakly towards the busy school hallway she could see through the glass doors on the other side of the small room.

'Don't be scared,' Julia told her, with unexpected understanding. 'What I told you earlier – don't worry about it. You'll be fine. We're here and we've got your back.'

Gray didn't know what to make of this new bodyguard. She was professional but also seemed to really care, in a way the other guards hadn't. She didn't keep her distance.

'I'm not scared,' Gray insisted. 'And, I wanted to say – thank you for being honest about everything. No one else is.'

'Well.' One eyebrow raised, Julia glanced at Ryan, who was talking with the receptionist. 'Not everyone would agree, but you need to know this stuff.' She turned back to Gray. 'Now I'm going to ask *you* a favour. The information I told you is secret. You shouldn't share it with anyone else.' She paused, a wry smile lifting her lips. 'Your mother wouldn't thank me for telling you.'

'I can keep a secret,' Gray said.

Julia studied her face and then nodded, as if satisfied with what she'd found there. 'I trust you.'

Those three simple words sent warmth through Gray's heart.

'Oh, I almost forgot. Can I see your phone for a second?' Julia held out her hand.

When Gray handed it to her, the bodyguard typed something quickly. 'I've added my number to your contacts. If anything strange happens – anything at all – call me. Day or night.'

'I will,' Gray promised, just as Ryan walked up to join them.

'It's all set. We'll meet you right here after your last class,' he said. 'Don't leave the school building without us. Ever. Understood?'

The difference between his authoritative tone and Julia's approachable style was striking. Internally, Gray bristled, but she didn't argue. 'Understood.'

Julia seemed to hear the undercurrent in her voice because she nudged her. 'It's going to be tough in there.' She tilted her head in the direction of the crowded school corridor on the other side of the glass door. 'They'll all have seen the papers. But keep your cool. Let it roll off you.'

Gray had never been great at keeping her cool, but suddenly she wanted to. If only to impress this increasingly interesting bodyguard.

'I will,' she promised.

A bell rang through the hallways, jolting her. It was time.

Taking a deep breath, she turned and walked into the school maelstrom.

SEVEN

As soon as Gray walked away, Ryan spun to face Julia. 'What the hell were you thinking?' He looked furious. 'You had no right to tell her.'

'She needed to know.' Julia's voice was measured.

'That wasn't your decision to make,' he snapped. 'If she tells her mother…'

Julia motioned for him to shut up. The receptionist was returning to the desk, a worried-looking man in a suit right beside her. He had to be the head teacher.

'This isn't over,' Ryan hissed as she strode away to meet him.

Julia hoped she'd made the right choice by telling Gray about the threat. It had been a spur of the moment decision. Raj had told her to get close to the girl – to earn her trust. And she suspected that the child of the prime minister would not get a lot of truth from the adults around her. A little honesty about something that really mattered could be enough to convince Gray to trust her.

That had been her thinking as the car wound through the city streets, with Gray glowering from the back. But she didn't have Raj's permission to tell her things that her mother had chosen not to, and this could easily backfire. Still, she didn't like being lectured by Ryan.

She hurried her pace to get to the head teacher before her partner, and held out her government-issued identification. 'I'm Julia Matheson," she said, politely, as Ryan shot her a glare. "This is Ryan Collins. We need to talk to you about Gray Langtry.'

The conversation wasn't long – Raj had already contacted him with the basics. Understandably, he was terrified of an attack on his students, and offered all the help they could possibly need. Already, the school had set aside an office normally occupied by volunteers, which the two of them could use as a base. Within an hour, they had passcodes to every locked door.

As soon as they had the access they needed, they got to work, bringing in the supplies from the boot of the car, and setting up a station inside the small office. After that, they separated to install tiny, wireless cameras at all the major access points. Hartford High School was a private school. It was low-profile and modern compared to exclusive schools such as Eton and Cheltenham Ladies' College, and particularly popular with politicians and journalists, many of whom sent their children there. The grounds held several buildings and about an acre of green playing fields. More than 300 students were enrolled, so it wasn't feasible to watch all of it, all the time. But they could cover a lot. They mounted wireless cameras at the main entrance and exit doors, and a few in the busiest hallways.

Within hours, their small, windowless office was a bustling hub of laptops, mobile phones and radios connected directly to headquarters.

Julia could hear Secret Service chitchat through the earpiece she wore inside her right ear. The prime minister was meeting the home secretary this morning, and had driven to Parliament a couple of hours ago. This involved a lot of agents, and a lot of talk. She found herself trying to block it out, while still listening in case someone tried to contact her.

Across the table, Ryan stared at his own array of computers. He'd been terse and disapproving since the car journey.

She knew her conversation with Gray had been risky. If the prime minister found out and didn't like it, Julia could be out of Number 10. But Raj hadn't sent her here to become friends with the prime minister. He wanted her to be friends with her *daughter*. And Julia saw something in Gray she thought she recognised from her own youth. The girl was clearly intelligent —her school record was largely excellent. And she was bitterly angry about her parents. Julia didn't yet understand the whole picture, but she could sense that Gray was stifled by the political world she'd been thrust into, and the way it had limited her life.

And she'd definitely been right about the honesty thing. There'd been real gratitude on Gray's face when she knew someone had told her the truth. It didn't look like much, but it could be a first step.

In the Army, she'd learned to think fast and to be inventive under pressure. Even before that, at school, she'd been a natural leader. Someone who took risks, but they were almost always the right risks. That's what she hoped she'd done today.

Ryan, though, was a problem.

She didn't know what to think of him. So far, he seemed capable but unimaginative. Still, Raj didn't put people together at random. There had to be a reason he'd chosen the two of them for this job. She just needed to figure out what that was.

'Look,' she said, turning sideways in her seat. 'About earlier. I'm sorry. I should have talked to you about it first.'

He flicked an unforgiving glance her way. 'Damn right, you should have. It's not our place to question the decisions of the prime minister.'

'It was a judgement call.' She kept her voice even.

His face hardened. 'Well, I question your judgement then.' He turned towards her. 'I can't understand why you'd do something like that.'

'Last night, Raj told me my specific role was to win Gray over," she reminded him. 'To be her friend. Someone she can trust. That's what I was trying to do.'

Ryan squinted at her. 'I heard him. But how on earth could you possibly think telling her something like that would be a good idea?'

There was so much Julia could have said then: Because I know what it's like to be lied to by your parents. I know what it's like to be treated like a problem. To be deceived. To be underestimated. I know what I wanted adults to do when I was her age.

But, of course, she didn't say any of that. 'Because I think I know her.' Julia held his gaze. 'I know how she thinks.'

'I don't understand what you're saying.' Ryan didn't hide his confusion. 'How do you know her? You just met her. I know her as well as you do.'

Julia didn't like to talk about her past. She hated sharing her story. But Ryan wasn't going to let go of this without knowing more.

'I stayed up half the night reading her file. Her parents are divorced. Her dad works for the Foreign Office and isn't around much. Her mother remarried a year ago. She started acting out after the election. Up until then, she was a perfect student. A perfect daughter.' She paused, looking for the right words. 'Given all of that, I think I know how to reach her, and I want to try.'

Ryan gave her a dubious look, but she kept going.

'Look, everyone lies to kids. We don't even think about it. We tell ourselves we're protecting them – that it's for the best. I was lied to so much when I was a teenager, if an adult ever told me the truth, I valued that. And I listened to them. We need her to listen or she's going to get herself hurt.' She pointed at the wall behind them. 'I don't know why her mother doesn't want her to know what's happening out here. You heard Raj. This isn't a bunch of amateurs. If that girl keeps sneaking out and lying to the people trying to protect her, she could die.'

Motion on the screen beside her caught her eye and she glanced at it. On the laptop she could see students flowing down a wide hallway. Gray walked in the middle of the crowd with her friend Chloe beside her – they looked distinctive together, both with long dark hair.

Easy to pick out in a crowd. Vulnerable.

'The only way to keep her safe,' she said, pointing at the screen, 'is to convince her to let us help.'

Ryan studied her for a long second, his face hard to read. Finally, he sighed. 'Look, if you're going to pull something like that again, at least discuss it with me first, OK? We're supposed to be partners.'

'Agreed,' she said, relieved.

'And, don't tell her any more about this,' he pressed. 'We can't just choose to defy her mother. I won't be part of this team if you refuse to follow the rules.'

Julia hesitated. If there was one thing she'd learned in the military, it was that the rules weren't always right. But Ryan was a born cop. And cops were rule followers.

As if he knew what she was thinking, his intense brown eyes met hers. 'I appreciate you've got good instincts, but I've been in this game longer than you. I can help you – if we work together. I'm not your enemy.'

'I know that,' she said.

'Do you?' He watched her narrowly. 'I hope so. Because Gray needs us both. In fact…' He paused. 'Her life depends on it.'

EIGHT

As Gray walked through the crowded corridor of Hartford School she felt the stares slide across her skin like hot water. The hissing of whispers followed her as she hurried around a corner towards her locker.

'Did you see the pictures?' A girl's voice giggled somewhere nearby. 'Imagine puking in front of the cameras like that.'

'My dad says he's not going to vote for her mum if she can't control her own daughter. Which is just stupid, but…' someone replied.

'Honestly. When we came out of the Bijou it was like…'

She didn't hear the end of that sentence, because Chloe appeared from nowhere, long hair flying as she ran up and grabbed her arm. 'We have to talk.'

Without waiting for a reply, she steered Gray down the hallway towards the girls' toilets. 'What's going on?' Gray asked.

'Not here,' Chloe hissed.

The toilets were busy with girls putting on make-up, brushing their hair. It smelled of perfume and the coconut sweetness of dry shampoo.

'Nothing to see here. Mind your own business,' Chloe announced at a volume that served only to attract more notice as she manhandled Gray into a cubicle.

'Chloe, what the hell?' Gray grumbled, squeezing into a corner by the toilet.

Ignoring her complaints, Chloe closed and locked the door behind them before facing Gray with her arms crossed.

'I've been looking for you everywhere. Where have you been?'

'Trying not to listen to everyone gossiping about me,' Gray said. 'It's absolutely hideous.'

'I know.' Chloe looked furious. 'Everyone needs to *get a life.*' She raised her voice as she said the last few words, to make sure the girls at the sink wouldn't miss it.

They both heard the uncomfortable shuffling of feet and whispering as this advice was absorbed.

'Anyway,' Gray sighed, 'I'm fine otherwise. Except I'm grounded forever, and I have new bodyguards that are supposed to stick to me like glitter from now on, which is obviously my favourite thing.' She glanced at Chloe. 'What about you? Were your parents angry?'

'Well, your mum had called my mum, so she knew the whole story by the time I got there, and she was not happy. But...' She shot Gray an apologetic look. 'I mean, my mum's not as strict as yours. And nobody in the press cares where I go at night. So, I'm not grounded or anything. Also, she printed out that picture of us from the *Daily Mail*. Not the one where you're puking,' she added hastily. 'The one after that, where we look more normal.'

'She's keeping it?' Gray was horrified. If she had her way, all the photos that had been taken last night would be fired into the sun.

'I know, but I don't get in the papers as often as you do. This could be my one chance,' Chloe said. 'Also my mum is ridiculous.'

Chloe's parents ran a successful art gallery, and were incredibly laid back about their children's lives. Her older brother was currently backpacking around India. Chloe had no curfew. It was why Gray liked spending time with them — they listened to cool music and went to see interesting plays. Their house was filled with art. It was very different from her own life, where the rules were so strict and every infraction was treated like a crisis.

'God. That is so unfair.' She sagged back against the cubicle wall. 'My mum's acting like I murdered someone live on TV.'

Chloe's smile faded. 'Yeah, here's the thing. I've got more bad news. There's a rumour going around, and I wanted you to hear it from me before some random told you.'

Leaning close enough for Gray to smell the mint of her chewing gum, Chloe lowered her voice to a whisper. 'People are saying the person who told the paparazzi you'd be at Aidan's party was Jake McIntyre.'

Gray stared. 'You can't be serious.'

'Serious as a heart attack,' Chloe assured her. 'They say Jake set you up to help his dad. That's why he left when he did. He gave them some sort of signal.'

Gray felt sucker-punched. Because the one person in the whole school who could really understand what would happen if the photographers took those pictures was Jake.

Jake's father was the leader of the other political party. Her mother had defeated Tom McIntyre in the election eight months ago. Jake had been through everything Gray had gone through – except becoming the child of the prime minister.

Up until the election, the two of them had not exactly been friends — his father hated Gray's mother, and vice versa. And that made it hard to form a real friendship. But they'd never been enemies. Since the election, he'd avoided her like a virus. And she hadn't minded, exactly. It was completely awkward. Everything just felt weird, so she hadn't reached out to him.

Still, he didn't seem the kind of person to sabotage her like that.

'I don't believe it,' she said, and yet she could hear the uncertainty in her own voice. Because who else could have done it, if it wasn't Jake?

'Well, I heard it from three guys who were at the party,' Chloe told her. 'One of them said he was laughing about it.'

Gray flinched. She thought of Jake watching her with disapproval across the bar as she held the shot. Could he be that bitter?

Out in the hallway another bell rang shrilly. The girls at the sinks grumbled and trooped out. Gray could hear their voices receding as the door swung shut.

'Is he at school today?' she asked.

'Jake? Yeah, he's here but he'd better be careful,' Chloe said. 'Everyone says some guys from the party are planning to beat him up if they see him.' She gave Gray a wry look. 'Look at it this way, at least everyone's talking about this instead of you puking in front of the Bijou.'

'Oh, believe me. They're talking about that, too,' Gray said dryly, remembering the voices in the hallway.

The bell rang again and Chloe unlocked the cubicle door. 'We better go.'

'Wait.' Gray followed her out. 'Which guys are going to beat up Jake?'

'Tyler Bolino and his brother,' Chloe said, as they moved swiftly through the hallway, which was quickly emptying as students poured into classrooms.

Gray made a face. 'Are they the only ones saying Jake did it? Because I wouldn't believe them. They were as drunk as us last night.'

Chloe stopped outside the biology lab and looked back at her. 'I know, but ask yourself this: how did the photographers know you were at the Bijou? Someone must have told them. And, other than Jake, who else would even know who to call?'

All morning, the rumours about Jake swirled through the school corridors, following Gray through every class, shrouding her day like fog. As the hours passed, the collective mood shifted — soon she heard less talk about her throwing up, and more about Jake setting her up.

She was on her way to politics class when Tyler Bolino lumbered up to her – so tall and broad-shouldered he blocked out the light. 'That was a hell of a party. I'm so hungover,' he laughed. 'How's your head?'

Gray had felt fine after eating the toast and drinking some water, and she shrugged. 'I'm good.'

'Listen,' he told her confidentially, 'don't worry about McIntyre. My brother and me — we've got it covered.'

Gray gave him a warning look. 'I don't need your help, Tyler. I can fight my own battles.'

His smile was secretive. 'Yeah. Sure.'

As he walked away, Gray called after him, 'Don't do this, Tyler. You don't have any evidence.'

He didn't look back.

For his part, Jake was nowhere to be seen. She didn't pass him in the hallway once, and he didn't show up for the sole class they had together.

His absence was remarked upon by everyone. Mostly it was held up as proof of his guilt. If he wasn't the one who called the photographers, stood the reasoning, he'd be here defending himself.

Gray wasn't sure who to believe. It seemed unlikely. And yet, Chloe had a point.

By one o'clock, when she spotted Aidan in the distance, she was determined to know the truth, and she ran after him. He was Jake's best friend, and he must know what had really happened.

'Hey, Aidan,' she called. 'I need to talk to you.'

He stopped and waited for her. 'What's up?'

He was tall in that way of guys who'd suddenly grown and didn't know what to do with themselves. His hands always seemed to be in the way. His freckles had always made him look younger than he was, but lately he'd been growing into them.

The two of them had a complex history. They'd been friends since she first came to Hartford School, three years ago. Last year, though, he'd suddenly developed a thing for her. She'd pretended not to notice – hoping it would go away. And then he tried to kiss her at a party. When she told him she thought of him as a friend, he'd been crushed. That was months ago, and still he barely spoke to her.

More than anything, Gray wished everything could go back to the way they'd been when they were younger. But she couldn't undo history.

'I couldn't believe last night,' she said. 'It got pretty crazy. Your dad was so nice to let us all into the club.'

'Yeah.' His shrug was noncommittal. 'Ever since my parents divorced, he likes to do this super dad thing now and then. It was a pretty good party though.' He gave her a look. 'I heard about the puking. How're you feeling?'

'Like an idiot.' Gray grimaced.

They smiled at each other and, for a second, the last year melted away.

'Yeah, those bloody photographers.' He pushed his auburn hair out of his face with one hand. 'Dad says they're always causing problems at Bijou. Showing up whenever someone famous is there.'

Gray took a step towards him, lowering her voice. 'Aidan, have you heard what everyone's saying? You don't think Jake tipped off the photographers, do you? Would he do that?'

He shook his head, hard. 'It can't be him. That's just not who Jake is. Tyler Bolino's just looking for a fight, maybe trying to impress you. Don't believe him.'

'If it wasn't him, though, how did they find out I was there?' she persisted. 'Someone must have told them.'

Aidan held up his hands. 'I wish I knew. I was really pissed off when I heard.' He gave her an apologetic look. 'I feel terrible that it happened at my party. Your mum must have been so mad.'

'You could say that.' Her tone was dry. 'But it wasn't your fault. Maybe it was just bad luck.'

'Either way. I hope things aren't too bad.' His eyes searched her face.

Suddenly, Gray was conscious that she was standing close to him. She took a clumsy step back. 'Well, I better go.'

His expression cooled.

'Yeah,' he said, distantly. 'Me too. See you.'

He loped away down the hallway, shoulders high around his ears. Turning in the opposite direction, Gray made her way back through the labyrinthine school corridors, kicking herself. She just didn't know how to talk to him anymore. She wished she could force him to be her friend. To not have feelings for her beyond that. But she couldn't.

The smell of food from the dining hall made her stomach rumble but she couldn't face the packed room and all of the gossip. Instead, she stopped at the small kiosk outside the cafeteria and bought a sandwich and a drink, and headed off in search of a quiet place.

Rounding a corner, she saw the library in front of her and decided to go in.

When she pulled open the door, the long, modern room appeared completely deserted. It was utterly silent. Even the librarian's desk was unmanned. Gray headed for the back, where she knew a table was tucked away. Food wasn't allowed here, but nobody would see her back there.

It was one of those libraries with more computers than books, but there were still a few rows of shelves behind which she could disappear for a while.

When she reached the shadowy section though, the table wasn't empty after all.

Jake McIntyre sat on a tilted back chair, his boots propped on another chair.

Gray froze, her stomach tightening.

He hadn't noticed her – the carpet had hidden her footsteps. His eyes were fixed on a book opened in front of him. The light glinted off his straight brown hair.

She stood, mid-step, wavering.

Should she run before he saw her? Or stay and challenge him about the rumours?

Sensing someone watching him, he glanced up.

He'd positioned himself so his face was mostly in shadow. Gray couldn't make out his expression but she was sure it had that sardonic look it always wore when he looked at her.

Squaring her shoulders, she forgot all about fleeing. 'So, this is where you're hiding,' she said, dropping her bag on the floor with a thud.

'I'm not hiding.' His flat, northern accent gave this low-key statement a withering edge.

'Sure you are.' She sat in a chair across from him. 'At the back of the room. In the dark.'

He waved one hand in her direction. 'Well, if I'm hiding, what are *you* doing? You're at the back of the room in the dark, too.'

The hint of amusement in his voice made her hackles rise. 'I'm having my lunch.'

Defiantly, she opened her bag and, pulling out the sandwich and bottle of water, set them on the table.

'You're not allowed to eat in here,' he reminded her.

'You're not allowed to put your feet on a chair in here,' she retorted.

'Touché.'

He was always saying things like that. Things teenagers never said to each other. Like he was a thirty-year-old trapped in a seventeen-year-old body.

Frowning, she unwrapped the sandwich, but she was too upset to take a bite now. Shoving it aside, she leaned forward, hands sliding across the smooth wood of the tabletop. 'Did you do it? Did you tip off those photographers that I'd be at the Bijou last night? Everyone's saying it was you. But I just…' Her voice trailed off.

At first, he looked at her without expression, as if he might refuse to say anything at all. But then, he closed the book and set it down on the table.

'No, I did not,' he said, firmly. 'And I'd really like to know who did.'

Lifting his feet off the chair, he dropped them to the floor, and sat up straight, moving into the light. Only then did she see the damage. A bandage was taped across the bridge of his nose; his left eye was swollen and puffy. A bruise tinged his cheek with blue.

Gray covered her lips with her fingers. 'Oh my God. What happened?'

'Tyler Bolino happened.' He touched his cheek gingerly. 'He was really excited to defend your honour.'

The wounds looked raw and painful. Gray felt sick. That idiot Tyler.

'I'm so sorry,' she said. 'I didn't know. I didn't ask anyone to do that. I wouldn't.'

'I know that. He just likes hitting things.' He held her gaze. His eyes were so dark they were almost black. 'It really wasn't me who called the photographers. I would never do something that cruel to you.'

Gray searched his face, finding no signs of deception. His eyes were steady. But she still had unanswered questions. 'I don't understand, though. You left earlier than me. Didn't you see them out there? Why didn't you warn me?'

'I didn't see anyone.' He paused. 'That's not entirely true, actually. There were some blokes standing around a van across the street. But it was dark, and I was angry about the conversation I'd had with you and Chloe, and I just wanted to go home.'

Gray was surprised. 'You were really cross?'

'Cross with myself,' he told her. 'I thought I acted like a twat. Still do, actually.' He pointed at her sandwich. 'Are you going to eat that, by the way? I haven't eaten all day. I'm starving.'

Caught off guard by the sudden subject change, Gray, who'd almost forgotten about the food, blinked.

'I'll split it with you.' Taking one half for herself, she slid the other across to him.

'Thanks.' He took a gigantic bite, and gave a happy sigh. 'I've been too terrified to go to the dining hall,' he explained, with his mouth full. 'The Bolinos might beat me up again.'

This admission of weakness was so unexpected, for a second Gray didn't know what to say. All she came up with in the end was, 'I can't blame you. But I think they're idiots.'

'They're *strong* idiots,' he corrected her, with a wry smile. 'Anyway, I don't think Tyler really thought it was me who tipped off the photographers. I think he just wants to impress you.'

Gray made a dismissive sound. 'I doubt it. He's more Chloe's type.'

'Come on.' Jake pointed the sandwich at her. 'Everyone wants to go out with the PM's kid. Get their face in the papers. I wish they'd just buy you flowers. Do something a bit less violent. My dad raised me to be a pacifist, you know.'

Gray laughed. The tension between them had eased. In fact, this was the most they'd talked since the night of the election.

'I'll have another word with them. Get them to back off,' she promised.

They finished the sandwich quickly. When they were done, he brushed the crumbs off the table top, before asking, hopefully, 'I don't suppose you have any more food?' When she shook her head, he sighed. 'I could eat two more of those sandwiches.'

Watching him, Gray picked at the label on the water bottle. It was so nice not feeling tense around him. She kept thinking about last night, and how badly it had all ended.

'Hey,' she said, before she could lose her nerve. 'About the party…'

He glanced at her, caution written on his face. 'Yeah?'

'I'm the one who blew it. I drank too much, and I said some stupid things. I just… I wanted to say I'm sorry. Not just for me, but for Chloe, too. She can get fierce about defending me.' Feeling disloyal, she added quickly, 'She means well.'

He picked up the sandwich packet and threw it into a nearby bin. 'Well, I'm sorry, too,' he said, after a second. 'If I hadn't been so caught up in my own problems, I would have noticed those photographers were out there and warned you.'

'Next time,' Gray told him.

Their eyes met across the table.

'Next time,' he agreed.

Warmth kindled in Gray's chest, like the sun coming out on a dark afternoon.

His lips curved up. 'This is weird, isn't it? Tom McIntyre's son talking to Jessica Langtry's daughter. And not wanting to kill each other. The photographers would *love* this.'

'I won't tell if you don't,' she said.

'It's a deal,' he agreed.

They exchanged a smile.

'It would make my skin crawl, being followed around by photographers like that,' he told her. 'Do you hate it? All that fame stuff?'

'There are good things, I guess,' she said. 'There are interesting people around sometimes. I get to do things I would never do otherwise. I mean, I met all those rock stars at that fundraiser last summer. And my mum and I went to a party at Buckingham Palace, which was just really weird.'

He held up his hands, jokingly. 'Now I'm jealous again.'

'But it's not normal, you know?' she said, after a second. 'It's not the way I wanted to spend my life. With bodyguards going everywhere with me, and the newspapers making fun of me. I mean, I basically live in my mum's office. Who *does* that?'

She glanced at him from under her lashes, poised to be hurt if he criticised or laughed at her. Instead, he looked thoughtful. 'When my dad was campaigning, I tried to imagine myself living in Number 10 and it just seemed ... I don't know. Hard to even think about. Not awful. But hard. Like you said. Not normal. I don't know if I could do it.'

'Yeah. I still don't know if I can.' She drew a breath. 'I've been assigned new bodyguards — they're actually here right now, in the building. And, today my mother started talking about sending me to boarding school so... I don't know if she thinks I can do it either.'

'Boarding school?' His eyebrows rose. 'Would you want that?'

She shook her head. 'We had a massive row. Her press officer is probably arranging it all now. If I don't come in tomorrow, they've sent me there, kicking and screaming.'

'That sucks,' he said. 'Parents, huh?'

She tilted her head. 'What about your dad? Do you get caught up in his world?'

'Nah. We're grand,' Jake said, bitterly. 'As long as I don't mind being his unpaid assistant, and agreeing with him on everything.'

His eyes held hers with a kind of defiance. As if daring her to ask more questions. They'd never talked like this before. Being truly honest. Last night seemed to have changed things. It was as if it had pushed them together.

'It's that bad?' she asked, hesitantly.

His mouth twisted. 'It is what it is. His job is his marriage and his children. The only thing I'm not sure of is where that leaves me.'

He sounded so unhappy Gray didn't know how to reply.

Out in the hallway, the volume was rising. Gray glanced at the clock on the wall. Lunch break was nearly over.

Jake was also aware of the time. 'And just like that, the moment passed,' he said.

To her own surprise, Gray didn't want it to be over. It had been strangely therapeutic talking to him. Which was not something she'd ever expected from Jake McIntyre.

'I have to go or I'll be late for my next lesson.' She stood reluctantly, picking up her bag from the floor. Jake stayed where he was, flipping through the pages of his book without looking at them.

'Aren't you going to class?' she asked, frowning.

'Well, it's a tough one.' He brushed his fingertips across the bandage on his nose. 'If I go out there, I might get the shit kicked out of me again. If I stay here, I have an entire library full of peaceful books to learn from.'

She gave him a doubtful look. 'You can't stay here all day.'

'Don't worry,' he said. 'The head knows what's going on. He wants me to stay in here for a while until they can sort out Tyler.'

'Well. I hope nobody else beats you up today,' she said.

'You and me both.'

The fervency in his voice made her laugh. She turned for the door.

'It's been nice talking to you, Gray,' Jake called after her. 'We should do it again sometime.'

She glanced back.

'It was nice talking to you, too,' she said. 'At least one good thing came out of last night. We don't have to hate each other anymore.'

She turned and headed across the room. She was nearly at the door when he spoke again, his words so quiet she wondered later if she'd imagined them.

'I never hated you.'

NINE

It wasn't until Saturday that Gray's new reality truly sank in. Her mother made it clear she wasn't joking about the grounding. Gray wasn't allowed to leave Number 10 at all. She had to cancel her plans to go to Chloe's house and, instead, work on her history essay at the kitchen table, where her mother kept an unsubtle eye on her.

Because she wasn't allowed to leave the building for any reason, her bodyguards were dismissed for the weekend. After all, Number 10 is protected by armed security guards. Gray was definitely not getting out and nobody was getting in.

Chloe sent regular messages promising that the whole world was boring this weekend and that she wasn't missing anything, but Gray knew better. She had weeks of isolation ahead of her.

She was so jealous of Chloe, out in the world, living a normal life. It was completely unfair.

Worse, her mother had refused to talk about the security situation Julia had told her about. No matter how Gray approached the subject, choosing her words carefully to make sure she didn't betray Julia, she just cut her off. But she was certain it had something to do with why she was grounded for so long.

Of course Richard, who was working in the living room for much of the day, made matters worse. He took pleasure in pointing out that working harder at the weekends would help her grades.

'I don't do this for fun,' he said, tapping his laptop screen. 'I do it to improve myself. I hope you can see the benefit of bettering your mind.'

'Sure, Richard,' she replied, a sardonic edge to her voice. 'I love learning.'

His expression soured. 'Changing your attitude could change your life.'

It was one of his favourite phrases. She was willing to bet he had a poster of it on the wall in his sleek skyscraper office at the insurance headquarters where he worked.

'Awesome,' she said, holding up her book. 'Well, I better get back to this. I need some more change.'

Pointedly, he closed his laptop and left the room. A few minutes later, he and her mother exchanged whispers in the hallway. The apartment was small and although their voices were low, they weren't low enough for Gray not to hear him say, 'I keep trying. But she doesn't want to engage with me.'

'I know, darling,' she heard her mother say. 'Give her time. She'll come around.'

The sympathy in her mother's voice set Gray's teeth on edge. Why was she always on his side? Gray had been here long before Richard had appeared on the scene, with his advice and boring platitudes.

Muttering under her breath, she shoved her earbuds in, cranking up the music to drown everything out.

It was a relief when, later that evening, the two of them prepared to go to a charity fundraiser.

For half an hour, some of the tension between them dissipated. The flat was alive with urgency as her mother searched for the right shoes and earrings, and Richard needed help with his tie and cufflinks.

When they finally stood at the door, ready to leave, Gray had to admit they looked good together. Richard was born to wear a tuxedo. Meanwhile, her mother was elegant in a designer dress.

Richard said something Gray didn't hear and her mother rested a hand on his arm, leaning in – they gazed at each other with a look so private, Gray felt uncomfortable seeing it. She cleared her throat, reminding them that she was still there.

'You both look so glam,' she told them from her spot on the sofa.

Her mother cast her a grateful look.

Richard didn't hide his surprise. 'Thank you, Gray.'

Someone knocked on the door. When Richard opened it, a young man in a dark suit stood in the hallway. 'Your car is ready,' he told them.

Richard walked out to join him, but Gray's mother lingered in the doorway. With her hair up, and sparkling earrings framing her face, she looked elegant and happy. The tension that had often tightened her face lately was momentarily gone.

Gray knew her mother's work had been pretty awful lately. The government had passed some new policies that hadn't gone down well. Her mother said the cuts to welfare and education were necessary to balance the budget, but a lot of people thought they went too far. There'd been protests in Parliament Square and at the entrance to Number 10. Gray had seen placards calling her mother a 'murderer' and a 'baby killer'. Meanwhile, on her own side, there'd been grumblings. Members of her own party wanted more cutbacks, and her mother was resisting. Things had been tense since the summer. So it was rare to see her looking relaxed.

'Have fun,' Gray told the two of them.

Her mother smiled. 'Have a nice evening, darling.' She paused before adding, 'I should mention — the security guards have been told you're not to go out tonight. I can rely on you to stay in the building, can't I? They work very hard, and I'd rather you didn't make them worry about you, as well.'

Any warmth Gray had felt the moment before evaporated, leaving a cold and resentful residue in its place.

'I don't have any choice, do I?' she said. 'I mean, they've got actual guns.'

With a sigh, her mother took a step away. 'Let's not do this now and ruin everything. We'll be out late. There's plenty of food in the fridge. Don't wait up.'

Then the door closed and she was gone.

'I wasn't going to,' Gray muttered.

She was glad to see them go. And yet the place felt oddly empty without them.

After pacing around for a few minutes, she sent a text to Chloe:

What are you doing? Want to come over?

Chloe's reply was instant:

Soz. Going to a film with Will.

Will was Chloe's on-again, off-again boyfriend. There was no point in trying to compete with him.

Gray had other friends of course, but Chloe was the only one she regularly invited to Number 10. The others were too awed by it all, or too weirded out, or too gossipy. Chloe, on the other hand, was fine with it. Even the first time she'd visited, she'd wafted through the gates, flirting with the guards as her bags were searched, before dashing up to the apartment with her hands full of takeaway coffees and a bag of muffins as if it were all absolutely normal.

Maybe it was because her parents were so cool, and because they'd always taken her with them when they travelled in Europe and abroad to America since she was a baby. She was just kind of unimpressible.

The two of them had been friends since the day they first sat next to each other in French class when they were both 14. But their friendship had grown stronger recently.

When Gray's mother first became prime minister, everyone else had looked at her differently the next day at school. They kept her at arm's length, as if she had somehow changed because of her mother's job.

By contrast, Chloe's main response had been a simple and accurate, 'Holy shitballs, girl! You're going to need a new wardrobe.'

Everyone at school had got used to the whole prime minister thing eventually. But by then, Gray had found she needed one person she could rely on at all times and completely trust. Chloe was that person. The two had become as close as sisters. Except when Chloe had a date.

With no choice but to be alone, Gray listened to music, ate something random for dinner, and tried to cheer herself up. But she'd been locked inside all day. And as it got later, and quieter, she felt increasingly trapped.

The idea of twenty more days spent staring at these four walls was suffocating.

And was it all truly because she'd gone to Aidan's party and puked in a plant? Or was the real reason the threat Julia had told her about? The one nobody would talk about? Was her punishment an excuse to keep her inside and away from danger?

Even Julia had refused to tell her more that afternoon when she'd asked. 'It's all pretty top secret,' she'd said vaguely. Gray got the feeling she wanted to say more than she had. Ryan still looked cross about it all. And her mother had pretended not to know what she was talking about when she'd hinted at it.

But what if that threat was the real reason she was grounded? After all, punishing her was a terrific way to keep her locked up.

Jumping to her feet, she crossed to the window, and looked down at a courtyard below. During the day it was busy with Number 10 staff bustling through or having lunch in the sun. At night, though, it was empty. Directly across the courtyard stood another government building. Some of the lights were still on, and through the windows she could see long corridors and ghostly rows of empty desks, neatly aligned.

Gray pressed her forehead against the cool glass, observing the building through the warm clouds made by her breath.

There was more to the threat than Julia had said. Everything that had happened on Thursday night – the police motorcycles, the military operation to bring her home... That was not normal.

Whatever was going on, it had scared people who didn't usually get scared. Scared them enough to make them lock her away. To make them lie to her. But how would she ever find out the whole story? Not one person was willing to tell her.

Out of nowhere, an idea appeared fully formed in her mind: *I could go and find out for myself.*

Instantly, she dismissed it. She couldn't just walk through government offices looking for information. The buildings were huge – she wouldn't know where to start.

And yet the thought wouldn't go away.

Her mother's office was impossible to get into; it would be locked and protected constantly. But that building across the courtyard – those were internal doors. They might be unlocked. Those offices held the people who worked in her mother's government. There could be something there — some information about the threat Julia had mentioned. If it was such a big deal, surely other people knew about it.

She could just look around. See what she could find that could explain what was going on. Nobody would ever know.

Without giving herself time to think about whether this might be a truly terrible plan, she walked across the living room to the family's front door and slipped out into the hallway.

She could hear no voices from below as she tiptoed down the stairs. It was Saturday night — most of the staff who filled the building during the week would be at home now.

The main problem was patrolling security guards. But she could avoid those if she was careful. Probably.

At the foot of the stairs, she hesitated. Turning left would take her to the main lobby, which always had a team of police guards by the door. She turned right.

Moving fast, she half-ran down the silent corridor, past a couple of small offices, until she reached a short hallway ending in double glass doors.

There, she paused. On the other side of the glass was the courtyard she could see from her room. It looked bigger from here, with several benches, and trees in huge planters, their few remaining leaves shivering in the breeze.

She glanced over her shoulder. The hallway behind her was still empty.

She pushed the door open.

Cold, damp autumn air flowed in. To Gray, it smelled like freedom. Excitement rushed through her veins like a drug. She was exploring. She was going where she wasn't supposed to be.

Did anything in the world feel better than that?

She walked into the darkness, letting the door swing shut behind her.

TEN

It had rained earlier. In the pale light from the lamp posts, the rain slick paving stones glistened like oil. Slightly shocked by her own audacity, Gray stood at the edge of the courtyard.

She couldn't see anyone through the windows above. Nor were there any obvious CCTV cameras. But she knew the police at Number 10's front desk watched feeds from cameras placed in strategic hidden locations. They could easily be watching her now.

Just in case, she kept her head tilted slightly down as she crossed the wet paving stones to the door on the other side, hoping that in dark trousers and a grey top, she'd pass as late-working member of staff.

Hesitantly, she reached for the cold metal handle. The door made only the faintest shush – a breath of movement – as it opened.

It was warm on the other side. In the soft darkness of the unknown office building, Gray stood very still, listening for any signs of life. She could hear nothing but her own heart pounding.

If she got caught now, her mother would absolutely murder her. But she wasn't about to go back.

Cautiously, she took a step forward. As if she'd flipped a switch, a bright array of overhead lights flickered and came on.

Motion detector lights, she reminded herself. Some of the corridors at Number 10 had them too.

With the lights on, she could see the corridor stretched only a short distance, ending where it intersected with another hallway, beyond which lay darkness.

Emboldened by the fact that, so far at least, she'd not seen a single person, Gray strode confidently down to the end. As she stepped into the dark hallway the lights came on there too.

This hallway was much longer, and just as nondescript. There were no signs on the clean white walls indicating whose offices these were. It had the faceless look she'd come to recognise in government buildings – studiedly bland.

To the right, the hallway widened out. That looked the most promising, so she set off in that direction. If she wanted to find information, she needed offices, but not any old office. She needed offices that involved security or police work. Something like that, she decided. And she had no idea if she was in the right place.

Now that she was here, the size of the building was daunting. Also, it was better secured than she'd expected. There were a few closed doors along the way but most were locked. The one that did open proved to be a men's washroom, and she hastily closed it again.

When she reached the elevators, she stopped. She must be getting near the front doors now, and there would be guards there. If she couldn't go forward and she'd already been back, the only direction was up.

She pushed the call button and waited, checking over her shoulder constantly. But the hallway remained empty.

Seconds later, the elevator arrived, giving a cheery chirp that seemed to echo in the silent building like an alarm. Gray jumped inside and punched the button to close the doors.

At random, she chose floor six – the top floor.

Only when it was moving did it occur to her that, while the bottom floor was empty, for all she knew the top floor could be filled with all the members of her mother's cabinet having some sort of top-secret meeting. It was after ten, but that didn't matter. Sometimes her mother worked until the early hours of the morning.

She reached for the row of buttons to choose another floor but then stopped, her hand hovering above the numbers. No floor was guaranteed to be safe. Now that she was moving, all she could do was hope.

Biting anxiously on the edge of her thumbnail, she glimpsed her reflection in the polished metal door. The shiny surface softened and distorted her face, making her eyes huge and dark.

What am I doing? she wondered. There was no way she was going to find what she was looking for. And she risked even more weeks of punishment. Despite that, though, she felt no desire to go back. To stop. The buzz of exhilaration from doing something rebellious felt too good. Besides, she wasn't a child. She had a right to try and understand what was happening in her own life. Her mother was always telling her to be confident and to take charge.

Well, don't look now, Mum…

The lift juddered to a stop, bouncing softly, as if suspended on rubber bands. A mechanical female voice intoned, 'Sixth floor'.

When Gray stepped out and the automatic lights came on. She was in a central lobby of sorts. From somewhere she could hear the distant rumble of a vacuum cleaner. Otherwise, the building was profoundly quiet. No sign of security. No official voices.

Ahead, she saw several open doors. With a quick glance over her shoulder, she hurried towards them.

The first door she reached opened into a large room with rows of blonde-wood desks. Each had an identical black office chair and a silver-framed computer monitor.

She walked through the rows, looking for any papers that might be useful, but most of the desks were empty. The only items left out were framed family photos. Virtually all of those pictures were of babies or small children.

As Gray explored the rows, seeing one cherubic face after another, it struck her that not one desk had a picture of a teenager on it. In fact, none of the children in any of the photos looked older than about eleven.

After that age, she thought, I guess we're not as much fun for them.

She wondered if her mother had her picture on her desk. She doubted it.

The realisation made her feel hollow. They'd been so close once. When had they lost that?

When you're little, they can't bear to spend the day at work, knowing you're at school without them. Who knows what adorable thing you might be doing? Once you're old enough to speak your mind and make your own decisions, parents don't see you as their little darlings anymore. You're not what they created. You're your own person. That's when they start to view you as a problem.

It happens gradually. Probably nobody in this room had noticed they had stopped putting pictures of their kids on their desk when they got to be thirteen. But every single one of them had.

Frowning, Gray made herself stop thinking and start focussing. She was here for a reason, after all. To snoop.

Finding a desk with a stack of papers next to the phone, she rifled through them. The letterhead read 'Departmental Security Unit, Cabinet Office'. A black government crest in the corner showed a lion and a unicorn. Her heart jumped. This was a good place to search. Security was what she was looking for.

Hurriedly, she skimmed the papers, but they were all memos about meetings and directives.

She moved on, checking the other desks but finding nothing about security threats. The room was lined with beige filing cabinets, and she tried a couple of them, but they were all locked tight.

It was disappointing, but she'd known this was a long shot. Still, there were other offices.

After peeking out to make sure the corridor was still empty, she slipped out and into the next office. She found more papers there – but again, not the right ones. Nothing that would help.

The last office in the hallway was a long room with about fifteen desks neatly aligned. Spotting one with a stack of papers by the keyboard, she went straight for it. The letterhead read, 'Eleanor Johnson, Security and Intelligence Division.' It was stamped 'CONFIDENTIAL' at the top.

It was just a few paragraphs, and Gray skimmed it rapidly at first, slowing as she realised what she was reading. It was a note that had been sent out to members of something called 'COBR'.

'Protocol 13 is applied effective immediately for protection at Number 10 Downing Street. Talos Inc. has been brought in for personal security duties. The threat organisation is unknown, but its methods would connect it to the Russian intelligence service. MI6 identify this threat as: CREDIBLE.'

Gray didn't always pay attention when her mother talked about work, but she knew enough to get that this was important. COBR – which everyone called 'Cobra' – was the secret government group in charge of dealing with emergencies. And MI6 was one of the most famous spy departments in the world.

Given that, this letter indicated that everything Julia had said was true. But it didn't tell her why someone wanted to hurt her family. She knew people were angry about the government's decisions, but this didn't seem to be a British threat. It was bigger than that.

Pulling her phone from her pocket, she snapped a picture of the letter before hurriedly returning it to the stack where she'd found it, and leafing through the rest of the papers. She was utterly focussed on finding out everything her mother hadn't told her. Maybe that was why she didn't hear the guards approaching until it was too late to run.

'There's another light on in here,' a male voice said, so suddenly and so close that it made her jump.

Gray fought back a gasp. The voice was right over her shoulder. He had to be directly on the other side of the thin partition wall.

'Anyone working in here tonight?' the unseen man asked.

Gray stood up as carefully as she could and looked frantically for somewhere to hide. But there were no closets – no cupboards. Everything was open. She was trapped.

'Not as far as I know.' The person who responded sounded only vaguely interested. 'Sometimes the air from the heating system activates the lights.'

'It's probably that,' the first man said. 'I'll just take a look.'

With no other alternatives, Gray ran to the end of the room farthest from the door, moving as quietly as she could. She crouched down low between two chairs, trying to lose herself in the shadows.

At the other end of the long office, she heard the soft shush of footsteps on carpet.

Gray couldn't see him. Her entire body was curled up into a protective ball. She kept her eyes fixed on the black plastic wheels next to her and huddled up, expecting to be found. Surely the guard would walk up behind her at any moment, grab her by the arm and haul her to her feet?

At that moment, the awful thought occurred to her that she hadn't put her phone on silent. What if Chloe called to check on her? Or her mother?

There was nothing she could do. If she moved at all he'd see her. And if the phone rang, everyone in the building would know she was here. She kept the volume turned up loud.

She couldn't seem to breathe. It felt like she was choking on her own fear.

Finally she heard the man say, 'Looks OK to me.' His voice came from outside, in the hallway. 'Must be the air. Why do they keep it on when no one's here, anyway?'

'They don't pay me enough to know the answer to that question,' the second man said. Their voices gradually faded as they moved down the corridor.

Still crouched, Gray let out a long shaky breath. That was too close. It was time to get out of here.

ELEVEN

Only when she was certain they were long gone did she climb to her feet and sneak back down the hallway, scuttling from doorway to doorway. Knowing they were in the building made her too afraid to use the lifts so she took the stairs, flying down one flight after another, her trainers thudding as fast as her heartbeat.

The ground floor, when she reached it, was as dark and quiet as when she'd first arrived. Wherever the guards had gone, it wasn't here.

Breathless, she ran the short distance to the double doors, hurtling out into the rain-streaked courtyard and pelting across the paving stones to the warm, empty hush of Number 10. Three minutes later, she was safely back in the family apartment.

Only then did she have time to think. Pulling out her phone, she read over the paper she'd found once again. '*MI6 identify the threat as: CREDIBLE.*'

No wonder her mother had been so frightened when she'd called that night, her voice shaking. No wonder she'd forgotten to be angry until time had passed.

But she wasn't the only one who was furious. Gray had been kept in the dark, when her own life was at stake.

Well, her mother wasn't the only one who could keep secrets.

When she and Richard returned after midnight, Gray was stretched out on the sofa in her pyjamas, a book open in front of her, diligently working on her English essay.

Gray blinked at them. 'I had no idea it was so late.' She yawned luxuriantly. 'I must have lost track of time.'

Her mother strolled through the living room to the kitchen, straightening a cup here, moving a jar there. Her movements were casual but Gray knew she was looking for signs of what she'd been up to while they were away. She also knew she'd find nothing but a few clean dishes next to the sink, already washed and drying.

Closing the book, she began stacking her things into a neat pile, her expression angelic. 'I just thought I'd take advantage of the quiet and get this essay done. Did you have a nice time?'

The two of them exchanged looks. It was Richard who replied. 'It was a good night. Your mother gave another brilliant speech. They all loved her.'

'Oh, it was nothing,' Gray's mother demurred, as she hung her coat and scarf in the closet near the door. 'Just the usual nonsense.'

But she looked pleased.

'That's great,' Gray said. 'I wish I could have seen it.'

Her mother smiled at her, eyes bright. 'Well,' she said. 'It's late, and I'm dead on my feet.' She headed towards the master bedroom, her heels clicking on the floor. 'Don't stay up too long, Gray.'

At first, Richard moved to follow her, but he stopped just outside the bedroom door and glanced back. 'Have you really been working the whole time we were gone?'

Gray forced a cheeky smile. 'No way. I watched loads of TV earlier. To be honest, I just got bored and thought I might as well do some work.'

That seemed to satisfy him. 'I promise I won't tell your mum,' he said, as if they were friends.

After he followed her mother into the bedroom, Gray sat on the sofa for a while, listening to the sounds of them getting ready for bed. She heard the rumble of Richard's voice. The low, musical sound of her mother's laughter.

If someone had asked her, she couldn't have said why she didn't like Richard. He was nice enough. He didn't order her around or ever get weird with her. In some ways, he was really quite patient.

He just wasn't her dad. And there was nothing he could do about that.

She got up and walked down the short hallway past the guest bedroom to her own room at the end, and stacked her books on the desk before sitting down on the simple wooden chair.

She'd been thirteen when her parents had split up. And despite everything – all the clues and warnings she could easily see in retrospect – the divorce had blindsided her.

Her father had been away a lot that year. The Foreign Office kept sending him places: Pakistan, Kazakhstan, Ukraine.

Periodically, without warning, she'd come home from school to find his battered leather bag in the hallway. Then she'd run into her parents' room for a hug, and to collect whatever small gift he'd brought her – a heart-shaped box made of cinnamon wood that smelled of rich spice. A tiny alabaster elephant, hand carved.

Her mother was an MP then, and she'd had to handle Parliamentary work and her daughter all by herself. The strain had taken its toll on their marriage. Whenever Gray's father was in the country the two of them had squabbled and snapped at each other.

On the night her mother had won her first election, Gray's father had been away. Her mother had celebrated with Gray and her campaign staff.

That was probably, Gray thought later, when their marriage had really ended.

After a while, it had become clear her mother was happier when he was away. She loved being a member of Parliament – she had soon begun to make a name for herself. Climbing the political ladder so quickly.

By that Christmas, they had both been too unhappy to keep up the pretence any longer. It had been a cold, difficult time, with frost inside the house as well as outside. Still, they'd kept it together until the tree was down, and the ornaments put away. That's when they'd told Gray they were separating.

Gray didn't want to think about that day. She got up and went to the bathroom, and began to brush her teeth. Her mind, though, kept going back to those days. It was like she'd opened a door, and the memories were flooding out.

Her father had stayed in the country for months as they all adjusted to the separation. He had rented a flat in Battersea, not far from where she and her mother lived, and Gray would visit him at weekends, walking along the Thames and talking about school and life.

At the same time, she and her mother had developed a closeness that came of needing each other. Gray had taken on more responsibility, helping to cook meals and clean the house. Her mother had devoted herself to her new role in parliament and her daughter.

Gray had spent weekends with her dad. He'd seemed vulnerable then – as if the collapse of his marriage had sheared away some of his pride. They'd gone to football games together –

he was a Chelsea fan. ('For my sins,' he liked to say.) Afterwards, they'd go out for hamburgers at a greasy spoon he liked. Strolling back across the Chelsea Bridge on warm summer nights, watching the boats pass on the River Thames below – those were her fondest memories of that year.

Then, one day, he'd told her he was being sent to Russia.

'It's a new placement,' he'd explained. 'A real opportunity for me. You understand, don't you?'

She had seen the excitement in his eyes – he couldn't wait to go.

And she knew that all of this – hanging out with her, just being a dad – that wasn't enough for him. It didn't make him happy. Not like his job. The realisation had hit her like a punch.

'Sure, Dad,' she'd said, forcing a smile. 'I know it's important.'

Gray rinsed out her mouth and headed back to the bedroom and closed the door.

Her dad had promised that he'd come back every month. 'And you can come and visit me,' he'd assured her. 'See Moscow. It's a fascinating city.'

The promised trip did happen. She'd flown to Russia to meet him. She'd found Moscow very cold, and very crowded. But also beautiful, with graceful buildings along the river.

After that, though, she never went again. And his trips home had become less frequent. It had been months since she'd seen him. On the phone he apologised and told her work was intense right now. 'A lot going on'. And she understood that. He was a diplomat, and relations between Britain and Russia were tense. But still. She missed him.

Gray climbed into bed and pulled up the covers. She opened a book she'd been reading — *City of Bones*, it was called. It was good. But tonight, the words swam on the page. Her mind was elsewhere.

Richard had appeared on the scene the year her father moved to Russia. He had picked her mother up in a car that cost nearly as much as their south London flat was worth, taking her out to plays and to dinners at expensive restaurants with glamorous city views.

After a whirlwind romance, they'd married in the country garden of the friend who'd introduced them.

It had all happened so fast, there hadn't been time to really process it. But it had been impossible for her not to see how happy her mother was that day. She'd glowed with it. She'd never looked that happy with Gray's father. Ever since then, Gray had tried to accept Richard as part of her family. And failed.

After they moved into Number 10, things had got harder. The little apartment, the constant scrutiny, the fact that Gray was pursued by the press, the frequent attacks on her mother by Tom McIntyre and also by members of her own party, unhappy that a woman had been selected to be prime minister – it all raised tensions at home.

It seemed to Gray that, somewhere amidst all of that, her life – and what she wanted – had got lost. Or at least, become less important. Her mother's job was what really mattered.

But now that she knew there was real danger out there, specifically targeting the two of them, even her petty acts of rebellion were lost to her. She couldn't keep sneaking out to parties anymore. Everything was far too serious.

She only wished she and her mother could talk about it, like they used to talk. But it seemed those days were over.

With a sigh, she set the book down on the floor beside the bed. And reached up and turned out the light.

TWELVE

On Monday morning, Julia waited for Gray at the foot of the stairs.

It must have been a quiet weekend – she'd had two full days without any phone calls from Raj. She'd actually managed to get some sleep and to do her laundry for a change.

The rest had done her good. She felt invigorated. Ready to win over both Ryan and Gray.

As if she'd summoned her by thinking about her, Gray bounded down the stairs, as out of place in this office building as a kitten in a fish tank. She wore jeans tucked into knee-high boots – almost exactly the same clothes that Julia had chosen for the chilly, rainy weather.

'Nice outfit,' she observed lightly, as the girl approached.

Gray smiled brightly. 'You too.'

'We're going out the side entrance today,' Julia told her. 'Ryan's waiting for us.'

'That's cool,' Gray said, and they headed in that direction.

She seemed to be in a good mood as they walked down the hallway, and across the busy front lobby, with its checkerboard floor. Certainly, she looked happier by far than she had last week. Gone were the gloomy frowns and miserable sighs. There was a lightness in her step.

Julia wondered what had happened to cheer her up so much. After all, she was still grounded for weeks to come.

'Get into any trouble over the weekend?' she asked, glancing at her. 'I looked for stories about you in the tabloids but I didn't see anything.'

'I'm grounded,' Gray reminded her, innocently. 'How could I possibly get into trouble?'

Julia gave a dry laugh. 'Trust me when I tell you, I am perfectly aware that being grounded doesn't mean you stay home.'

It was a joke, but Gray didn't seem amused. Instead, she looked defensive. 'I didn't do anything,' she said. 'I was home all weekend.'

Julia held up her hands. 'Hey, don't worry. I was just joking. I'm not accusing you of anything.'

Gray paused as if surprised, before saying airily, 'Oh, I know that. I was joking, too.' But her cheeks reddened, and she wouldn't meet Julia's eyes.

Quickening her pace, she strode ahead. Julia watched her go, a frown forming above her eyes.

She'd never seen anyone look so guilty.

What did you do? she wondered.

She'd checked the records when she came in. There was no mention of Gray leaving the building at all since Friday. If she had sneaked out somehow, nobody knew about it.

The thought sent a chill through her.

It shouldn't be possible for Gray to get out of Number 10 without anyone noticing, but she'd already proven she was innovative when it came to eluding her security team. And Julia knew there were a lot of exits in this place.

If she'd found a way to get out of the building without her mother finding out, she could get herself in a lot of danger.

She caught up with Gray, touching her arm to slow her down. Gray's head snapped up.

'Hey,' Julia said, quietly. 'If anything did happen, anything weird at all, you can always tell me, OK? I won't tell your mother. I promise. I just need to know.' Seeing the rebellious look in Gray's eyes, she added, 'I'm trying to keep you safe. Things are dangerous out there.'

The two of them stopped walking, stepping aside from the office workers who glanced at them curiously as they passed.

Gray searched Julia's face as if looking for something. 'Can you tell me more about the threat against my mum and me? Why do they want to hurt us? What do they want? Is it about the cutbacks or something?'

Julia hesitated. 'To be honest, I don't know a lot about it. I've only been told the basics. I know there's a threat, and I know my bosses are keeping an eye on it. But you shouldn't worry. It's my job to worry about this stuff, not yours.'

It was the wrong thing to say.

Gray's face closed. 'Fine. I understand. We should go.'

Turning, she strode off, leaving Julia to scramble after her.

'Hang on, Gray,' she said. 'I'm telling you the truth. I really don't know any more. Please, tell me what's going on.'

The girl looked at her strangely – a wistfulness in her expression. But when she spoke, her tone was steady. 'It was nothing. I just want to know and my mother won't tell me anything. I feel left out. It's no big deal.'

It was a lie. Julia was almost certain of that. But it was plausible enough that she felt she had no choice but to accept it. If Gray felt attacked or harassed, she'd shut down further. She needed to give her time.

All the same, worry settled on Julia's shoulders. What was Gray hiding?

When they reached the unmarked door, two armed police officers glanced up at them. She recognised one of them from training camp.

'How's it going, Matheson?' he asked, holding out a machine for Julia to swipe with her ID. 'Raj keeping you out of trouble?'

'For now.' Her reply was absent, her focus on the teenager next to her.

Gray seemed lost in thought as the guard opened the door to reveal a quiet side street.

It was a short walk to where Ryan had parked. He stood by the open door of a dark Jaguar. His eyes surveyed the road for any sign of trouble, while Gray climbed into the back seat.

Julia got into the passenger seat and spoke into the microphone on her wrist. 'Firefly in transit.'

'Copy that,' a voice said into her earpiece.

In the back seat, Gray looked out of the window and said nothing. Her expression was smooth, but something was wrong.

The restful weekend seemed long ago already. Gray was hiding something, and Julia knew she should take her suspicions straight to her boss. But doing that would ensure the girl would never trust her. And trust might be the only thing that would save her life.

Somehow, she had to get Gray to talk. But how?

THIRTEEN

After her Saturday-night adventure, Gray's week quickly fell into a new kind of normal. Knowing what she knew, she could no longer fight the terms of her confinement at Number 10. Julia was right, there really was danger out there. Yet she was still angry at her mother for not telling her the truth. And she didn't know what to do with the information she did have. Everyone seemed to be telling her to be afraid, and do nothing.

Which was a pretty awful thing to ask.

She hadn't attempted to sneak out of the flat again. After all, she had proof that there was a real threat and that her mother was keeping it from her. She was unlikely to stumble across anything else. So her life became nothing more than going to school and then going home again.

Occasionally, she saw Jake McIntyre in the hallway. His bruises had faded from purple to yellow. The fuss about the party at Bijou had faded in much the same way. This week, everyone was talking about how Sally Lemington had lost her virginity on Saturday night in the back seat of Jared Longacre's dad's car.

Gossip moved fast.

She hadn't spoken to Jake again, and at times she wondered if she'd imagined their talk in the library. But sometimes when they passed each other in the crowded corridor, he caught her eye. And only once, but memorably, he smiled at her when no one was looking – a secret, just-for-her flash of light that warmed like the sun.

She'd told nobody – not even Chloe – about their discussion. The gossip factory knew perfectly well that his father hated her mother, and would have loved for the two of them to defy their parents and get together. Even becoming friends would have been enough to get everyone talking. Somehow she knew that too much attention would cause this tiny thread of connection between them to break. Neither of them wanted to be dragged further into the spotlight than they were already.

After her mother had won the election, there'd been a huge buzz about the two of them being in the same school. One newspaper had even published an article about it — The Romeo and Juliet of British Politics, the headline had read, to Gray's absolute mortification. For a while, whenever they'd passed in the hallways, things would go quiet, and she could sense the eyes on them. That was why, until now, she'd avoided him completely. It was the only way to avoid the damaging whispers. Eventually, the spotlight had moved on.

Now, though, she feared its return.

Aside from that though, she welcomed almost any distraction from her ongoing imprisonment. For the first time she could remember, there was no reason to look forward to the weekend. As she and Chloe walked down the corridor to the exit after their last class that Friday, the mood around them was boisterous and giddy. It was Halloween weekend. Some of the younger kids were in costumes – she saw a Katniss Everdeen, with her bow and arrow, and several versions of Doctor Who.

As Gray watched them run by aglow with excitement, she envied them so much. All that awaited her was another weekend at Number 10, by herself.

At her elbow, Chloe was fairly bouncing as she walked. 'My vampire costume finally arrived — I honestly thought it wouldn't make it in time. It took three weeks! And Will is going as Robin Hood.'

'Robin Hood and a vampire is a wild combination,' Gray commented, trying to show some enthusiasm about the party everyone would be going to except her.

'He refused to be a vampire too. *Refused.*' Chloe wrinkled her nose. 'But he'll be a cute Robin Hood.' She touched her upper lip. 'He's growing a little moustache.'

Another crowd of younger students shoved past them and ran for the exit, full of sugar and energy.

Gray turned to look at Chloe. 'Are you and Will getting more serious?'

'I mean, maybe? Or not really?' Chloe's cheeks turned pink. 'Basically, without you around I don't know what to do with myself so we've been going out more. I still don't think he's the one. I guess he's sort of the one who calls, which isn't as romantic.'

Maybe this was true, but she looked happy. A strand of worry tightened around Gray's heart. If she lost Chloe to Will, what would she do?

'There's no way your mum'll back down, is there?' Chloe asked, hopefully. 'I mean, it's getting ridiculous. You've served your time.'

Gray gave a dark laugh. 'Have you met my mum? She doesn't change her mind.'

'Well, I think it's bloody unfair,' Chloe said. 'It's Halloween weekend, for God's sake. You're only sixteen on

Halloween once. Besides, Amy's party won't be any fun without you.' She linked her arm with Gray's and squeezed her tight.

Although her intentions were good, this made Gray feel worse. She had ordered a witch costume in early October – low cut, with a short skirt. It had arrived a few days ago and was hanging in her closet now, along with its matching pointy hat. But her hints to her mother that she might be allowed out for one night only had been rebuffed that morning over breakfast.

'I think you've been to enough parties. You should have thought about this before you lied to me,' she'd said, snapping her laptop shut to signal the end of the conversation. 'Consequences have actions. You're grounded for two more weeks.'

Gray knew better than to keep fighting her. 'She won't back down,' she told Chloe now. 'She never does.'

Just then, Chloe's phone rang. 'Hang on,' she said, 'It's my dad.' She stepped aside to take the call.

As Gray waited, she glanced ahead to see Jake standing with Aidan on the school's front steps. Aidan was talking animatedly. Jake was looking into the distance, his lips very slightly curved up in a half-smile that made it hard to tell if he really thought what Aidan was saying was funny.

As Gray watched him surreptitiously, he must have felt her gaze, because he turned. Their eyes met. Gray felt that look like an electric shock. As if something tangible and real crackled on the air between them. The look on his face was complicated. It was as if there were things he wanted to say. Lots of things. Chloe couldn't seem to tear her gaze away. She wanted to talk to him again like they had in the library. Like friends.

'Are you hearing a word I'm saying?' Chloe nudged her with her shoulder, breaking the connection.

'I'm sorry,' Gray said, flustered. 'What did you say?'

'I said my dad's stuck in traffic, and he's going to be late.' Chloe's eyebrows drew together, and she gave Gray a perplexed look. 'What's going on?'

'Nothing,' Gray insisted, turning sideways, hoping her friend wouldn't notice Jake and put two and two together. 'Do you need a lift?'

'No, he's going to pick me up at the coffee shop.' Her brow creased. 'I wish you could come with me.'

'Me too.'

Julia walked up to them, blonde hair swinging above her black top. 'Time to go,' she told Gray, cheerfully. 'Enough education for one day. Put down those books and prepare to chill.'

The two of them said goodbye to Chloe, and Gray followed her bodyguard to the side door.

The whole way that look stayed with her, like a dream you can't quite forget. But as the afternoon stretched out into evening, she became convinced she'd imagined it. There was no way Jake McIntyre liked her. And surely – *surely* – she didn't like him? She couldn't. He'd been a thorn in her side for years. She was slowly going crazy, she decided, locked away by herself night after night.

Still, she couldn't get him out of her mind. And that evening, as she sat with her mother and Richard at the dinner table, she found herself saying aloud, 'I had a talk with Jake McIntyre the other day.'

She instantly regretted it.

Her mother's smile tightened. 'I keep forgetting he goes to your school.' She took a sip of wine. 'What on earth did you talk to him about?'

Our parents, Gray thought, but she didn't say that.

'Some guys thought he was the one who told the paparazzi I was at Aidan's party.' Gray kept her tone mild. 'It wasn't him. But he still got beaten up.'

'How do you know it wasn't him?' Richard leaned forward, watching Gray's face. 'Are you certain?'

Gray thought of Jake's utterly honest voice in the library when he had told her it wasn't him. The way his gaze had never shifted.

'I'm positive,' she said. 'He didn't do it.'

'I don't see how you can be positive,' Richard argued. 'God knows he's got the contacts. His father is a past master at calling the tabloids with lies about your mother.'

Gray was nonplussed. She didn't know Jake's dad had done that. But she recovered enough to say, 'Jake isn't his dad. They're two different people.'

'Of course they are,' said her mother. 'But he could have access to that information. And his father might well ask him to do things he doesn't want to do. I hear his father uses him as an assistant in his office.'

'Jake hates that,' Gray informed her quickly, as she felt the conversation slipping from her control. 'He doesn't want to work there. He's really angry about it.'

A new interest kindled in her mother's eyes. 'That's a surprise. I'd always heard the two of them were very close. His parents' divorce was notorious.' She glanced at Richard. 'A complete meltdown.'

Gray's brow furrowed. Other than what he'd told her, she knew little about Jake's family, aside from the fact that his father was always speaking at rallies and talking about how terrible her mother was. All the kids at school loved him. Even Gray thought he was totally right about climate change, although she'd never say that to her mum.

'Why was their divorce notorious?' she said, although she felt a tiny bit disloyal for asking for gossip.

'Well, I suppose it's common knowledge.' Her mother paused, as if choosing her words. 'His mother had an affair with another woman. Tom reacted very badly to it. He sued for custody and fought like a demon to get Jake.' There was a faint hint of satisfaction in her voice at telling a terrible story about her political enemy. 'Somehow he won the court case, and he took Jake out of his school in Leeds in the middle of the term and dumped him in Hartford High School, where he knew nobody. The poor kid.' She paused to finish the Chardonnay in her glass before adding, 'I've always suspected he chose that school because he knew I sent my daughter there. It wasn't like him to choose a private school.' She glanced at Gray. 'Honestly, it wouldn't surprise me at all if he asked his son to spy on you.'

Gray was dumbstruck. Suddenly it all made sense. The way Jake had just appeared a couple of years ago. His loathing for his father. The way he always stuck to the fringes of things, shoulders hunched, hands in his pockets.

It put her own parents' divorce into perspective, leaving her almost embarrassed about how dramatic she'd thought it was. She'd had no idea it could have been so much worse.

'Tom McIntyre's a piece of work,' said Richard, who had got up and walked to the fridge while her mother was talking and brought the wine bottle over. He topped up her glass and pressed a hand against her shoulder. 'I feel sorry for his son.'

'So do I,' her mother agreed, before turning to Gray. 'But, if I'm completely honest, I'd really rather you didn't spend time with him.'

Gray's jaw dropped. 'What? *Why?*'

'I know it sounds paranoid, but he does work in his father's office. And, regardless of what he says, that means he works for the opposition. And his father is determined to destroy my career.'

She stood and took the plates to the sink, as Gray stared at her back, stunned. Whatever she'd expected, it wasn't this. 'Jake's not a politician, Mum,' she said. 'You can't treat him like… like…' She gestured at her mother and Richard. '…one of you.'

'Darling, I know. And I know it's hard to understand why it matters.' Still infuriatingly calm, her mother raised her voice above the running water and the clatter of plates. 'The simple truth is, Tom McIntyre loathes me. It's a kind of obsession. And I wouldn't put it past him to ask his son to get close to you and find out anything he can. Even if he hasn't done that, you still know a lot about my work — we talk about it all the time. You might say something that could hurt me and Jake could pass it on to his father. You simply can't trust him.'

Gray opened her mouth to argue, but her mother continued, 'I talk freely around you, and often conduct business here. You hear things. And you don't know what's secret and what's free to share with your friends.' She held up a hand, fending off arguments Gray hadn't yet delivered. 'Now, obviously, you would never intentionally hurt me, but someone who knew more about politics could convince you to reveal things that could be damaging to me. I can't risk that. Things are quite fragile at the moment.'

'I wouldn't tell him anything important,' Gray said, offended. 'We talked about school and the things people were saying about him. That's it.'

But even as she said it, she knew it wasn't true. They'd also talked about her mother and her relationship. About her father.

A knot of worry formed in her chest. Could her mother possibly be right? Would Jake try to get information about her? Had she said too much? If she'd inadvertently betrayed her mother, everything could get so much worse in her life.

Unaware of her inner turmoil, her mother reached for a tea towel. 'You can see why I would prefer it if you didn't speak to him at all from now on,' she said. 'If you can't avoid talking to him for some reason, be very careful about what you say. Remember who his father is. And how much he hates me.

'I know I can trust you to do the right thing.'

FOURTEEN

Gray's mother was scheduled to travel to Brussels the next morning. A gala dinner was planned, and she would be staying the night. Richard was also travelling that day, heading to New York for business meetings. In better times, Gray would either have gone to stay at her dad's or with Chloe, but with her dad still away and Gray grounded, there was no alternative save to leave her alone at Number 10.

When she walked into the living room that morning, still in her pyjamas, her hair standing on end, her mother was standing at the mirror by the door applying lipstick, a small suitcase at her feet. She wore a dark jacket over a silk top and a statement necklace in heavy silver. Gray knew she wore that necklace when she was anticipating a fight. Clearly, Brussels wasn't going to be much fun for her.

'You look fierce,' she told her as she headed to the kitchen in search of coffee.

'Oh good, you're up.' Putting the lipstick away, her mother turned to her. 'Are you sure you don't want me to have someone come and stay with you? I know your Aunt Laura said she was busy, but she would do it if I told her I was worried about you. I hate the idea of you here all by yourself.'

Gray nearly dropped the cannister of coffee. 'I don't need a babysitter,' she said, her voice rising. 'God, Mum. I'm nearly seventeen years old. I can make my own *supper*.'

'I know precisely how old you are, thank you.' Her mother's voice held a hint of defensiveness. 'And there's no need for you to make dinner. I asked the cook downstairs to make you some of that chicken and rice you like. It's already in the fridge. All you have to do is heat it up.'

Her sudden surrender caught Gray off guard. She'd been preparing to argue. Now she had to calm down, abruptly. 'Great,' she said. 'Then there's no problem.'

Her mother hesitated. 'I know you can take care of yourself, Gray. I'm just... Well. If you need something you'll call downstairs, won't you?'

Gray made a face. 'I promise.'

But her mother didn't let it drop. 'If anything makes you nervous, call the security desk immediately. Or use the panic button.'

This wasn't like her. It wasn't the first time Gray had spent the night alone at Number 10. Suddenly, though, she thought she understood. This was about the threat. And all the things her mother knew and hadn't told her.

Suppressing the urge to point out how much safer she'd be if her mother was honest, she walked over to her.

'Mum, come on.' She gave her mother a quick hug, feeling the heavy necklace cool beneath her chin. 'I know how to call security. I also know there's a panic button in the kitchen, and I promise to use it if I get hungry or bored.'

Gray was trying to make her smile, but it didn't work. Up close, the fine lines around her mother's eyes appeared deeper than normal. She looked stressed.

'This is the most secure building in the country,' Gray reminded her. 'I'll be safe.'

'Of course you will.' Her mother smoothed her expression. 'Well then. I should go. My driver will be waiting. Richard's already downstairs.'

She gave Gray a quick hug and then headed for the door, heels clicking on the polished oak, the rolling suitcase rumbling at her side.

Suddenly, unexpectedly, Gray missed her terribly. She missed the way they used to be.

When her mother had first been elected to Parliament, she had sometimes taken Gray with her on work trips. And their afternoons spent exploring some new city together were among her fondest memories. It had been such an adventure, having a politician mother. She missed that feeling – the bond between them, once so strong, seemed with every passing day to grow more brittle.

'Mum?' she called, on impulse.

Her mother turned to glance at her.

'Knock 'em dead, OK?'

A smile lit up her mother's face. 'You know I will. See you tomorrow, darling.' She opened the door. In the hallway, Gray glimpsed an anonymous staff member, shoulders stiff with anticipation, waiting to take her bag. Then the door closed again, and she was alone.

Gray walked around the island to the open-plan kitchen and put the kettle on to boil. Her hands moved slowly but her mind was working.

After the dinner conversation, she'd been unable to sleep. She kept thinking over what her mother had said about Jake and his father. She didn't really believe Jake would use her to get information about her mother. He seemed too honest a person for that. Too real. But the truth was, she didn't know him at all.

And she knew better than most the kind of pressure a political parent can put on their child. She'd lived it.

She was 'discouraged' from posting political views on the internet. So strongly discouraged, that her mother had told her once: 'If you want to ruin my life, and your own, become an activist.' And Gray knew the papers would have a field day if she started posting about equal pay for women or the evils of capitalism — things her mother's party didn't believe in.

It would have been great revenge when her mother was being dictatorial, but she never did it. She didn't want the explosion of attention any more than her mother did.

Besides, whatever her own views, she was loyal to her family.

Why shouldn't Jake be the same?

He'd made it clear he and his dad didn't get along, but that didn't mean he wouldn't do things to support his father's political success.

She still didn't believe he'd called the press that night at Bijou. He would have had to be a great actor to fake it that day in the library. But as to whether he might pass on a tidbit of information if she accidentally revealed things — she just didn't know.

The realisation that she wasn't at all certain that she could trust him left her confused and a little angry. Was there nobody in the world aside from Chloe that she *could* trust?

She wished Julia was around to talk to, but the bodyguard didn't work weekends, since there was no need for personal security when Gray couldn't leave the building.

Maybe that was what started her thinking about going exploring again.

She wasn't sure what she'd be looking for now — she already had the proof she needed about the threat. But she didn't want to sit in this flat all alone with her thoughts for the next twenty-four hours. She needed a distraction.

She spent the afternoon web chatting with Chloe, who was getting ready for Amy's party, dressing as a vampire queen in a tight black mini-dress with a high peaked collar.

'I can't belieff you're not coming wiff me,' Chloe lisped, through plastic pointed teeth. 'It'th going to be therrible.'

'It's going to be great,' Gray corrected her. 'And I expect you to get all the gossip, and call me tomorrow.'

Chloe beamed at her through the phone screen, a perfect, ruby drop of fake blood glistening below her lips.

Fleetingly, Gray considered telling her about her plans. She hadn't mentioned the last expedition into the nearby building, because she didn't want her to freak out about the threat. In the end, she decided to say nothing. It would be hard to explain, and Chloe was caught up in preparations for her night out.

If anything exciting happened, though, she would tell her. If it all went well, maybe the next time she went exploring Chloe could come with her.

After they hung up, she worked on the plan – sketching out how it would work. She had to have a good story ready, because there was no way to get where she needed to go without going right by the police guards.

First, though, she had to wait. The timing had to be perfect. As night fell, she heated up the chicken and rice her mother had left, and ate it at the kitchen island while reading the Instagram posts Chloe and Amy were putting up online of the party. Each colourful image of a friend in a hilarious costume grinning at the camera made her more determined to get out of this apartment. Whatever it took.

By eleven o'clock, she was filled with such an electric mixture of adrenaline and loneliness she forgot to be scared as she opened the front door of the family's apartment and paused to listen.

She heard no voices – no footsteps. The building seemed to breathe around her, slow and steady. As if it were asleep.

The hallway wall sconces – which were always left on – cast a faint golden glow as she crept out. Her glittery, rubber-soled shoes made no sound at all on the stairs.

The hardest part, as far as she could tell, would come right at the beginning, when she had to get by the police who guarded Number 10's front door twenty-four hours a day.

When she reached the ground floor, the building was very quiet. She could hear the low murmur of the officers talking – the faint, plastic sound of fingers typing on a keyboard.

She increased her pace, heading purposefully across the main entrance hall where the guards sat at a bank of computer monitors, where the CCTV screens showed different parts of the building.

She'd nearly made it past when an official voice called out behind her, 'Excuse me, Miss?'

Gray stopped. Swallowing hard, she turned. 'Yes?' she asked, innocently.

Three guards looked at her. One stood between her and the desks where they worked, having obviously got up to follow her. He was tall and trim, and a similar age, she guessed, to her father. He wore a white police uniform shirt, with a black bullet-proof vest strapped over the top that made his chest look bulkier than it was.

'Can we help you?' His tone was polite, but also authoritative, with a hearty underlying helping of '*Don't mess with me*'.

Gray had prepared for this but now that she was in it, she had to fight to keep her composure. She tried to appear guileless. 'I'm just going to the kitchen to see if they have any chocolate. We've run out upstairs and it's Halloween, you know?'

'We could have someone check and bring it up to you, if you like?' the officer said. 'The kitchen staff are on call.'

They were all watching her with more interest now.

Gray forced her face muscles into a smile. 'Actually,' she said, in what she hoped was a confiding tone, 'I really want to nose around the kitchen and see what they've got to eat. I'm starving. And I won't know what I want until I see it. Is that OK?'

There was a pause as the main officer considered this. He was clearly the boss of the three. Finally, though, he tilted his head towards the kitchen.

'Go on, then,' he said. 'Bring us back some chocolate if you find some.'

'Or a box of digestives,' one of his associates called out.

'You're supposed to be on a diet,' the third officer teased him.

'It's Halloween, mate,' the dieting guard said, defending himself. 'I'm a growing boy.'

'Thanks! I'll see what I can find.' With a wave, Gray headed off in the direction of the kitchen, relief coursing through her in such a rush it made her feel dizzy. She could hear the police good-naturedly bickering behind her. They'd obviously accepted her story.

The kitchen was still some distance away when she stopped in front of a nondescript door. It was the door Julia had taken her through on that first day, to avoid the photographers. The secret one that led to the tunnels and, through them, to other government buildings.

Gray was going to find out what else was down there.

FIFTEEN

Julia stood outside the Houses of Parliament, shivering in the cold as Big Ben tolled eleven times. She was so close to the clock tower, she felt the vibration of the bells through her feet.

Normally, she'd be home now watching TV, but Raj had called just before six and asked if she'd mind pulling a bit of overtime. 'There's a dinner party in Parliament,' he'd said. 'A lot of famous politicians in one place can be attractive to the bad guys. A lot of targets. It'd be good to have all hands on deck.'

Something told her he didn't want her there just to stand around with a bunch of police watching drunk people walk across Parliament Square dressed as Frankenstein or cowboys.

She rubbed her hands together, trying to get some feeling back in her icy fingers. Why had she left her gloves behind? Her jacket was in no way thick enough to withstand the freezing wind blowing off the River Thames, which flowed just behind the famous building.

She'd had to get ready fast – trading in the school-friendly wardrobe she wore when working with Gray for neat black trousers, her hair pulled back.

A group of tipsy young women stopped to pose for a picture with the front gate officers. Amiably, one agreed to the photo, and smiled broadly as the women fluttered around him, butterflies to nectar.

If I see one more sexy witch, Julia thought, her expression cool and blank as a laughing woman offered her pointed hat to the cop, who politely declined to wear it.

'It looks better on you.' His smile was pleasant but his eyes remained observant.

If there was one thing Julia had learned in the last couple of hours, it was that Parliament cops had the patience of saints. It took everything in her not to shout at the crowds, 'Can you just keep moving? Haven't you ever heard of *terrorism*?'

Moments later, she spotted Raj emerging from one of the stone archways. He was talking to a man in a suit who had his back to her. The two had a strange body language – Raj was half-turned away, as if he didn't want to get too close to the other man, and yet he was listening intently.

When his companion turned so his profile was in the light, her breath stopped in her throat. She hadn't seen his face in years, but she recognised him instantly.

She turned quickly away. She felt colder than before, her mind whirling through the possibilities. Something was very wrong here.

Minutes later, a voice came from behind her. 'Crazy night.'

Julia spun around to find Raj standing next to her, watching the crowds stream by. His black leather jacket didn't appear any warmer than her own, but the freezing wind didn't seem to affect him as he watched her steadily, as if anticipating what she was going to say.

'Why were you talking to Nathaniel St John?' she asked, an accusation underlying her words.

'Before you jump to conclusions, he asked to meet.' His voice was coated in distaste. 'Frankly, I'd prefer never to speak to him. But as you know, he has connections. And, it turns out, he's been hearing some of the same rumours I have. He wanted me to know he wasn't involved, but that he thinks the rumours are true.'

Julia wasn't mollified.

Nathaniel was a friend of her parents, and he was one of the reasons she was estranged from her family. Their extreme politics and selfish decisions had driven her away when she was young. She still despised them.

'Rumours about what?' she asked. 'Raj, you know better than anyone that he lies.'

'I know what I'm doing, Jules.' It was the first time he'd used the nickname she'd been known by as a teenager. 'This situation with Firefly and her mother is worse than we thought. The second we increased our security, these guys changed their tactics. We adjust again, and find they've already changed. It's almost as if they know what we're going to do before we've done it.' He paused. 'You should know that thc latest messages we intercepted mentioned you, specifically.'

Julia's heart kicked. 'They know my *name*?'

He nodded.

For once, she was speechless. Talos Inc. and everything she and the other guards did was top secret. Nobody knew except the prime minister and her closest aides.

'Raj,' she said, breathless with shock, 'that means someone inside is working against us. Someone very highly placed.'

'Yes, it does.' His voice simmered with quiet fury. 'That's why I'm telling you this. You need to know that we're operating under Protocol 9 from now on. We're going off the books. Nothing we do will be reported to anyone except the prime minister, who has agreed to keep it entirely out of her public office.' He paused. 'Also, I'm going to need you to move to a safe house. Tonight. The address is here.' He handed her a slip of paper.

She stared at it, the words it held momentarily meaningless.

From the street, she heard a sudden burst of raucous laughter and shouts. A double-decker bus sounded its horn irritably at a crowd lingering too long in the street. But it all seemed far away.

Protocol 9. A war protocol, so rarely invoked it took Julia a moment to remember. It meant radio silence. Nothing else they did would be known by anyone in government. Nobody would know what their job was. And if they got in trouble – or killed – nobody in government would claim them.

'Not one other person will have access to this,' he assured her. 'Nor can you share it with anyone. I'm breaking protocol by telling you as much as I am. But you need to know for your own safety. You'll stay in the safe house from now until I tell you otherwise. After you collect your things tonight, you may not go home again for any reason until I personally say it's safe.'

Julia's mouth was suddenly dry. This was all much worse than she'd imagined. 'What about Ryan?' she asked. 'Did they identify him?'

He gave a crisp nod. 'He'll be moving tonight, too. I'm speaking to him next.'

Julia found herself struggling to fully process what he was telling her. There was a spy inside the highest level of the British government. Possibly inside the prime minister's office. And this person was working with the new Russian terrorist group that wanted to kill the country's leader, and her entire family.

Nothing like this had ever happened before, as far as she knew.

'Does this mean Gray's in more danger than we thought?' she asked, the words spilling out. 'If they're on the inside they can…'

He cut her off before she could say another word. 'We always knew she was under threat and that has not changed. Our work to protect her remains the same. She's not safe anywhere outside of Number 10 Downing Street.' He looked past her, his eyes as dark as the sky. 'And yet, she keeps trying to get out.'

He let out a breath that clouded in the cold air and stepped closer to her, his voice growing urgent. 'Julia, you have to convince Firefly to trust you. Confide in her. Tell her your own secrets. Listen to hers. Be her *friend*. She's young and lonely. She can't possibly fully understand what danger she faces right now. We need her to tell you what's going on. What she hears. She might not recognize a threat if it came to her. She's been too shielded by her mother.'

'There's one other thing.' He paused. 'You should know that her father works for MI6. He's on long-term assignment in Russia. I can't tell you any more than that. But it may be connected to what's happening right now. This could be all about him.'

'Does Gray know this?' Julia asked, her brow creasing.

He shook his head. 'She doesn't have a clue. She thinks he's a kind of diplomat. Her mother doesn't want her to know. That's part of the problem. The girl's old enough to understand but her mother still thinks of her as a child she wants to protect. And you and me?' He held out his hands. 'We're stuck in the middle.'

'I'll make sure she's safe,' Julia promised. 'But her mother needs to stop lying to her daughter.'

He shot her a warning look. 'Like it or not, we work for the prime minister. She makes the rules. And we abide by them.'

An icy wind blew in off the river, cutting through Julia's jacket to her skin, making her shiver.

'I strongly disagree with not informing the girl of what's really going on at this stage,' she said, tightening her muscles against the cold.

'It's not your decision, Matheson.' His tone told her to drop it.

'Understood.'

'Right now, we need to get you safe.' Some of the ice left Raj's tone. 'Go home. Get your things. Make sure you're not followed. Use the usual methods. Remember your training.'

'Yes, sir.'

A loud *bang* split the night, and they both jumped. Behind the towers of Parliament, blue, red, and gold lights exploded into tiny falling stars, as the fireworks show began. The crowds on the street cheered.

Raj looked up at the huge clock face of Big Ben, glimmering gold against the dark winter sky, beneath a shower of coloured sparks.

'These are dangerous times,' he said. 'But this building has lived through worse. It'll be here when this threat passes.' His gaze shifted to her. 'Follow my rules, and so will you.'

With that, he strode away, heading for the tall arched entrance into Parliament.

As she watched him go, Julia felt the first real prickle of fear up her spine. She'd worked in intelligence in the military – she could hear everything he wasn't saying. The mission he'd described was virtually impossible, and he knew it.

The threat was organised and credible and had penetrated the British government at the highest levels. No one could protect Gray if someone inside that building wanted her dead.

The thought made her angry.

Gray was just a child. If they wanted to take her out, they'd have to go through Julia first. And she was going to enjoy stopping them.

SIXTEEN

The lights were already on in the tunnel when Gray reached the bottom of the stairs. Maybe they were always left on. Or maybe someone else was down here.

The thought made Gray's heart twist. She knew she hadn't thought this through. This was much riskier than sneaking into an empty office building. This was walking into the unknown.

It was unnaturally quiet below ground. No sounds of traffic, no faint whoosh of heating through vents. No voices or footsteps aside from her own. In fact, the only thing she could hear, apart from her own breathing, was an occasional irregular light tapping sound – like someone dancing far away with no sense of rhythm.

Thick electrical cables ran along the ceiling above her head, along with a dozen plastic pipes.

The pipes are making the noise, Gray told herself, because it's what her mother would have said, although she had no idea what would make pipes sound like that.

Determined not to give up this early, she hurried her pace, half-running into the tunnel, retracing her steps from last week. The air was cold and damp, with the musty, stale smell she remembered.

Sooner than she expected, she reached the intriguing old-fashioned doors with frosted glass windows. With their hand-painted numbers and blackened doorknobs, they looked like doors into the past. As if she could open one and step straight into World War II Britain, with bombers buzzing overhead.

Pressing her face against the frosted glass, she tried to peer inside one, but could make out nothing but shadowy shapes. Tentatively, she tried the handle.

It rattled at her touch but refused to turn.

Locked.

She tried the next one. And the door after that. All locked.

She wanted to try all of them, but time was short. The police upstairs would notice, eventually, that she hadn't come back. Her plan was to try to reach the end of one of the tunnels and find out where it went, and then get back fast. She would allow herself no more than half an hour underground.

When she got back, she'd show up at their desk with chocolate biscuits, say goodnight, and head upstairs. No one would ever know.

She resumed her journey through the tunnel, jogging steadily. After the doors, the chipped, whitewashed walls were blank. No warning signs or notices. Anyone who came down here was meant to know where they were going.

Ahead, a square opening appeared on the right. When she reached it, she saw that it was a second tunnel. It looked very much like the one she was in. Same lighting. Same dusty walls. At the arched entrance, a faded, hand-painted sign pointed into the distance. It looked for all the world like a street sign. It read: 'Foreign Office.'

Gray hesitated. Her father was a diplomat for the Foreign Office. If she got in there, maybe she could find out something about him, and the work he was doing. He never told her much about his job. Only that it was important, and secret.

NUMBER 10

In the end, she kept going straight on. One thing she knew about diplomats – they worked all hours. She was unlikely to find that building empty. It was too risky.

She'd walked some distance when she noticed the ticking sound had come back again, from behind her. It sounded like high heels clicking against a stone floor.

Her breath caught. What if someone else really was down here?

She broke into a full run, hurtling through the tunnel at such speed, the walls beside her blurred. She was moving so fast, she almost missed the next intersection. When she passed the opening, she skidded to an abrupt stop, losing her balance in the process, and slamming her hands against the nearest wall to catch herself. The stone felt damp and slimy beneath her fingers, and she jerked her hands away, rubbing her palms hard against her jeans.

The musty, damp smell was much stronger here. It smelled of mould and decay. Of years without light. It was a graveyard smell.

This tunnel didn't look at all like the other one she'd encountered. The entrance was arched, for one thing, instead of square. The walls were uneven – she could see chisel marks on the stones. No cables or pipes ran along the ceiling.

It had lights, but these were not the dirty fluorescent tubes that lit up the first tunnel. Instead, an unsteady glow came from dangling incandescent bulbs that flickered in the darkness, sending shadows skittering across the old walls like spiders.

At the entrance, a hand-painted arrow pointed into the tunnel next to an old, faded sign that read only: 'Q'.

Q? Gray thought, her brow furrowing.

Nothing in government was called Q. There was no office of Q. Or Department Q.

What could it mean?

Whatever it was, it had to be secret. The Foreign Office tunnel had been clearly marked. This office, whatever it was, had a code name.

Her stomach tightening, Gray peered into the narrow space with its moving shadows and swinging lights. Part of her wanted to pass it by. Another part wanted to turn back.

But her curiosity got the better of her. There had to be a reason this tunnel wasn't clearly identified. And she wanted to find out what that was.

Cautiously, she turned into the tunnel and began to walk.

The first thing she noticed was how cold it was. The ceiling was very low and damp. Droplets of water pattered onto the stone floor like rain. Puddles had formed in places, forcing her to wade through icy water.

It was much narrower than the other tunnel – if Gray stretched out her arms she could touch both sides. It was older, as well. Cracks split the stone here and there, in jagged cuts that revealed nothing except more grey rocks. The stone floor was dirty – grit crunched beneath her shoes.

In some places, pale stalactites hung down. Most were small and spindly – needles of hardened minerals. A few were long enough to pick at her hair like bony fingers as she ducked beneath them, shuddering.

The walkway wasn't straight. It bent and curved, sometimes quite sharply. The floor undulated up and down. Soon she was cold, wet, and lost.

Still, she trudged on. She wasn't sure how long she'd walked when she noticed an ominous darkness ahead. The closer she got to it, the darker it seemed. When she reached the end of the light, she stopped.

NUMBER 10

From this point on, it appeared the old lights that hung from the ceiling had all burned out.

Gray hesitated for a long moment. She didn't want to walk into that unknown. She'd never seen darkness so complete. It was as if she were in a cave.

She could see her breath now. Her hands felt numb. Fear uncurled inside her.

Her chest tightened as she leaned forward, as if on a precipice, and peered into the gloom. There could be nothing down there at all. Maybe the tunnel just ended.

But she hadn't come this far for nothing. And she didn't really believe any of these tunnels went nowhere. They'd all been built for a reason.

'Come on, Gray,' she whispered to herself. 'Don't be a coward.'

Julia wouldn't be afraid to walk in the dark. She'd been a soldier. She didn't seem to be afraid of anything.

Reaching into her pocket, she pulled out her phone and turned on the flashlight app. It cast a weak, bluish glow into the thick black that threatened to envelop her.

Bracing herself, she took a step into the darkness.

Almost instantly, her shoes sloshed into water.

Gray gave a small cry of surprise, shining the light down.

This section of the tunnel must have flooded after all the rain last week. The water was ankle deep, ice cold, and black as pitch.

Gritting her teeth, she waded through it, trying not to brush against the oozing walls. Clouds of breath appeared and then faded in the faint light from her phone. Everything echoed. The splashing of her feet, the rasping of her breath, even the pounding of her heart seemed to rebound off the walls.

After a minute, though, she noticed a faint light ahead.

Her heart quickened. She hurried her steps, sending cold water up over her ankles in her haste.

She was almost there, when she heard something scuttle through the water behind her.

Suppressing a scream, she spun around to look. The phone flew from her numb fingers, landing in the water with a *splash*. Its light blinked out.

'Bollocks,' Gray breathed. The word echoed back to her in a raspy whisper: *Bollocks... bollocks... bollocks.*

She wanted to run but she couldn't leave her phone there. Someone might find it. With its sparkly gold case, it didn't look like something a prime minister's staffer might have dropped.

There was only one thing to do.

Reluctantly, she crouched, dipping her fingers into the icy water with distaste, feeling the rough stone under it.

'Oh God,' she whispered aloud, and her voice echoed back. *Oh God. Oh God. Oh God...*

'This is so disgusting.'

Disgusting. Disgusting ...

Setting her jaw, she swished her hand until at last her fingers encountered something slick and metal and definitively modern. Grasping it, she snatched it from its watery grave, holding it up triumphantly. Cold water ran down her arm.

Its screen was blank, and it stayed that way no matter how many times she pushed the on switch. But at least she had it. And it was easier to explain a waterlogged phone than one that had somehow disappeared forever in an apartment she wasn't supposed to leave.

With damp fingers, she shoved it into her pocket. Determined now to get out of the cold and damp, she ran towards the light. To her relief, the ground was drier here. The air smelled fresher. And it was definitely getting warmer.

She was close to something. But what?

Sprinting, she rounded a bend to find the tunnel ended abruptly in front of a solid oak door.

Gray studied it curiously. This wasn't like the doors near Number 10. It was much older.

An old metal light fixture arched above it, curled like a snake. The wood of the door was thick and scarred. The huge black hinges appeared to be made from iron.

Instead of a doorknob or handle, it had a solid iron ring.

Gray reached out with both hands to grasp it. It was heavy, and oddly warm to the touch.

It turned smoothly, as if it had recently been oiled.

The door swung open.

SEVENTEEN

Cautiously, Gray stepped into a well-lit underground corridor.

Conduits carried thick ropes of electrical wires in vivid rainbow colours – red and blue and yellow – along the low ceiling. Stacks of pipes ran along the walls.

It was old, like the tunnel, but heavily used. Clean and dry. There was no musty smell of decay here.

There were modern signs everywhere. 'Low Ceilings: Mind your head!' 'Don't Touch! Risk of Electrocution!'

The stone edges of the ceiling were ornate and carefully carved. It looked sort of like a church, maybe. Or a palace.

God, what if she'd ended up in Buckingham Palace?

The thought was both exciting and terrifying. You couldn't just sneak into that building without expecting to get arrested.

Still, it was unlikely. She was sure she hadn't walked that far.

Eager to find out where she was, she sped through the basement, looking for a way to get upstairs, trying every side door, until she finally came to a set of plain stone steps, leading upwards.

She dashed to the top, and pushed the door open a crack.

What she saw on the other side made her jaw drop. It was glorious. The walls were panelled in polished oak. The floors were covered in vivid red carpet. Old drawings of London at various stages in its history hung in elaborate gilded frames on the walls.

The air smelled of lemon furniture polish and leather. The scent was rich and filled with promise.

She could see bookshelves fifteen feet high in the distance, lined with volumes in bindings of tooled maroon leather with gilded lettering. The heavy curtains on the arched windows were made of scarlet and gold silk. The painted oak ceiling soared high above her head.

There was no question where she was. Only one place in London looked like this. She'd been here plenty of times with her mother. She wasn't in Buckingham Palace at all. She was in The House of Lords.

She'd just sneaked into Parliament.

Gray was so shocked she found herself laughing in a mix of terror and exhilaration. If she got caught now, it would mean so much trouble. This was the country's seat of power. And she'd walked right into it.

It took a real effort to make herself calm down enough to think practically.

The most important thing was to be sure she could find her way back out again. Parliament was a massive palace-like structure. And like a castle, it was rambling. Filled with long, confusing corridors. It would be very easy to get lost.

She turned a slow circle. The door she'd come out of was marked with the letters 'BL-141'. She memorised that, along with other landmarks near it – the towering bookshelves, an ornate grandfather clock.

Not a sound came from any direction. The building seemed to be completely empty. It wouldn't be, of course. It had to be patrolled all night by police and security guards, just as Number 10 was. And she knew parliamentarians often worked very late. There were people here, somewhere.

I should go back, she thought.

After all, she'd done what she had set out to do. She'd made it to the end of the tunnel – she knew where it went. She should run straight back to Number 10 before anyone knew she was gone.

But now that she was here, her curiosity was fired. She'd never been here by herself before. It was one of the grandest buildings in the world, and she had the run of the place. She'd always wanted to explore its many twisting hallways and narrow stone staircases. There were so many intriguing unmarked doors and gilded passageways.

Ten minutes, she decided, ignoring the voice in her head that told her to go home now. I'll just spend ten minutes looking around and I'll run all the way back.

With no time to spare, she began walking in the direction of those bookshelves. She could use them to help find her way back – like giant breadcrumbs.

She strode down the hallway, her shoulders back, walking like she owned the place.

The building dazzled her. It was like something out of a fairytale with its marble tables and tall arched windows and doors, each framed in elaborately carved stone or oak.

When she reached a window weighted curtains fringed in gold tassels, she paused to look out – Big Ben's tower loomed so gigantically close she had to lean back to see the time.

Eleven thirty.

A crowd of police officers and black-clad security guards were clustered at the base of the clocktower. One of the female officers looked familiar. Gray squinted, trying to make out her features. With her short blonde ponytail, she looked like Julia. But then the woman walked away before she could get a better look.

Reminding herself that time was short, Gray dropped the curtain and hurried down the hallway, past oversized throne-like chairs and long tables topped with heavy urns and books the size of encyclopaedias.

Each turn seemed to reveal something amazing – a life-sized suit of armour gleaming in a corner. A sword as long as she was tall, in a glass case. And everywhere more paintings and books.

The hallway ended in an extraordinary lobby, where four corridors met through high archways. Overhead, huge chandeliers were ablaze, highlighting the floor, tiled with a star design at the centre. On all sides, marble statues surrounded her. Some were on plinths, others were mounted into the walls between the huge doorways. Their blank eyes seemed to regard her with disapproval as she paused, trying to get her bearings. The atrium was circular, with four hallways sprawling off in different directions. She'd been here before, but never alone.

She was trying to decide which corridor to take when she heard voices approaching.

Everything echoed off the stone and tiles – it was impossible to tell where they were coming from. The hall contorted the sound.

But they were getting closer.

Gray's chest tightened.

Panicking, she turned left and then right, looking for a place to hide – but there was nothing. There were no windows. No curtains. Nothing to get behind. No way to disappear.

Now she could hear the sound of heels clicking against the wood floor nearby. A deep male voice grumbled, 'Henry couldn't get that bill through with a sledgehammer if you ask me…'

Desperately, Gray dashed directly across the lobby, through the high, open doorway on the other side, and into another wide hallway. She had no idea where she was going, but all that mattered was that the voices were fading behind her.

She kept running, her heart racing, until she couldn't hear them anymore. Finally, when it was quiet again, she allowed herself to stop and look around.

This corridor was significantly less opulent than the one she'd come out of. The walls were plastered instead of covered in panelling, and the ceiling was lower and plain white. It was lined on both sides by what looked like normal business offices.

The plainness of it told her that she'd walked into the House of Commons.

Parliament is made up of two houses. Everything in the House of Commons is green and quite simply decorated. Everything in the House of Lords is red and ornate.

Her mother's office had been in the Commons until she became prime minister and moved to Number 10.

I wonder if I could find her old office? Gray wondered, as she looked around. The place was a labyrinth. The old office had been on the first floor, and she considered going up there, but when she reached the stairs, she caught a glimpse of someone heading up, and her breath hissed between her teeth as she hastily turned back.

No, she decided, I'd better stay down here.

Besides, she was already running out of time.

The hallway was lined with small doors, each marked with a mixture of numbers and letters on it that told her nothing about what might be inside.

She tried the first door on her left, more out of curiosity than hope. To her surprise, it opened easily, revealing a small office.

Whoever worked here had left the lights on.

On an impulse, she slipped inside and closed the door behind her.

She turned around to take in her hiding place.

The office was small and nondescript. There was little room for more than a desk and a chair, along with shelves lined with files. A small TV hung above the door, its screen black.

Turning her attention to the desk, she found it was annoyingly neat. Aside from the computer and phone, there was only a letter opener, and two framed pictures of chubby-cheeked children.

Having tried the desk drawers and found them all locked, she was checking the side shelves for any useful papers, when she noticed the door. It was not the door she'd come in through.

Thinking it was a closet of some sort, she tried it. It opened to reveal a much larger office.

Inside it was dark, but enough light came in through the open door for her to see that this one had a bigger, fancier desk, with a more comfortable-looking chair.

Whoever occupied the smaller office – this room belonged to their boss.

Gray felt along the wall until she found a light switch. When she turned it on, a large executive office sprang into view.

The walls were painted dark grey, and the floor was covered in plush matching carpet. Expensive-looking lamps provided subtle lighting from every corner. Across the room from the desk, a long table was surrounded by six chairs, each upholstered in green leather, with the logo of Parliament – a castle gate shaped like a hashtag with spiked edges – on the back in gold.

Stepping back, she glanced at the door again – there was no sign to indicate whose office this was. But it was clear they were important. This office was *swank*. Gray's mother's office had never been this big – or this nice – when she was in Parliament.

It would be extremely bad to get caught in here.

But… it was also kind of fun.

Pushing her luck, she walked around the desk, and sat down in the black leather chair, picking up a heavy glass paperweight to see the bubbles trapped inside.

Suddenly, she felt utterly empty. This would all have been fun, she thought, if someone else were here to explore with her. On her own, it felt pointless.

She wondered what all her friends were doing right now. If the party was fun.

Pulling her damp phone from her pocket, she pressed the on button hopefully. But the screen stayed stubbornly dark.

'Of course,' she muttered, and her voice sounded loud in the silent office.

Her gaze fell on the black office phone sitting on the desk. When she picked up the receiver it felt cool in her hand, and the low, reassuring hum of the dial tone greeted her.

She dialled Chloe's number from memory. Propping her wet silver trainers up on the desk, she waited.

It rang four times.

Five.

She was about to hang up, when suddenly Chloe's voice sounded in her ear.

'Who is this?' she asked aggressively.

'Oh my God,' Gray said. 'You're so suspicious.' Hearing her best friend's voice had brightened her mood instantly.

There was a brief pause. 'Gray? Is that you?'

'Who else?'

'This isn't your number.' Chloe's tone was accusing. She wasn't lisping anymore – she must have taken the plastic teeth out. 'Where are you? Who are you with? Did your mum let you out of prison?'

'Not exactly.' Gray grinned. 'I broke out.'

'You did?' Chloe cheered. 'Where are you? Come and meet me.'

It struck Gray that she couldn't hear any telltale sounds of a party in the background. 'Wait, where are *you*?' she asked. 'Why aren't you at Amy's party?'

'It was grim,' Chloe sighed. 'Her parents were there.'

'You're joking.'

'Yeah. That was not fun,' Chloe said. 'Her mum made pizzas. Like, what are we? *Twelve*? Everyone just sat around in costumes looking at their phones. I left as soon as I could. Amy was so embarrassed.'

'Oh, drag.' Gray tried to sound sympathetic but she couldn't stop smiling. She hadn't missed out after all.

'Yeah,' Chloe sighed. 'It was the worst. Complete waste of time.' Her tone shifted. 'I did have a *very* interesting conversation with Jake Macintyre, though.'

Gray's heart kicked. 'Jake was there? What did he say?'

She failed to keep the urgency out of her voice, and Chloe clearly noticed that.

'Well,' she drawled. 'First, can I say he's so much more interesting than I thought. And cuter. How did I not notice those cheekbones?'

The hot burst of jealousy Gray felt on hearing this was so unexpected it shook her.

'Hello? Are you still there?' Chloe tapped her phone with her nail.

Gray cleared her throat. 'Yeah, I'm here. I was just... So, what are you telling me? That you like Jake now?'

'God, no,' Chloe said, 'He's not my type at all. What I'm trying to tell you is, all he wanted to talk about was *you*. How is Gray doing? Is she still grounded? When will her mum let her out? Is she seeing anybody...?'

'He really asked you that?' Gray cut her off. 'He really asked if I was seeing anyone?'

Dropping her feet to the floor, she leaned forward. She felt warm with happiness.

'Why do you sound so surprised?' She could hear Chloe's amusement over the phone. 'I keep telling you you're smokin' hot. *Of course* he likes you. The question is, do you like him? You guys were not liking each other at Aidan's party, as I recall.'

Heat rose to Gray's face. 'Yeah, but we've talked since then,' she confessed.

Chloe gasped. 'Wait. And you were going to tell me this when?'

'Now,' Gray said, flushing.

'So, you do like him?' Chloe sounded thrilled.

Gray wasn't sure how to answer that. Mostly, Jake confused her. Why did she suddenly not hate him? What had changed?

She was looking for the right words, when she heard voices.

'Let's go in here,' a man said. The air shifted as a door swung open.

Gray's heart stopped.

Someone had just walked into the outer office.

EIGHTEEN

'Chloe,' Gray whispered urgently. 'I have to go.'

Faintly, she heard Chloe say, 'Why? What's wrong?'

But there was no time. She set the phone down on the base as quietly as possible, and jumped to her feet.

'I'm sorry to take you away from the party,' a man's voice was saying in the adjacent office. 'But I wanted to speak to you about that matter we were discussing earlier.'

Another man chuckled dryly. 'I rather thought you might.'

The door to the outside office still stood ajar. Through the gap, Gray saw shadows moving her way.

Her body had begun to tremble, but she couldn't panic. She had to do something. She couldn't let them find her standing here, too terrified to move.

Forcing herself into action, she raced across the room to the only other door. When she opened it, she saw a small cupboard, filled with supplies. There was just enough room to squeeze inside.

'Let's go into my office,' she heard the first man say as the voices neared. 'We've only got a minute or two, unless we want the others to notice we've left.'

Gray pulled the cupboard door to *just* as the door to the adjoining office swung open. She prayed that the darkness had hidden the movement.

'Let's have a seat,' the first man said.

Through the door, she heard the muffled sound of chairs being pulled out as the men sat down. They were so close, she could have reached out and touched them.

She breathed as quietly as she could, praying they wouldn't notice. Even the sound of blood rushing through her veins sounded deafening.

But the men were intent on their conversation.

'I take it this means you intend to go forward with it?' The second voice sounded surprised.

'Ah, good. Straight to the point then.' The man's voice was a rich baritone. He sounded like someone she might have heard on television before, although she couldn't place him. 'Yes. We're going forward with it. That's why I wanted to talk to you. I hope you'll be part of it too. We want you in. More than that.' He paused, as if carefully choosing his words. 'We would very much like it if your organisation could get involved.'

Gray's brow furrowed. There was an illicit edge to this meeting. Both men were deliberately keeping their voices low. They were alone in an office in a largely empty building and yet they were still trying to be quiet. The only reason to do that was if they were hiding something.

Thinking logically was calming. She focussed on staying still. She wanted to hear more.

'Well, this is a great honour.' The second man sounded more cautious than pleased. 'Obviously, I'd need to know more details first.' He paused. 'What's the plan?'

'I can't tell you everything until I'm certain you're in.' There was an unpleasant edge to the first man's voice now. 'You understand what we're discussing is extremely … delicate.'

'That's certainly one way to describe it,' the second man said coolly. 'You're talking about revolution.'

'Don't be absurd.' The first man's tone was dismissive. 'We are setting things back to where they should be. Correcting an error made by a few foolish individuals. That is all. Revolution is for students.'

Gray's pulse began to race. She didn't understand what they were talking about but she knew something very wrong was happening in this room. There was a tang of poison in the air.

'Tell me.' The second man sounded dubious. 'How do you plan to get rid of her? You've tried to convince the party to remove her, but they've refused. You've tried to convince her to step down and she's refused. What actions are left to you? You can't force a prime minister to resign if neither she nor her party want her to.'

Gray drew in a quick, silent breath. They were talking about her mother.

The thought was so shocking, she didn't hear the next few things the men said. The floor seemed to lurch beneath her feet. Who were these men? Why did they want to get rid of her mother? What was going on?

At the table, the men were still talking. The first one was explaining something in that oddly familiar, plummy voice.

'As you say, we've tried the traditional route, and it hasn't worked as we'd hoped,' he said. 'We've decided it's time for something bigger. Something that would drive the country to us. Make them choose us. They trust us in times of upheaval. If we give them a crisis, they will come to us for safety.'

'I'm not sure I understand,' the second man said. 'What crisis can you create?'

There was a long pause.

When he spoke, the other man's voice was so low she had to strain to hear. 'If something were to happen to her…' he said, slowly and deliberately, '…we believe that would drive the public to us.'

'Something?' The second man sounded uncomfortable. 'What are you talking about, precisely?'

'Isn't it obvious?' The baritone-voiced man sounded impatient. 'I think you know. After all, a lunatic with a shotgun killed a member of parliament on the street not all that long ago. It's easier than you think.'

Gray's blood turned to ice. The threat to her mother – these men were part of it.

A voice in her head said, *But they're not Russian.* And yet she knew it didn't matter. She was listening to an assassination plot. Inside Parliament.

'You have someone in mind,' the second man said, and his voice seemed to come from the far end of a tunnel, hazy and shrouded in echoes, 'to do the work?'

I need to calm down, Gray thought. I need to listen.

But her mind couldn't seem to do what she wanted. What was she doing here? She shouldn't be in Parliament. She should be in her bedroom. She'd promised her mother. She'd sworn she wouldn't leave. If she'd just done what she'd said, none of this would be happening.

But she had to be here. She had to hear this. And she had to save her mother from these men.

'Does this mean you're interested?' the baritone voiced man asked, avoiding the question.

There was a pause before the reply came. 'I am interested.'

'Excellent.' Gray heard the triumphant smile in the first man's voice. 'She's attending a charity fund-raising event in

Oxford in two weeks' time – it's private, so her security will be light. We're looking at that and –'

Someone knocked at the door.

Gray flinched.

'Bloody hell,' the second man breathed. 'Who is it?'

'Calm down,' Baritone hissed, sharply. 'I'll handle it.'

Gray heard the creak of his chair as he rose to his feet. The whisper of his shoes on the carpet. The air shifting as he opened the door.

'Yes? What is it?'

She couldn't believe how cool he sounded.

'You told me to let you know when they were asking for you.' The voice sounded distant and muffled.

'Thank you,' the man said, crisply. 'I'll be there shortly.'

There was a pause as the messenger departed. Someone exhaled audibly.

'We'll have to continue this conversation another time,' the baritone-voiced man said, finally.

'That was too close.' The second man rose from his chair and walked to the door. 'Let's discuss this outside of Westminster next time, please.'

The first man gave a low, sardonic laugh. 'You're going to have to get used to this if you plan to join us.'

The lights went off. The door closed. Gray couldn't hear the second man's response.

Squeezed inside the cupboard, she listened as the two of them walked away. She could hear the faint rumble of their voices, but their words were lost to her now.

Then the voices faded altogether. And the building was silent again.

Cautiously, she emerged from her hiding place to find the room empty.

She rushed to the door and peered into the small dark office on the other side. It, too, was empty.

Her heart ached in her chest. She felt as if a weight were pressing against it.

She needed to get out of here. She had to warn her mother.

Opening the office door, Gray checked the long, brightly-lit hallway. It looked just as it had when she'd first arrived — simply painted and lined with office doors. But it wasn't the same at all. It was as if the conversation she'd overheard had left an oily residue behind.

As she stepped out into the corridor, she fought her instinct to run. She could not attract attention now. So she made herself walk, shoulders stiff, as she retraced her path to the central atrium with its statues of kings and queens. It took everything in her to move steadily, hands clenched at her sides, her mind trying to process the sickening conversation she'd overheard.

She hadn't gone far though, before she heard footsteps ahead.

Her heart sank. She drew back, cowering in a doorway, too tired and scared to do anything else.

The steps clicked crisply on the stone floor in the atrium just ahead of her. Shivering, Gray waited to be caught. But the man never looked her way as he crossed the wide room. If he had, he would have seen the shock in her eyes. And he would have recognised her.

Because it was Richard.

NINETEEN

When her stepfather had passed out of sight, Gray stepped out of the doorway again. Hurrying to the atrium – heedless of being seen – she stared after him. What was he doing here? He was supposed to be on a business trip. He'd left first thing this morning for New York. And yet, here he was, in Parliament. It didn't make sense.

She thought briefly about following him, but talked herself out of it just as fast. She needed to get home, get safe. Call her mother.

As she resumed her journey across the parliamentary palace, she began to doubt her own eyes. Maybe it wasn't him. Men all looked the same in those suits. He'd been a good distance away at the end of the hallway.

But it had looked exactly like Richard. Same long, arrogant stride. Same carefully styled hair.

In the stone-walled lobby, the statues in their long cold marble dresses and flowing pale cloaks gazed down at her imperiously as she paused, trying to remember which corridor would take her back to the cellar.

You shouldn't have come here in the first place, their blank faces seemed to say. You caused this. Your mother will hate you even more now.

Tears scalding her eyes, she headed blindly across the lobby, her head down. The great building was so quiet, the soft scuffing of her shoes on the ancient stone floor seemed deafening as she entered the hallway on the other side.

There, the familiar, ornate oak panelling appeared, and the heavily-decorated ceiling. She was back in the House of Lords. Heading in the right direction.

Her mind kept replaying everything she'd just heard. With every step she doubted herself. Doubted she'd understood.

Why would anyone in this building actually plot to kill the prime minister? It would be insane. Such a thing hadn't happened in hundreds of years. She must be wrong. She had to be.

But even as she told herself that, she knew that conversation had been tinged with a palpable sense of evil. There had been a gleeful vindictiveness in the first man's voice – as if he'd wanted to do something like this for a long time. And at last, he was getting his chance.

If only she'd seen his face. She'd been too close to dare to look out. The men had been right in front of her. There'd been no nameplate on the door of the office. All she had were voices in her head making terrible plans. No proof.

As she slipped past the ticking grandfather clock she'd used as a landmark earlier, she found herself wondering how on earth she was going to explain any of this to her mother.

And then there was Richard. Should she mention seeing him? *Had* she really seen him? What if she was wrong?

Numb, she made her way past the towering bookcases, with their beautifully-tooled leather volumes, past the crimson curtains and throne-like chairs, barely seeing any of it. It was hard to imagine that half an hour ago she'd been so excited to be in this building. Now, she just wanted out.

When she finally came across the small, plain door marked BL-141 she yanked it open with relief, hurtled down the narrow stone steps to the low-ceilinged corridor, hurrying to the wide ancient door with its iron ring handle.

Grabbing the handle with both hands, she turned it hard, blinded by tears.

The icy, cold tunnel didn't seem frightening at all now. Not after what she'd just experienced. It felt safe by comparison. As the door closed behind her, she broke into a run, racing into the darkness. Her already soaked feet splashed through cold water but she didn't feel it. She just ran faster, her breath coming in sobs.

Heading back seemed much faster. In no time, she was at the point where the two tunnels met beneath a sign marked 'Q'.

She paused, panting.

Her chest burned, and her body ached from running, her feet were numb from cold and damp.

But she didn't stay for long. She knew she had to keep going.

By the time she reached the short staircase at the end of the tunnel, she was breathless. Panting, she climbed up to the door, and stepped into the normal, late-night hush of Number 10.

There, she stopped, leaning against the wall. Sweat ran down her back as she pressed her fingertips against her forehead, trying to force herself to calm down. She needed to *think*.

What am I going to do? How do I explain this? she thought.

Down the hallway, she could hear the guards in the front lobby talking. One of them laughed. The sound seemed jarring.

Should I should tell them? she wondered, dazed. After all, they're the police.

But she'd passed them less than an hour ago and said she was going to the kitchen. How would it look if she appeared now, tearful and panicked, covered in dirt and sweat and talking about assassinations?

They'd think she was insane.

Frantically, she straightened her top and swiped the tears from her cheeks before walking steadily down the corridor. When she reached the black-and-white tiled floor of the lobby, she forced a tight smile and waved at the guards before turning away quickly.

'Good night, miss,' one of them called.

'Did you forget our chocolate?' another joked.

They all laughed.

Her jaw tight, a frozen smile fixed in place, Gray continued steadily down the hallway until she'd rounded a corner and they could no longer see her. She ran the rest of the way, up the stairs, and through the door of her family's apartment, slamming it behind her.

Everything was just where she'd left it. The room was warm and dry. But the dangerous information she'd learned was like a bomb with its fuse alight, and she had no idea what to do with it.

There was only one person who might know. She ran for the landline, snatching it off the base, fingers fumbling with the plastic.

A tear slipped down her cheek and she struck it away with the back of her hand.

She hit zero. It rang only twice, and then a crisp female voice answered. 'Reception. How can I help you?'

Gray swallowed hard. 'This is Gray Langtry,' she said. 'I need you to put me through to my mother... Please.'

If the woman was surprised that the prime minister's daughter was calling her mother in the middle of the night her voice didn't betray that.

'Of course, Miss Langtry,' she said, her tone unchanged. 'I'll put you through.'

There was a click, and then somewhere in Brussels, a phone rang.

And rang. And rang.

Gray clutched the phone, her hand slippery. She could hear the ringing and her own uneven breathing in her ear.

Where is she?

Maybe her mother had turned her phone off for the night. But that didn't make sense. Her mother never turned her phone off.

She couldn't still be out – it was an hour later in Belgium.

Just as she was giving up, the ringing stopped. 'Hello?' Her mother sounded groggy. 'Who is this?'

'Mum.' Gray fought back the tears that threatened to overwhelm her. 'I'm sorry to wake you.'

'Gray?' She sounded muffled – half asleep. Sometimes when she travelled she took sleeping pills. Otherwise, she said, all she did was lie in bed and think. The distant note to her voice indicated that this was one of those nights. 'What time…?'

'It's late,' Gray said. 'I'm sorry.'

She heard rustling as her mother rolled over.

'What's the matter?'

Gray searched for the words she needed.

I broke into Parliament. I heard two men plot to kill you. I don't know who they were. I don't know where I was. And I think your husband might not be in New York after all.

She couldn't say any of that.

'Gray?' Her mother sounded more coherent. She was waking up. 'Is something wrong?'

'When are you coming home?' Gray heard herself ask.

'Tomorrow afternoon.' A hint of irritation entered her mother's tone. 'You didn't call me in the middle of the night to ask me that, did you?'

'No,' Gray whispered, trying not to cry. 'I'm sorry I woke you. I'll tell you tomorrow.'

'Tell me what?'

'Nothing. Go to sleep.' Gray breathed in, gripping the phone tightly. And then she heard herself say, 'I love you.'

She hung up before her mother could ask anything else.

Lowering herself onto one of the kitchen chairs, she dropped her head to her hands.

What was she going to do now?

TWENTY

That night, Gray hardly slept. She spent the long hours trying to find a way to explain what had happened. By the time her mother walked into the flat early on Sunday afternoon, she was so relieved, she could have thrown herself into her arms. But her mother's cool expression stopped her.

Leaving her bag by the door, she crossed the living room to where Gray was seated on the sofa.

'We need to talk.'

Gray searched her face. 'What's the matter?'

Her mother's expression grew disbelieving. 'What's the *matter*? What on earth was that phone call about? It was after one in the morning in Brussels. What were you thinking?'

Gray's lips moved but it took a second for words to come out. 'I just … needed to talk.'

Her mother sat down in the chair across from her, her face serious. 'Did you sneak out last night?'

All the air left Gray's lungs. How did she know?

Did someone see me after all?

It took her a second to find words. 'I… what do you mean?'

'Oh, come on.' Her mother's gaze was imperious. 'No games, please. I know everything.'

'You know what?' Gray asked, unsteadily.

'After you hung up, I couldn't get back to sleep. I called security to make sure you were safe.' She stood next to the sofa, her eyes blazing, looking down at her daughter. 'They told me you went to the kitchen and didn't come back for more than an hour. They said you looked strange – dishevelled.' She folded her arms. 'Richard told me he thought you'd been sneaking out more than I knew. I didn't want to believe him but now I think he was right. Tell me the truth. You were angry about not being allowed to go to that party, and you found a way out, didn't you? When you came home you were afraid I'd find out, so you called me.'

Gray couldn't seem to catch her breath. She'd been up all night worrying about what to do. How to explain what she'd overheard. And now she had to defend herself to Richard, who wasn't even here.

'I didn't meet my friends and I didn't drink,' she insisted, heatedly. 'That's a complete lie.'

'Then give me an explanation for what happened last night.' Her mother's voice rose. 'Where were you? The guards checked the kitchens — you weren't there.'

'I went to Parliament.' Gray half-shouted the words. 'I was just exploring, OK? I was all by myself.'

In the light filtering through the blastproof curtains covering the windows, she saw the colour leave her mother's face. 'What are you talking about?'

'I'm telling you the truth,' Gray said. 'I went into the tunnels and I got lost and dropped my phone in a puddle and eventually I ended up in Parliament.' Her words tumbled out in a rush of unexpected, dizzying truth. 'Some men came along and I was afraid of getting into trouble, so I hid. I overheard them talking. They talked about you, Mum. They *threatened* you.'

'Gray.' Her mother's face hardened. But she didn't stop.

'They said they were going to kill you. I swear to God.'

'Gray, *stop*.' Her mother looked horrified. 'Why would you say something like that? How do you even know about the tunnels?'

Gray grew defensive. 'Julia took me through the tunnels last week to get to the car when the photographers were looking for me. I didn't know they went to Parliament. It was an accident – I just wanted to see where I'd end up. I knew it was safe. But then I heard the men talking and I didn't know what to do.'

Her mother was watching her with cool disbelief, and Gray found herself panicking, trying to find words that she'd accept. 'I'm not lying, Mum. It happened. They threatened you. You have to believe me. You're not safe.'

'Who threatened me, Gray?' Her mother's powerful voice silenced her. 'Who were the men?'

There was a long silence. This was the moment Gray had dreaded.

'I don't know,' she admitted.

'You don't know.' Her mother's tone was contemptuous. 'What did they look like? Surely you can at least describe them.'

It was a completely reasonable question. And Gray knew she had no answer.

'I didn't see them,' she whispered.

'You didn't see them.' The disbelief in her mother's tone was scalding.

Tears of frustration filled Gray's eyes. She didn't trust herself to speak. It was like her worst nightmare was unfolding and there was no way to stop it. There was no way she could even think about mentioning Richard now. The whole conversation would explode.

When she didn't speak, her mother let out a long breath and crossed the room to the window. She turned her back to the glass, facing the living room. The soft daylight formed a halo around her, making it hard to see her expression. But Gray didn't have to see it to know she was hurt and angry.

'I don't understand what's wrong with you.' Her mother sounded as bewildered as Gray felt. 'Is it attention? Is it because I'm so busy I can't spend time with you like I used to? You've told lies in the past, but never anything like this. You've sneaked out, but never so recklessly. I'm so worried about you right now.'

'I'm not lying,' Gray whispered, dully. 'I was hiding. That's why I couldn't see…'

'Stop this.' Her mother pressed her fingertips against her temples. 'Please. I'm too tired to argue with you. If you really did sneak into Parliament, you risked getting arrested. You risked exposing me and my career to…' Her voice grew unsteady and she paused, shaking her head. 'There are real threats out there. Awful, dangerous things. Truly deadly people. And for you to say something like this just to get yourself out of trouble.' She shook her head slowly. 'It's disgraceful. You should be ashamed of yourself.' She drew a breath. 'I'm ashamed of you.'

Hot tears ran down Gray's face. 'You've got to believe me,' she implored, her voice trembling. 'I didn't see their faces because I was hiding. I was scared. There was no name on the door…'

Her mother stood abruptly, cutting her off. 'I worked until midnight last night,' she said quietly. 'I was up at dawn this morning for meetings that impact our entire nation. My job *matters*. I can't live like this, worrying about you getting into trouble every time I turn my back. I feel like I can't trust you at all right now.'

Gray could think of a thousand arguments to defend herself, but it was pointless. Her mother wouldn't believe anything she said. Worse, she could almost understand why. She had no proof. And her past lies had destroyed the trust between them.

When she didn't respond, her mother nodded, as if her silence had confirmed her worst fears. She strode towards the kitchen, still talking. 'Tomorrow morning I'm going to talk to the boarding school I mentioned. I think it's time for you to go somewhere else for your education. You need discipline, and attention I can't give you right now. Richard is right.'

Gray felt every word like a slap. Her mother was really doing it. She was going to get rid of her. Richard had probably wanted this from day one, and now he'd get his way.

Richard. Who might well be lying about more than either of them knew.

The thought sent heat into her blood, and she jumped to her feet.

'Why won't you send me to live with Dad?' she said furiously. 'At least he still loves me.'

But she didn't get the reaction she'd expected. Instead of arguing, her mother gave her a pitying look. 'Gray,' she said softly. 'You know why.'

For some reason, that hurt most of all. Her mother didn't even care enough to fight with her about it. Gray could barely see through the blur of tears. She felt like she couldn't breathe.

Everything was ruined. Somehow, she'd managed to lose both her parents. And now her mother might die, all because of her.

'You should believe me,' she whispered. 'I wouldn't lie to you about this.'

Her mother delivered her response with genuine sadness. 'Sometimes I think you'd lie to me about anything.'

It took all Gray's strength to turn and walk away. Moving with slow deliberation, she stumbled the last few feet to her bedroom.

There, in the small space that still felt like a stranger's room, she sank to the floor, and sobbed as if her heart had broken.

TWENTY-ONE

On Monday morning, Julia arrived at Number 10 half an hour earlier than usual. With little to do until Gray came downstairs for school, she headed to the staff dining room for coffee. Fighting a yawn, she filled the largest cardboard cup and added a generous slosh of milk.

She needed this. She hadn't got much rest over the weekend.

After her talk with Raj on Saturday night, she'd gone home to pack a bag. It had felt very strange being in her own flat – not knowing when she'd see it again. She had found herself cleaning it quickly, putting every dish away. As if she were going on a long journey.

An hour later, she'd returned to the Talos office to pick up the keys for the safe house. From there, it was a bit of a blur. She'd switched cars, and taken a deliberately twisting, turning route across the city to ensure nobody was following her.

The safe house proved to be a featureless modern one-bedroom flat on a quiet street just north of the city centre. It was a perfectly fine place, equipped with everything she'd need. And yet she'd hardly slept since she'd moved in.

She hated to admit it, but she was rattled. The idea that someone inside the government was plotting against the prime minister sent the danger level off the charts.

Whatever Raj had said that night, the warning beneath his words was clear to her. 'Don't trust anyone in Number 10 except the prime minister and her daughter. Don't trust anyone in the government. Don't trust the police.'

This was why she hadn't slept.

Just as she turned away from the coffee urns, Ryan walked up.

'Good weekend?' he asked, a hint of irony in his voice.

'Wonderful.' Her tone was dry. She watched as he grabbed a large cup and turned to the coffee. Unlike her, he appeared rested. She could see the damp comb marks in his short dark hair as he poured coffee. 'How about you?'

'Busy.' He opened three sugar packets at once and poured them into his cup.

They walked out of the canteen together, pausing in the doorway. Government workers sped by them, already caffeinated and frantic at eight o'clock, clutching phones like weapons. None of them paid any attention to the two bodyguards.

Julia considered her partner. While she wasn't sleeping, she'd had time to think about things, and one element of her life she wanted to fix was their working relationship. It had got off to a rough start. But if things were as bad as they seemed, the two of them needed to have each other's backs.

'So … did you talk to Raj?' she asked, quietly.

His eyes flickered to hers. 'Yeah.'

'You in a safe house now?'

'I moved Saturday,' he said, lowering his voice. 'You, too?'

She nodded.

'I'll tell you what, this job just got a hell of a lot more dangerous,. Ryan shot her a piercing look. 'He told you what he suspects?'

'Yeah,' she said. 'It's not great.'

'No it is not,' he agreed.

'Look,' said Julia, 'I know you don't know me. And I've done things you don't agree with. But please believe I did them for a good reason. I intend to do this job well, and to take care of Gray. That's all I want to do.'

He listened without speaking, his sharp eyes giving nothing away.

'I might not always do this job the same way you would, but please believe I have the same goal,' she finished. 'We're on the same side.'

He blew on his coffee, and took a long sip before replying. 'I believe that,' he said finally, looking down the hallway. 'You should know I had the same partner for five years. We worked every job together. Last year he quit. No warning, nothing. Just said he'd had enough.' His jaw was tight. 'I worked alone for a while after that, and then Raj assigned us to work together.' He glanced at her. 'I was rough on you, that first day. And I'm sorry about that. I'm just used to doing things my way.'

This felt like progress, and Julia rushed to build on it.

'Don't apologise. I should have told you what I was going to do,' she said. 'Ryan, I'd like to start over if we can. Gray needs us to get it together. I will if you will.'

She held out her hand. He looked at it with something like surprise, and then met it with his own, gripping her fingers firmly.

'It's a deal,' he said. 'We've got enough people to fight without fighting each other.'

Some of the tension left Julia's shoulders. This was better than she'd expected.

'Right.' He dropped her hand to glance at his watch. 'It's showtime. I'd better go and get the car. Meet you at the side entrance in ten.'

'See you there,' she said.

He strode away through the crowd of harried workers, easily two inches taller than the tallest man he passed, shoulders broad and unyielding.

It was a relief to have him on her side now.

Julia downed the rest of her coffee as she hurried to the foot of the stairs, arriving just as Gray walked down from the family's residence. The shadows under her eyes said she hadn't slept much either this weekend. Her face was pale with worry.

Moving into the safe house had only made Julia more sympathetic to Gray's situation. The sense of being followed, observed. Of having to live in a house that wasn't her own. Of having her life upended. It was as if, for the first time, she'd had a real glimpse of what the last year had been like for her charge.

'You OK?' she asked, throwing her empty cup into a nearby bin.

'I'm perfect.' Gray's tone was short.

Julia's brow creased. But all she said was, 'I can see that.'

Gray turned away quickly, and the two of them headed back down the hallway toward the side entrance.

As she walked, Julia shot her a puzzled sideways glance. Gray appeared genuinely upset. Something must have happened over the weekend.

The weekend report, which had been emailed to her that morning, contained nothing unusual except an odd paragraph about the girl spending a long time in the kitchen on Saturday night, which Julia had discounted as superfluous information.

Now, though, she wondered.

'Gray,' Julia said. 'I know something's going on. I wish you'd let me help.'

'Nothing's going on,' Gray insisted, but her voice was unsteady and she wouldn't meet her eyes.

Julia reached for her arm, pulling her to one side. Her face was puffy, as if she'd been crying. Her lip trembled.

Something must have happened.

'Please, let me help you,' she said gently. 'You can trust me. I'm on your side. I know it's hard to believe this, but I feel like I understand some of what you're going through. I want to help.'

This time, Gray did look at her. Julia thought she saw conflict in her gaze, but all she said was, 'I'm sorry. I'm really fine. Just an argument with my mum. Can we go? I don't want to be late for school.'

Julia knew better than to push harder. 'Of course,' she said.

As they returned to the flow of hallway traffic, Julia stuck close to her charge, keeping her expression impassive until they reached the side entrance. She showed her pass to the armed guard, who opened the door for them.

Ryan stood by a dark blue car, scanning the street for danger.

From the corner of her eye, Julia saw Gray take a deep gulp of London air – as if, even with its sooty tang of exhaust, it felt good in her lungs. It occurred to her the girl might not have been outside at all since Friday afternoon.

What a way to live, she thought.

'Good morning, Gray. Nice weekend?' Ryan asked as Gray approached. Behind her back, Julia caught his gaze and shook her head. His eyebrows rose.

'Not really,' Gray said, bending over to get into the back seat.

'Oh.' Glancing at Julia, he mouthed, 'What's wrong?'

She made a helpless gesture. Shrugging, he tossed her the keys and she caught them expertly in midair.

As Julia pulled out into the road a minute later, she glanced at Gray in the rearview mirror. What could have gone wrong? She'd been fine on Friday. Sad about a party she couldn't go to. But otherwise, a normal bouncy teenager.

Between then and now, everything had changed.

As she shifted into gear, she met Gray's eyes in the rearview mirror. 'You know, if you need to talk, we're good listeners.'

In the mirror, Gray met her gaze. Again, there was something in her eyes – a kind of longing for understanding. Then she blinked hard. 'It was just a bad weekend,' she said, wearily, and turned her head away.

After that, the two of them left Gray alone with her thoughts as the sleek car crept across Westminster Bridge. The autumn sun was high, and the river glittered blue and silver beneath them.

When they pulled up in front of the school, Julia waited in the car as Ryan got out to check the area. Gray, who'd put dark sunglasses on, stared blankly ahead.

Outside, Ryan signalled – one finger pointed up. All clear.

Julia climbed out, and stepped back to open Gray's door. 'Let's go.'

Gray didn't look at her as she left the car, and the three of them walked to the door in a loose line.

NUMBER 10

Julia was last, scanning the crowd of students and parents moseying into the three-storey red-brick building without any sign of urgency. Her narrow gaze sought anything unusual. Rubbish bins were all in the usual place and had been emptied. Nobody lingered near the footpath. No one looked at Gray. It all appeared normal. Still her heart raced.

Ryan walked in first through the visitors' door and paused to say hello to the woman at the reception desk, who seemed to melt in the light of his attention.

While they chatted, Gray stood doll-like, hands hanging still, her heart-shaped face hollow. She'd removed her sunglasses. She looked bereft.

Resolving to try one more time, Julia stepped closer. Gray regarded her warily.

'Whatever it is, you can tell me,' Julia said quietly. 'I promise I won't tell your mother. I won't even tell Ryan.'

Gray gave her a tormented look. 'What does it matter?' she whispered, tears filling her eyes. 'No one would believe me.'

Before Julia could reply, the girl turned and ran through the double doors into the main school corridor.

Julia stared after her, warning signals firing in her mind.

Something had scared that girl. And how had it happened when she hadn't left the building?

TWENTY-TWO

School seemed to come at Gray from far away. She had hardly slept. Every time she closed her eyes, she heard the low rumble of men's voices making awful plans. Heard her mother telling her she was sending her away. Saw Richard striding through Parliament, where he should not be.

She'd been very tempted to tell Julia what was going on. She believed the bodyguard wanted to help. But she knew how it would go. If she told Julia everything, she'd take the information straight to Gray's mother. She had to.

And her mother would say, 'Don't listen to Gray. She lies.'

Julia would look at her differently after that. She'd look at her like she was a liar. Then she'd have nobody on her side.

Everything that had happened made school seem less important. Somehow, she went where she was supposed to go, walking woodenly to her first few classes, where she sat with a pen in her hand, staring into the distance as the words floated around her.

It was nearly lunch hour when Chloe ran up to her in the hallway.

'What happened on Saturday night?' she demanded. 'You disappeared.'

Gray hesitated. How much could she say? It all sounded so crazy.

'I thought I was about to get caught but … nothing happened …' Her voice trailed off.

She loved Chloe, but she wasn't someone who could help. And she didn't want to scare her with the truth.

But her friend wouldn't give up. 'Did you really break into Parliament?' she persisted, as they made their way into the crowded lunchroom. 'What was it like?'

'Empty.' Gray's tone was curt, and Chloe looked up at her in surprise. 'It wasn't as much fun as I thought it would be,' Gray amended herself, adding quickly, 'Sorry to be so bitchy. I haven't slept.'

'You weren't bitchy.' Chloe drew back, really looking at her for the first time. 'What's the matter? You look awful. Did something happen?'

The two of them drifted to a stop, letting the other students flow around them.

'Nothing, really,' Gray said. 'Just my mum and I had this big fight on Sunday.'

'What did you fight about?' Chloe's eyes widened. 'She didn't find out you left, did she?'

'Sort of.' Gray lowered her voice. 'The security guards told her I was out of the flat for an hour. She accused me of sneaking out with you. I had to tell her where I really went. She lost it.'

'That blows. But what can she do to you?' Chloe reasoned. 'You're already grounded. What's left?'

'Boarding school, apparently,' Gray said.

'She can't be serious.' Chloe looked aghast.

Gray thought back to the long, lonely hours on Sunday afternoon. The chilly Sunday dinner they'd both picked at in near silence. The brochure about a boarding school that she'd found on the kitchen table this morning.

171

'I think she means it,' she said.

Suddenly the smells from the lunchroom curdled her stomach. She couldn't have this conversation right now.

She took a step back, nearly running into someone behind her. 'Actually, you know what? I'm not that hungry and I didn't finish my psych paper last night because of everything. I think I better work through lunch.'

Chloe's brow creased. 'You sure? I could come with you if you want?'

'If you come with me, we'll keep talking about this and I really don't want to.'

A hurt look crossed Chloe's face. Gray felt instantly awful.

'I'm sorry. I didn't mean that. I just need to be alone for a little bit, OK? I promise I'm fine.'

Chloe was clearly reluctant, but she could see Gray meant what she'd said. 'You sure you'll be OK?'

If there was one thing Gray wasn't sure of, it was that. Instead of answering she gave a half-hearted wave and turned away.

Leaving the bustle of the lunchroom behind her, she walked slowly down the long school corridor.

A headache hammered at her temples. She needed time to think. She'd figure this out. Come up with a plan.

Her feet seemed to have a will of their own, taking her towards the sanctuary of the library. When she pushed the door open, the room had a hollow, breathless feel – as if nobody had been here in a while. It was as quiet as a church.

Gray let the silence envelop her.

After a second, she made her way through the tables, chairs and computer carrels towards the round table at the back of the room, in the shadowy corner where she'd sat with Jake a week ago. This time she'd sit there alone, and work this through.

But as she passed the crowded bookcases in the history section, she saw the edge of the table, two chairs with their backs to her. And someone's feet, clad in dark trainers, resting on one of them.

Her heart beat faster.

Jake was stretched out in the same seat as before, his head propped on his hand. A book lay open in front of him. His long dark lashes cast smoky shadows on his cheeks.

He appeared to be asleep.

Gray studied him, remembering the things Richard and her mother had said. That he couldn't be trusted. That he would use her for information.

What if it was true? She'd feel like such an idiot.

But then, if that was Richard she'd seen in Parliament, *he* was the liar.

She stood by the table, uncertain whether to wake him or turn back and pretend she'd never seen him in the first place. She was still making up her mind when his eyes opened, and met hers.

He had the most startling eyes – dark as chocolate and impossible to read.

'Hey,' she said.

His eyebrows rose, just a little. 'Hey?'

Her face grew hot. How did he always manage to make her feel as if she'd done something bizarre?

'I didn't know you were in here.' Her tone was defensive. 'I thought it was empty.'

'Yeah, well.' He cleared his throat. 'I had a bad weekend. Don't feel like school today. But for some reason, they don't give us days off for that.'

He sounded as weary and defeated as she felt. Gray set her bag down. 'I had a bad weekend, too. I came in here to hide.'

There was a pause and then he said, 'I guess we could hide together.'

As she sat down across from him, she remembered something Chloe had told her in that brief, dangerous phone call from Parliament, before everything changed.

'All he wanted to talk about was you.'

The thought gave her some solace, and she rested her chin on her hands. 'Why was your weekend so terrible?'

'Had a row with my dad.'

'What did you fight about?'

He waved one hand. 'My grades. My inadequacies. My unacceptable plans for the future.' His flat, northern voice made it sound like it was no big deal. But his bleak expression told a different story. 'Apparently, I lack seriousness.'

'God,' Gray said, bitterly. '*Parents*. Why can't they mind their own business?'

'Good question.' He looked at her. 'Right, then. Tell me about your bad weekend. Someone else's misery might cheer me up.'

She searched for words to explain but couldn't find them.

Maybe it was the exhaustion. Maybe this was just the breaking point. Whatever the reason, to her horror, her eyes filled with tears.

All the amusement left Jake's face. 'Shit.' He leaned towards her, one hand reaching out but not quite touching her. 'What the hell happened?'

Mortified, she forced a laugh. 'I'm so sorry, I don't know what's happening.' She scrabbled in her bag for a tissue. 'It's just, I haven't slept and ...'

She couldn't do it. Couldn't pretend it was nothing. Just a normal argument with her mother. She needed to tell someone the truth. And out of everyone she knew, maybe Jake would understand.

And she just didn't care what her mother thought about him right now. Not one little bit.

'Something happened,' she said, wiping her cheeks. 'Something really, really bad. I haven't told anybody.'

He tensed visibly, although his expression didn't flicker. 'Did someone hurt you?'

'No,' she assured him. 'It wasn't like that. I heard something. Something terrible. Some men, planning to do something to my mother.' She had to force her mouth to form the words. 'I think they want to kill her.'

Jake's eyebrows drew together. She could see the confusion in his face as he tried to process the information. 'I'm sorry,' he said. 'I'm not sure I understand. What exactly did you hear?'

Now that there was someone listening, Gray wasn't sure how to begin.

'Well, first,' she said. 'did you know there are tunnels leading from Number 10, to Parliament?'

Jake looked surprised. 'There are rumours about tunnels. I always thought it was bollocks. Are you telling me they're real?'

'They're real,' she said. 'I went through them on Saturday night.'

'By yourself?' He sounded surprised. 'They let you do that?'

'No one saw me,' she said. 'It was really late. I was just exploring. I didn't know where I would end up. I've only been down there once before, with my bodyguard, and we didn't go far.

I wanted to see where the tunnels went. In the end, I kind of ended up in Parliament.'

Jake gave a low whistle. 'So it's true,' he said, obviously impressed. 'There is a tunnel direct to Number 10. That's so cool.'

'Yeah,' she said, with a ghost of a smile. 'That was the good part.'

He grew serious again. 'So, what was the bad part?'

In the quiet of the empty space, amid the safety of a room filled with books, she told him about walking the halls, hearing the voices, the panicked dash for a hiding place.

He listened, rarely interrupting, his fingers under his lips in an unconscious gesture.

'It was like one man was trying to convince the other to join him,' she explained. 'And he told him he'd be part of something by getting rid of my mother – killing her, I think. He said they'd cause people to panic, and if they panicked they'd vote for their candidate. One of them used the word "revolution".'

'Wait, wait, *wait*.' Jake pushed himself back from the table. He looked horrified. 'They didn't really say that. Did they? Don't bullshit me, Gray.'

'I'm telling you the truth. They want to do it. I can't get their voices out of my head.' She shuddered. 'They're going to kill her. And I don't know how to stop them.'

He stared at her. 'They really said that? Just the way you told me?'

'I'll never forget it for as long as I live,' said Gray.

'Did you tell your mum?'

Gray nodded. 'She thinks I'm lying.' Her voice was measured. 'She thinks I'm trying to get attention.'

He looked baffled. 'Why would she think you'd lie about something like this?'

Gray hesitated, but decided to tell it straight. 'I've lied to her in the past,' she confessed. 'A lot, actually. About parties and curfew – who I was out with. She doesn't trust me, I guess. My stepfather …' She stopped herself, thinking of Richard walking across Parliament in the dead of night. 'Well. That's another story.'

Jake's gaze swept across her face as if looking for something. 'Who were the men? Did you recognise them?'

'That's the worst part. I didn't see them,' she admitted, miserably. 'I had to hide, and I could only hear them.'

This was where she'd lost her mother, but Jake merely listened, his brow knitted with concentration. 'Describe their voices. Did they have accents? Northern? Southern?'

'They were just English. Posh. Neither of them had an accent like yours. One was older, though. I think I was in his office.' She searched her mind for more details that might be helpful. 'I think the younger one was being recruited by the older one. He sounded kind of … I don't know. Shocked, maybe.'

Jake's brow furrowed.

'Gray, are you sure about all of this?' he asked. 'You couldn't have misheard them?'

She leaned forward, willing him to believe. 'I'm positive. I hear their voices in my head constantly. I can't sleep for hearing them. I will never forget the things they said.'

Silence fell. jake stared into the depths of the quiet library as if it might hold the answers to their quandary.

'Do you believe me?' she pressed. 'Do you think I'm telling the truth?'

When he replied, he chose his words carefully. 'I believe that you believe it.'

Gray sagged back in her chair. She regretted every lie she'd ever told. Anything she'd ever done that had made people doubt her.

'I wouldn't lie about this,' she said, fighting the despair that threatened to overwhelm her. 'I never, ever would.'

'I believe you're not lying,' he said. 'But maybe ... maybe you misunderstood them.'

She gave him an incredulous look. 'How could I misunderstand that? I told you just what they said.'

He rested his fingers beneath his lips again – a gesture she was starting to recognise as something he did when he was anxious. 'The thing is, Gray, people really don't like your mum.'

'I know that,' she said, dismissively. 'It's politics.'

It was impossible to miss. The newspaper headlines, the TV news stories. Lately, at weekends, protesters had been gathering outside Number 10, carrying placards with her mother's face on Satan's body. Or the Tin Man from the Wizard of Oz, with her mother's hair and clothes, and 'If I only had a heart' written on a sign around her neck.

'It's worse than you think,' Jake said. 'It's more intense. My dad...' He paused, looking down at the table. 'My dad thinks he can win the next election. Some people on your mum's side are helping him.'

Her jaw dropped. 'Why are they helping *him*?'

'They want to force your mum out. Everyone does. My dad's just trying to take advantage of it but...' His voice trailed off.

'But what?' she asked.

'I don't like these guys,' he said, after a second. 'I don't trust them. My dad shouldn't trust them.'

'Why is he working with people like that?'

His shrug was expressive. 'He wants to win. At any cost.'

Around them, the library was lost in shadows. There were no sounds from the corridors back here. No voices at all. They seemed to be all alone.

'Why are you telling me this?' asked Gray.

'What if you overheard *those* guys?' he said. 'You could have misunderstood what they were saying. Maybe they were talking about working with my dad.'

'I didn't misunderstand a thing,' she said firmly. 'It was clear what they wanted. It wasn't confusing at all. They planned to kill her to create chaos and take power. They talked about that MP who got shot a few years ago. The older one talked about how easily it was done.'

Jake rubbed a hand across his face. 'It's *insane*, though. Why would they…?'

'They don't care.' Gray leaned forward to catch his gaze. 'Don't you get it? They want her dead. They want to hurt people. They want everyone to be scared. They were *ice cold*. They were monsters.'

At a loss for words, Jake just stared at her.

For Gray, this was something at least. At last, someone understood.

'What about your dad?' she suggested. 'Could we tell him? Would he help?'

There was a long pause before he replied. 'The thing is, my dad would benefit a lot if your mum weren't around.' He spoke so quietly that at first she thought she'd misunderstood.

'He wouldn't want her to be hurt, would he?' she asked, genuinely confused. 'I mean, it's just politics. It's like this big stupid game.'

He lifted his head. There was regret in his eyes.

'I wish I could say that I know my dad, and that he has integrity and honesty, and you could trust him. But I can't say that, Gray. He won't help. And if he knew about this, he'd find a way to use it to help himself.' He drew a breath. 'We can't ever tell him.'

Gray didn't know what to say. If nothing else, Jake had just proved one thing at least. He was not spying on her for his father.

'I always thought your dad was so cool,' she said, after a while. 'He seems so laid back compared to my mum. Everyone likes him.'

'Yeah, well.' His mouth twisted. 'Don't believe everything you see on TV. You want to know the truth? My dad is everything people say your mum is. He was cruel to my mum. He made me stay with him when they divorced because it would look better if he was a single dad. I'm a prop to him. I can't even imagine what he'll be like if he ever makes it to Number 10. It'd be a nightmare.'

Whatever she'd expected him to say, it wasn't that.

With his hipster glasses and casual style, Tom McIntyre gave the appearance of being young and approachable – completely different from normal politicians, with their expensive suits and ties. Students loved him. In every mock election Hartford High School had ever held, Tom McIntyre had always won, hands down.

If he was really as bad as Jake said, and Gray's mother wouldn't listen, who was left for her to turn to?

Julia, a voice in her head reminded her.

But before she could suggest telling her bodyguard, Jake began talking with a new energy. 'I think the first thing we need to do is to figure out who those guys were. I know the Houses of Parliament better than my own home. I've spent enough time there.

Maybe if you describe what you saw, and where you walked, I can figure out whose office it might have been.'

Hope flared in Gray's chest. So she told him about the little plain door, and the grandfather clock, the throne-like chair and the window looking out at Big Ben.

'It was a long hallway in the House of Lords. It's pretty wide, but there are big bookcases that make it seem crowded. The walls have this wood panelling – really glossy. And sketches of the city back in the past.'

'That describes most of the House of Lords,' he said, doubtfully. 'What else?'

She squinted, trying to remember her path. 'I walked until I reached this big stone room where lots of hallways met. I've been there before but I can't remember what it's called. It had a really high ceiling and all these statues of kings and queens.'

'Central Lobby.' He said it as if there was no question. 'I know right where you were. I've been there a thousand times.'

At that moment, a bell rang, loud and shrill.

The noise made Gray jump. She'd almost forgotten they were at school. Lunch break was over.

They both heard the library door open, and the unmistakeable sound of heavy footsteps.

'We should go,' she said, reluctantly.

'Yeah. If I skip class again they're going to give me detention.' He stacked his books. 'You said you dropped your phone. Have you got another one yet?'

'I dug my old one out.' Gray reached into her bag, and pulled out a battered phone in a cracked pink case. 'It's crap but it works.'

'Give me your number. I'll call you later so we can talk more. Figure out where you were.' Jake held out his phone.

Gray typed in her number, and then handed the phone back.

Nothing was fixed, everything was still awful, but she felt better all the same. He believed her. She wasn't alone with this.

'Thank you,' she said, as she handed it back. 'For believing.'

He put his books in his bag, and then looked at her with those thoughtful eyes. 'As far as I know, you've never lied to me, Gray. Why would I doubt you?'

That simple statement meant so much, she didn't trust herself to speak. It had a been long time since anyone had said something like that to her.

He put his bag on his shoulder. 'Now, all we have to figure out is how to stop this.'

TWENTY-THREE

After her conversation with Jake, Gray felt physically lighter. As if a weight had been lifted from her. The sense that she was not alone stayed with her through her classes and even as she walked with Chloe to the visitors' entrance to meet Julia.

If her bodyguards noticed the change in her mood, neither of them commented on it.

All Julia said was, 'You alright?'

'I'm fine.' Gray even smiled at her as she climbed into the back seat of the Jaguar.

The fact that Jake had believed her made her think again about confiding in her bodyguards. But unlike him, they still worked for her mother. If she ordered them not to believe her, they had to assume that she was lying.

No. She wouldn't tell them now. Not until she had some sort of proof.

So she said nothing as they drove across the city. The sky was an ice cold blue, and the city looked bright as they crossed Westminster Bridge, over the Thames, past the hulking fortress of Parliament with its crowds of tourists angling for the best photograph, and souvenir stands peddling Union Jack flags and pictures of the princes.

The city's Christmas lights were up, but not turned on yet. That was still a couple of weeks away. By then, Gray was certain, this would all be over. Her father would be back. Her mother would be safe.

Everything would be fine.

Ryan stopped the car at the spot near the side entrance to Number 10 where Gray usually alighted.

Julia got out first, checking the street was safe before opening the door.

Humming to herself, Gray stepped out into the icy air and the two of them walked towards the building.

'You seem happier than earlier,' Julia observed.

'I am.' Gray turned to tell her something – what, she would never remember. Because that was when the man appeared, running around the corner shouting her name.

'Gray! Gray!' He gestured wildly, lumbering towards them. 'I have to talk to you!'

He was heavyset, wearing a rumpled white shirt under a faded green jacket. His eyes were wild. He held something in his right hand. Something metal.

Gray froze. She knew she should run, but her feet felt suddenly heavy and unwieldy. She tried to scream but all that came out was a whisper.

'Julia…'

But the bodyguard was already there, leaping in front of her so quickly that all Gray saw of her was a blur.

'No, you don't, mate,' she said, icily, heading towards him, one hand outstretched to him, the other motioning to Ryan.

'I just want to talk to her,' the man insisted. Then he lifted the knife.

Suddenly, Ryan was behind him, grabbing the man by the wrist. The two of them struggled for control of the blade.

The man punched Ryan in the face. His head snapped back, but he held on fiercely.

'Drop it,' he said between gritted teeth. 'Don't be stupid.'

To Gray's surprise, Julia didn't help him. Instead she threw an arm around Gray's shoulders and hustled her towards the building speaking into a microphone attached to the lapel of her leather jacket as they ran. 'Intruder at entrance three. Code Blue. Repeat: Code Blue.'

Gray twisted around to see behind them. The man raised his fist to punch Ryan again. This time, though, Ryan was ready, forcing his arms behind his back.

The man screamed and clawed at the guard, shoving his shoulder in his face. Ryan didn't seem to be aware of the blow. He wrapped his free arm around the man's throat just as the side door of Number 10 flew open and three police officers in bullet-proof vests rushed out to help.

Julia pulled Gray inside, moving her so fast her feet barely seemed to touch the ground. Gray looked back through the open door. The man was lying on his front, his hands handcuffed behind his back, police all around him. His face was red. He was weeping. A knife lay on the ground a few feet away, glittering in the sun.

'I love you, Gray!' he sobbed, craning his head to see her.

Julia slammed the door shut, cutting off her view.

In the hallway, Gray stood unmoving. She didn't even think she was breathing.

This was everything she'd been afraid of. The threat Julia had warned her about. It was coming true.

Her bodyguard pressed the small microphone connected to her jacket. 'Firefly secure. Suspect in custody.'

It was warm inside but Gray was trembling. She felt odd. Distanced from her body. She couldn't seem to feel her fingertips.

Julia looked at her worriedly. 'You OK?'

She tried to reply but nothing came out. She felt woozy.

The bodyguard rubbed Gray's arms up and down briskly, as you would if someone had been out in a snowstorm for too long. 'We're fine,' she told her, soothingly. 'Safe as houses.'

Three police officers thundered down the hall past them. Gray shrank back against the wall with a gasp. The movement brought breath back into her body. But that only made the shaking worse.

'Come on.' Julia took her arm, and led her away from the door. 'It's all under control. Let's get out of the way.'

'Why am I so c-cold?' Gray heard herself ask.

'You're in shock.' Julia's voice was matter-of-fact. 'Let's get a cup of tea inside you, shall we?'

Gray wasn't going to be distracted by tea. Her thoughts were muddy. She needed to understand what had just happened. 'The man. Did he h-have a knife?'

'Yes, he did.' Julia guided her steadily down the hallway. 'But he didn't hurt anyone. And we are all safe.'

Gray slowed, turning to her. 'Ryan's OK?'

'Don't worry about Ryan. He's fine. He's dealt with much worse.' Julia pulled her through the double doors into the building's main kitchen.

The room was industrial, with huge stainless steel refrigerators and giant ovens. The air smelled faintly of whatever they'd been cooking a couple of hours ago. A team of workers – all in white shirts with black trousers – were scrubbing the countertops.

NUMBER 10

From the hallway, Gray could hear the thumping of running feet, voices calling commands through walkie-talkies. Sounds of chaos. An alarm had begun to ring insistently. Here, though, everything was normal.

Julia gave the kitchen staff a jaunty wave as she led Gray to where two large urns steamed quietly.

Dropping tea bags in two mugs, she filled them with hot water, and put two sugar cubes in each.

'Sugar's what you need for shock,' she explained as she topped both mugs with generous slugs of milk. 'Adrenaline messes with your head. Sugar is the antidote.'

She dropped the used tea bags into the bin and, leaving Gray propped against the counter like a broom, hurried over to another cupboard and pulled down a plastic container filled with biscuits. Taking a few, she returned to Gray and placed a mug in her hand.

'Here you are,' she said.

Hardly aware she was doing it, Gray clutched the hot mug tightly. She followed obediently as Julia led the way out of the kitchen to the empty dining room, to a table in the corner, away from all windows, and gently pushed her down into a chair.

She kept thinking about the man outside. '*Gray, I love you…*'

It turned her stomach.

The bodyguard dropped into a seat, and slid a biscuit across to her. Gray stared at it, as if she'd never seen one before.

Julia said, 'Gray. I need you to drink your tea. Just a sip. I promise it will help.'

Obediently, Gray raised the mug to her lips and took a shallow sip. The sweetness and heat flowed into her body, thawing her.

Julia gave a satisfied nod.

'See? Works every time.' Leaning back, she took a sip of her own tea. 'Man, that guy was big. I'm glad Ryan was there. I could have brought him down, but it would have been messy.'

'How?' Gray heard herself asking the words that were in her head. 'How could you take him down?'

Julia considered this. 'Well, he's probably having a psychotic episode, so he's not going to look for unexpected moves. I'd go for his knees first – see if I could knock him down by kicking them out from under him.' She took a bite of her biscuit and chewed thoughtfully. 'If that didn't work, I'd go for his bollocks.'

To her own surprise, Gray found herself giggling.

'That's better.' Julia smiled at her approvingly over the top of her mug. 'There's a little colour in your face. You were white as a sheet a moment ago.'

Now that her mind seemed to be working again, Gray found she had a lot of questions.

'Who is he? Is he part of the threat you told me about? Against me and my mum?'

'It's too early to say,' Julia told her. 'We'll look into his background. But… I don't know. It doesn't feel right to me. This is different.'

'How?' Gray pressed. 'He had a knife.'

'I know. But the way he acted.' The bodyguard shook her head. 'This guy has some sort of fixation on you. He might have been walking around the area for hours hoping to get a glimpse of you. Then we pulled up at just the wrong time.' She glanced back at Gray, and her hazel eyes held no deception. 'The threat – that's more organised. Professional. This guy's no professional, that much is clear.'

Gray had begun to feel more like herself. Her head was clearing.

'You were great out there,' she told her guard. 'Thank you for being so fast.'

Julia waved that away. 'It's my job. I'm just sorry he frightened you.' She cocked her head, studying Gray. 'It must be so hard for you, to have to deal with this when you're so young. I'm sorry you have to go through things like this.'

'It's funny – when my mum first got elected, I thought it was the greatest thing. She'd worked so hard for it. But then all this stuff happened.' Gray gestured at the sprawling staff dining room around them, with its rows of tables and empty chairs. 'I mean, this is basically my kitchen now. Who lives like this?'

'I couldn't do it,' Julia admitted. 'I couldn't live with all the attention. I think you're doing better than most people.'

Gray gave a humourless laugh. 'My mum isn't that impressed. She thinks I'm messing it all up.'

'Your mother has a lot on her mind, Gray,' Julia said gently. 'Give her a break.'

'She should give *me* a break,'' Gray fired back. 'She doesn't trust me at all. And it's …'

At that moment, Julia's phone rang. 'Two seconds,' she said. 'It's my boss.'

She stayed in her seat as she answered it. 'Julia here.' She listened for a second and then said, 'Firefly is fine. I'm with her right now.' She gave Gray a quick smile. 'The suspect is in custody The police will be identifying him now. You can reassure her mother that she's fine.' She listened again, growing serious. 'Copy that, sir. I'll pass that on.'

As she talked, Gray stole glances at her bodyguard. Her skin was clear and unlined. She didn't look very old at all. And yet she'd handled the attack like she'd seen it all a hundred times. She'd known just how to deal with the aftermath.

Julia ended the call and put the phone away. 'Sorry about that,' she said. 'Where were we?'

Gray couldn't quite remember. Instead, she said, 'Can I ask you a question?'

'Shoot,' Julia told her.

'How did you get this job? You don't seem very old.'

'I started young. Right after I finished school, I joined the military. Intelligence branch.' Clocking Gray's blank expression, she explained, 'I was a bit of a spy, really.'

'How old were you?'

'Nineteen.' Julia took a long drink of tea.

'Why did you do that?' Gray asked. 'You didn't want to go to university?'

Julia set her cup down carefully. 'I don't get along with my parents,' she said after a second. 'I wouldn't ask them for money or help. I needed a job quickly, and I wanted to do something that mattered. Something useful. I wanted to serve my country.' She glanced up at Gray. 'Does that make sense?'

It did make sense. When she'd joined the army, she'd been less than three years older than Gray was now. The realisation was daunting.

But it also made her think. If Julia could handle the military at that age, surely Gray could deal with the situation she was in now.

'It must have been hard, going from school to the army,' she said.

'Best thing that ever happened to me.' A wry smile crossed the bodyguard's face. 'You wouldn't believe what I was like at your age. I was a prefect, you know, in my school. Really into rules. I was such a pain in the arse.'

'But the army changed you,' Gray guessed.

'I learned what I was capable of. I learned I was stronger than I knew. A better person than I'd ever thought. It tested me.'

'How did you end up here?' asked Gray.

'I knew my boss, Raj Patel, when I was your age. After I got out of the military, he invited me to work for him at Talos.' She popped the last bit of biscuit in her mouth.

Talos. Gray had heard that name before. It took her a second to find it in her memory.

Talos Inc. has been brought in for personal security duties. The document she'd seen in the Cabinet Office. She hadn't known what Talos was then. Now, it made sense.

'So Talos is like, personal bodyguards?' she asked.

'Talos is security of all kinds.' Julia gave her a meaningful look. 'You see, my job is to keep you safe no matter what threatens you. I work for *you*, Gray. Not your mother. You are my client.'

Her voice was steady – convincing. Gray found herself thinking again about telling her the truth of what she'd learned. Julia was young and brave. She'd already risked her life once today for her. If anyone could help, surely it was her?

She put her own cup down. 'If I told you something in confidence,' she said, 'would you have to tell my mother?'

'I would not...' Julia paused and then rephrased. 'I wouldn't tell her. But if I felt you were in danger or in any way threatened, I'm obliged to tell my boss. And he works for your mother. So he would want to tell her.'

Gray shifted back in her chair. That was what she was afraid of.

Julia searched Gray's face, a frown above her eyes. 'If anything's scaring you, please tell me. We'll work something out. I'll find a way to fix it.'

Gray was torn. She wanted more than anything to confess everything. To get Julia's help. Telling Jake had felt so liberating, but he wasn't in a position to protect her mother. Julia was.

And yet, without any proof, without even knowing the names of the men involved, telling Julia would be pointless. Her mother would dismiss it out of hand. If she could just identify the men she'd overheard, she could take that to Julia. That was all she needed. Their names.

'Please tell me, Gray,' Julia pressed. 'I'd really like to help.'

'No. Never mind,' Gray said. 'It's nothing. Just school and boys.' Before Julia could ask again, she stood up. 'Look, I better go.'

Concern shadowed Julia's face, but she stood up too. 'Fine,' she said, reluctantly. 'I'll walk you to the stairs.'

In the main lobby, everything was still in upheaval. The front entrance had been locked – no one was being allowed in or out. Staff crowded in the corridors, trying to figure out what was going on.

With Julia at her side, Gray walked behind the crowd, unnoticed in the hubbub as she turned into the quiet stairwell. Julia touched her arm to stop her.

'Gray, if you ever need to talk to me about anything, I'm here.'

'I'll remember that,' Gray said, meaning it. 'And thank you so much for protecting me.'

She climbed the stairs alone, aware that Julia was still standing at the bottom, making sure she was safe. When she reached the family apartment, it was empty. She'd hoped her mother would be here – that someone would have told her, and she'd have rushed back from her meetings to see her. But – of course not. The two of them were barely speaking.

It was only when she sat down on the sofa that she realised she was utterly exhausted. She had so much to do – an essay for history, and French homework she hadn't even thought about – but she couldn't concentrate.

Every time she picked up a book, her mind made the danger spin around her like a roulette wheel, stopping on knives, or threats, or police with machine guns.

When her mother finally called to check on her, they had a stilted conversation that didn't make Gray feel any better.

'They told me you were fine,' her mother said. 'I'm very sorry security failed in this way.' Her tone was condemning.

'My bodyguards were great.' Gray felt suddenly protective of Julia and Ryan. 'They saved my life.'

'Well,' her mother said stiffly, 'I understand the man had a psychotic episode. He's being treated now. He won't ever come near you again.'

Crazy man with a knife or not – the two of them were simply at loggerheads about everything right now. And Gray didn't know how to fix that. Her mother still hadn't mentioned the threat against their lives – even now, when a man was in hospital for attacking her.

After they hung up, she checked the internet on her phone to see if news of the attack had reached Twitter. Of course it had. There were pictures of the streets around Number 10 blocked with police cars, their lights flashing.

'Attempted attack on PM's residence,' claimed one newspaper.

Gray scrolled through the short reports of what she'd just experienced.

'Prime Minister's daughter, Gray Langtry, is said to be uninjured.'

'Man in custody.'

'Police refuse to say if the attack was terrorism.'

When her phone rang again a while later, she picked it up reluctantly. She'd had enough of her mother for one day. But it wasn't her mother's number on the screen. It was Jake's.

Fumbling with it in her haste, she punched the answer button.

'Hey,' she said, nonchalantly.

'Gray, I just heard what happened. Are you OK?' His voice had all the panic and worry she'd hoped to hear in her mother's.

'I'm fine,' she assured him. 'My bodyguards got to him before anything bad could happen. He put up a fight though.'

'You must have been terrified,' said Jake. 'Did it have anything to do with the threats you told me about? Was it those guys?'

'I don't think so,' she said. 'Everyone seems to think he's a random crazy guy. Not a...' What was the word Julia had used? '...professional.'

'Your mum must be losing her mind over this,' he said.

Gray looked around the otherwise empty apartment. 'Yeah, well. Not so much. She's still at work. I'm still her least favourite daughter.'

'Well, I've an idea that might help,' Jake said.

'Really?' Gray sat up straighter. 'What is it?'

'There's a big bill going through Parliament tonight. I'm going to be there late, working for my dad,' he said. 'If you can get over there again through the tunnel, we could retrace your steps and find the office you were in. Figure out who it was. Then you'd have the proof.'

Gray hesitated. The last thing she wanted to do was go through the dark tunnels again. But she needed proof. And there was only one way to get it.

'OK,' she said. 'I'll be there.'

TWENTY-FOUR

That night, just before nine o'clock, Gray opened the door of the apartment. The great sprawling office building was hushed as she slipped into the corridor and down the stairs.

After what had happened last time, she didn't want to go back into the tunnels. She didn't want to go anywhere near Parliament. But if she could find proof, it would change everything.

Still, she couldn't walk past the front door guards this time. They'd definitely be on the lookout for her. She had to find another way into the tunnels.

She'd spent the evening trying to think of a way around them. And she'd come up with a plan. The only problem was, she wasn't sure it would work.

When she reached the foot of the staircase, instead of turning left towards the front door, she turned right, as if she were going back to the building across the courtyard.

She could hear the guards talking from down the hallway as she half-ran around the corner. Without hesitating even long enough to make sure there was no one around, she shoved the double doors open and ran out into the icy night.

Instead of running straight across the courtyard though, she turned right.

NUMBER 10

This was the part where it might all go wrong. She was gambling that there must be another way in.

She could see her breath in the cold air as she hurried past the spindly winter trees, searching the blank stone wall near the kitchen. When she spotted a door, her heart began to race.

She reached for the handle, praying it was unlocked.

It turned easily. She let out a sigh of relief.

Yanking the door open, she stepped back into the quiet, muffled warmth of Number 10 and looked around. She was in a short corridor she'd never seen before. If it was where she thought it was, she should be past the guards.

She held her breath and tiptoed down the faintly-lit hallway to where it intersected with the building's central corridor. There she stopped, and leaned out.

She'd been right. The door leading down to the tunnels was right beside her.

Moving fast, she opened the door and stepped inside, unnoticed.

There was no time to linger. If anyone was going to catch her, they could catch her running. She hurried down the stone steps, and when she reached the tunnels she began to run.

Her breath burned her lungs, but she kept pushing it, her feet pounding on the stone floor of the tunnel. It took no time at all, or so it seemed, to reach the first intersection with the tunnel to the Foreign Office. Heartened, she kept going, moving faster.

She was halfway to the tunnel marked Q when she heard something.

Panting, she skidded to a stop. But with her breath rasping and blood roaring in her ears it was hard to make anything out.

She could see nothing in the long straight tunnel ahead. Certain that she must have imagined it, she took a step.

Then the unmistakeable sound of a man laughing echoed around her, mockingly.

The fine hairs on Gray's forearms rose.

She spun around, scanning the tunnel in both directions. She could see no one.

For a second, she hesitated – uncertain whether to continue forward or run back to the safety of Number 10.

But this was her one chance. Jake wasn't going to be in Parliament every night at this hour. Her mother wouldn't work late every evening. Richard wouldn't be away every night. This could be her one chance to try to figure this out. She couldn't throw it away just because she was scared.

Forcing her feet forwards, she began to run again, slowly at first, and then faster. With every step, she scanned the way ahead.

When the narrow entrance to Q tunnel loomed to her right, she let out a relieved breath, and hurled herself into its dank shadows.

This time she was prepared for the darkness. She resisted the urge to look behind her, no matter what she heard. She had to keep going. The faster she moved, the sooner she'd be through to the other side.

When she reached the blacked-out section of the tunnel she knew she was almost there. Gritting her teeth, she splashed through the freezing water, trying not to think of what might be submerged there. Running in the dark instead of risking using her phone to illuminate the way. She could see enough, and she knew there was light ahead.

At last, the old arched door appeared in front of her.

Breathless, sweat streaming down her back despite the chill, she grasped the iron ring and turned it. The door swung open.

NUMBER 10

When Gray emerged into the elegant, panelled hallway from the same nondescript door she'd used before, she instantly noticed that the feel of the building was very different from her last visit.

There was no hollow emptiness. Instead, it felt warm and alive. She could hear voices, see people in the distance bustling about. Everywhere there was a sense of urgency.

The grandfather clock told her it was just after nine, but it could have been the middle of the day. Jake had told her everyone was working late, but she hadn't realised exactly what that would mean.

She could see men in suits up ahead. In jeans and a dark pullover, and with soaking trainers, she'd stand out.

When she reached a ladies' room she dived inside, and hurriedly locked herself in a cubicle. Pulling her phone from her pocket, she called Jake's number.

He answered on the first ring. 'Where are you?'

'I'm in the loo,' she whispered.

There was a pause.

'Which loo?' She could imagine his arched eyebrow.

'Somewhere in the House of Lords,' she clarified.

'That's a big place. Can you find Central Lobby? The one with the statues?'

'Yeah, sure. It's a straight shot from here,' she said, hoping she was right. 'I just have to not get caught on the way. I feel really obvious.'

'Don't worry, all the MPs have interns working for them,' he assured her. 'No one will look at you.'

'Come on, Jake,' Gray said. 'I'm *me*. Everyone notices me.'

'Oh, right.' He sounded almost embarrassed. 'I forgot about that. Well, if anyone recognises you, tell them you're visiting your mum. She's been here all evening.'

That gave Gray pause. She knew she was unlikely to run into her mother in a building as big as this one, but if she were that unlucky, she'd be profoundly busted.

Still, there was nothing for it.

Before she could reply, she heard the sound of a door creaking, and then high heels tapping on the tiled floor.

'I have to go,' she whispered. 'See you in five.'

Hanging up, she shoved the phone in her pocket.

A woman was at the sinks, humming to herself. 'You look terrible, Jo,' she murmured.

Gray heard the distinctive sound of someone rummaging in a handbag, and then things fell silent for a moment. Finally, after what seemed like forever, the woman's heels tapped across the floor. Then the cubicle door next to Gray's opened and closed again.

As soon as she heard the lock connect, Gray opened the cubicle door and sprinted from the room.

The distance to Central Lobby wasn't as far as she'd remembered. When she walked in a few minutes later, Jake stood in the middle, beneath a gilded ceiling painted with entwined red and white roses.

'I don't believe it.' His voice echoed off the stone walls. 'You're really here.'

She could see how impressed he was. 'I told you,' she said, smiling.

He grew serious again. 'You're sure you're OK to do this after what happened today? You're not too... I don't know. In shock?'

'I'm fine,' Gray insisted, holding out her arms. 'Unscathed.'

'Alright then.' Jake held out a plastic card dangling from a lanyard. 'Here's your key to the magic kingdom.'

Gray examined the cream card with the green symbol of Parliament on it, and the word VISITOR in large letters.

'Wear that and security won't even look at you,' he said as she slipped it around her neck.

Ignoring the magnificent room around them, he rocked back on the worn heels of his trainers, and tilted his head.

'Right. Now, let's go and find out who wants to kill your mother.'

TWENTY-FIVE

The two of them stood in the centre of the ornate octagonal room as Gray tried to remember which way she'd run the last time she'd sneaked into Parliament.

Four huge arched doorways dominated the walls around them. Each had a thick stone frame that soared twenty feet high, surrounded by statues of royal figures.

'Waddya reckon?' Jake asked, when she didn't speak.

'I think I ran straight across,' she said, slowly, her voice echoing off the stone walls. 'So, if I came in through that hallway…'

Jake pointed to the opposite doorway. 'You must have gone out that way. Let's try it.'

He strode purposefully across the room, ignoring the busy parliamentary workers who scrambled out of his way. He seemed more comfortable in Parliament than he was at school, moving with confidence. Like he belonged here. Like this was his home.

She'd been obsessed with her own problems but could tell his life was no more normal than her own.

'Why does your dad make you come here so much?' she asked, walking beside him.

'To piss off my mum.'

Gray wasn't sure how to reply to that. Taking her silence as a need for more information, he explained. 'Dad didn't want me to live with him, not really. He just wanted to hurt my mum because she left him – particularly because she left him for a woman. That hurt his pride. And besides, like I said, I'm useful to him. He's a noble single father.'

His tone was condemning.

Gray thought about her mum and Richard, and how she'd felt after the divorce.

'Do you like her?' she asked.

'Who, my mum?' He gave her a puzzled look.

She shook her head. 'Her girlfriend.'

'Louise?' He lifted his shoulders briefly. 'She's alright. The thing that matters to me though, is how happy she makes my mum. That's what I care about.'

His words hit Gray hard. She thought about how happy her mother was with Richard. Much as it pained her to admit it, they had a better marriage than her parents had shared. The thought was sobering.

'If you could choose, you'd live with her, wouldn't you?' she guessed.

'In a heartbeat.' He tilted his head at her. 'What about you? Would you live with your dad if you had the choice?'

Gray thought of her dad's fourth-floor flat near the Thames. It had a comfortable, worn feel to it. His deep leather chair by the windows, lots of bookcases. The funny old lady downstairs who sometimes let Gray walk her pug in the park across the street.

It had been a long time since he'd spent much time there. Nearly a year. She missed him so much. But he obviously didn't want her in his life enough to come home more. He certainly wouldn't want her living in his house. He loved being a diplomat as much as her mother loved being prime minister. Their jobs were more important than she was.

Her throat was suddenly tight. She disguised the pain with bitterness. 'No one cares what I want,' she said shortly.

After that, they walked in silence for a while. Then, out of nowhere, Jake said, 'We're very alike, my mum and me. I think that's why my dad acts like he does. I remind him of her. I have her eyes.' A lock of hair fell into his face and he pushed it back impatiently. 'See, my dad thinks my mum'll hate it if I become like him, so he drags me to work all the time. Makes me come here after school every day to work in his office.' He shrugged. 'Nothing I can do about it, though. He has custody until I'm eighteen.'

'How old are you now?' she asked.

'Sixteen,' said Jake. 'Just a year, six months, three weeks and two days to go and I'll be free.'

It struck Gray they were both trapped. Him with his dad. Her in Number 10. Until they could grow up enough to get out.

While they talked, they'd been walking. Now they had reached an intersecting corridor Gray had never seen before. She looked around, her heart sinking.

'None of this looks familiar,' she told him. 'I think we've come too far.'

'Right then.' He turned around. 'Let's go back.'

As they retraced their steps, Gray studied the doors, trying to remember which one she'd gone in that night. At first, nothing looked right. Midway down the corridor though, she saw one that appeared promising.

'This one,' she said eagerly, pointing at it. 'I think I've seen it before.'

It was cracked open.

Motioning for Jake to wait, she gently pushed the door open a bit more so she could see inside. It was a small office, with two desks crammed into it. A young woman sat at one of them, talking on the phone.

She glanced up at Gray, who looked past her.

There was no door connecting it to a larger room. It wasn't the right office.

'Sorry,' she whispered at the girl, and backed away apologetically.

Turning to Jake, she shook her head.

They checked door after door – some were locked, some were open – and after a while, they all looked the same to Gray. And she could remember so little about the office she'd gone into.

She'd started started the night with hope but it was ebbing away.

When they made it back to the lobby where they'd started, they paused.

'I guess it could be a different hallway,' Jake suggested.

'I guess.' Gray looked at the other long hallways stretching off Central Lobby, each one lined with doors. 'There are a lot of offices here.'

'Hundreds,' he said.

Gray checked the time on her phone. It was already a quarter to ten. 'I only have half an hour left if I'm going to get home before my mum.'

'We'll go faster,' he promised.

They raced down a different hallway, checking the doors, but finding nothing that looked as she recalled. It was as if she'd somehow ended up in some other Parliament by mistake that night. Some dangerous parallel version of it.

They passed people periodically, and Gray always glanced away at the last second, hoping not to be spotted. At one point, a crowd of six walked towards them, talking and laughing, and she stopped abruptly to look at a filing cabinet shoved against one wall. She didn't look up again until the crowd was gone.

When she straightened, Jake was watching her with a look she couldn't read.

'I'd hate that.' He tilted his head at the crowd. 'Worrying about being noticed all the time.'

'Yeah. It's weird,' she said. 'It's always going to be weird.'

He shot her a sideways glance. 'The papers were always going to go crazy if the PM's kid was a pretty teenage girl. It's red meat to them.'

Gray was so flustered about his use of the word 'pretty' it took her a second to focus.

Jake didn't seem to notice. 'This is weird, right? I mean, me being Tom McIntyre's son. And you being who you are. I wouldn't have thought we could be friends.'

Gray smiled. 'Me neither.' She thought for a minute and then confessed, 'My mum told me not to hang out with you.'

'Did she?' He looked at her. 'Because of my dad?'

'She told me I couldn't trust you. That you were probably spying on me for your dad.'

From beneath her lashes, she observed his reaction. He didn't reply for a long time. There was something complicated in his expression. A kind of intensity that made her chest feel tight.

'What did you say to that?' he asked.

'I told her I choose my own friends,' she said, firmly. 'Also, I told her you were not your father.'

A slow smile brightened his angular features. Gray found herself smiling back without even realising she was going to do it.

He stepped closer. 'Gray, I...'

'Jake!' A brash voice cut him off.

They turned to see a man hurrying towards them. He wore a dark suit with a crooked tie and carried a large envelope in one hand.

Jake froze. All the animation left his face. He flicked a warning look at Gray, who stepped back, trying to lose herself in the shadows. She didn't recognise the man at all, but she got the feeling Jake didn't want him to see her.

'Where have you been?' the man demanded. 'I've been looking for you everywhere. You can't go disappearing on a night like tonight. It's a bloody nuisance.' He had a northern accent, thicker than Jake's. 'Why didn't you answer your phone? Everyone's working their arses off. This is no time to be picking up girls.'

Jack's mouth tightened but he said nothing as the man thrust the envelope at him.

'Take this to your dad's office, right away.'

'Fine.' Jake snatched the envelope.

'And for God's sake, answer your phone next time,' the man chided. 'If your dad finds out you're hanging out with...'

He peered past Jake to Gray. She'd made herself as small as possible but there was no way to become invisible. The man's voice trailed off. He stared at her with an expression of almost comic surprise.

'Hang on. Isn't she...?'

Jake didn't let him finish. 'We have to go,' he said, reaching for Gray's hand. 'I have the envelope. You need to get back, Mike.'

But Mike didn't move. He stood, watching with frank astonishment as the two of them hurried away.

Gray let Jake take the lead. He seemed to be walking at random – left, then right, right again, then left.

She had no idea where they were. She wasn't sure Jake did either. But it didn't matter. She'd seen the look on Mike's face. He'd tell Jake's dad. Word would get around.

Midway down the next hallway, Jake abruptly turned into a room, motioning for her to follow. It was an empty meeting room. Blue chairs were arranged in a horseshoe shape around a long table. Slim silver microphones were arranged in front of each seat.

Closing the door behind them, he leaned his back against it and raked his fingers through his dark hair. There were hectic spots of colour high on his cheeks. 'I really wish that hadn't happened,' he said.

'Who was that guy?' Gray asked him.

'Mike.' He said it with contempt. 'My dad's clerk and chief arsehole. He despises me nearly as much as I hate him.'

'Will he tell your dad he saw you with me?' she asked.

The look on his face told her everything she needed to know.

Gray sagged back against the wall next to him. 'My mum's going to find out, isn't she?'

Jake didn't reply. He didn't need to.

She thumped her head back against the wall. 'I can't believe this is happening.'

'Same.'

They were side by side, backs to the wall. Jake turned his head to look at her. They were so close, she could feel the warmth of his breath on her cheek. 'The worst part of this is, Mike is such a massive wanker.'

Despite everything, Gray found herself laughing. And once she started, she couldn't stop.

Jake gave her an incredulous look. 'What is so funny?'

She kept trying to stop laughing, but couldn't. Was this what hysteria felt like? She was helpless. 'It's just… He really is.'

Then Jake was laughing, too. Reluctantly, like it pained him. Which only made her laugh harder.

It took them a full minute to regain control. When they did, the seriousness of their situation hit them hard.

'I'm sorry,' Jake said, his face falling back into sombre lines. 'I guess tonight wasn't a great idea. It was always possible we'd be seen. I just thought with everyone so busy –'

'Don't apologise,' she said. 'I'm glad we tried.' She searched his eyes. 'What will your dad say when he finds out?'

He lowered his voice to a fair approximation of his father's northern growl. 'I want you in my office every day, workin' where I can see you. Can't be trusted on yer own.' He sighed. 'The usual. What will your mum say?'

She gave him a bleak look. 'Welcome to boarding school, Gray.'

'We'll figure something out,' he promised. 'It'll be OK.'

Gray so wanted to agree. But she knew it wasn't true.

Trouble was coming. And she was no nearer to figuring out who was behind it.

TWENTY-SIX

The next morning, Gray emerged cautiously from her bedroom to find the apartment empty. Wintery daylight streamed through the kitchen windows onto clean granite countertops. The warm kettle told her that her mother had already had her morning cup of tea and gone to work.

She relaxed a little. If her mother had had any clue she'd been out the night before, she would definitely have stayed around for a fight.

After their encounter with Mike, Jake had walked her back to the door leading down to the tunnels. They hadn't spoken much. Everything had already been said. They'd agreed to keep in touch today – alerting each other as soon as word got to their parents.

Gray had run home through the tunnels without incident, slipping back into Number 10 the same way she'd gone out. She'd climbed into bed exhausted, and never heard her mother come home.

She was sitting at the kitchen table, eating a slice of toast, when her phone buzzed.

A message from Jake.

Mike still hasn't told my dad. It's torture.

NUMBER 10

Dusting toast crumbs off her fingers she typed back.

Maybe he won't tell.

The response came instantly.

He'll tell.

Julia was waiting for her as usual when she got downstairs. In jeans and a loose black peacoat, she appeared younger than ever.

'You look chipper,' she said, as Gray hurried over to her.

'I'm *not* chipper,' Gray objected.

'Well, you look as bright as a button, then,' Julia amended herself, as they threaded through the throng of staff arriving for work. 'Did you talk to your mum about what happened?'

'No,' she said. 'I haven't seen her.'

Julia's eyebrows winged up. 'You haven't seen her since yesterday afternoon?'

Gray gave a loose shrug. 'She had to work late last night. Some big immigration bill. I was asleep when she came in. And she went back to work today before I got up.'

'Right.' Julia sounded disapproving. 'So you don't know about the guy.'

Gray's breath hitched. 'What about him?'

'The police gave us a report late last night. He's not part of any known threat. He has a history of mental illness. He only climbed over the fence to talk to you.'

'With a *knife*?' Gray's voice rose.

'He claims the knife was in case someone tried to stop him from meeting you.' Julia's tone was dry. 'Apparently he had big plans for scaring them off with it.'

Gray gave her an incredulous look.

'Look, I'm not saying I believe him,' Julia said. 'All I'm telling you is, he wasn't part of any organisation. This isn't the big bad thing we've been worrying about.'

'Oh good.' Gray's tone was ironic. 'I guess I'm safe now.'

Julia opened the door leading to the side exit. 'You are, as long as you're with me.'

Gray wasn't looking forward to going outside again through the same door where it had all happened, but as soon as they walked to the end of the corridor she could see that security was visibly more intense. Instead of just one police officer at that door, there were two.

Nodding to Gray and Julia, one of them opened the door. The clean smell of cold rain flooded in. Three uniformed police officers, two of them armed, were arrayed between the door and the car where Ryan stood waiting, a bruise shadowing his cheekbone where the attacker had punched him.

There was something about the increased security that made Gray feel a little better. She and her mother weren't speaking right now. But these police officers, guarding her like a jewel, were a message from her mother to her.

I care.

It might have been a first step towards forgiving each other, if Gray hadn't known that her mother would undoubtedly find out later today that she'd broken her rules.

And everything would go right back to being terrible again.

All day long, Gray waited for the axe to fall. But as time passed without a phone call or any indication at all that Mike had talked, she began to relax, just a little. When she and Jake met in the library at lunch time though, he remained convinced his father's clerk would talk.

'Mike's a spineless tosser,' he said, crushing his empty sandwich box vehemently. 'He's just clinging to this little shred of ammunition, so he can use it when it will have the biggest impact.'

Gray wasn't convinced. 'Why didn't he say anything last night though?'

'My dad was busy with the bill. It wouldn't have been a good time to tell him.' He gave a wry laugh. 'I almost respect that idiot Mike for his strategy. It would have been the wrong move to run straight to him. He's waiting to hold it over my head as blackmail, or to use it for maximum effect.'

But all day long, nothing happened.

When school finished, Gray lingered on the front steps talking to Chloe, who was having a crisis of conscience about Will, her on-again, off-again boyfriend.

'The thing is, I don't really love him,' Chloe said earnestly. 'I just like having someone to go out with, so I'm not alone at parties while you're grounded. But I get the feeling he's really into me.'

'I think you have to listen to your stomach,' Gray advised.

Chloe blinked. 'My stomach?'

'Do you get butterflies in it when you see him?' Gray asked. 'Hearts can be deceived but stomachs don't lie.'

Chloe wasn't convinced. 'Maybe, but…'

'Gray.' Julia walked up, interrupting them without warning. 'The car's waiting.' She looked tense, her mouth set in a disapproving line.

Gray's brow creased.

'OK, I'm coming.' She gave Chloe a quick hug. 'Call me later.'

By the time she turned around, Julia was already striding impatiently towards the visitors' entrance. Gray had to run to keep up with her.

'What's the matter?' she asked.

'Your mother called,' Julia told her, quietly. 'She said to bring you straight back home.'

Gray's heart twisted. 'Did something happen?' she asked, as she climbed into the car. 'Is she alright?'

'Everyone's fine.' Ryan started the engine and pulled into traffic. 'She just wants to talk to you.'

Gray didn't buy his soothing tone. Her mother wouldn't ask to have her brought straight back unless something was wrong.

A voice in her head asked, What if she knows about last night?

But Jake hadn't heard anything from his father yet. It made sense that he would hear first. Pulling out her phone, she sent him a quick text:

Mum asked to see me. Something's wrong.

Does your dad know?

His text came through almost immediately.

Still nothing here. Good luck.

The car journey took place in near silence. All of them seemed to sense that bad news was coming.

NUMBER 10

At Number 10, three officers greeted them outside the side entrance, guns at the ready. Julia and Ryan escorted Gray through the busy corridors. Ryan had left the car in the street and walked in with them – something he'd never done before. All Gray's warning signals were flashing now.

When they reached the main lobby with its police in full uniform and CCTV screens, they didn't walk straight across it towards the family apartment. Instead, Ryan turned into another staircase. This one was grander, with a long curved banister. Its lemon-yellow walls were lined with portraits of previous prime ministers.

They were taking her to her mother's office.

In her pocket, her phone buzzed insistently. She checked it as they climbed up. The message was from Jake. She knew what it would say, before she looked.

Mike talked.

'Put it away, Gray.' Julia gave her a stern look. 'You know the rules.'

Reluctantly, Gray shoved the device back into her pocket without replying. Nobody was allowed to use phones in this part of the building – not even the PM's kid.

At the top, they walked down a long corridor, past a number of rooms. Through open doorways, Gray glimpsed spacious meeting rooms that looked like Edwardian parlours.

When they got to the end of the hallway, Julia reached for the handle, pausing to glance at Gray.

'Ready?'

Gray gave a stiff nod.

They walked into a small waiting room, filled with tasteful chairs and couches with silk and linen covers in neutral shades. A television mounted on the wall showed BBC News with the sound off. A receptionist sat at one end. The door behind her led to the prime minister's personal office.

The receptionist glanced up at them. When her eyes settled on Gray, her expression changed almost imperceptibly. 'Oh, Miss Langtry,' she said, with the bland distance of a doctor. 'Your mother's in a meeting but she asked for you to wait. I'll let her know you're here.'

She typed something into her computer. Ryan and Julia turned back to the door.

'You're not staying?' There was a touch of desperation in Gray's voice.

Ryan shook his head. 'Our part is done.'

'Good luck,' Julia told her, not without sympathy.

Gray perched on an armchair as far from the receptionist as possible. Her back was rigid, but her right foot jittered nervously. Each second ticked by with excruciating slowness.

When the door to the inner office finally swung open, she twitched.

She heard her mother's voice. 'I appreciate you coming out today, John.'

Climbing to her feet, Gray stood stiffly, waiting her turn.

'Of course. I'm grateful for your time, Prime Minister,' a man said. 'We'll get this done for you.'

His voice was a distinctive baritone, deep as the grave.

Gray's blood turned to ice.

She knew that voice. She'd heard it in Parliament when she was hiding in a cupboard.

It was the man who'd threatened her mother's life.

TWENTY-SEVEN

Her feet felt rooted to the floor. She couldn't seem to move. To breathe.

The man that emerged from her mother's office was tall – over six feet – and bulky. His greying hair was neatly combed. His suit was impeccable. His angular face familiar.

It was John Ashford, the deputy prime minister. She'd seen him on television. He and her mother weren't friends, but he was part of her cabinet. He'd been at the gala dinner with her mother and Richard last week – she'd seen him on the news, sitting at the top table just a few seats away.

Why would he want to kill her mother?

Before she could work any of it through, her mother appeared in the doorway of her inner office. 'We must get together soon,' she said, pleasantly. 'It would be lovely to see Annabelle.'

He replied, but Gray didn't hear what he said.

Her mother was so close to him he could have stabbed her and nobody would have had a chance to stop him. But all he did was smile.

Gray watched as he spoke briefly to the receptionist and strolled to the door.

Just before he walked out, he glanced around the room. His gaze fell on Gray, who stared at him, hands curled into fists. His pale blue eyes were cool and blank.

'Gray.' Her mother's impatient voice pulled her attention back. 'Come in, please.'

Torn by indecision though, she didn't move.

What could she do? Chase him down the hallway? Tell Julia to tackle him? They'd think she was insane.

Maybe she was going crazy. How could it be him? He was her mother's colleague.

'*Gray.*' Her mother gave her a warning look.

Casting one last tormented look in the direction of Ashford, Gray crossed the room to where the prime minister waited.

In ominous silence, her mother closed the door behind her.

Her office was spacious. The tall windows lining the far wall were protected with blast-proof curtains, through which the last of the grey afternoon light filtered. The ornate white marble fireplace was unlit. The panelled walls were painted pale blue. A heavy, ostentatious desk sat across from the windows. In front of it, four leather chairs surrounded a low table.

'Take a seat.' Her mother gestured at the chairs, seating herself primly in one.

Numbly, Gray did as she was told.

'We need to have a talk.'

Her mother brushed a piece of lint from her navy pencil skirt. She was disturbingly calm. 'I've had some information come to me from Tom McIntyre,' her mother continued in that same mild tone. 'He phoned me personally to say that you were seen in Parliament last night. Of course, I told him this couldn't be true. As far as I knew you were home, as we'd agreed.' She met her daughter's eyes directly. 'Do you have an explanation for this?'

NUMBER 10

Gray didn't see any point in lying. It wouldn't matter anyway. It was time to tell the truth.

'Yes. I was there,' she admitted, stammering slightly. 'I was working on something.'

'Of course you were.' Her mothers' tone told her what she thought of that explanation. 'And who were you working with?'

Gray was recovering her focus now. The familiar cut and thrust of arguing with her mother was steadying, in a way.

'You know already, don't you?' Gray leaned back in her chair. 'Or you wouldn't be dragging me out of school and making such a huge deal out of it. I was with Jake.'

Her mother leaned forward. Her eyes were chips of ice. 'Grayson Langtry. What the hell were you thinking? Sneaking into Parliament at night with the son of the leader of the opposition? While you are grounded. In direct contravention of my orders. Are you completely out of your mind?'

'I'm not out of my mind.' Gray stood her ground. 'Jake's helping me try to figure out what's going on. Who's trying to hurt you. I told him what I heard that night and, unlike you, he believed me.' She drew a breath. 'If you won't try to figure this out, I will.'

Her mother was shaking her head. 'Gray, this is getting out of hand. You've broken every rule I've set for you. If you're now dragging the opposition in to this, I'm going to have to…'

'Jake isn't the opposition.' Gray spoke over her. 'He's a sixteen-year-old student at my school.'

Her mother made a dismissive gesture. 'His father is the opposition, and you know what I meant. Don't try to distract me.'

'I'm not distracting you,' Gray said. 'You keep confusing Jake and his dad. He's not his dad. He doesn't even *like* his dad. They're different people.'

'Regardless of how many people Jake and Tom McIntyre *are*.' Her mother layered on the sarcasm. 'The point is, you're now dragging them both into this absurd story about murder plots in Parliament. And you're ignoring my restrictions.'

'I'm doing it for you, Mum,' Gray told her. 'I'm trying to help you because you refuse to believe me.'

Her mother rounded on her. 'I don't believe you because you lie, Gray. And I do not need your *help*.'

Gray drew a sharp breath.

Her mother must have known she'd gone too far, because she paused. When she spoke again, she was calmer. 'I don't want to fight with you. Whatever you went into Parliament for last night doesn't matter right now. What matters is, you shouldn't have been there. You're grounded. You broke the rules I set for you. Didn't you?'

Gray gave her a steady look. 'Yes.'

For a long second, her mother held her gaze. Then, to Gray's surprise, she rubbed her forehead. 'Oh, Gray,' she said softly. 'I feel like I've let you down.'

Nonplussed, Gray searched for a response.

'How?'

'I heard about what happened yesterday. The attempted attack.' Her mother lifted her head. 'I was furious that anyone got that close to you. Raj assured me you were fine but…' Her voice trailed off. Suddenly, she looked tired and defeated. 'If anything had happened to you, I don't know what I would have done,' she said softly. 'I dragged you into this building against your will, and now I'm scared you're going to get hurt because of me.'

Gray swallowed hard. 'I'm fine,' she said. 'Julia and Ryan were there.'

Her mother nodded, but her lips were still tight. 'Do you understand how hard it is to keep you safe if you sneak out whenever my back is turned?' She leaned forward, hands clasped on her knees. 'Do you know how much that scares me?'

'Yes, but I'm trying to help you.' Gray's voice quivered.

'I don't want you to help me with this, Gray. This is *my job*. Not yours.' She straightened. 'I would like you to reconsider the boarding school we spoke about.' Seeing Gray's mutinous expression she held up her hand. 'Not as punishment. But as a safe place. I don't think it's fair to make you live in a hothouse like Number 10. It's fine for adults. It's not fair to you.'

'Oh, sure.' Heat rose to Gray's face. 'This is all about making things better for *me*. It has nothing to do with how much easier *your* life would be if you could put me away somewhere until I grow up. Let me out at Christmas for family photos. Then institutionalise me again, so I don't embarrass you.' She went for the jugular. 'Why did you even have me in the first place, Mum, if the only thing you really love is your career?'

Years of taking and giving blows on the floor of the House of Commons had taught her mother to hide her emotions. But Gray knew her better than anyone. And she saw the red stain creep up her neck. Noticed the very slight flinch.

And she didn't feel sorry.

'I don't want to go to boarding school. Bring Dad home. Send me to live with him. It can't be the case that neither of you want me. I'm not *that* awful. I only lied to you about parties, for God's sake.' Gray's voice grew unsteady. She was going to cry, and she couldn't bear for her mother to see that.

Jumping to her feet, she ran for the door.

'Gray.'

She turned to see her mother standing in front of the low chairs. She didn't look angry anymore. She looked sad. 'I'll try to reach your father. He's on an important job, and it's not easy to get him. But I'll try.'

Gray choked back a sob. Even getting what she wanted hurt. Because it meant her mother was willing to let her go. It felt like her world was falling apart.

But her mother wasn't finished.

'I need you to stay away from Jake McIntyre,' she continued firmly. 'For your own sake as well as mine.'

Gray was speechless.

There was no point in continuing this argument. Anything she said would just make things worse. Turning, she headed for the door.

But when her hand touched the cool metal of the handle, the thought of John Ashford's oily voice stopped her. How amused he'd sounded as he described the plot to murder her mother. How could they be fighting about Jake when things were so dangerous?

She turned back. Her mother hadn't moved.

'That man who was in here earlier – Ashford,' Gray said. 'Don't trust him.'

Her mother gave her a puzzled look. 'I don't trust anyone, Gray. Why are you worried about John?'

Gray hesitated. She could tell her without any proof. And her mother would call her a liar. And discount every word.

But she had to say something.

'He's dangerous,' Gray said.

There was a long silence as her mother studied her.

When she spoke again, she changed the subject as if Gray had said nothing at all.

'I need to be certain you're safe right now, Gray. So I've asked your bodyguards to stay with you in the apartment until I get home.'

Gray was stunned. 'What are you telling me? They're my prison guards now?'

'Please, Gray. Just go home. I've got work to do.' Her mother turned away.

But Gray stood where she was. 'You know, it's funny,' she said. 'There's so much I want to tell my mother. So much she needs to know. But I don't want to tell *you* anything.'

Spinning on her heel, she flung the door open and stormed from the office, and out into the long office hallway, where Julia and Ryan were waiting for her.

TWENTY-EIGHT

When Gray went in to see her mother, Julia and Ryan positioned themselves in the corridor outside to wait.

'Looks like the kid's in trouble again.' Ryan said.

The two of them had been getting along much better ever since their talk. They'd worked smoothly together when the attempted attack had happened, and since then, there'd been more trust between them.

Julia glanced at him. 'Do you have any idea what she did?'

He shook his head. 'All Raj told me was get her back here in double-quick time. Said her mum was fuming.'

Julia couldn't imagine what Gray might have got up to inside Number 10 that would have resulted in her mother calling the security chief personally.

When the office door opened a few minutes later, they both looked up. But it wasn't Gray who emerged. Instead, it was John Ashford, the deputy prime minister.

They stepped aside to give him room.

As he passed, his eyes met Julia's briefly. His predatory gaze was familiar to her – any ex-soldier would have recognised it. She'd seen that sort of look before, on both sides of conflict. It was a hunter's look.

When he'd disappeared down the hallway, she said quietly, 'I don't like that guy.'

'Who? Ashford?' Ryan shrugged. 'He's just another politician, isn't he? They're all pretty terrible.'

Julia didn't agree. Politicians were human beings. Some were good. Some were bad. She knew which camp Ashford fitted in. She could see it on his face.

Julia's radio crackled through the earpiece she wore whenever she was inside Number 10.

Raj Patel's voice filled her head.

'Unit C-5. Please verify, is Firefly with Swan?'

'Swan' was the security code name for Gray's mother. Richard was 'Wolf'.

Julia answered before Ryan could, her voice low and curt. 'Affirmative.'

'I have new orders for you,' Raj said. 'You're to stay with Firefly at all times until Swan returns home. Repeat: at all times. Please confirm you understand.'

Julia and Ryan exchanged a puzzled look.

'Clarification,' Ryan said into his radio. 'Does this mean we should be *inside* the family residence?'

'Affirmative. At least one of you must be inside at all times. Eyes on.'

Julia blew out an audible breath. Whatever Gray had done, it must have been bad.

'Copy that.' Ryan's voice betrayed no emotion, but when he turned to Julia, he looked exasperated. 'What the hell did that girl do?'

When the office door flew open a few minutes later and Gray torpedoed out, they jumped to attention.

'Ready to…' Ryan started, but Gray powered by him without a look. '…go…?' He finished the sentence, looking at Julia, who ran after Gray with Ryan right behind her.

Gray stormed to the end of the corridor and thundered down the stairs, heedless of office staff coming the other way who had to dive to one side to avoid her. On the ground floor she hurtled down the corridor and up the second flight of stairs, running into the residence and slamming the door behind her so hard the wall shook.

Ryan and Julia, who had stayed right behind her all the way, stood uncertainly outside the door.

'What the hell is going on?' Ryan asked.

'This is war,' Julia told him grimly. 'Mother versus daughter. And we are right in the middle of it.'

Neither of them touched the doorknob.

'We have to go in.' Ryan didn't sound happy about the prospect. She didn't blame him.

'I'll do it.' Julia reached for the door. 'You mind staying out here?'

The look he gave her was almost comic. 'I'd rather be in a coal mine than in that apartment right now.'

Julia tapped on the apartment door twice and opened it without waiting for an answer. Gray stood in the middle of the living room, her school bag at her feet. She didn't appear to have moved since she first entered the flat.

Her eyes were dry, but her face was red and blotchy. Whether that was due to rage or hurt, Julia didn't know.

Gray shot her a glare. 'What do you want?'

'One of us should be inside with you.' Julia kept her tone apologetic, but Gray's face darkened.

'Come in. Stay out. It's not up to me, is it?'

Leaving Julia standing there, she ran down the short hallway and slammed a door.

Finding herself alone in the prime minister's personal living space, Julia had absolutely no idea what to do with herself. Surrounded by the sleek, tasteful furniture in soft shades of cream and grey, she felt like an intruder.

It was surprisingly small. There was no formal dining room – just an open-plan arrangement with a long kitchen table serving as the dividing line between the kitchen and the living area. A flat-screen television was mounted on one wall. Everything else looked like a magazine ad for a tasteful urban home.

Cautiously, she perched on the edge of a chair. She was thirsty but couldn't imagine wandering through the kitchen, opening the prime minister's cupboards to find a glass.

She kept listening for sounds from down the hallway, but she heard nothing. No sounds of crying. No sign that Gray was phoning friends to complain about her mother. The quiet was eerie. What was she doing in there?

Mostly, Julia was angry at her boss for putting her in this position. He had to learn how to say no to the prime minister now and then, or she and Ryan would end up living in Gray's bedroom with her. She wouldn't put it past the mother right now.

It seemed to her that Gray and her mother were two stubborn women, carved from the same unyielding stone, and when they fought, no one won.

If she was in the middle, she'd go down, too. She wasn't going to let that happen.

Pulling her phone from her pocket, she called Raj's number.

'Everything OK, Julia?'

'All fine,' she told him, crisply. 'She's in her room.'

'What can I help you with?'

Raj was a good boss. Focussed and clear in his assignments. An excellent judge of character. And she was grateful to him for finding her, however he'd done it, and freeing her from a boring life of paper pushing. She'd never had to stand up to him before. And she swallowed hard before speaking.

'Boss, we can't do this,' she said quietly. 'I can't be a prison guard for a sixteen-year-old girl. I'm sitting in the prime minister's living room and I do not belong here. Permission requested to wait outside.'

There was a long pause. 'Permission denied,' he said after a moment. But he didn't sound angry. 'Look, I agree with you. I'm going to try to get us out of this. Right now, I'm dealing with a furious mother whose kid somehow got out of Number 10 last night, past the cops and the guards, and into Parliament to hang out with the son of the leader of the opposition party.'

Julia closed her eyes and let out a breath. 'You're joking.'

'I wish I was.' She could hear the frustration in his voice. 'Obviously, her mother blames us and every cop in the city, and she wants to send a message to Gray. I'm hoping if we give her a little time, she'll realise that this is unsustainable. Until then, you or Ryan must be inside the apartment at all times whenever she's away.'

'Understood,' she said. After a pause, she added, 'Do you think it would be OK for me to get myself a glass of water?'

There was a pause. 'Send Ryan down to the canteen,' he said. 'Have him bring back whatever you need. Try not to move around the apartment. Got it?'

She wasn't supposed to get comfortable. At all.

'Yes sir.' she said, crisply.

When she hung up, she leaned back in the chair. There had to be something she could do to fix this.

She needed to talk to Gray.

TWENTY-NINE

From inside her room, Gray heard the faint sound of voices as Julia talked to someone, and then, after a while, silence.

She was so angry. So frustrated with her mother. She wanted to cry. To scream. But her eyes stayed stubbornly dry.

Boarding school.

She'd known it would happen. She'd even told Jake it would. That didn't make it any easier to accept.

'How can she do this?' she whispered.

It suddenly struck her that, if it was this bad for her, it must be worse for Jake. Every time she tried to phone him though, the calls went straight to voicemail.

She needed help. She needed advice. But who could she trust?

Slowly, as if in a daze, she scrolled to her father's number, her fingertip hovering over the word 'Dad'.

Why didn't he call? Why didn't he come home?

Shoving her hair back from her face, she typed quickly into her phone.

Mum's in trouble. Someone's going to kill her. No

one will listen to me. I heard something in Parliament. I

think Richard…

She paused for a long moment, and then carefully deleted the last three words. She wasn't even sure it was him she'd seen. She couldn't confuse things. Not right now. She continued typing.

She won't listen. It's John Ashford. Do you know

anything about him? She doesn't want to believe it. Please

call me. Or come home. I love you.

Before she could change her mind, she hit send.

She waited for a few minutes, staring at her phone. There was no response.

Of course there wasn't, she thought, with dull acceptance. No one in my family listens to me.

Swallowing her pain, she dialled a different number. Chloe answered on the first ring.

'Gray! What happened? Your guards dragged you out in a huge rush. It was like you were being *arrested.*'

When she heard her best friend's familiar airy voice, something in Gray's chest loosened.

A sob shook her. 'I'm in so much trouble,' she said, her voice trembling. 'I don't know what to do.'

Instantly, Chloe grew serious. 'What's happened? No one tried to hurt you, did they?'

'No, nothing like that.' Lowering herself onto the bed, Gray dropped her head into her hands. 'There are things I should have told you before, but I didn't want to scare you. I wanted to tell you today too, but it's just so weird. Now everything's all messed up.'

'Gray,' Chloe said gently. 'I'm your friend. You can tell me anything.'

'But this is big,' Gray said. 'Bigger than us.'

'Well, try me.'

Slowly, brokenly, she explained what had happened that night in Parliament. The men she'd overheard.

'Oh Gray, no.' Chloe sounded horrified. 'Did you tell your mum? What did she say?'

'She didn't believe me. She thinks I'm lying to get out of some kind of trouble.' Gray's tone was dull. 'Ever since, I've been trying to find proof to take to her, so she'll believe me. Jake's been helping me.'

There was a telltale pause before Chloe said, 'Really? You told *Jake*?' Her voice was an odd mix of shock and hurt.

'I didn't mean to leave you out,' Gray said quickly. 'It's such a weird situation. I wasn't sure I trusted myself. I thought Jake could help because of who his dad is, you know?' She drew a gulping breath of air, feeling terrible. 'Last night, I sneaked out to meet him in Parliament to try and figure out who wants to hurt my mum. But we got caught, and now my mum thinks I'm more of a liar than ever. And she's going to send me to boarding school and I won't see you anymore. I'll be all alone. And I think I know who wants to kill her but Mum won't believe me and she's going to get hurt. I know it. I just know it.'

Finally, the tears arrived. She dropped onto the bed, clutching the phone in one hand and covering her face with the other as she sobbed.

It took Chloe a moment to absorb all of this. 'Gray, babe, listen to me,' she said, firmly. 'You have every right to cry, but we

231

need to work through this. Have you talked to Jake since you got home?'

'He's not answering his phone.'

'OK, I'll try to reach him,' Chloe said. 'If we're going to come up with a plan, we'll need him.'

Surprised, Gray wiped tears from her cheeks. 'A plan?'

'If your mum won't listen to you, and you think you know who's behind this, we have to find someone else who can help.'

Chloe – the former head of her Girl Guide group, and class leader two years running – was kicking into gear.

'You can't tell anyone but Jake,' Gray warned her, panicking. 'This is so secret I shouldn't even be telling you.'

'Don't be ridiculous.' Chloe sounded insulted. 'I won't tell anyone. Not even my parents. But of course you should tell me. I'm your best friend. I've got your back.'

This made Gray want to cry all over again. But Chloe was already working on the problem. 'Did you say the men mentioned attacking your mother at some fund-raiser in Oxford?'

'Yes,' Gray said, digging in her pocket for a tissue.

'When is it? The fundraiser, I mean.'

Gray stopped to think. 'I think it's this Saturday.'

There was a pause. When she spoke again, Chloe's tone was firm. 'You should tell your bodyguards,' she said. 'This is what they do.'

'I can't,' Gray said, miserably. 'They'll never believe me.'

Chloe didn't back down. 'I know you're upset and you feel hopeless, but you have to do this. I want you to promise me you're going to tell them.'

Gray lowered her head to her hands. Her mother had looked at her like she was insane five minutes ago. Now she had to go through that all over again.

But Chloe was right. It was time.

'I'll do it,' she said, finally.

Still, she couldn't bring herself to do it right away. She stayed in her bedroom as the afternoon light slanting through her window faded to black. In the courtyard below – the one she'd now thoroughly explored – she could see office workers in their coats, leaving.

Eventually, it was quiet and empty. No one walked beneath the skeletal winter trees shivering in the freezing November wind.

She kept rehearsing things she'd say when her mother came home. Honing her line of argument. But she had no hope that it would work. Nothing she said got through to her mother right now. They'd never been further apart.

Several times she tried to call Jake, but his phone went straight to voicemail again.

When her phone beeped just after 7:30 pm, her heart skipped. But it wasn't him. It was a message from her mother.

> **I'll be late. Richard's flight is delayed.**
> **There's food in the fridge.**

With a contemptuous flick of her wrist, Gray threw the battered old phone onto the bed.

Guess she doesn't want to talk to me either, she thought.

By then, though, she was starving. And hunger nibbled away at her pride.

If her bodyguards were going to be there, she'd just have to deal with it. She wasn't going to starve to death for them.

When she walked into the living room a few minutes later, Julia was sitting alone on one of the armchairs. Spotting her, the guard stood up awkwardly.

'How … are you?'

'Ravenous.' Gray headed for the kitchen. 'I'm going to make some food. Are you hungry?'

The brief pause before Julia responded was the only hint Gray got that she was surprised.

'Famished,' the bodyguard said.

Opening the fridge, Gray saw that her mother had left another dish from the cafeteria downstairs.

She lifted the foil lid to peek at it, and called out to Julia, 'I think it's shepherd's pie. Is that cool?'

'To be honest, I could eat a shepherd at this point,' Julia told her.

Gray gave a short laugh, and the ice between them broke, just a little.

The bodyguard walked into the kitchen. 'I'll turn the oven on. You get a baking tray.'

They prepared the meal with a kind of unexpected camaraderie. Julia made a salad ('Literally the only thing I know how to cook'), while Gray set out plates and glasses on the breakfast bar.

When it was ready, they sat across from each other at the table, eating.

The food was good. Shepherd's pie was one of the dishes the cooks excelled at. To her surprise, Gray had an appetite, despite everything.

She kept thinking about what Chloe had said. But she could imagine the disbelief on Julia's face if she told her everything. And the words wouldn't come.

Julia kept the conversation going, asking Gray questions about school and homework, avoiding sensitive subjects. She didn't seem at all judgemental. In fact, talking to her was sort of like talking to a friend.

'I like Chloe,' Julia said at one point. 'I wasn't sure at first, but she seems really together.'

'She is,' Gray assured her. 'People judge her because of how she looks, you know? Because she's so pretty and cheerful. But she is incredibly smart. She's the one person I trust.'

Julia got up and refilled their glasses from a jug on the counter. 'You have to deal with that too, don't you?' she said. 'I mean, you get a lot of attention because of the way you look.'

Gray wrinkled her nose. 'It's ridiculous. I'm sixteen, and the tabloids want to talk about my clothes. I get them from the same shops everyone else does, and they don't look that great on me anyway.' She took the glass Julia held out to her. 'Thank you. I mean, if my mum wasn't prime minister no one would look at me twice.'

Sitting across from her, Julia studied her soberly. 'You have such a good head on your shoulders, Gray. I just don't get why you're always in trouble.' When Gray didn't answer, she gestured at the apartment around them. 'Look. You should know that none of this was my idea. I don't want to invade your space. I don't even know why I'm here.'

Gray set her fork down. 'You're here because I sneaked out and went to Parliament last night. I met a friend. Jake McIntyre.' She paused. 'You know who he is, right?'

Julia nodded. If she was surprised by the information she'd just learned, it didn't show in her expression.

'Anyway,' Gray said, 'someone saw us together. Mum lost it. She's using you to punish me. I'm sorry you have to waste your time on this.'

'Don't apologise,' Julia said. 'It's not your fault I'm here. You were just doing what any girl your age would do. It's perfectly normal.'

Gray toyed with the knife on her plate. 'It didn't used to be like this,' she said. 'Mum and me, we always got along. Even after Dad left. But lately things have been … bad. Since Richard came along.'

Julia didn't look surprised.

'I'll tell you something,' she said. 'If there's one thing I understand in the world it's what it's like to have trouble with your parents. When I was your age, I couldn't be in the same room with mine. They basically ruined my life. I absolutely get it.'

Gray couldn't imagine this capable, intelligent woman not getting along with anyone.

'Do you and your parents talk now? Is it better?' she asked.

'Not at all.' Julia shifted the subject. 'What about your dad?'

Gray sighed, wondering how to explain. 'We used to be close,' she said, after a moment.

'He's in the foreign service, isn't he?' Julia tilted her head, watching her.

'Yeah,' Gray said. 'He sort of lives abroad now.'

'That must be hard.'

'I think if he were here, things would be easier.' Gray looked down at her empty plate. 'I'd have a place to go when Mum's busy or when I need to get out of this building. Without him, I'm sort of…'

'Trapped.' Julia finished the sentence for her.

This was precisely the word Gray would have used. When Gray looked up, there was a depth of understanding in Julia's expression.

'Yes. Completely trapped. And my dad never even calls anymore.' Gray sank back in her chair. 'I don't think he cares what's happening here.'

'I know it's a tough way to live.' Julia's tone was gentle. 'But your parents' work – both of them – what they're doing is really important.'

Gray made a face. 'My mum's work is important. But my dad isn't a big deal. He's just a diplomat. There's no reason for him to disappear. He just prefers being away.'

The bodyguard gave her a strange look.

'What?' Gray demanded. 'What don't I know?'

Julia looked past her, as if deciding how to handle this.

'Everything isn't as it seems with your father,' she said carefully. 'I can't tell you much. All I can say is that he's doing something very dangerous and incredibly brave. This is why you're not hearing from him. He's serving his country.'

Diplomats didn't do dangerous work. Gray opened her mouth to argue but then something made her close it again.

Memories came to her fast and thick – bags in the hallway, her father's sudden disappearances, his whispered arguments with her mother, gifts from exotic places she didn't even know he was going. The way he never went to the office when he wasn't on assignment. How tired he'd looked the last time she saw him.

All the pieces fell into place and suddenly she knew. 'My dad's a spy, isn't he?' Julia didn't answer, but Gray knew she was right. 'Oh my God.' She dropped her head in her hands. 'Do my parents tell me the truth about *anything*?'

'Gray.' When she lifted her head, Julia was leaning forward, watching her. 'You're tougher than you think. You can handle this stuff. You're smart. Give your parents – and yourself – a break. Your life is not normal, but try to see that they love you.

Their work is just extremely unusual. And they want you to fit in it, safely.'

But Gray didn't feel tough. She felt deceived. Everyone wanted to protect her from the world by not telling her the truth, even as reality rushed at her, with blades and cameras and threats of murder.

Julia carried the dirty dishes to the sink. After a moment, Gray got up to help. Neither of them talked much. Julia wasn't a chatterbox like Chloe, filling the air with amusing stories and gossip, but there was an openness to her. She was approachable and honest in a way few adults seemed to be.

If anyone would understand, it would be her.

As they finished washing the last dishes, Gray spoke tentatively. 'Can I ask you something else?'

'Of course.' Julia glanced at her.

'If someone threatened my mum, could they be arrested?'

Julia turned off the water. Her eyes were suddenly alert. 'Yes, they could. I would make sure of it.'

'But, you'd need proof, right?' Gray pressed. 'It couldn't just be someone saying, "I heard something bad." It would have to be more.'

'There would need to be some valid information,' Julia conceded. 'But the person who heard the threat doesn't have to be the one to find the proof.' She tapped her chest. 'I can do that.'

Gray hadn't considered that. Maybe even if her mother insisted she was a liar they'd still have to investigate if Julia believed her?

'Gray.' Julia took a step towards her. Her eyes were intent. 'Did you hear someone threaten your mother?'

'I…' Gray began, but she never got the chance to finish the thought.

The apartment door swung open and her mother walked in, carrying a glossy black briefcase. Richard was right behind her.

Gray's mouth snapped shut.

She saw her mother take in the two of them standing in the kitchen. Saw her notice the clean dishes on the counter, the dish towel in her hand.

'Oh good,' her mother said coldly. 'You had dinner.'

She gave Julia a look of pure dismissal. 'Thank you for your help. You can go now.'

Julia hesitated, her eyes on Gray, a question on her face.

Gray shook her head, very slightly. She would not discuss this in front of her mother and stepfather.

With obvious reluctance, Julia walked to the door. 'See you tomorrow, Gray,' she said. Turning to the prime minister, she added, 'Thank you, Ma'am.'

As soon as she left the room, the air grew frigid.

'We have to talk,' her mother told Gray.

Gray wasn't about to talk to her right now. 'We've talked enough.' Dropping the dish towel, she headed towards her bedroom.

'Don't be rude to your mother,' Richard called after her.

Thinking of the man she'd seen in Parliament who looked very much like him, Gray paused long enough to give him a withering stare. 'Don't tell me what to do, Richard. Who are you, anyway?'

'Gray. Stop this.' Her mother followed her down the hallway. 'You're sixteen and you're acting like a child.'

'I'm sixteen,' Gray countered, 'and you're treating me like one.'

She closed the bedroom door firmly, shutting her mother out. Through the door, she heard her mother and Richard talking.

'She's impossible,' her mother said. 'I can't take much more of this.'

Gray couldn't make out her stepfather's reply.

After a while, she heard the two of them moving away from her door. Their voices faded.

Pulling her phone from her pocket, she checked to make sure she hadn't missed a call from Jake – but the screen was empty.

Dropping the phone on her desk, she sat down heavily.

Her mother wouldn't listen. Her father wouldn't either. But Julia would.

THIRTY

The next morning, Julia was waiting for Gray at the foot of the stairs when she came down.

'Let's go,' she said abruptly.

Gray could sense the tension – Julia moved with absolute purpose as she guided Gray out of Number 10's main entrance, rather than the usual side door they'd been taking since the night of Aidan's party.

'Why are we going this way?' Gray asked, as they passed a cluster of police officers.

'We're switching things up,' Julia said. 'We'll be changing doors a lot from now on.'

Outside, it was cold and sunny. The usual black government car was parked directly in front of the door. The photographers and reporters standing in the fenced-off area where they waited for politicians paid little attention as Gray ducked into the car. The incident at Bijou was old news.

Ryan took the wheel, his eyes hidden behind dark sunglasses. Instead of getting in the front passenger seat, as she usually did, Julia got into the back with Gray.

Nervous, Gray clipped her seatbelt in place and waited. A hundred unspoken questions hung heavily in the air as Ryan pulled the car out into heavy Westminster traffic.

Julia turned to Gray. 'We need to finish the conversation we started last night.'

Gray shot a nervous glance at the front where Ryan was listening as he drove.

'You can trust us, Gray,' Julia promised. '*Both* of us. What you alluded to last night is incredibly serious. And I need you to tell me everything.'

Removing the sunglasses, Ryan met her eyes in the rearview mirror. 'We work for you. Whatever it is, let us help. Protecting you and your mother is what we do.'

In truth, they didn't need to convince her. The idea of sharing the burden was such a relief, she could feel a tension inside her begging her to do it.

'The first thing you need to know,' she told them, 'is that last night wasn't the first time I sneaked through the tunnels into Parliament.'

Throughout the journey she talked fast, trying to leave out nothing. Ryan and Julia mostly listened quietly as the story poured out. Julia's face displayed no reproach. If anything, she seemed absorbed in the details, occasionally asking for more information, especially about the two men Gray had heard.

When Gray told them one of the men was John Ashford, the only sign of surprise they betrayed was an exchange of glances in the rearview mirror. And the way Ryan's grip tightened on the steering wheel.

When she finished, the bodyguard turned to her, her expression grave.

'You did the right thing,' she assured her. 'Thank you.'

But Gray knew more than she did about what would happen next.

'If you go to my mum with this, I guarantee she'll tell you I'm lying. All I can tell you is, *I'm not*. You have to believe me. Every word is true.'

To her surprise, Julia reached over and squeezed her hand. 'Gray, listen to me. We do believe you.'

When they walked into the school a few minutes later – Julia in front, eyes searching the crowd – Gray felt free. She'd handed the burden to people who could do something. Her mother would be safe. She could go back to some sort of normality now.

She left the two bodyguards at reception and half ran into the school, practically skipping with relief.

Chloe was in her usual place near the double-doors, and her expression was grim. She grabbed Gray's arm as soon as she saw her and pulled her into a corner, out of the crowded hallway.

'Why haven't you answered your phone?' she asked. 'I called you three times.'

'I'm sorry,' Gray said, surprised. 'I was busy. What's wrong?'

'Have you heard about Jake?' Chloe asked.

'No. What happened?'

'His dad's pulled him out of school.'

Gray felt as if she'd been punched.

This is all my fault, she thought. I shouldn't have told him what was going on.

'Where is he? Is he here?' she asked, looking at the throngs around them with something like panic. 'Has he already gone?'

'I think he's meeting with the head,' Chloe said. 'No one knows if he's just going to send him straight home or let him go to class.'

The first bell rang. Crowds of students began flooding into classrooms.

'I need to find him.' Gray raised her voice to be heard above the noise. 'If you see him, call me right away.'

Chloe gave her an odd look. 'Is it because of what you told me? About sneaking into Parliament?'

'I don't know,' Gray said. 'But I think so.'

All that morning Jake was nowhere to be found. Not during morning lessons. And not in the hallways between them. As the day went on, Gray grew increasingly concerned.

By midday, she'd convinced herself he was already gone. He still wasn't responding to her texts, and a small voice in her head wondered if he blamed her as much as she blamed herself. Maybe he thought it was her fault, too.

Desolate, she moved down the school corridor alone, pushing her way through the lunchtime crowd. She had no idea what to do now. How to reach him.

That was when she saw him in the distance, talking with Aidan.

He looked tense and angry. Aidan seemed to be trying to calm him down.

Gray stopped in her tracks. The crowd swirled by her like water flowing around a stone. Someone complained loudly ('Could you, like, move?') and Jake glanced up.

Their eyes met through the crowds. Even from where she stood, she could see the relief on his face.

Saying something to Aidan, Jake left him standing in the hallway and strode towards her as Gray pushed her way through the crowd to him, her heart in her throat.

There was still time to say goodbye.

When they reached each other, they stood in the middle of the corridor, oblivious to the people around them.

Jake's gaze swept her face. 'You heard?'

She nodded. 'I'm so sorry. If I hadn't involved you, none of this would be happening.'

'It's not your fault,' he said. 'What about you? Is your mum punishing you?'

'She's sending me to boarding school,' Gray said.

'Our bloody parents.' He said it with real anger.

It was so unfair. They were just trying to do the right thing. And they were both having their lives destroyed.

'Is this really your last day?' she asked.

'This is it. Dad has it all arranged.' His voice was taut with repressed emotion.

They stared at each other, helplessly.

'I hate that this is happening,' she said. 'It's so unfair.'

A bell rang, signalling the start of the lunch break.

Neither of them moved. Jake looked down the busy corridor.

'Let's get out of here,' he said.

They walked to a side hallway, and then to a set of double doors leading out of the school into the playing fields behind it.

Gray didn't know where he was taking her, and she didn't care. The crowds thinned with every step. Most students were heading to the school cafeteria.

By the time they stepped outside, they were alone.

The sky was a vivid wintery blue. The trees around the school had shed the last of their golden and russet leaves, creating a thick carpet the two of them walked through, their feet sinking in, as Gray told him what her mother had said – that boarding school could give her freedom.

'So much freedom they need walls to keep it all in.' Jake gave a sardonic laugh.

'What about you?' She shot him a sideways glance. 'Where is your dad sending you?'

'He's giving me what I asked for a year ago. He's sending me back to Leeds to live with my mum.'

Gray let out a breath. That was so smart of Tom McIntyre. He could give Jake what he wanted and get rid of him at the same time. It was a move of true malice. But at least he'd be with his mum.

'Are you … happy?' she asked, tentatively. 'I mean, you wanted to live with her.'

Stopping abruptly, he turned to face her.

'Happy? I hate him for this.' He looked furious. 'He's doing it now, in the middle of term, to make it as hard as possible. And mostly to get me away from you.' He looked away, a muscle working in his jaw. 'I spent half the morning arguing with the head about whether I could stay and finish my studies if I moved in with Aidan.'

Hope fluttered in Gray's chest, but faded swiftly when she saw his glum expression.

'He said no?'

'He doesn't want to get between me and my parents.' His voice was bleak. 'Without their permission, it's impossible. And my mum is so excited…'

His voice trailed off as they left the shelter of the trees and walked out across the sport fields, a vast expanse of emerald shot with autumn gold. The sunshine, the cool air, the sound of London traffic getting closer as they neared the edge of the grounds – all conspired to give the afternoon a strange sense of magic. Maybe they could run away, and be whoever they wanted to be, someplace else.

But even as the thought entered Gray's mind, she let it go. It wasn't possible.

'What are we going to do?' she asked, as much to herself as to him.

They'd reached the fence at the back of the school grounds. Jake grasped the top bar, and raised himself up and over in a smooth, quick move. From the other side of the fence, he gave her a rakish look.

'We're going to get some coffee,' he said.

Gray glanced over her shoulder – the school looked small in the distance. She knew Julia was in there somewhere, and she'd be furious if she knew Gray was going off without her. She wasn't supposed to leave the grounds without her, ever.

But she wouldn't go far. And right now, she and Jake needed to be on their own.

She put her foot on the bottom bar and climbed over to join him.

THIRTY-ONE

After Gray walked into the school that morning, Julia and Ryan shut themselves in their small office. Two computer screens showed multiple images from the CCTV cameras they'd mounted at the school exits and in corridors but they weren't looking at them.

'What do you think?' Julia asked. She was sitting on one of the hard plastic chairs the school had allocated.

'She was very specific.' Ryan sounded cautious. 'But she has to be wrong about Ashford. I mean, so the voice sounded the same.' He turned his hands over. 'That's not a positive identification.'

'She was convinced,' Julia said.

'I know. But that's not enough. Not with someone like Ashford.' He leaned back in his chair. 'Also, we have to consider the slight possibility that she's a fantasist. I mean, there's got to be a reason her mother doesn't believe her.'

Julia bristled. 'She's never lied to us. Not once.'

'Oh, come on. She didn't exactly inform us she was leaving Number 10 and sneaking into other buildings,' he pointed out.

'That's not lying. That's being a kid,' Julia said hotly. 'All teenagers break the rules. Didn't you?'

'Not like her,' he said.

Julia was beginning to regret bringing him into this situation. Now that he was in, though, she couldn't just walk away. She needed him on her side, or Gray's situation could get even worse.

After all, the two of them had worked on Raj last night to get him to convince the prime minister that they didn't have to be in the apartment with Gray every minute. And she'd agreed that being in the building would be enough. This had given her hope that they could work on other things – more important things. But she had to figure out how to convince him.

'Look.' she said, striking a more conciliatory tone, 'I don't want to argue. I agree that we haven't got enough, but it's Wednesday now. If by some crazy chance Gray's right and someone's going to attack her mother on Saturday at that charity event in Oxford, we've got three days to sort something out to protect her. We can't assume she's wrong.'

He studied her for a long moment across the desk, his eyes dark. 'We should tell Raj everything,' he said, finally. 'Let him decide.'

It was a gamble. Raj could take everything straight to the prime minister. Order them not to investigate further. But Ryan was right; there was nowhere else for them to go. Raj was the expert.

The only problem was, he was out of town and couldn't be reached all morning.

It was midday before they he finally returned their calls. By then, Julia was so anxious she could barely sit still. She put the call on speakerphone so they could both talk with him.

'What's going on?' Raj asked. 'Is Firefly secure?'

'She's safe,' Julia assured him, glancing as she said it at the computer screen, to see the kids pouring out of class for lunch into a rushing, shoving, shouting stream of bodies. 'I had a long talk with her last night. I gained her confidence enough that this morning she divulged what's been happening. I understand why she's been acting out. And it's not good news.'

She and Ryan told him everything Gray had told them. He listened quietly until they mentioned John Ashford. The second Julia said the name, he cut her off.

'Was she certain it was him?'

Julia thought of Gray's terrified, desperate expression. The way she'd looked at Julia like she knew she wouldn't be believed. And Ashford's emotionless eyes, sweeping across her face like a razorblade. 'Yes, sir. Very certain.'

Raj swore quietly. 'Could she be wrong?'

'Sir,' Ryan interjected, 'she didn't see his face. We're relying on her ability to recognise his voice.'

'You have doubts, Ryan?' Raj guessed. 'Tell me.'

Julia met Ryan's eyes across the table.

'She's just a child, sir,' Ryan said. 'And she cannot positively say she saw him that night, because she couldn't see anyone from her hiding place.'

Julia bit her tongue.

To his credit though, Ryan added reluctantly, 'But she seems completely convinced, I must admit.'

'Dammit,' Raj swore. 'If she's right, what are we dealing with here? A coup?'

There was a long pause. 'Something like that,' Ryan conceded.

For several seconds none of them spoke. Julia knew Raj was absorbing everything they'd told him. Finally, he spoke.

'I have to take this to the prime minister. I have no choice.'

'She and her daughter are not in a good place right now,' Julia reminded him.

'What part of "I have no choice" do you not understand?' His voice rose. 'There are rules, Matheson. And I have to follow them.'

Wincing, she fell silent.

'I'll speak to her as soon as I can and get back to you,' he continued, gruffly. 'If she agrees, we'll pass her daughter's allegations on to the Secret Service. If she doesn't, we have to let it go, regardless of what the girl says.'

'Yes sir,' Julia and Ryan chorused, but Raj never heard it. He'd already hung up.

Julia rubbed the skin above her eyes. 'Well, I guess that could have been worse.'

But Ryan didn't seem to hear her. He was focussed on his computer.

'Look at the side door on your screen,' he said. 'Is that Firefly?'

Julia scanned the moving images filling the wide screen in front of her, searching for what he saw. It took a second, but she found it.

It was definitely Gray, in the blue top and black skinny jeans she'd worn that morning, boots up to her knees. She was holding hands with Jake McIntyre.

They were running out the door.

THIRTY-TWO

'What exactly happened after school yesterday?' Gray asked. 'I kept texting you and you didn't reply.'

Jake's face darkened. 'It was just what I expected. Dad lost it. Said I was a traitor. That I was betraying the party for a girl. I could bring down his leadership, ruin his career.'

'Sounds like my mum,' she said. 'I'm so sorry.'

'Well, it's fair to say I didn't handle it well.' He grimaced. 'We had a row and that was when he told me he was sending me to live with my mum. He told me to pack. Then he took my phone and laptop away so I wouldn't be 'tempted' to contact you. That's why I never got your texts.'

They were sitting at a table in the far corner of a busy coffeeshop, two coffees cooling between them. The stereo was playing a jaunty pop tune and Gray wished someone would turn it off.

'What about your mum?' Jake's gaze swept her face. 'He told me he called her and told her everything. I'm sorry he did that.'

'Oh, you know.' Gray shrugged. 'She told me I was childish and selfish. That I was only friends with you because I wanted to hurt her.'

Jake gave a dry, humourless laugh. 'They only think about themselves and their stupid careers. Our whole lives are sacrificed to make them more electable.'

Suddenly she realised what he didn't know. In all the drama that day, she hadn't told him about John Ashford.

'Oh my God, I haven't told you.' She filled him in on what had happened in her mother's office.

Jake's jaw dropped. 'He's your mum's deputy.' He looked shocked. 'Why would he…'

He stopped mid-sentence, thinking. 'He wants to be prime minister, doesn't he?' he said. 'They won't choose him because nobody wants a grouchy old man to run the country. But if everyone was scared – if something terrible happened – the party would choose him. They'd think he's a safe pair of hands. It's almost the only way.' He looked horrified. 'My God. How do we take on someone that powerful? The only person with more power than him is your mother.'

Gray gave him a look. 'I told my bodyguards today.'

His eyes widened. 'Everything?'

She nodded. 'Chloe told me I should, and I think she's right.'

'What did they say?'

'They believe me,' she said. 'They're going to do what they can to help. Get the Secret Service involved.'

He exhaled. 'That's great. They can sort it out. Ashford's not that smart.'

'I hope so,' Gray said. But doubt still nagged at her. Despite all her attempts, she knew she had no proof. It was her word against one of the most powerful men in the country.

'Gray…' Jake was reaching across the table towards her, when a woman walked up, looking at Gray with a kind of hungry eagerness.

'I'm sorry to interrupt.' She smiled at both of them and then turned to Gray shyly. 'Aren't you Gray Langtry?'

The woman was small and slight. She had brown hair that hung over her shoulders and she was clutching a newspaper in one hand.

Gray bit back a sharp reply. All she'd wanted was five minutes to be normal. Five minutes without being hunted. She'd had enough of it. Enough of being the daughter of the prime minister for one day. For one life, actually.

'No,' she said. 'I'm not.'

'Really? You look just like her.' The woman gave her a suspicious look. 'Exactly like her.'

'I get that a lot.' Gray gave her a guileless smile. 'I think it's the hair.'

Jake chuckled quietly. But the woman must have heard, because suddenly her mood changed. She took a step towards them, the paper crumpling in her fingers.

'Oh, I get it. You think you're too good to talk to me. You want to make fun of me.' Her voice rose. 'What gives you the right?'

Suddenly, all Gray could see was the man shouting 'Gray, I love you!' with a knife in his hand. Her heart began to race and she sank back in her chair. Her skin felt clammy with fear.

'No,' she whispered.

'Hey,' Jake objected. 'Leave her alone.'

The other people in the coffeeshop had fallen silent and turned to watch the spectacle.

Jake got to his feet, trying to get between the two of them, but the woman shoved him aside, looming over Gray.

'You're as bad as they say in the papers,' she shouted. 'You selfish, spoiled –'

The door to the coffeeshop flew open so hard it banged against the wall. Startled, the woman jumped back as Julia and Ryan stormed in. Julia glowered at her, an avenging angel with attitude, and flipped open a leather wallet holding a badge.

'I need you to step back right now,' she said, her tone almost daring the woman to argue.

Blanching, the woman shuffled a few steps back, bumping into the table behind her, knocking a glass of water over so it splashed onto the floor. The people at the table hurried out of the way.

'I was just trying to get her autograph,' she insisted. 'I wasn't going to hurt her or anything.'

'You request an autograph,' Julia snapped. 'You do *not* demand one.'

As she escorted the woman well away, Ryan turned to Jake and Gray, his eyes as hard as chips of slate.

'Get up,' he said. 'We're going.'

THIRTY-THREE

Julia was so angry she could barely breathe. Angry at Gray for sneaking out *again* and risking her life for a boy. Angry that a middle-aged woman would harass a child for an autograph, as if she were a celebrity instead of just a girl trying to have five minutes with a guy she liked.

She took the woman's name and address, writing them down for a later security check while Ryan escorted Gray and Jake to the door. When they were safely outside, she followed, stuffing her notebook back in her pocket. At the door, she paused to turn back and face the silent and startled room, where the only sound was the music still pouring from the speakers.

'Please excuse us, everyone,' she said, raising her voice. 'The situation is safe. You can all get back to your coffees now.'

As the door closed behind her, she heard the buzz of excited conversation start up.

Outside, an icy wind blew her hair into her eyes. A cloud had moved across the sun, darkening the sky.

Gray stood at a distance. She looked ashen and angry, arms folded across her chest.

Jake was nearby, shoulders hunched against the wind. Neither of them had a jacket on, despite the weather. He, ill-advisedly, leaped to their defence. 'We were just talking –'

'Don't you dare.' Julia shut him down with a glare that could have frozen water. 'Don't say anything.'

For a second, it appeared Gray might step up to argue, but then she seemed to contract in on herself, becoming physically smaller. Her chin dropped.

'It's my fault, Julia,' she said quietly. 'I shouldn't have gone without telling you.'

'You're damn right you shouldn't have,' Julia fumed. 'You know about the danger, and you left the school and walked off alone for no reason.' She gestured at Ryan. 'We would have gone with you. All you had to do was ask.'

Gray gave her a reproachful look. 'You would have told me I couldn't go and you know it.'

That was true enough, Julia thought.

'Fine,' she conceded. 'But at least you would have been alive.'

'I'm alive *now*,' Gray pointed out, her earlier chagrin fading.

An older woman walking by with a small dog turned and watched them with interest.

Jake held up his hands. 'Guys. Can we not fight here?'

'Shut up,' Julia said, heatedly. 'No one asked your opinion.'

'Julia.' Ryan's voice was easy but she didn't miss the cautioning note in it.

She let out a puff of air and tried to calm down. 'Fine. Let's get going.'

They walked for a few minutes down a quiet pavement towards the school before Gray spoke again.

'Can I ask - how did you find us?'

'How we found you isn't the issue,' Ryan interjected. 'The issue is that you could have got yourselves killed.'

'We were careful,' Jake assured him.

'Oh good. They were careful.' Julia's voice was sarcastic. 'Well, I guess there's no need for us to worry, as long as two sixteen-year-olds, one of whom is the daughter of the prime minister, are *careful*.'

'I know all about the threat,' Jake informed her. 'I was keeping an eye out.'

Julia gave Gray a withering look.

'Everyone, calm down.' Ryan stepped between them. 'Let's get back to school. We can take this up again later.'

They made the rest of the journey back in near silence.

If she were honest, Julia couldn't have explained why she was so angry. Mostly, she was hurt. And that surprised her. She'd honestly thought Gray wouldn't do something like this. Not after their conversations. Not with all that she knew.

For the first time, she wondered if maybe the prime minister wasn't entirely out of line when she said her daughter had problems with the truth. Maybe Gray couldn't be trusted after all.

The thought made her stomach twist.

But then she remembered how scared Gray had been when she told her what she'd overheard. And all the details she'd recalled so clearly.

No. Gray wasn't a fantasist. She was just impulsive.

Besides, she reminded herself, no other teenager would get in so much trouble for going for a cup of coffee. It was this Gray rebelled against. And could she really blame her?

When they reached the school building, she held Gray back while Ryan escorted Jake to his classroom.

'I'm sorry I shouted at you,' she said, when they were alone. 'You scared me.'

'I know.' Gray bit her lip. 'I'm very sorry. It was stupid. It's just that Jake's dad is sending him away because of what happened. I only wanted to say goodbye.'

She looked so hurt and lonely it tugged at Julia's heart.

So that was it. The parents again. Pushing the kids so far, they took risks.

'I get it,' Julia told her, softening her tone. 'But please trust me enough next time to ask me to go with you. I will sit across the room and not look at you at all. I just need to be there in case another weirdo wants you to sign her copy of the *Daily Mail.*'

Gray gave a tremulous smile. 'I promise.'

She escorted Gray to her next lesson, waiting in the hallway until she went in.

As she walked back down the quiet school corridors, she could hear teachers' voices through the doors, and the faint sound of students answering questions. It reminded her of her own school days, which seemed so long ago. She'd been honest with Gray about her past. She had once been a prefect at a boarding school, until her parents had yanked her out, against her will. They too had been playing games with her life, much like Gray and Jake's parents were doing now.

She remembered how helpless that had made her feel. How angry and resentful.

Parents forget that teenagers want and deserve some control over their own lives. They are, after all, months away from being adults. And yet all too often, they're treated like infants. And when that happens, there's almost always trouble.

When she got back to the room she and Ryan used as an office, he was on the phone.

'Hold on,' he said, motioning for her to shut the door. 'Julia's here. I'm going to put you on speaker.' He clicked a button. 'Go ahead, Raj.'

Julia pulled her chair back and sat down, trepidation growing.

'Julia,' their boss said from the phone, 'I was just telling Ryan. I've spoken to the PM. I explained the situation. She was very clear. She does not want us to investigate Ashford.'

Julia's heart sank. 'You told her everything?'

'Everything,' Raj said.

Across the table, she and Ryan exchanged a long look.

'She doesn't want us to nose around at all?' he asked. 'Even to check phone records? We could do that without him ever knowing.'

'She has authorised no investigation by Talos at this time.' Raj's voice betrayed no emotion. 'We have no official approval for anything except protecting Firefly. That is our primary focus. Understood?'

'Yes sir,' they both said.

'What about the fundraiser in Oxford?' said Julia. 'The one where they threatened to act. Can we at least send some extra security to that?'

'The PM doesn't want the charity to have to deal with too much red tape.' This time she thought she heard disapproval in their boss's voice. 'She's asked for only her normal protection to go with her.'

'That's a bit of an iffy call,' Ryan said. 'Don't you think? Given the threat level?'

'I'm going to work on her about this one,' Raj conceded. 'But for now, assume we're not getting any extra hands on this. I'm counting on you to give me all the time you can.'

When the call ended, the two of them sat amid the computer monitors with their flickering images of empty hallways and closed doors.

'Well, hell,' Ryan said, flipping a pen in one hand. 'That's a bit of a kick in the teeth.'

Julia didn't reply. She stared at the screen. Her mind was working.

The call had been odd.

What had Raj said? No official approval. Our primary focus.

He'd used a lot of careful wording. It didn't sound like him. Normally he was a blunt speaker. Everything was always crystal clear. But that hadn't been. In fact, he'd said many things in that conversation – one thing he hadn't said was 'No'.

She sat up straight, looking at Ryan. 'I have an idea.'

THIRTY-FOUR

For Gray the worst part was, she hadn't been given the chance to say goodbye to Jake. They had both been hustled to their respective lessons and she didn't see him in the corridors at the end of the day. She didn't even know if he was still in the building or if he'd gone home.

Chloe, of course, thought it was thrilling. She cheered when Gray told her about their escapade at the coffee shop, as they walked slowly to the front door. 'That is the most romantic thing I have ever heard. You are Romeo and Juliet. You are Tristan and Isolde. You are –'

'We are never going to see each other again,' Gray told her bluntly.

Chloe flung an arm around her shoulders. 'Oh, come on. He's not moving to Borneo. He's only going to Leeds. You'll find a way.'

Gray, who had just spotted Julia threading her way through the crowded hallway, didn't reply.

When she reached them, Julia nodded to Chloe and turned to Gray. 'We have to go now,' she said, an ominous note in her voice.

Chloe gave Gray a supportive look as she turned to follow the bodyguard through the hallway.

Julia was silent as they left the school building.

Gray was disappointed. She'd thought they'd made up already, and she'd hoped the guard wouldn't still be angry.

'I'm really very sorry about what happened,' she reiterated.

'I'm sorry too,' Julia said, and something in her voice sent a warning prickle down Gray's spine.

Ryan was waiting by the door, and the three of them speed-walked to the car. As soon as Gray was inside, the car pulled away so fast she was thrown back against the seat.

They drove for five minutes in absolute silence before Gray couldn't take it anymore. 'If you need to shout at me some more, please just do it,' she pleaded. 'I know I deserve it. I shouldn't have left the school without telling you. I won't ever do it again. Please, don't hate me.'

The two bodyguards exchanged a quick glance. Ryan, who was driving, motioned for Julia to handle it. She turned to face Gray.

'There's something we need to tell you.' The cool fury from that afternoon was missing from her expression. She looked worried. 'We took the information you gave us to Raj Patel. We told him everything you told us.'

Gray knew the truth before she even said it. 'He told my mum, didn't he?'

Julia nodded, her lips a tight line.

'What did she say?'

'She told him we were not to take this investigation any further under any circumstances.'

Gray dropped back, the last strands of hope slipping away. 'I told you this would happen. I guess you don't believe me either.'

'We want to believe you.' Ryan glanced at her in the rearview mirror. 'But I've got to say, you're not giving us much evidence that you can be trusted.'

Gray's voice rose. 'I just went for a coffee with Jake to say goodbye. Can't you understand that?' She gave them a look of pure pain. 'My mum could die now, all because of that.' She turned away. 'I don't understand anything.'

There was a long silence. She could sense the bodyguards were having some sort of silent exchange in the front seat but she didn't raise her head to look at them. She didn't want to see their anger or their pity.

When Julia spoke again, her tone had changed. 'Can we trust you, Gray? Are you really telling us the truth about Ashford?'

Gray lifted her head. 'You don't have to believe anything else I ever say,' she told her. 'But I swear on my life I'm telling the truth about what I heard. On my *life.*'

Julia held her eyes with a cool, assessing look. Then, as if she'd seen all she needed, she nodded.

'OK, then,' she said, briskly. 'Here's what's going on. Your mother ordered Raj not to pursue any investigation into your allegations. He has to do as he's told.' She paused before finishing the thought. 'We, on the other hand, don't.'

Gray was confused. 'You don't?'

Ryan glanced at her in the rearview mirror. 'We're willing to look into this further, on our own time. Quietly.'

Gray sat up straight, pressing her hands against the backs of the front seats, the leather smooth and cool against her fingertips. They were going to help.

Julia turned to look at her. 'We're going to look into Ashford's phone records, and see what we can find. We'll nose around a little bit into his background. See if there's anything dodgy.'

Excitement flashed through Gray. 'The Oxford fundraiser is this Saturday,' she said, eagerly. 'It's supposed to happen then. Can you help?'

There was a pause.

'We brought this up with our boss.' Julia glanced at Ryan.

'Your mother told Raj to send only her usual bodyguard,' he explained, his eyes on the road. 'She said the building is secure and she doesn't want to cause a distraction.'

'She always does that. But he has to convince her.' Gray leaned forward, imploring them. 'Or you have to be there. He can't give up because she says no. These guys know she won't bring security. They're counting on it.'

A bus pulled into their lane and Ryan braked sharply.

'Raj is going to try to change her mind,' Julia said as he manoeuvred around the red double-decker. 'But she doesn't seem the flexible type.'

'What happens if she doesn't say yes?' Gray pressed. 'Would you go to Oxford to help her? She'd be safe if you were there.'

'We'll do all we can,' Ryan said. 'In the meantime, we'll look into Ashford's background. See if we can find links to the Russian organisation. Try to understand what he might be up to.' In the mirror, he held her eyes. 'But that's as far as we can go. We can't go rogue without permission.'

Gray turned to Julia, beseeching her.

'We'll work on Raj,' Julia promised. 'I'm sure he'll listen.'

Gray turned to look out of the window. Clouds were building in the east, blocking out the sun.

What Julia and Ryan were offering wasn't enough. There had to be people on the ground at that party. People who knew someone was going to try to hurt her mother, and who were ready to protect her.

Gray liked Julia. She trusted her. But she wasn't going to leave her mother alone at that party. As the car neared Number 10, she came to a decision.

If Ryan and Julia couldn't go to that party in Oxford to look out for her mother, there was only one solution.

And that was for her to go to Oxford herself.

THIRTY-FIVE

The next day, she told Chloe what was going on, about Ryan and Julia not being able to go to Oxford, and about her plan to go herself. To her surprise, Chloe didn't even try to change her mind. In fact, all she said was, 'I'll go with you.'

They were in the lunchroom at school, talking in low voices. The cacophonous room was half forgotten, the remnants of their lunches in front of them.

'You can't,' Gray said. 'You'll get into trouble. I'm not going to be responsible for that.'

She was still battling her own guilt about planning to do something she knew would upset Julia. It felt like a betrayal. But she had no choice. If Raj Patel wouldn't let the bodyguards help her mother, and her mother wouldn't help herself, then Gray had to step up and do it. She'd thought about it half the night.

There was no other way. But she didn't want Chloe on her conscience too.

Chloe, though, wasn't about to back down. 'You can't go on your own. It's too dangerous. You need me there.'

'What about your mum?' Gray said. 'What will you tell her?'

'I'll tell her I'm going with friends to visit Oxford because I'm thinking about applying for university.' Chloe shrugged. 'She'll be thrilled.'

The idea of going with Chloe was comforting enough that Gray could push the danger out of her mind, at least for now. Besides, there was plenty to worry about.

There was still the problem of how to get inside the event. The party was an annual fundraising gala, with celebrities, music, art, and lots of glamour. Tickets had been sold out for months. It was the hottest event in town. They couldn't just waltz in.

'Maybe we could buy tickets from one of those re-selling websites?' Chloe suggested.

'It would cost hundreds of pounds,' Gray told her. 'I've got my emergency credit card but I can't put something like that on it. It's too much.'

As she speared a French fry with a fork, Chloe considered this. 'I don't see why you have to pay at all,' she mused. 'You're the prime minister's bloody daughter. If that doesn't get you into a party, I don't know what does.' She popped the fry in her mouth.

Gray stared at her, an idea unfurling inside her mind.

Chloe stared back. 'What?' she said, swallowing. 'What did I say?'

A grin spread slowly across Gray's face. 'I'm the prime minister's bloody daughter. Why didn't I think of that?'

Chloe's eyebrows drew together. 'I'm so confused right now.'

'I'll just tell them sort of the truth. I'll call the event organiser and ask if she'd set aside two tickets for the prime minister's daughter, who would like to surprise her mother by attending,' Gray explained. 'There's no way they can say no.'

'You have a devious mind, Gray Langtry. That's what I like about you,' Chloe said, approvingly. She paused. 'We could use some help with this, though, given how messed up everything is. Do you think Jake would come with us?'

'I don't know. I haven't heard from him. I think he still doesn't have his phone back. I've emailed, but he may not have a computer either.' Gray sighed and pushed her empty plate away. 'Besides, I kind of feel like I've done enough damage to him already, you know?'

'You can't blame yourself for what's happening,' scolded Chloe. 'It's his dad's fault, not yours.'

'Maybe,' Gray said, unconvinced. 'But I think we need to plan to do this on our own.'

'Right, then. Let's plan.' Chloe pulled out a notebook and began to make a list. 'Who will get tickets? I could call and pretend to be your assistant?'

'I'll handle that,' Gray said.

'Gray to get tickets,' Chloe murmured, writing it down. She glanced up. 'Then we need to figure out how we get to Oxford.'

'Train,' said Gray.

'Chloe to order train tickets,' Chloe said as she wrote. 'And as this is the party of the year we can't exactly go in jeans. We need frocks and shoes to fit in. Shall I go shopping?' She blinked at her expectantly.

Gray laughed. 'I knew it. This was all an excuse for you to buy a new dress.'

'I deny that,' Chloe said. 'But I will buy a new dress.'

'I'll wear the one I wore to the last thing my mum made me go to.'

'Oh, that was the one where you met that band!' Chloe enthused jealously.

269

'And they treated me like a ten-year-old.' Gray flushed at the memory. 'Mortifying.'

'Gray to wear mortifying dress,' Chloe said, writing. She looked up, tapping a finger against her cheek. 'So, I guess now all we have left to do is figure out how you're going to get out of Number 10, how we get to the party without causing a national emergency, and how we protect your mum when we're there. And then how we get home in the middle of the night.'

'Easy peasy,' said Gray, with a weak smile.

When she got home from school that afternoon, the apartment was empty and quiet, light filtering through the bomb-proof curtains.

She poured herself a glass of juice and opened her laptop, navigating to the website for the fundraiser in Oxford. The words SOLD OUT were stamped across the homepage. On the contact page, she found a number for the organiser and called it immediately, before she could lose her nerve.

She and Chloe had worked out exactly what she was going to say. They'd decided it would be best if she didn't say who she really was. Instead, she was going to pose as her mother's assistant.

She was ready, the words already in her throat. But the call went straight to voicemail.

Rather than leave her phone number, she hung up immediately.

She decided to give it half an hour and try again.

While she waited, she examined the website about the event. The annual gala raised millions of pounds for three arts charities. It always attracted celebrities and well-known politicians. This was the first year her mother was attending – she would be giving a keynote speech. The images on the site showed women in designer ballgowns and men in black tie. Everyone looked incredibly glamorous.

As she flipped through the photo gallery, Gray began to doubt their plan. How were they going to look like they belonged at that sort of party? It was so adult.

Running to her room, she yanked the closet doors open and rifled through her clothes, before pulling a blue silk dress from the very back. She held it up.

On a whim, she shucked off her school clothes and stepped into it.

The fabric felt cool against her skin, and light as air. She had to contort her body to reach the zipper.

Stepping in front of the mirror, she considered the result. The dress had a full skirt and a nipped-in waist.

She turned backwards and forwards, studying herself. She didn't look like a movie star. But it would do.

Suddenly, she became aware that her phone was ringing in the kitchen.

Still in the silk dress, she ran across the apartment, the skirt swishing behind her like wings, and snatched it from the table.

The number wasn't recognised

'Hello?' she said, panting. 'Who is this?'

'You sound breathless. Are you running from something?' That familiar northern accent, all flat-vowels and sharp consonants, made her heart flutter.

'Jake!' she exclaimed. 'Is this really you?'

'It's really me.' She could hear his smile through the phone. 'I have bravely sneaked away from my keepers and purchased a burner phone. They can't keep a Yorkshireman down.'

Gray leaned against the kitchen island, her bare toes cool against the tiled floor as she smiled.

'It's so good to hear your voice,' she said. 'I thought they'd have put you on a prison bus to Leeds by now.'

'The prison bus doesn't leave until Sunday,' he said cheerfully. 'I'm being held hostage at my father's office non-stop until then, as far as I can tell. Good times will be had by none.'

'Are you there now?' Gray asked. 'Is it safe to talk?'

'I will have you know I'm currently hiding in a Parliamentary gentlemen's changing room,' he informed her loftily. 'It's very grand. There are places to leave your sword.' He paused. 'Yes, it definitely says "Sword".'

Gray was smiling so hard it hurt her face. 'At least it's a nice jail.'

'Look,' Jake said, growing serious, 'I'm sorry we didn't get a chance to say goodbye. We were kind of rudely interrupted.'

'Yeah, I'm sorry about that too,' she said. 'I was enjoying our escape. How are you handling everything? Is it awful?'

'Nothing's changed,' he sighed. 'Dad still won't listen. How'd your mum take it when they told her about us leaving school?'

'Actually, my bodyguards didn't tell her,' she said. 'I owe them one for that. Anyway, I've hardly seen her. There's something going on at work and she's never home.'

'Yeah, it's all kicking off over here. Haven't you watched the news?' He sounded surprised that she wasn't more aware and for some reason that made Gray defensive.

'Things have been kind of busy,' she reminded him. 'I haven't really been into the news.'

'Sorry,' he said. 'It's just that all of Parliament is obsessed with what's going on right now. I forget that everyone doesn't spend all day wrapped up in this stuff.'

'Why? What's happening?'

'It's a nightmare for your mum, basically,' he said. 'Members of her own party are openly against her on this immigration bill. Some of them are voting with my dad's party to try and bring it all down, and maybe bring her down with it.'

Gray felt suddenly cold. 'Bring my *mum* down? You mean, replace her as prime minister?'

'Well, yeah. That's the plan, anyway,' he said. 'Might not happen but it's not looking great for her right now, if I'm honest.'

Gray couldn't think of anything to say. No wonder her mother had been so tense and snappish lately. She was fighting for her career. 'She's only had this job a year, Jake. And they already want to get rid of her?'

'Yeah, this is one of the reasons my dad flipped out when he heard about us. Anything that could distract from tearing your mum to pieces is the last thing he wants right now.'

Gray shuddered. 'Did you ever notice that when you talk about politics you make it sound like actual war?'

'Politics is war,' he told her bluntly. 'Anyone who says otherwise is lying.'

There was a pause.

'Is she really in trouble?' Gray's voice was small. 'Is she losing the war?'

Jake hesitated. 'The thing about your mum is – she's a lot like you. She's a fighter. Just when you think you've got her down, she gets back up again and comes at you harder than ever. It's why

273

my dad hates her so much.' There was reluctant admiration in Jake's voice. 'He can't beat her.'

An unexpected burst of pride sent warmth to Gray's heart. 'It's a bunch of men trying to get rid of her, isn't it?' she said. 'Men like Ashford. She always said they hated having a woman in charge.'

'It always is men,' he said. 'You ladies are going to have to do something about that one of these days.'

'Give me time,' Gray told him.

'I don't doubt it for a minute.' She could hear his smile through the phone. 'Look, I've got to get back soon. Bloody Mike will be looking for me.'

'Wait,' Gray said. 'There's something I need to tell you.' She took a breath and said it all in one flood of words. 'Chloe and I are going to Oxford on Saturday, to be at the fundraiser to protect my mum. We could use your help.'

There was a long pause as he absorbed this. 'You're going to slip your security detail?'

'That's the idea,' she said. 'They've been told they can't go to Oxford. I've got to be there to help her. I really think something bad is going to happen.'

'Gray…' She could hear the doubt in his voice. 'Isn't this too dangerous?'

'She's taking one bodyguard, Jake.' Her voice rose. 'Maybe that will be enough. Maybe not. If I go, my bodyguards will come to get me. They have to. It's their job. The police will probably come too. Don't you see?' She pleaded with him to understand. 'If I go there, a ton of security will come after me. Nobody will dare hurt her then.'

'I can see your point,' he said. 'But people will recognise you. And if your mum's in danger, you could be too.'

Gray waved this away. 'I'll do something with my hair – wear a hat. Chloe's really good at disguising me.'

There was a pause before he replied. 'I don't like the sound of this. At all.'

After Chloe's acceptance of her plan, Jake's resistance took her aback. If anyone was going to say no she hadn't expected it to be him.

'Well, I'm going,' she said, defiantly. 'And Chloe's coming, too. It's the only thing we can do. The event is tomorrow.'

The pause that followed was so long, she thought he might have hung up. Finally, he spoke. 'I'm not letting you do this alone. If you're going, I'm going.'

Gray punched the air. 'Are you sure? How will you get away?'

He made a dismissive sound. 'Let me worry about that. I'm really quite wily, you know. What's the plan?'

Gray told him what she and Chloe had concocted. 'I've got to call the person back as soon as we hang up, make sure I can get tickets. We have to dress up. It's insanely posh. Do you have a tux?'

'Yeah,' he said. 'But it makes me look like a stretched penguin.'

She laughed. 'Well, wear it on Saturday and we'll look ridiculous together.'

His tone changed. 'You know all hell will break loose when you go missing, right? The prime minister's kid can't just disappear without warning for an entire day. They'll have every cop in the country looking for you.'

'That's the plan,' she said. 'I want them to follow me. Just make sure you're at Paddington Station at two o'clock tomorrow. We'll get the train together.'

'I'll be there,' he told her. 'Look, I'd better go. Mike will be organising a search party. And no one's left a sword in here for me to use to defend myself.'

'Jake,' she said. 'I don't want to get you in more trouble than I already have. Are you sure about tomorrow?'

His reply came without hesitation. 'It'd be worth it to see you one more time before I go away.' He paused. 'Pissing my dad off is an added bonus.'

THIRTY-SIX

As soon as Jake was off the line, Gray called the event organiser again. This time, the woman answered on the first ring.

'Sarah Morgan.' Her tone was brisk, and Gray's heart sank a little. She didn't sound like someone who'd be easily fooled.

Gray tried to make her voice sound just as dismissive and rushed. 'Hi, Sarah? This is Emma Reilly, special assistant to the prime minister.'

'Oh, hello. I've been trying to reach you. I hope everything's OK for tomorrow?'

'Everything's perfect.' Gray enthused, trying to adopt Emma's perky-but-efficient tone. 'The prime minister is looking forward to it. We've just a little request, if you don't mind.'

'Of course.' Sarah sounded instantly cautious. 'What can I do?'

'Mrs Langtry's daughter, Gray, would like to surprise her mother by coming to the event on Saturday night and I wondered if you could arrange tickets for her.'

'How lovely.' Sarah didn't sound as if it was really lovely. 'The ticket situation is very tight, as you know, but I'm sure we can find space for her daughter.'

'She'll need three tickets, actually,' Gray said.

'Oh.' Sarah sounded regretful, 'I'm afraid three will not be possible. We're just fully booked, you see, and we don't want over-crowding. It wouldn't be safe.'

Damn. The whole point of Jake and Chloe coming was so that Gray didn't have to do this all by herself.

'She'd be fine with two,' she blurted, forgetting momentarily to sound like her mother's assistant.

There was a pause, as if Sarah had noticed the change. 'We could manage two,' she said, after a moment. 'But absolutely no more than that.'

Two tickets would mean one of the three of them would not be able to go inside. But there was no time to think about how that would work right now.

'Two will do,' Gray decided. 'Oh, and this is going to be a surprise for her mother – please don't mention anything about it to the prime minister.'

If Sarah thought this was odd, she didn't let on. 'Understood,' she said. 'I'll leave two tickets at the front desk in her name. It's "Gray", isn't it?'

'Yes,' said Gray.

'Perfect. Well, she can collect them on Saturday at the front desk. Now, I have a few questions for you, if you don't mind. And I really must have your answers now. Time is running out. We have been leaving messages all week.'

Gray heard the sound of papers rustling across the line.

'We still need a precise time for the prime minister's arrival.' Sarah sounded very firm. 'I've still got this as TBA, and we're just one day out. Can you be more precise at this point?'

Thinking fast, Gray repeated something she'd heard the real Emma say in similar circumstances. 'As you can imagine, the prime minister's schedule is very busy. I'm still trying to pin down everyone on her team about Saturday. I might have to circle back with you on this first thing tomorrow.'

'Right.' Sarah didn't sound like she liked waiting. 'Emma, I hate to press, but at this stage things are getting quite difficult without knowing...'

'How about I have a word with her press officer and get a precise time for you?' Gray was desperate to get off the phone before she said something terribly wrong. Already there was the likelihood Sarah and Emma would realise that this conversation had happened and had not involved the actual Emma. 'Can I ring you after that?'

'Of course.' Now Sarah didn't sound happy at all. 'This affects our entire schedule for the night, and I'm sure you can understand how problematic...'

'Right you are,' Gray agreed. 'I'll get back to you as soon as I can.'

'There's just one more thing...' Sarah began.

But at that moment, Gray heard the unmistakeable clicking of high heels on the floor of the hallway. Her mother was back early.

'I'll call you tomorrow on that as well,' she said hurriedly. 'Thank you so much.' She hung up just as her mother walked in the door.

'Hi!' Gray said, too brightly.

Her mother gave her a doubtful look. 'Hello.' She was alone – no sign of Richard. At least there was that.

'I was just talking to Chloe,' Gray explained unnecessarily.

Her mother's eyebrows drew together. 'Oh? How is she?'

'Great!' Gray couldn't seem to control her enthusiasm. Nervousness was turning her into some sort of hyperactive cheerleader. 'Well, you know,' she amended herself. 'Busy and stuff.'

'Busy and stuff.' Her mother set her briefcase down by the door. 'I can relate to that.'

By now, Gray had calmed down enough to notice things like, what was her mother doing here? She'd hardly seen her all week. And according to Jake she was under attack from all sides. 'You're home early,' she observed. 'I mean, ish.'

Her mother kicked off her heels, leaving them lying by the briefcase. 'I spilled coffee on my blouse,' she explained, pulling her jacket back to expose the offending brown stain on her cream top. 'I decided to take the opportunity to have a break.' She stretched her arms above her head and yawned. 'I've got to go back down in a little while.'

Shadows underscored her eyes. Gray also noticed that the jacket hung looser on her than it had a few weeks ago. For the first time in a long while she felt a pang of worry about her mother.

'Can I get you a cup of tea?' she offered.

Her mother gave her a look of absolute surprise. 'Sure,' she said, after a beat. 'That would be lovely. I'll go and change this top and come right back.' She disappeared into her bedroom, unbuttoning the blouse as she walked.

Gray filled the kettle and turned it on. She made the tea the way her mother liked it – strong, with just a little milk and one sugar. 'Proper builders' tea,' her mother always said.

She was dropping the tea bag in the bin when her mother walked back into the kitchen with her head down, looking at something on her phone. In the bright overhead lights, Gray noticed subtle new lines on her forehead. She was sure those hadn't been there a few weeks ago.

'Is everything alright?' she asked.

NUMBER 10

Her mother set the phone down with a sigh. 'Fine. I'm sorry, darling. It's been a hell of a week.'

Gray handed her the mug. 'I saw the news,' she told her. 'It sounds like it's been awful.'

Her mother's gaze swept her face. 'It has been extremely unpleasant.'

'Everything's going to be alright, isn't it?' Gray asked. 'They won't vote you out over this.'

'I'll get through it,' her mother said. 'Don't worry about me. The worse they act, the better I get.'

That mixture of assurance and cockiness – this was the old her. It reminded Gray how different things used to be between them. When they used to have each other's backs.

Her mother must have been thinking something similar, because out of the blue she said, 'I know I've been hard on you, these last few weeks. I'm sorry things got so ugly. If I'm absolutely honest, I over-reacted because I was afraid. The security situation is more serious than you know. There have been a lot of very credible threats. Against me. Against you. I got scared. And I took it out on you.' She paused. 'I know you want a life of your own, and a little freedom. Living like this…' She gestured at the small apartment. 'I know this is like a prison for you. And for me, if I'm honest. But I chose this life.' She touched her chest. 'I made that decision, you didn't. And I'm sorry if it's been hard on you.'

Gray was stunned. Whatever she'd expected her mother to say, it wasn't this. She wanted to hug her, but she kept her hands at her sides.

'Well, I'm sorry I've made things worse for you,' she said. 'I didn't mean to hurt you – I want you to know that. All I wanted to do was just be a normal person.'

'It might surprise you to know that I understand that.' A melancholy smile crossed her mother's face. 'The thing is, I can't bear to let you go out in a world where you're in danger because of me.' She looked down at the mug of tea clasped in her hands. 'I don't think you'll ever be able to understand how guilty I've felt about putting you in this position. I hate what it's done to your life.'

This was all Gray had wanted to hear for months. Her eyes welled up. 'Mum, I'm so proud of you. And I'm sorry about everything.'

'Don't be.' Putting down her mug, her mother pulled her into a hug. 'You have a right to be a teenager. I need to remember that.'

Gray breathed in the warm, familiar scent of her Chanel cologne and rested her head on her shoulder. It felt like safety.

After a second, her mother let her go. She swiped her cheek with her hand. 'Remind me of this moment the next time I yell at you, agreed?'

'Will you listen?' asked Gray.

'Probably not.'

They smiled at each other, and some of the tension wound tight in Gray's chest eased. Then she remembered about Saturday.

'Mum,' she said. 'Tomorrow, would you…'

Her mother's phone beeped and she turned away to picked it up. 'I've got that fundraiser tomorrow, remember?' she said absently as she looked at the screen. 'And now I have to go back to work.' Grabbing the mug, she took a hurried sip and set it down again. 'What was it you wanted to say?'

Gray hesitated. But what would she say? Take extra security, I can't tell you why I know that you should? Be careful? Don't go? Any of those would result in an argument and misunderstandings. And they had just started getting along.

'Nothing,' she said.

'Well. Thanks for the tea.' Her mother half-ran across the room and slid her feet back into her heels. When they were on, she was three inches taller and somehow less exhausted. 'Don't wait up for me – it's going to be another long night. Richard will get in around nine. Do you mind making your own dinner again?'

'I'll be fine,' Gray told her. 'Don't worry about me.'

Scooping up her briefcase, her mother headed for the door. At the last second though, she stopped and looked back. 'I think you've been grounded for too long. This weekend we're back to normal. OK?'

This would make running away on Saturday so much easier, Gray thought with a hint of shame. And then they'd be right back where they started.

'Thanks, Mum,' she said. 'Good luck tonight.'

But her mother wasn't finished. 'Your bodyguards will go with you at all times, though. Until things calm down a little. I'm sure you understand.' With that, she hurried out of the door.

And Gray's hopes came crashing back down to earth.

THIRTY-SEVEN

'So, what are we going to do?' Julia set her pint glass down on the sticky tabletop.

She and Ryan were in a pub in Covent Garden – far enough away from Parliament to feel confident that they wouldn't bump into anyone from work. It was Friday night, so the place was packed. Nobody paid any attention to the two of them, sitting close together in a dark corner at the back.

'I think we need to go up to Oxford on Saturday, and try to get into that fundraiser,' Ryan said. 'It's the only way.'

Julia took a sip of beer, forcing herself not to look too relieved.

When he'd suggested meeting after work to discuss the situation with Gray, she'd been certain he was going to tell her they had to drop the whole thing. And on some level, she couldn't blame him. They'd both be putting their jobs on the line if they did this.

'How can we make this work?' She set the pint down. 'We can't let Raj know.'

Ryan rested his elbows on the table. 'If both of us disappear on Saturday, Raj might notice something's up. There's never been a weekend yet when we were both unavailable to be on call if needed. So I think one of us should stay here.'

'I want to go up to Oxford,' Julia said immediately. 'I know you've got more experience than me, but I feel like I've got a handle on this one.'

Ryan, to her surprise, didn't disagree. 'Fine. I'll stay in London in case anything happens here.' He reached for his drink, watching her over the top of the glass. 'Have you been following what's happening in Parliament this week? Looks like Ashford's making his move.'

'I've only seen the headlines. What's happening?'

'He's triggered an uprising inside the party,' he said. 'Because the immigration bill is a compromise with the Labour party. It's not as tough as he wanted. So he's getting everyone to agree she can't handle the job. If something were to happen to her right now, he'd be perfectly positioned to take over.'

She looked at him. '*That's* why you're agreeing to this. You think Gray's right and it's all starting to happen.'

His only reply was a loose shrug, but she knew she was right.

'If you go up to Oxford on Saturday, how are you going to handle it?' he asked, changing gears.

'It's tricky,' she conceded. 'I won't be able to get into that party. I'm not on the list of official security. Besides, I need to stay out of the PM's sight – she's not expecting me there.' She paused to think. 'I'll liaise with the local cops. They'll be clued in on everything happening inside. I'll see if they can get me in. If not, I'll flash my badge at the organisers – tell them it's an emergency.'

He gave her a cautioning look. 'If Raj finds out, you're fired.'

His words sent a chill through her. She had thought about it, of course. This was insubordination, however good her intentions. But this was about her country being manipulated, and a possible attempted assassination. Those were both more important than her job, as much as she loved it.

'I don't have any choice,' she retorted. 'Raj pays us to use our instincts and protect the prime minister and her daughter. That's what I'm going to do.' She leaned forward, holding his gaze. 'What do you make of all this, really? Some shadowy organisation nobody's ever heard of, plotting to kill a British prime minister and replace her with a puppet leader. This can't really be happening.'

'That's what I used to think.' His tone was dark.

'What's going on?' she asked. 'What made you decide to believe Gray? You've doubted her from the start. What do you know that I don't know?'

He fell silent for so long, she thought he wouldn't reply.

'I made some calls,' he said finally. 'Friends of mine in MI6. I asked how worried I should be.' He paused, shifting the glass on the tabletop. 'They told me to be very worried. They said it's bigger than we know, and more dangerous than we can imagine. Some of them think these guys have infiltrated the government at multiple levels. Some of them think it's even inside the spy services. They're suspicious of each other.'

Something cold settled in Julia's stomach. 'How could that happen?'

He lifted his shoulders. 'Money. Blackmail. It almost doesn't matter how. What matters is, if they've got John Ashford, there's nobody they can't get. They could win this thing. They could become the government.'

It was such a shocking idea, she found herself struggling to accept it. But she knew Ryan was right.

Raj had hired both of them for their instincts and they could feel it in the air – an icy wind was blowing through the heart of British democracy.

They had to stop it before it went too far. They had to keep Gray and her mother safe.

'So you go to Oxford, and I'll stay here and cover your back,' Ryan said. 'And somehow, we'll try to stop this thing.'

THIRTY-EIGHT

On Saturday morning, Gray was up early, wired and anxious from the moment her eyes opened.

She'd stayed up late the night before, messaging Jake and Chloe, putting the last pieces of their plan together. She kept going over and over it in her head. Walking through it in her mind. Getting to Paddington Station, and from there to Oxford, and to the museum where the event would take place, until she could see it all clearly.

As she brushed her dark hair and twisted it into a sideways braid, the blue eyes reflected in her mirror were sober. But there was no chance of her backing out.

Some part of her felt a twinge of guilt. Julia would never forgive her when she found out what she was doing. But she couldn't let herself think about that. Not if someone was going to try and kill her mother tonight.

If her mother survived and Gray survived, no one would doubt her story ever again. No one would call her a liar.

Everything would be different then. And she could apologise when it was all over.

When she walked out of her bedroom, dressed and ready to go, her mother and Richard were at the kitchen table, drinking coffee and looking at their laptops.

'Gray.' Her mother glanced up at her, smiling. Their talk last night had cleared the air between them. 'You're up early. Do you want breakfast?'

Too nervous to eat, she shook her head. 'I'll just have some juice.'

Richard barely glanced at her.

When today was over, she still had to deal with the problem of her stepfather. But that had to wait for another day.

One crisis at a time, she told herself, as she poured orange juice into a glass.

'What are your plans for the day?' her mother asked, as she carried the glass to the table.

'Actually, I was meaning to tell you. Chloe invited me to see a film at her place.' She gave them a look of wide-eyed innocence. 'But only if that's alright with you. Obviously, I'll take security.'

'Well.' Her mother glanced at Richard, who arched one eyebrow but said nothing. 'I think that would be fine. We're both out today – there's no reason for you to sit here by yourself. Just ask what's her name – Julia – to drive you.'

She was still openly jealous of Gray's bodyguard.

'Sure.' Gray kept her voice easy, but this was the first hurdle to going to Oxford. Her excuse for leaving the building. And her mother had given her permission.

She had to calm herself down before speaking again, making sure her emotion didn't show in her face.

'So, are you guys both going to Oxford tonight for this party?' she asked, after a moment.

The two of them glanced at each other across the table.

Richard cleared his throat. 'I can't go tonight, unfortunately.' He glanced at her mother. 'I'm sorry to miss what's certainly going to be a brilliant speech.'

'Richard has a work meeting he can't get out of.' Her mother was using that falsely positive tone she wielded when she was cross but trying to get over it. 'It's actually lucky, as it means you won't have to spend the night here alone.'

Gray observed Richard surreptitiously. His eyes remained on the screen, but they didn't move. It was as if he was staring at himself in the reflective surface. Waiting for the danger to pass.

Suspicion prickled at the back of Gray's neck.

A tiny voice in her head whispered: What if Richard isn't going tonight because he knows something terrible is going to happen? What if he's part of it?

That was crazy, though. Even she couldn't consider that possibility. He and her mother were happy.

She pushed the thought away, but it lingered, like an uneasy feeling after a bad dream.

Her mother always worked Saturdays, and Richard usually spent most of the day at his club. Today though, they seemed in no hurry to leave. Gray hid her impatience as the minutes ticked away, and the two of them chatted and pottered around.

Finally, just before noon, her mother's phone rang. After speaking to her assistant (the real Emma) for a minute, she sighed, and began gathering her things into her briefcase.

'I'd better get going,' she told her husband. 'I've only got a couple of hours before I need to leave for Oxford.' Kissing Richard lightly she said, 'Are you off to the club?'

'Yes.' He closed his laptop. 'I'll walk down with you.'

All morning, Gray's phone had been buzzing with messages. Chloe was already at the Westminster tube station waiting for her. Time was running out, if they were going to get to Paddington before two o'clock.

Lying on the sofa, a book open and unread in front of her, she gritted her teeth as the two of them gathered their things with no particular sense of urgency.

Finally though, they walked to the door, Richard with his bag over one shoulder, and her mother in flats and trousers – her signature weekend working clothes.

Stopping in the doorway, her mother looked back at her. 'Have a good time with Chloe. Be safe.'

'OK. Thanks!' Forcing a smile, Gray waved, every muscle in her body tense as she lay there languidly, as if she had no need at all to rush.

The second the door closed, she leapt to her feet. Grabbing a shoulder bag from the hall cupboard, she rushed to her bedroom, flinging open the closet door with such force it banged against the wall. The silk dress was there where she'd left it yesterday. Folding it as neatly as she could, she put it in the bag, along with a pair of heels she'd borrowed from her mother's closet.

Moving fast, she grabbed more supplies – sunglasses to disguise her face, a hairbrush, her make-up bag.

When she was ready, she pulled on her coat and scarf, switched her phone off, and hurried across the room, the bag thumping against her hip. There was no time for second guessing this plan. No time for doubt.

Keeping her pace unhurried, she strolled down the corridor to the side exit she and Julia used every day when she went to school. There was rarely more than one police guard there. So she'd only have one person to convince.

The officer at the side door recognised her instantly. Jumping off his chair, he gave her an almost comically confused look. 'Can I … help you?'

'I'm going out to meet a friend,' she told him airily. 'Everyone knows. My mother approved it.'

He looked doubtful. 'Are you sure, miss? Shouldn't someone go with you?'

'Julia's meeting me outside.' Smiling easily, she held up her hand, sunglasses dangling from her fingers. 'I'm going incognito.'

He didn't back down. 'I'm sorry, miss. I believe someone should walk out with you.' His tone was careful, but firm. 'For security.'

Julia would be nearby. She'd told Gray she would be on call all weekend. If he picked up the phone, she could be here in minutes.

Lifting her chin, she gave him an imperious look. 'My *mother* says it's fine,' she informed him, in an icy voice that sounded, she thought, a lot like the prime minister's. 'I don't want to argue with you. But her decision should be enough for everyone. She's in her office now, if you want to call her. But she doesn't like to be disturbed when she's working.'

The officer hesitated so long, she was certain he was going to call and check.

Her hands, hidden by the bag she carried, began to tremble but she kept her expression even.

After a long wait that seemed to last years, he made up his mind. Taking a reluctant step back, he opened the door. He looked troubled as he scanned the empty street. 'Where's Julia meeting you?'

'Right outside.' Gray gave an apologetic smile. 'I'm early.' She held up her phone. 'I'll tell you what,' she said. 'I'll call her right now – make sure she's close.'

'You do that,' he said.

Stiffly, waiting to be ordered back at any moment, Gray walked outside, her phone pressed to her ear as if she were talking to Julia. She could feel the officer's eyes on her, as she paused at the corner.

'Oh sure,' she said loudly into the phone. 'I see you!'

She waved as if someone ahead were gesturing at her. Turning to the officer who was still standing in the doorway, she said, 'She's right there. Thank you!'

Finally, he went back inside.

She was almost too nervous to breathe as she left the building behind and walked through the gates, out onto the sidewalk.

When the gate clanged behind her, the sensation was almost dizzying. She was completely alone. She hadn't been alone in public in weeks. It felt good. It felt liberating. And a little terrifying.

She threw her bag over her shoulder and headed out, her steps long and confident.

She'd just made it through the toughest part of the plan.

Everything else would be easy.

Westminster tube station was a sprawling post-modern construction of exposed rafters, rattling metal floors and long, industrial escalators. It wasn't the ideal starting point for someone who'd grown used to being protected and coddled. But Gray felt better by the time she reached it.

With every step she remembered more about what it was like to be an ordinary person. To not worry about stalkers and obsessives and photographers and psychopaths. To just be sixteen and on her way somewhere.

She'd forgotten how much she liked it.

In the subterranean ticket office, she spotted Chloe almost immediately, standing by the ticket machines, her head bent over her phone. She wore snug jeans and a loose black jacket. Her dark curly hair was tucked under a beret, and she had a bag over one shoulder. She didn't see Gray walking towards her until she tapped her on the shoulder.

'Are you loitering, young lady?' she asked, deepening her voice.

Chloe's face lit up. 'You got out! I was starting to think you wouldn't make it.'

'It was close,' Gray said, beaming. 'I had to talk a cop into letting me go. It took ages.'

Chloe held out a ticket. 'Here – you'll need this.'

Gray took it gratefully. 'Thanks. I have to find a cash machine. I've no money at all for anything.'

She didn't say that she didn't have money because, trapped in the house, she hadn't needed any for weeks.

'Have you heard from Jake?' Chloe asked.

'A while ago,' Gray said. 'He was having trouble getting out too.'

She showed her the text Jake had sent over an hour ago.

NUMBER 10

They're watching me like a hawk. But don't worry.

I'll find a way out.

'I hope he makes it.' Chloe checked her watch. 'Either way, we'd better hurry. We'll miss our train.'

Throwing their bags over their shoulders, they ran to the long escalator, descending into the bowels of the shadowy station. Chloe chattered giddily all the way down.

With her hair braided, and the scarf half hiding her face, nobody noticed Gray. She felt anonymous for the first time in months.

Still, when they got on the tube train, they chose the end of a car, near the rear doors, and stayed on their feet. Chloe arranged herself so she was slightly blocking the view of the other passengers. It was a system they'd developed months ago.

But the other riders were staring at their phones, or at newspapers or paperbacks. No one looked down to the end where the two teenagers stood, heads bent close together.

They remained unnoticed all the way to Paddington. As they rode the escalator up from the tube into the train station above, the normal London cacophony greeted them. Excitement chased Gray's doubts away. She was beginning to believe that they might actually do this.

They'd arranged a meeting place inside the coffee shop near the platform for Oxford. When they walked in, Jake was leaning against a table.

'Finally,' he said. 'I thought you'd never make it.'

They rushed at him, all of them laughing and talking at same time.

'You made it!'

'I thought you were trapped?'

'How did you get here?'

For all of them, the relief of having made it this far was heady. Gray had never felt so strong. So independent. So *normal*.

Three coffee cups sat on the table at his elbow. Chloe pointed at them. 'Please tell me one of those is mine.'

'Oh yeah,' he said. 'I got everyone coffee. Figured we'd all need it.'

'You star.' Chloe grabbed one and took a long sip.

'Have you checked on the train?' Gray asked as she picked up her own cup.

'It doesn't have a platform number yet,' he said. 'We've still got twenty minutes.'

Instantly, Gray's euphoria evaporated. Twenty minutes was too long. They needed to get moving. By now, someone might have figured out that she hadn't left with Julia. That Julia didn't, in fact, have any idea where she was. As soon as that happened, the police would be looking for her. And Paddington Station was crawling with police.

Gray looked up at the tall metal beams around them. There was a CCTV camera just across from her. Another, a short distance away. There was even one, she realised, behind the counter of the coffee shop.

Swallowing hard, she tilted her head down.

Once they were on the train, they'd be safe.

'Was it hard getting out?' Jake asked, glancing at her.

'It was … interesting,' she said, keeping her voice steady enough to hide her concerns. 'What about you?'

'As far as Mike knows, I'm having a real digestion problem,' he said mischievously. 'I've been in the gents' for an hour now.'

Chloe's phone rang. Glancing at the screen, she made a face. 'It's my mum – be right back.'

Out of all their parents, Chloe's were the only ones who had any idea where their child was going to be that day. The only one who didn't have to hide.

So Jake and Gray didn't worry when she stepped outside, holding the coffee in one hand, pressing the phone to her ear with the other.

'Where's your mum?' Jake asked. 'I gather she's not home.'

'She's working. My stepfather's at his club,' Gray said. 'I should have time...' Her voice trailed off. Outside, Chloe was gesturing wildly at them. 'Hang on. Something's wrong.'

The two of them ran to where Chloe stood, just outside the door, her phone in one hand. All the humour had left her face.

'What's wrong?' Gray asked, her brow furrowing.

Chloe gave her a helpless look. 'Someone just called my mum from Number 10. They were looking for you.'

Gray drew in a sharp breath. 'What did she say?'

'She said she had no idea where you were. That I was spending the day with another friend looking at colleges. But...' She gave Gray a warning look. 'They asked for my number. It's almost like they know.'

At that instant, her phone began to ring again. They all stared at it, aghast. Her ringtone was a snippet from a bouncy pop song – the one they'd danced to at Aidan's party. It played over and over, its cheery tune jarring.

'Gray!' Chloe was panicking. 'What do I *do*?'

'Don't answer it,' Jake told her firmly.

'I can't just ignore it.' Chloe looked from Jake to Gray, holding her phone far away from her body, as if it might bite her.

A deep, echoing voice over the tannoy began announcing the train to Oxford.

Finally, the phone stopped ringing.

A second later, it began ringing again.

'They know something's wrong. They'll figure it out.' Gray could feel the moment of freedom slipping away.

'You have to decide what you're going to do.' Jake held her gaze. 'Do you want to go home and sort things out with security? Or do you want to go to Oxford and do this thing? We can do either, I promise.'

Gray hesitated. Some tiny, scared part of her wanted to run home as fast as she could. She didn't want to be dragged off a train by police. Humiliated in public.

But she would never run. This was her only chance to prove to everyone she was telling the truth.

Ironically, the only way to be trusted was to lie.

'I'm going to Oxford,' she said, firmly.

'Right, then.' Jake took Chloe's phone and removed the battery, handing it back to her in pieces. She stared at it blankly. Then he did the same to his own phone.

Gray pulled out her phone to do the same, but then hesitated.

'I'm going to turn my phone on,' Gray decided. 'Just long enough to tell them I'm safe. Remember, I want them to follow me to Oxford. I need them not to panic.'

'They can trace it,' Jake warned her.

'I know,' she said. 'But they have to know I haven't been kidnapped. If they know I'm safe the search will be different. Do you understand?'

He nodded. 'Do it.'

The other two watched sombrely as she turned on her phone. Immediately, it began to ring – a shrill, steady warning. Taking a deep breath, she hit answer.

'Gray.' It was Ryan. She could hear the relief in his deep, measured tone. 'Where are you?'

'Look, Ryan, I'm fine.' Her voice was calm. 'I'm perfectly safe. I'm not in trouble. I'm being careful. Please tell Julia not to worry.'

The loud tannoy voice announced the train again.

'Which station are you in?' Ryan asked instantly. 'I won't stop you, Gray. I just need to come with you.'

'I know that's not true,' she told him. 'I know you'd just take me home, and I can't let you do that. I'm with friends right now. We're absolutely fine. Don't call the police and start a crazy manhunt. Protect my mother, Ryan. She's the one who needs you. She needs all of us.'

She could hear him talking as she turned her phone off.

She would have been more worried that they might find her, but this wasn't her normal phone. That phone, which undoubtedly had a tracking device on it somewhere, had been destroyed in a puddle. She'd switched the SIM cards. This was the phone she'd used before her mother was prime minister. She didn't think anyone even knew she still had it.

Hoisting her bag to her shoulder, she looked up at her friends.

'OK, then. Let's go.'

THIRTY-NINE

Julia was just getting into her car outside the safe house when her phone rang. Ryan's name was on the screen.

'What's up?' she asked.

'You're not going to like this,' he said. 'Firefly is in the cold.'

For a second, Julia couldn't get her brain to accept what he was saying. 'You can't be serious.'

'She told the door cop she was going to have coffee with a friend, and that you were going with them.' He took a breath. 'I got her on the phone a few minutes ago. She was in a train station.'

Julia closed her eyes. Oh Gray, what have you done?

She tried to put herself in the girl's shoes. Where could she be going with Chloe that was so important she'd risk everything?

In the end, it wasn't a hard question to answer.

'She's going to Oxford.' There was no doubt in her voice. 'The little idiot's going to go up there and try to save her mother.'

Straightening, she started the car and slammed the door. She had to stop Gray before she got herself killed.

'Are you still in London?' Ryan asked.

'Yeah, why?'

'Come and pick me up,' he said. 'I'll be outside Number 10.'

Julia threw the car into gear. 'I'm on my way.'

Fifteen minutes later, she drove up to Ryan where he stood on Whitehall, a short distance from Number 10. He got into the passenger seat, his face grim.

He was still putting his seatbelt on when she pulled out into the traffic.

'What's she playing at?' he asked. 'Does she want to die?'

Julia, who had thought of nothing else on the way here, shook her head, her eyes on the road.

'I think she wants us to go to Oxford and protect her mother. I think this is her plan. You and me in a car, racing to the place we were told we couldn't go.' She slowed to a stop at a red light at the edge of Trafalgar Square.

Ahead, Nelson's column jutted upwards into the clouds. Such a silly place to put a statue, she'd always thought. So high no one can actually see it.

The lions beneath the column glowered into the distance as a crowd of young people tried to climb up onto their old stone backs.

Behind them was Parliament. To the left was Buckingham Palace.

This was the power centre of the country, and yet she felt so helpless.

'Dammit,' she muttered, slapping her hand on the steering wheel. 'Why doesn't she just tell us she's going to do this, instead of running off like this, putting so much at risk.'

'I told her I'd go with her anywhere she wanted to go,' said Ryan. 'She said, "I know that's not true."'

Julia shot him a sideways glance. 'She wasn't wrong, was she?'

His mouth twisted. 'Of course not. I would have taken her straight home.'

The light turned green, and Julia signalled left, tailgating a taxi.

'That is the problem,' she said, as they turned. 'She knows too much about us. She knew we couldn't help her do this unless we had no choice. She's left enough breadcrumbs to show us where to go, but that was all she could give us.'

Ryan sank down in his seat. 'Kid's too smart for her own good.'

'Tell me about it.'

For a while London traffic took all of her attention. When they reached another red light, she turned to him. 'When do we tell Raj? You know what he'll say.'

'I've just been trying to decide,' said Ryan. 'Let's get to the edge of the city, and then tell him. Let's say no police until we get there.'

Julia didn't have to ask why. 'If word gets out that the PM's kid is on the run, the press will be everywhere.'

Ryan put on his sunglasses as the light turned green.

'And cops,' he said, 'have the newspapers on speed dial.'

FORTY

Just before six o'clock that evening, Gray stood in a cubicle in the ladies' washroom at the train station, struggling into the silk dress. Her skin was clammy and cold, and the filmy material kept sticking to her.

Through the walls, she could hear the sounds of a busy evening. The deep, ground-shaking rumble of trains coming and going. Voices passing outside the door.

As she tried to pull the delicate fabric without tearing it, her heart thrummed with a low but constant sense of apprehension. Either she was right, and someone would try to kill her mother tonight, or she was wrong, and had sparked a manhunt without any reason.

At least she assumed there was a manhunt. They'd spent the day dodging the police, and had seen no sign of massively increased security. But then they had been very careful.

She just hoped Julia and Ryan were in town by now, and that her plan would work.

'How's it going in there?' Chloe's voice came from outside the door.

'I'm almost done.' Hopping up and down, she kicked off her ankle boots and socks, trying not to touch the ice-cold floor, and wiggled her feet into sharply pointed high-heeled shoes.

Unlocking the door, she tottered out, holding her bag in one hand. 'I can't walk in these things. They're instruments of torture.'

Chloe gazed at her with open admiration. 'Who cares? They look fantastic.'

Still grumbling, Gray made her way unsteadily to the sinks and examined herself in the hazy mirror.

With its full skirt, the blue dress gave the illusion of an hourglass figure. She looked fine, but her face was damp and her hair was going everywhere.

Someone knocked at the door. 'We're in here,' Chloe shouted.

A voice on the other side complained but neither of them paid much attention.

'You look gorgeous,' Chloe insisted, turning back to Gray. 'Let me do something with your hair.' She dug through her bag, pulling out a brush. 'You should wear it loose,' she decided. 'In waves.'

Gray watched as she removed the braid with expert twists of her fingers. 'I wish you could come in with us. You don't mind, do you?'

As there were only two tickets, they'd agreed that Jake and Gray would go in. Chloe was going to stay outside, looking for trouble.

Chloe shook her head. 'Don't be silly. Jake will be more help inside. He knows who everyone is. I'll be more use outside.'

Watching her work, her lip caught between her teeth, Gray's heart melted. She was such a rock. Through everything that had happened, she'd been there. Cheering her up when she was down. Refusing to let their friendship be threatened by the changes in Gray's life. Sticking with her when it all got weird.

Ducking the brush, Gray turned to face her. 'You're the best friend ever. You know that? Thank you so much for being here.'

'I'm just doing what anyone would,' Chloe insisted, but her cheeks reddened. 'Now, be still, while I make you beautiful. After all, you're the prime minister's bloody daughter.'

When the two of them walked out a few minutes later, Jake was waiting by the station entrance. He didn't notice them right away.

'Blimey.' Chloe nudged Gray. 'Look at him.'

The dinner jacket suited Jake's long, angular body, and made him appear older. And very cool.

'Cor! You look like James Bond,' Chloe told him as they walked up.

'Do I?' He tugged at the dark fabric of his lapel. 'I think I look like a git.'

His gaze swept across Gray in a lingering way that made her cheeks warm. 'You look stunning.'

Chloe had fussed over her hair until it stopped frizzing, and polished her make-up.

Not wanting him to notice her blushing, she turned away and her gaze immediately encountered the curious eyes of a passing woman. The man behind her was also staring.

The dress was attracting attention. She might be recognised. Quickly, she wrapped her scarf around her neck, lifting it up over her chin.

'We'd better go,' she told the others.

In the dark, Oxford felt different. As they made their way to the museum, they lost their way twice and had to backtrack. The landmarks they'd noticed earlier – a row of blank-eyed statues separated by spikes of metal, a tall, jagged tower – seemed sinister now.

As they turned back into a quiet street, Gray shivered under her warm coat. Her mother's shoes had begun to rub blisters on her heels. She couldn't wait for this night to be over. Her stomach was tight with trepidation.

Jake must have been feeling the same nerves – his head was down and his shoulders hunched. He'd stuffed his jacket into his bag and wore nothing over his tux.

'Aren't you cold?' she asked.

He shook his head. 'I'm northern. I don't mind the cold.'

But his hands were shoved deep into his pockets.

When they rounded the next corner, the museum appeared ahead of them.

Bright lights set the grand central portico aglow, while the wings on either side were lit with deep blue. A row of expensive cars idled out front, blocking traffic as they paused briefly to unload women in flowing gowns and men in black tie, before moving on.

'Just two cops,' Jake said, tilting his head at the front gate.

Tension rising in her chest, Gray scanned the people nearby for familiar faces. 'No sign of my bodyguards.'

Her heart felt heavy. If her bodyguards didn't come, they'd be all alone trying to save her mother. She was counting on Julia to understand what she was doing.

She had to.

They paused at the corner, and she turned to Jake and Chloe. 'This is it,' she said. 'Last chance to go home. I promise I won't blame you.'

Jake didn't hesitate. 'Don't be daft. We've got to do this.'

Chloe, in a pink bobble hat, cheeks red from the cold, nodded hard. 'Jake's right. I'm not going anywhere.'

'Where will you wait?' Gray asked her.

Chloe pointed to where a small cluster of photographers had gathered near the museum. 'I'm going to use them as my hiding place. I should be able to see everything from there.'

'OK.' Gray exhaled, looking at Jake. 'We should go.'

Taking Gray's icy hand in hers, Chloe gave it a squeeze. 'Good luck. Be careful.'

Jake and Gray headed to the crosswalk. As they waited for the light to change, he glanced at her. 'You ready?'

She nodded. She was scared but also relieved that this was finally happening. No more unknowns. They stood close together. In the darkness, his fingers found hers and he took her hand.

The light turned green.

They stepped into the crowd heading for the museum. For once, even with the paparazzi there, Gray kept her head up. She didn't mind if they photographed her now. She didn't care what they thought.

They'd already been punished for being friends. And it wasn't going to stop them.

Jake squared his shoulders, as if he'd had the same thought. They moved in sync through the crowd, the silk of Gray's dress fluttering.

As they neared the front gate, they fell in behind a white-haired man in a tuxedo and a woman wearing a mink coat.

From beneath her lashes, Gray studied the two police officers at the museum's front gate. They weren't armed, but they were clearly alert for trouble as they studied everyone who walked in.

She forced herself to walk steadily in the unfamiliar heels. She kept her eyes turned away as she passed the two officers, but she thought she could feel them watching her.

With every step, she expected someone to grab her arm. To shout her name or pull her aside. But no one did.

When they were a safe distance away, she let out an audible breath and slowed her pace.

She fought the urge to look over her shoulder – to make sure they weren't following her.

Leaning towards her, Jake said quietly, 'There aren't enough cops here.'

He was right. As they climbed the stairs to the grand portico, there was nobody in sight who didn't look like they were here for a party. Those two cops at the front gate *were* the security.

Everyone was wearing thick coats, scarves – it would be so easy to hide a weapon.

She'd been wrong earlier when she thought this place looked safe. This was a great place to kill someone.

The museum's entrance hall was crowded. As people gathered in the warmth, their voices echoed off the marble walls and soaring ceilings. Music was coming from somewhere – something classical.

As they approached the front desk, a dark-haired woman in her forties wearing an elegant suit looked up. 'Can I help you?'

'There should be two tickets on hold for me,' Gray told her.

The woman reached for a box of cards, divided alphabetically. She was distracted – she'd hardly glanced at Gray's face. 'Name please?'

'Gray Langtry.'

The woman visibly twitched. 'Of *course*.' Her frosty demeanour melting, she beamed at her. 'Miss Langtry, I have your tickets right here. We're so pleased you could join us tonight. Your mother is such a supporter.'

Pulling an envelope from a drawer she took out two tickets on thick card and handed them to her. Gray gripped them tightly.

'I hope you enjoy the event.' The woman paused. 'By the way, your mother hasn't arrived yet. When she does, should we let her know you're already here?'

Smiling, Gray said, 'Please don't tell her. My being here – it's a surprise for her.'

The woman gave her a conspiratorial smile. 'I won't say a thing. Enjoy your evening.'

As they walked away, tickets in hand, Jake gave her a sideways look of sheer admiration.

'You have the calm of a true criminal,' he said.

'Thanks... I think.' She smiled at him, removing the scarf.

They left her coat at the coat check, and showed their tickets to a young woman at the entrance to the main museum. She motioned for them to pass.

They followed the music through a gallery lined with marble statues, to a glass bannister overlooking a sculpture gallery below and stopped to look down. The party was already packed.

Waiters dressed all in black moved smoothly between statues and other ancient pieces of art, wielding trays with sparkling flutes of champagne. In one corner, a string quartet played music that seemed to dance on the air.

A stage had been set up for the speeches later.

Gray's stomach clenched as she looked at the throng below. Anyone there could be the killer.

Next to her, Jake was frowning at something.

'What is it?' she asked, following his line of vision to the crowded floor below.

'Ashford.' Keeping his hand low, he pointed to two men who were huddled together.

One of them she recognised instantly as the deputy prime minister. His thick, silver-streaked hair was distinctive. His mouth was turned down. He and the other man seemed to be quarrelling.

'Who's the man with him?' she asked.

The man was younger than Ashford, maybe forty years old. He was just as blow-dried but somehow more polished. He didn't seem afraid of Ashford. If anything, he seemed to hold him in contempt.

'I know him. He's always in Parliament. My dad hates him.' Jake thought for a second. 'I think his name is Nathaniel St John – something like that, anyway. He's a money guy. Not a politician.' He turned to her. 'Look, my dad won't be here, but people who know him are definitely here. If they see me with you, things could get tricky. I think we should separate.'

The thought wasn't pleasant, but Gray could see the logic. There might be friends of her mother here as well. If she was with Jake, they'd attract attention.

'OK,' she agreed. 'Just be careful.'

'Don't worry about me. You're the one who needs to look out for yourself.' He glanced back over the bannister. 'It's too crowded. It would be easy for some lunatic to get close to you.'

'I'll be fine. We'll stay where we can see each other,' she said. 'Just keep an eye on my mum.'

Behind them, a chorus of voices, laughing and talking, moved down the walkway towards them. They had to get moving.

'You go first,' Jake told her. 'I'll be right behind you.'

Gray moved to the top of the stairs and paused, looking down at the throng below.

It was time to do what she'd come here to do. To prove she wasn't lying. To save her mother. To save herself.

No more excuses.

Holding her head high, she walked down to the party.

FORTY-ONE

On the busy street outside the Ashmolean Museum, the dark government car pulled up with a screech of brakes, parking behind two police cars that had also just arrived.

Ryan and Julia jumped out, running to join the four officers gathered just inside the museum's imposing metal gates.

Their breath preceded them in icy white clouds.

'Holy hell, it's as cold as a witch's door knob,' Ryan said.

Julia didn't reply. She hadn't spoken in quite some time. They'd got caught in two huge traffic snarls on the way here, which had delayed them by more than an hour. What if they'd missed Gray?

They'd called Raj as soon as they were out of central London. He'd exploded when they told him the news.

'How the hell could something like this happen?' he'd demanded. 'What idiot police officer let that girl walk out of there alone?'

'We're on our way to Oxford now,' Ryan had told him. 'We think she's going to that event with her mother. She wants to protect her.'

There'd been a long silence as Raj absorbed this.

'We can't put out a red alert,' he'd said, finally. 'The press would put her in more danger.'

'That's what we think,' Ryan had agreed. 'We need a soft warning to the Oxford police. Just have them look out for her, but don't search. She's not missing. She's... visiting.'

Raj had sworn softly. 'This is a disaster waiting to happen. Get to Oxford. Do what you can. I trust you to handle it.'

They'd put out a low-key warning to the Oxford police to look out for the prime minister's daughter, but Julia knew they wouldn't find her. Gray was too smart. Besides, it was a big event – it would be easy for her to lose herself in that crowd.

So far, Raj had managed to keep the situation under wraps. Only the security services, the prime minister's office, and the local police knew that she was missing.

For now, at least, they could hope that whoever it was out there who wanted to kill her thought she was safe at home.

She was still angry at Gray for deceiving her like this. But part of her admired the girl's gumption. However dangerous this was, it was also bloody brave.

When they reached the officers at the gate, she and Ryan showed their identification and asked about Gray.

'We haven't seen her,' one told her shortly. 'And with you standing in my way, I won't see her if she walks by right now.'

'We need to get in there.' Ryan pointed at the building behind them. 'We should be inside when the prime minister arrives.'

The top-ranking officer of the group shook his head. 'Our orders are: nobody gets in who's not on the list provided by the government. You're not on the list.'

Julia had learned to stay calm in the face of bureaucratic idiocy when she was in the military. That skill served her well now.

'If we get permission from the prime minister's team, will you let us in?' she said.

He gave her a sour look. 'If the prime minister adds you to her list, you can go inside. Until then, you stay out here in the cold with the rest of us.'

Julia and Ryan stepped back.

'What are you going to do?' Ryan asked.

Julia dialled Raj's number. 'Get some help,' she said.

Raj answered in a tense tone she'd come to associate with bad news.

'We're here. The local plods won't let us inside to look for Gray,' she explained. 'Can you get me in?'

'Give me ten minutes,' he said. And hung up.

Ryan gave her an enquiring look.

'He's on it.' She turned to scan the crowd. 'Let's make sure she's not out here first.'

She swept the courtyard with a critical eye. She could see from here how unacceptable the security was. Four cops and a handful of museum security for hundreds of guests.

If the killer really was happy with either mother or daughter, Gray could be dead before her mother even walked in the door.

What Gray didn't understand was that either of them would do. There was no way her mother would stay in office if Gray were killed. And Ashford would get what he wanted anyway.

How did you explain that to a sixteen-year-old girl?

You tell her, a voice in her head said. You treat her like a grown-up.

But it was too late for that. All the grown-ups had decided to keep Gray safe by lying to her. And now she could die because of it.

For the first time she allowed herself to be afraid for Gray. She was in way over her head.

'I have to get in there, Ryan.' Quivering with impatience, she looked up at her partner. 'She can't be in there alone.'

He kept his eyes fixed on the flow of people entering the museum in their evening gowns and crisp suits.

'You will.' His voice held absolute assurance.

But would it be soon enough to save Gray?

FORTY-TWO

Gray descended the long staircase to the gallery, walking as if she belonged at the party. As if she were expected. With each step though, her eyes swept the crowd for signs of trouble.

Everything looked normal. The music was louder here – amplified by the wide space and the stone floors.

John Ashford was still in the corner, talking to the money man, Nathaniel something. Their argument seemed to have got worse now. Gray slowed her pace to watch. The money man was leaning in, his face red, saying something that Ashford did not like. Ashford made a dismissive gesture. The younger man turned abruptly and stormed away.

When he'd gone, Ashford stared into the distance for a moment.

Then he looked up. Their eyes met. Even from across the room, she saw the recognition on his face.

Her heart pounding, Gray tore her gaze away and hurried to lose herself in the crowd. The place was packed, the voices an indistinct roar around her. Gray fixed a smile on her face, as if she were having a wonderful time.

After a few minutes, she chanced another look in Ashford's direction. The deputy prime minister had disappeared.

'Champagne?' A waiter stopped in front of her, a tray of golden flutes in one hand.

Like all the other waiters, he was dressed in chic black. He had short dark hair and an attractive oval face. His expression was deferential.

She started to say no automatically. Then it occurred to her that everyone else in the room was holding a glass. Champagne would help her fit in.

'Thank you.' She took a glass from the tray.

With a polite nod, the waiter turned away, but not before Gray saw the recognition in his face. He knew who she was.

It didn't matter at this stage, of course. The charity knew she was here, and other people were likely to recognise her. It would be fine as long as she stuck to her story. She was here to surprise her mother. That was all.

It was nearly seven now, and the room was much more crowded. When she turned to look for Jake, it took her a while to find him in the crush.

When she spotted him, he was standing by a statue of a woman on a high plinth. Like her, he held a glass of champagne, and affected a casual air as he scrutinised the people around him.

'It's ghastly,' she heard a woman say over the noise of the crowd. 'Because the PM's coming and that singer everyone's talking about, half the country wanted a ticket. Now it's heaving.'

Just then, Gray was jostled by a woman in a dark green silk dress. She had to lift her glass high to avoid spilling the champagne she hadn't yet touched.

'Oh, I'm so sorry,' the woman said. 'It's absolutely desperate, isn't it? I can't move without knocking into someone.' As she met Gray's gaze, her eyes widened in recognition and her face brightened. 'Oh my goodness. Aren't you Gray Langtry?'

'Yes.' She smiled politely. 'That's me.'

'I adore your mother,' the woman told her, motioning for a friend to join them. 'I just think she's so inspiring.' She looked around the room as if Gray's mother might suddenly appear. 'Is she here yet? I'm dying to hear her speak.'

'She'll be here any minute,' Gray told her.

'And you've come to support her.' The woman looked at her with admiration, as if coming to a party were a huge accomplishment. 'I think it's abominable how the press is covering her, I really do. I think it's sexism. They'd never treat a man like that. Male prime ministers get away with murder. But if a woman puts one step out of line, every newspaper in the country has a nervous breakdown.'

Gray wasn't sure how to respond to that. Before she knew she was going to do it, she heard herself say, 'I'm very proud of her.'

'Of course you are!' The woman's face fell. 'I wish I had something for you to sign. I'd love to have your autograph for my daughter.'

At that moment though, the phone in Gray's clutch bag began to vibrate.

'I'm so sorry,' she said, pulling her phone out. 'Excuse me. Someone's calling.'

'If it's your mother tell her I love her,' the woman called after her, beaming excitedly.

Gray lifted the phone to see Chloe's name on the screen. 'What's happening?'

'Head's up,' Chloe said, breathlessly. 'Your mum just pulled up. She's getting out of the car now.'

Gray's heart began to race. This was it. She'd have given anything to see Julia and Ryan right now. But without them, it had to be her.

'Thanks,' she said, and began to make her way towards where Jake stood at the foot of the stairs. 'Are you OK out there?'

'I'm completely fine,' Chloe assured her. 'What's it like?'

'Crowded. Lots of champagne.' Catching Jake's eye, Gray motioned for him to come over. 'I'd better go.'

'Stay safe,' Chloe ordered. 'Let me know if you need me. Oh, by the way. Your bodyguards are here.'

Gray's heart jumped. 'Both of them? Have they come inside?'

'Both. They're still outside. Standing at the gates, talking to the police.'

'Look, I don't know if it's possible, but if you can get to them,' Gray said hurriedly, 'tell them I'm in here. Tell them to come in.'

'On it,' Chloe said. 'Stay safe.'

Gray was putting the phone back in her bag when Jake reached her. 'What's up?'

'My mum's here,' she told him. 'And my bodyguards are outside, looking for me.'

'That's good news though, right?' He searched her face. 'You wanted them here.'

'It's really good news.' She smiled at him, some of her fear finally easing. 'If they come in, we can leave all the hero stuff to the experts.'

'Would you like a canapé?' The voice came from behind them. They both wheeled around to find a waiter holding out a tray of fat pink prawns, each impaled on a toothpick with a blood red cherry tomato.

It was the same waiter as before. 'No, thank you,' she told him, politely.

He pivoted and proffered the tray to a young couple nearby.

'We'd better separate again,' she told Jake quietly. 'I think that waiter recognises me.'

'It's not the waiters I'm worried about,' he said. 'I think Ashford saw you.'

'Yeah,' she said. 'I noticed that too.'

Just then, a murmur swept the room. Gray looked up to see her mother at the top of the stairs. She wore a dark, glittering dress, and her hair was pulled up into a loose twist at the nape of her neck.

The crowd burst into applause. Her mother smiled, her face glowing. This was exactly the kind of thing she loved, Gray thought. Adoration from an audience, and all for a good cause.

'I'd better go,' Jake whispered.

She nodded and watched him move through the distracted clusters of partygoers, and melt into the crowd on the other side of the staircase.

As her mother descended the steps, Gray slipped into the throng, trying to make herself invisible.

In the press of bodies it was hot, and she'd begun to perspire. Her throat was dry and she took a sip of champagne, which bubbled on her tongue.

She felt so much better knowing the bodyguards were here. Chloe would get to them. They would come in. Everything would be fine. All she had to do was stay close to her mother until they got her.

Just behind her mother's right shoulder was her press secretary, Anna. She wore a black dress and heels, and had a phone clutched in her hand, as always. Gray recognised the dark-haired man to her mother's left as Adam, one of her bodyguards.

She craned her neck to see behind them. No sign of Julia or Ryan. They must still be outside.

The main problem now was that the room was so crowded, it was hard to imagine how she could protect her mother if she were attacked. She needed to stay close to her without being spotted.

When her mother reached the gallery, the crowd parted to allow her through, creating a further crush as people stepped back. Gray squirmed through the mass of silk dresses and dark suits. Over people's shoulders, she caught glimpses of her mother as she moved across the room, pausing to shake hands or chat with well-wishers and acquaintances.

The bodyguard kept his eyes on the crowd around her but Gray couldn't see how he could protect her in this packed space. The sheer density of the crowd made security virtually impossible.

She was standing behind a statue of a headless torso, safely hidden by the crowd, when she spotted the waiter who'd recognised her earlier that night.

Now he carried no tray, but stood at the fringes of the crowd. He leaned forward, on the balls of his feet, as if poised to run. But it was his face that caught Gray's attention. His eyes were fixed on her mother, intently. He looked transfixed.

One of his hands was at his side. The other was hidden in the front pocket of his short, black waiter's apron.

With everyone focussed on her mother, no one but Gray noticed as he began to make his way through the crowd towards the prime minister. What was he doing? The other waiters had disappeared into the kitchen. He was the only one still on the floor.

Her heart began to race.

What if it was him? Turning, she balanced on her toes, trying to find Jake, but all she saw was a sea of strange faces.

The waiter was already disappearing into the throng. There was nothing else for Gray to do. She plunged into the crowd behind him.

'Excuse me… Pardon me,' she repeated, as she pressed her way through, trying to keep the man in sight.

Her heel landed on something soft.

The woman next to her flinched. '*Ouch*. Would you be careful?'

'Sorry!' Gray flung the word over her shoulder as she struggled to keep moving. She couldn't see the man anymore. She'd lost him.

Panicking now, she pushed past the last few people, bursting out of the crowd at the edge of the gallery, breathless.

There was no sign of the waiter.

She took a step back, to try and get a better view of the room.

That was when a hand grabbed her from behind, and a cold blade pressed against the side of her neck.

'Don't scream,' a voice whispered in her ear. 'Or I'll use this.'

FORTY-THREE

Squirming in the man's grip, Gray turned her head very slightly and saw the waiter's short dark hair, and black button-down shirt.

The arm he'd wrapped across her torso was as hard as steel. The knife was steady against her neck. She looked around, desperately.

They were behind the crowd. Everyone was looking the other way, to where her mother was just climbing onto the stage.

Nobody was looking at the back of the room.

Her heart hammered against her ribs so hard it hurt. 'What do you want?'

'Shut up. Stay still.' He hissed the words in her ear. The warmth of his breath against her skin made her shudder.

Instinctively, she turned her head to try and see his expression. He jerked her back with such force her feet left the ground. A startled cry left her throat, lost in the noise of the crowd.

'Don't look at me,' he hissed. 'Scream again and I'll end this right here.'

He had a strange accent. A mixture of London and Eastern European.

Gray began to tremble. 'Who are you?'

'I'm your worst nightmare, sweetheart.'

Gray couldn't move, couldn't think. She was hyper aware of the sharp point of pain on her neck.

He began to pull her backwards, half-lifting her from the ground as if she weighed nothing. One of her shoes tumbled off.

From somewhere behind her, she heard the distinctive metal click of a door opening.

Desperately, she scanned the rows of people standing just a few feet away, but their backs were turned to her. Her mother was about to speak.

Her other shoe fell off just before he pulled her through the door into a dark corridor. Beneath her bare feet the floor was cold and rough, like it was made of concrete.

'Where are you taking me?'

He jerked her body hard. 'Stop asking questions.'

He was still walking backwards. There were no lights. Gray let one hand dangle loose and in the darkness, touched the wall. It was concrete as well. They must be in a maintenance corridor behind the gallery.

She tried to think of anyone who would help her. But there'd be nobody back here this late at night. No one would come to save her. She had to do this herself, somehow.

But she couldn't fight   not with that blade pressed against her skin.

Make him talk, she told herself. Try to distract him.

Her throat was so dry and tight it took a minute for her to summon the words. When she did, her voice was shaky. 'What do you want from me?'

'I came here to kill the prime minister. That's not going to happen.' He pressed his lips against her ear. 'I guess you'll have to do.'

Gray was shaking so violently it was hard to speak. But she made herself talk. 'Who hired you?'

He jerked her up so her feet dangled above the floor. His arm was so tight across her lungs she couldn't get air.

'Shut up.' He said it almost casually, in that strange hybrid accent.

When he set her down again, bright spots of light flashed across her vision.

She wasn't going to get out of here. The thought sent a shard of ice through her heart. She didn't want to die. Not now. She was just a child. She had plans. She wanted to go to college. To do something interesting with her life. To see her father again. To see Jake.

Heedless of the knife, she struggled in his grip.

She tried to cry out, but the sound came out thin and airless. More a gasp than a scream. The knife pressed hard against her neck, sending a sharp, burning pain through her. She felt warm liquid run down her dress.

The pain shocked her. She was distantly aware that the liquid was blood. But there was so much.

In seconds, her dress was sticky with it.

'Help.' Her voice was thick. It seemed to come from far away. 'Someone.'

The darkness no longer surrounded her. It was becoming her – filling her. Her bones turned to water. Her heartbeat felt sluggish.

She reached out into the shadows, as if the walls could save her.

'I said shut up,' he snarled.

'That's no way to talk to a lady.' The voice – female, young – came from behind them.

The man swung Gray around, and yanked the blood-stained knife from Gray's neck, pointing it in front of them.

In the glowing light of the fire exit sign, Gray made out Julia's familiar face.

She stood with her feet apart, hands loose at her sides. Her stormy eyes were fixed on the waiter.

'Who the hell are you?' The man growled the words contemptuously. But Gray felt his body change – every muscle tensed.

'Listen. Here's the situation.' Julia's tone was rational. 'Right now, you're facing charges of attempted murder and grievous bodily harm. That's eight years. If she bleeds out, you'll do the full twenty. Let her go now. Take the shorter term.' She cocked her head, studying him with predatory alertness. 'There's one other thing you need to know. I will kill you if I have to.'

The waiter had gone still behind Gray. For a second, she wondered if Julia was getting through to him.

Then he spoke. 'I'll take my *chances*.'

As he said the last word, he shoved Gray hard to one side. She felt herself fall as if in a dream. Air whistling by and the ground rushing up. She couldn't seem to do anything to save herself. Nothing was working.

But unlike a dream, when she hit the ground it hurt.

She heard the breath leave her lungs as if from far away. Everything went dark.

When she came to, her nostrils were full of the smell of cold dirt and steaming, coppery blood.

The rough floor was pressed hard against her cheek. She didn't know where she was. It was dark and she was in pain.

Then she heard the unmistakeable sounds of a struggle. Fists slamming into flesh. Grunts of pain. And she remembered.

Julia.

She forced herself to roll over, to sit up.

In the faint glow of the fire escape light, she saw the two of them – Julia crouched low. The waiter with a blade glinting like a piece of ice in his hand as he shifted it left-right-left – almost too fast to follow. Then he lunged for her.

Julia feinted right then lunged the other way. As she passed, she grabbed his right wrist and twisted it violently.

The man shrieked but held onto the knife, kicking her in the abdomen.

Gray heard the audible whoosh of air leaving Julia's lungs, saw the shudder the blow sent through her, but she recovered quickly, whirling to face him and aiming a vicious, balletic kick at his head.

He held up his hand to ward off the blow, but not quickly enough. The kick caught his cheek with a *crack*. Before he could recover, the bodyguard launched herself at him, raining kicks against his back and side as he struggled to fend her off.

Gray thought she had him now. But then, snarling a curse, he dropped his hands and with almost uncanny speed, thrust the knife at her.

Gray screamed, her voice faint and hoarse.

Julia didn't flinch. She dropped and rolled on the ground, coming up behind him. In a smooth, practised move, she grabbed him by the throat and began throttling him.

'Drop the knife.' Her voice was ice cold.

An awful gurgling sound came from his throat as she pressed her forearm tighter against his windpipe, using her free hand to add to the pressure.

Then a tall shadow appeared, racing down the corridor, feet heavy on the concrete. Ryan flung himself at the waiter, grabbing his knife wrist, turning it until the blade slowly pointed sideways and then gradually down at the floor. The man's face was purple from pain and lack of oxygen.

He made an awful keening noise as the knife slipped from his fingers and clattered to the concrete floor.

Ryan kicked the blade away and pulled handcuffs from his pockets.

'Give me his hands,' he said.

Julia didn't loosen her hold. The sound the man was making turned to a rattle. Still she tightened her arm across his throat.

Ryan looked up at her. 'Give me his hands, Julia. Gray needs us.' His voice was almost gentle.

Slowly, she let go of the man's throat. Gasping, retching, the waiter slumped to the floor. Julia, her face flushed, pulled his hands behind his back; Ryan cuffed him quickly. The instant he was secure, Julia ran to Gray, dropping to her knees beside her, reaching for her hand.

'You OK?'

Gray wanted to explain that something was terribly wrong. There was blood on her dress, and she was so very cold.

But all she managed was, 'It … hurts…'

Julia traced the blood flow to her neck. When she found the wound, she pressed her fingers against it and turned back to Ryan. 'I need something. A cloth. Give me your shirt,' she told him urgently.

He pulled his black shirt over his head and handed it to her. Julia pressed the cloth against the back of Gray's neck.

'You're going to be fine, Gray.' But the quiver in her voice said otherwise. She glanced at Ryan. 'Where's the bloody ambulance?'

Pulling out his phone, he talked into it urgently, as Julia held his shirt against Gray's wound.

'You're OK,' Julia told her gently. 'Help is coming.'

She could hear other voices coming now, from the end of the hallway. A thundering of feet against the hard floor.

Ryan pulled out a flashlight and turned it on, waving it in the air. 'Down here,' he shouted.

Turning back to Gray, Julia said, 'They're on the way. Stay with me.'

'My mum,' Gray whispered, clutching her arm.

Julia's eyes were steady. She had the most honest face Gray thought she'd ever seen.

'She's safe.' Still pressing the cloth against her neck, she smoothed Gray's hair gently from her face with her free hand.

Relief made Gray feel weak. She thought about Chloe and Jake. Someone needed to tell them. They would be looking for her.

She wanted to tell Julia, but it was too late. A wall of darkness was closing in.

'How're you doing, kid?' Julia asked as the paramedics arrived.

But Gray was falling into the dark.

FORTY-FOUR

When she woke up, the light hurt her eyes.

She tried to blink but her eyelids were so heavy. Lifting them took huge effort. Her eyes felt gritty and her mouth was sour and dry.

At first, she thought she was in her own bed at Number 10. But when she tried to turn her head to look at her alarm clock, a burning pain in her neck made her gasp. And she remembered.

Turning just her eyes now, careful not to move her head, she took in the small, plain hospital room.

Her mother was curled up in a straight-backed chair next to Gray's bed, her head resting on her bent arm. Gray's father was next to her in another chair, his head tilted back. Eyes closed.

Gray blinked hard, thinking for a moment she must be dreaming. But when she opened her eyes again he was still there. She studied him wistfully.

He seemed older. A beard he hadn't had when she saw him last gave him a stranger's face. And there were new grey strands in his wavy dark hair. New lines on his familiar craggy face.

But it was definitely him.

She tried to speak but her throat was too dry. She had to try twice before any sound emerged. 'Daddy?'

She hadn't called him that in years. But somehow, that was what came out.

He went from asleep to wide awake in an instant. Every muscle in his body tensed, poised to leap into action.

Gray observed this with hazy concern. What had happened while he was away to give him a soldier's intensity?

'Gray.' He stood up and reached for her hand, smiling with clear relief. 'Hello, honey. You gave us quite a scare.'

His voice woke Gray's mother, who raised her head, running a hand across her face.

'Is she awake?' she asked her ex-husband, as if Gray weren't right there.

'She's fine.'

Gray's neck burned, and she reached up to touch the spot, but when she lifted her hand a number of tubes snaked with it, and she set it down again.

'He stabbed me.' It came out as a whisper.

'Yes,' her mother told her, reaching for her hand. 'You had surgery last night. You have some tendon damage but you're going to be absolutely fine.'

Gray's eyes flashed to her father. 'Surgery?' Her voice was a dry whisper.

Without answering, he reached to the side table for a plastic glass with a straw. 'Drink.'

The water was tepid and swallowing hurt, but she took a few tentative sips.

'The cut wasn't deep, but the knife nicked an artery,' he told her. 'That's why you lost so much blood so quickly. You gave us a scare.'

Gray's mother reached out to touch Gray's cheek. Both of them were touching her now, as if they needed some tangible proof of life.

'How?' Gray whispered.

'How what, darling?' Her mother bent over to hear her better.

'How did you find me?'

Her father answered. 'The bodyguard – what's her name?'

'Julia,' her mother told him.

He nodded. 'Julia. She figured out that you must have gone to Oxford to help your mother. Chloe found her in the crowd. Told her you needed help inside, and that you weren't answering your phone. She said Jake McIntyre was inside with you but that he couldn't find you.'

'It was the shoes,' her mother said, jumping in. 'When she went inside, Julia couldn't locate you in the crowd. But she saw shoes and your bag outside the maintenance door. When she checked the bag, your phone was inside.'

Her father squeezed Gray's hand. 'That was when a security team got your mother out of there.'

'I didn't know what had happened.' There was pain in her mother's voice, and more than a hint of anger. 'Nobody would tell me anything until we were in the car. Even then, all they would say was there'd been an attack and you were missing.'

'The rest, you know,' her father concluded.

'Jake? Chloe?' Gray whispered, clinging to his hand.

'Both fine. Both worried about you.'

'The man?' Gray was starting to feel more awake. 'Who was he?'

'We don't know everything,' her mother said, 'but we know he's a member of an extremist group with ties to Russia. He has no criminal record. He isn't on a watch list. He joined the catering company four weeks ago. They said he volunteered for this event.' Her voice tightened. 'He told his manager meeting me would be an *honour*.'

Gray thought of that first moment when she'd reached the gallery. The waiter by her side in an instant. That flash of recognition in his eyes.

'Ashford,' Gray whispered hoarsely, looking at her mother.

Her mother and father exchanged a look she couldn't read.

'We don't have proof that he's involved,' her mother said, after a brief hesitation. 'I've passed on everything you told me to the security teams. He'll be investigated, I promise.'

'If he had anything to do with this…' The words seemed to burst from her father's throat, low and savage.

'*If* he did.' Gray's mother stopped him with a stern look. 'He'll go to prison.' She turned back to Gray. 'Did the man say anything to you? Anything at all?'

Gray looked up at her but all she saw was a dark corridor; she felt an arm as hard as steel across her chest, and a knife at her neck.

When she spoke, her voice was unsteady. 'He said he came for you. But I would do.'

Her father stalked across the room to look out of the window, fingers raking through his hair.

Her mother leaned over to press her cheek against Gray's. 'You're safe now. I promise.'

She whispered the words in a voice Gray could remember from when she was three, and had fallen down and skinned her knee. When she was five, and woke up in the dead of night to find herself alone in the dark with a tummy ache. When she was seven, and some girls at school tormented her because they thought her name was weird. She said it in the voice that had always made everything better. A voice Gray seemed to have forgotten. Until now.

All the anger and the deception that had divided them for weeks dissipated into thin air. There was so much Gray wanted to say. So many things she wanted to apologise for. But she was so tired.

She'd have to tell her mother later that she was sorry for lying to her. Sorry for adding to the distrust and bitterness that had pushed them further from the close unit they had once been.

'I love you, Mum,' she whispered.

With the touch of her mother's hands still warm on her cheeks, she closed her eyes and slipped back into darkness.

When she woke again, it was later. The light through the blinds threw long shadows.

She could hear low voices. It took her a second to realise her parents were still in the room. They were talking.

Their voices were so hushed Gray had to strain her ears to hear them.

'Is it really that bad?' her mother was asking.

'It's worse.' Her father's tone was taut. 'This incident – an attempted assassination of the prime minister. An attack on our *daughter*...' His voice tightened. 'It's so aggressive – this will not be the end of it. The man you've caught is a foot soldier. You need whoever hired him. And whoever *he* works for. The generals are who you need.'

'We'll find them,' her mother promised. 'We'll get them.'

'You won't.' Her father's voice was flat. 'He probably doesn't even know who he works for. These are not amateurs, Jess. This organisation is the most dangerous I've ever seen. They've been flying under our radar for years. Quietly growing in strength. Spreading their tentacles all over the world. While we were looking the other way, they were taking over.'

Her mother wasn't having it. 'It can't be that bad. We can't have missed it. The security services cannot have been that blind.'

'They weren't *blind*.' Her father's voice rose just a little, and he paused. When he spoke again it was in a whisper. 'These guys were KGB, Jess. The best spy organisation in history. They are good. They are ruthless. They are organised. This whole thing – the attack on Gray – this is your warning. They have a plan. They're coming for us.'

Gray opened her eyes just enough to see the two of them through her lashes. They had pulled their chairs some distance away from the bed to avoid disturbing her. Her mother was staring at her father with that expression she got when she was figuring things out – eyes narrowed and intense.

'What do you think about Ashford?' her mother asked.

'I think he's joined them.' Her father's reply came without hesitation.

'He's the deputy prime minister, James,' her mother said. 'You can't believe that.'

'I do believe it. And you'd better believe it, too.' He reached for her hand. 'The security services have had suspicions about his connections to Russian money for a long time. You know about the parties on Russian yachts, the five-star retreats all paid for by oligarchs. He's corrupted. The time for doubt is over. This is real.

This is happening. You're the prime minister. You need to find a way to fight back. Before it's too late.'

'But if the security teams can't do anything…'

He cut her off. 'What do you think I've been working on for the last four months?'

He glanced at Gray, who quickly shut her eyes. 'Do you think I'd have voluntarily left my little girl for so long without a good reason? This is what I've been working on.'

At this, Gray's breath hitched. A tear began to roll down her cheek. But she stayed still.

'I've been trying to figure out what they were planning,' her father continued. 'In Moscow, nobody's talking. Not even contacts we've relied on for years will tell us what's going on. The best information came from Polish and Ukrainian security. They're the ones who told me how far it's spread.' He took a breath. 'How bad it really is.'

'You're seriously telling me they've compromised members of the British government at the top level?' Her mother searched his face.

'And the American government,' he said. 'And the EU government. They've people everywhere.'

'What do they want?' Her mother pointed at Gray. 'By doing something like this – what do they expect to gain?'

'All they want is to make us weak. To create chaos.' He threw his cup in the bin. 'And to get their people higher up the food chain. If they get rid of you, because you're traumatised or dead, Ashford is perfectly positioned to be prime minister. If he's working for him, that's all they need. Game over.'

'But they failed,' her mother said.

'This time. They'll try again.' He held her gaze. 'They'll try to get Gray again too. They got so close. They'll be emboldened.'

'How am I supposed to keep her safe, James? She has to have some sort of a life. I feel like I'm imprisoning her. It's awful to see her feeling so trapped.' Her mother sounded tormented.

'You don't have any choice, Jess,' he said. 'We have to send her to Cimmeria Academy. Let them protect her. It's what they do.'

'Is it really safe there?' Her mother didn't sound convinced.

'It has the best security of any school in the country,' her father said. 'It's our only hope.'

Her mother didn't reply right away. When she did, her voice was muffled. 'She hates the idea of boarding school so much. To take her away from Chloe, and this boy, Jake… They've become close. I don't know. '

Her father wasn't backing down.

'Explain it to her.' His voice was steady but firm. 'She's not a child anymore, Jess. She's sixteen. She's smart. She's capable. Tell her the truth. All of it. Let her decide. She'll make the right choice.'

Without warning, he turned and met Gray's eyes with an astute look that said he'd known she was listening all along.

'I have faith in her intelligence,' he said, and it wasn't clear to Gray whether he was talking to her or her mother. 'I always have.'

FORTY-FIVE

It was late on a Tuesday afternoon when Julia emerged from the tangled underground tunnels at Westminster Tube station, onto the busy London street. The November sun was already setting behind the jagged towers of Parliament, turning the old stone walls to a shimmering gold.

It had been a week since the attack in Oxford, but the newspapers hadn't tired of the story. Papers stacked in the corner newsstand held blaring headlines: 'WOULD-BE KILLER'S EXTREME GROUP NOT ON GOVERNMENT WATCHLIST' and 'MCINTYRE DEMANDS TO KNOW HOW POLICE MISSED KNIFEMAN.'

Somehow they'd managed to turn an attack on the prime minister's family into an attack on the prime minister, Julia thought, shaking her head.

The crossing light was green, and she jogged across the wide street as buses grumbled and belched impatiently, then threaded her way through the groups of tourists, commuters, and protestors, passing the tall iron gates outside Downing Street.

Recognising one of the guards, she raised a hand as she passed. He lifted his hand from his machine gun long enough to respond in kind.

But she didn't turn in to the prime minister's street. Instead she made her way past the monolithic government buildings, and turned down an unmarked private street, emerging sometime later, after showing her pass to another guard, in front of the quiet, tucked-away building holding Talos Inc.

Ryan stood waiting for her behind the security barrier, chatting idly with the guard until she walked through.

'There she is,' he said.

'Late as usual.' She finished his sentence with a rueful smile.

'Just a few days off and you become a slacker,' he teased. 'It happens fast.'

She and Ryan had worked 48 hours straight after the event, helping police identify the attacker and begin tracing who had given him his assignment. Central Oxford had been virtually shut down. With police standing guard outside the hospital where Gray was being treated, it had been mayhem.

Julia would never forget those long, dark hours. For nearly a day they'd waited just for the assurance that Gray would survive. The only way she had got through it was by burying herself in her work.

After two days, Raj had ordered both of them to take a few days off and rest. This was her first day back.

The suspect still wasn't talking, but it was beginning to be clear that he did not know the names of the people he worked for. Everything had been done through the dark web, making it virtually untraceable.

Julia and Ryan had a pretty good idea who was involved, though.

They took the lift to Raj's top floor office. The door was open when they walked in.

'Oh good,' their boss said, closing his laptop, and motioning for them to sit across from him. 'How are you? Rested?'

He directed the question to Julia.

'Yes,' she said. 'Ready to get back to work.'

'Good,' he said, giving her an approving look. 'I've got a new assignment for both of you.'

Julia straightened. She'd been expecting this moment. She wanted to stay on Gray's security detail. After all they'd been through, she felt connected to her. But she knew it was normal procedure to rotate out anyone who'd been involved in an attempted attack like the one in Oxford, and bring in a new team.

'As you may know, the prime minister and her ex-husband have decided to send Gray to boarding school. They've chosen one you and I are familiar with,' he said, with a glance at Julia.

Her heart kicked. Gray was going to Cimmeria. The school she'd gone to. The school her parents had pulled her out of against her will. The school where her friend had died.

'Where's that?' Ryan asked, puzzled.

'Cimmeria Academy. You might have heard of it. Its current student body includes the children of the leaders of Poland and Spain, as well as children from some pretty influential business families,' Raj said. 'It keeps a low profile compared to some private schools. But it has a strong security protocol in place.' He cleared his throat. 'I helped to set it up myself, back in the day.'

'Sounds like a good place for her,' Ryan said. 'So, what's our assignment?'

'You're a good team. But I'm splitting you up.' Raj looked back and forth between them. 'Ryan, I'd like you to join the police investigation into the attacker. You know all the background on the things Gray overheard that day, and the prominent people involved. It's a delicate situation, and we need someone to help coordinate, and feed information back to us.'

Julia hid her disappointment. This was the job she'd wanted. She knew as much as he did. It didn't make sense that Raj hadn't chosen her for that. All she wanted to do right now was dig into the organisation behind the attack. She had to know who they were.

Ryan gave a nod. 'You got it, guv.'

Raj turned to Julia, a speculative glint in his eye. 'Your assignment is different,' he said. 'I would like you to stay on as Gray's bodyguard. The two of you have formed a real connection, and I don't think anyone could do a better job protecting her. I want you to go with her to boarding school. It's a secure place, but I want someone who knows her to stay with her until we get to the bottom of this plot to replace her mother. For now, as far I'm concerned, she's not truly safe anywhere.'

Julia kept her expression neutral but she barely heard anything he said after the first sentence.

He's sending me back to Cimmeria, she thought, shocked. Out of anywhere in the world, why does it have to be there?

Suddenly, she realised he'd finished talking. He and Ryan were both looking at her expectantly, and she wasn't sure how long she'd been silent.

'Uh… Yeah,' she said, trying to focus. 'Are you sure it's necessary for me to go to school? I mean, she should be fine there with the security already in place. And I could help Ryan with the investigation here.'

'As I said, we need someone to be with her. In this office, nobody knows more about that school than you do, except me. You know the topography, how difficult it is to secure. You know its weaknesses.' Raj paused. 'You're the one for this.'

Desperately, Julia tried to think of another reason why she couldn't take this assignment. But she could see in his face that 'No' wasn't an option. He'd made his mind up.

Defeated, she said, 'You got it. When am I leaving?'

The look he gave her told her he knew everything she wasn't saying. But all he said was, 'In ten days. Firefly should have recovered enough by then.'

Ten days, Julia thought, with grim resignation. Ten days and I go back to the school I never wanted to see again.

'I guess I'd better pack.' Her voice was toneless.

'I'll have a plan of action for you by then,' Raj continued. 'And you'll need to come to London regularly for updates. Basically though, I think you need to be ready for the unknown. I just have a feeling this threat is still with us. And Gray is not safe.'

TEN DAYS LATER

Gray stood in the middle of her room, surveying the mess she'd made. Every piece of clothing she owned had been unceremoniously dumped on her bed. A suitcase lay empty on the floor nearby.

'What do you even take to boarding school?' she asked.

Chloe, who was perched on her desk, looked up from her phone. 'A motorcycle?' she suggested. 'A hot guy? Cake?'

'All excellent suggestions,' Gray conceded. 'But I only have one suitcase.'

'Definitely cake, in that case,' Chloe decided.

Gray picked up the dress she'd worn to Aidan's ill-fated party. It seemed like a hundred years ago. It had only been a few weeks.

Dropping the dress into the 'not going' pile, she sat down in a clear space on one corner of the bed. 'I guess I won't take much. The letter they sent said I have to wear a uniform, and they provide most of my clothes.'

'A *uniform*.' Chloe wrinkled her nose. 'What are you, twelve?'

Leaving her phone on the desk she walked over and joined Gray on the bed, draping an arm across her back. 'I wish you weren't going.'

'Me too.' Gray leaned her head against her friend's shoulder. Chloe's curly dark hair felt soft beneath her cheek. She smelled of shampoo and that trendy floral perfume she'd been wearing lately. She'd been amazing through all of this.

What was she going to do without her?

'I just don't understand why you have to do this.' Chloe turned to face her. 'I thought you and your mum were getting along better now.'

'We are,' Gray said. 'But I told you. It's a security thing. The group that attacked me – they'll try again.'

After she'd returned from the hospital, she and her parents had talked through her options. To her mother's credit, she'd left it entirely up to Gray.

'I will never make you go if you don't want to,' she'd said. 'And I feel terrible that you have to make this decision. The last thing I want is for you to go away.'

And yet it was clear that she had to go. John Ashford was still her mother's deputy. There was no proof of his involvement in the plot – he'd covered his tracks well. They had the assassin, but not the people who'd hired him. So the threat level was high. If she stayed at Number 10, her activities would be seriously limited. For her own safety – no parties, no trips to the movies, and constant bodyguards. She'd have to pre-book every trip out of the building. Security would sweep any building she entered.

And then there was the press. After news of the attack broke, their obsession with Gray had soared. When she was well enough, she and her mother had been filmed by BBC News in the living room at Number 10.

Gray had still been weak, and it had been stressful, but they'd hoped giving them some footage would diminish the press hunger for stories about her. In fact, the opposite had occurred.

343

Hundreds of cameras were permanently stationed outside Number 10, solely to get a picture of her. Her face had been on the cover of every newspaper. Anna, her mother's press agent, was fielding interview requests from the US, Japan, Korea.

At a school, hidden in the woods, on hundreds of acres of land, tightly secured, the press would never find her. And she would be all alone.

'I'll message you constantly,' she promised Chloe, as she made herself stand up and pack in earnest. 'You'll get so bored of hearing from me.'

'I'll never get bored of hearing from you,' her friend vowed. 'And if anyone gives you a hard time at that stupid school, you just remind them you're the prime minister's bloody daughter.'

They were both laughing when someone tapped on the door. They looked up to see Gray's father standing in the doorway.

'Sorry to interrupt,' he said, surveying the damage in her room with a rueful expression. 'I just wanted to have a minute to say goodbye to my girl.'

Gray's heart twisted, and her smile faded away.

Chloe jumped to her feet. 'I was about to go to the kitchen to get a drink anyway.'

She slipped out. Gray's father stepped inside and closed the door behind him. 'You all ready to go?' he asked.

'Not exactly,' she said, glancing at the mess around her. She gestured at the chair in front of her desk. 'You want to sit?'

He moved a pile of books out of the way and lowered himself onto the delicate white chair. There was something rugged about him that looked incongruous surrounded by the magenta feather boa she'd worn to a party a few months ago, and the sparkly necklaces she had draped from the edge of the mirror above it.

The two of them had talked a lot in the weeks since the attack. She knew for certain now that he worked for the government as a spy. This was why he had disappeared without warning, and couldn't return her calls. On many jobs, it wouldn't be safe to even take his phone with him.

Because of that, it hadn't been Gray's desperate text message that had brought him back this time at all. He hadn't seen that until he was back in the UK. It had been her mother, contacting him through the agency he worked for, who'd brought him back.

'So, are you ready to go?' He was smiling, but there was a melancholy in his expression that reflected her own.

'I guess.' Gray picked up a top from the stack beside her and folded it, just to have something to do with her hands. 'It seems so weird, going to a place I don't know at all, to like, live.'

'It is weird,' he agreed. 'But I do it all the time. And I promise it gets easier.'

She nodded, unconvinced. It was complicated trying to tell your dad your life was hard when he risked his own life all the time.

Misunderstanding her expression, he assured her, 'You're going to be fine. This new school sounds like an excellent place. You will make new friends.'

Gray thought about arriving at the school with a scar on her neck, and news programmes still flashing her picture across TV screens worldwide.

'I'll be fine,' she said. 'Julia's going with me. She'll fight off anyone who isn't nice.'

When he smiled, he looked more like his old self. He'd shaved the beard off, and that made him look younger too. But the silver in his hair was going to take some getting used to.

'What are you going to do now?' she asked. 'Are you going back to Russia?'

'Not right away. I'm helping with the investigation into this plot. I may go back in a month or so, if needed. But for now, I'll be around.'

Gray felt betrayed. *He's finally staying in London and I'll be gone.*

As if he knew what she was thinking, his face shadowed. 'I'm sorry I've been away for so long, kiddo. I feel like I let you down, being gone when all this bad stuff was happening here. If I'd known…'

'Don't apologise,' she said. 'You had to be there. And you came back when I needed you. That's what matters.'

She paused. From down the hall, she could hear Chloe and her mother laughing about something.

'Dad, what are we going to do about Richard?' she asked quietly. 'Was it him that night in Parliament?'

He looked away, a muscle flickering in his jaw. When he spoke, his voice was measured.

'We believe you were right, and it was Richard you saw that night. We've checked his flight records — he left for New York the day after he told you and your mother he was travelling. He was in the country that day, he spent the night at his club, and we've found him on CCTV inside Parliament.'

Gray stared at him. Out of everything she remembered about that night in Parliament, she'd most wanted to be wrong about stepfather. For her mother's sake.

'Is he part of the plot? You have to arrest him. Mum could be in danger.' She whispered it urgently.

'Hang on.' He held up his hands. 'We don't believe he *is* part of the plot.'

Gray's brow furrowed. 'Then why did he lie?'

Her father paused, choosing his words. 'It looks as if he has been working with a few members of your mother's party to get a bill passed to help his company. She knows nothing about this, and she does not support the bill.'

'I don't understand,' Gray said, puzzled.

'Basically, he's gone behind your mother's back to do something she doesn't want, because it will help his business and make him a lot of money.' He rubbed his jaw. 'And I have no idea how to tell her that, or even whether I should. It's none of my business, after all. But I can tell you, there is no evidence that he is one of the people trying to kill her.'

Somehow this made Gray feel even worse. That her mother was being betrayed by the man she loved over nothing. It wasn't even ideology. It was money.

'I hate him,' she said passionately. 'He's horrible. Why did she marry him? He's been dying for her to send me away since he got here. And he lies.'

Her father studied her with those wise eyes the same dark blue as her own. 'But your mother loves him.'

'Yeah.' Her face flushed. That was the problem.

'So. There we are.' He leaned forward, resting his forearms on his knees. 'Sweetie, there's a thing you're going to have to learn, about compromising when it comes to other people's choices. And this is a big one, because he's in your life. But I think you need to find a way to live with him. If he makes things better for your mother – that's not a bad thing.'

'But he's lying to her,' Gray pointed out.

Her father's face tightened. 'Yeah, OK. I don't like him much either. But I'm not married to him, and neither are you.' He reached across the space to take her hand. 'You are two years away from being eighteen, and being able to live wherever you want. And I think you're going to like your new life at this school in the meantime. Let your mother deal with her own choices. She can handle someone like Richard. Do you think you can tough out two years?'

Gray squeezed his sturdy, familiar hand, suddenly so grateful to have him here. To be able to rely on him. To tell him her problems.

'I can tough it out if you can,' she said.

'That's my girl.'

He stood. 'Right. I need to get back to work. Give me a hug right this minute.'

Jumping to her feet, she threw herself into his arms. As he held her tight, she closed her eyes, memorising this feeling of warmth and safety. Here, nothing could hurt her.

'I missed you so much,' she whispered.

'I missed you, too, sweetheart,' he said. And held her tighter.

Two hours later, Chloe had gone and Gray's suitcase was nearly full. She was putting the last things in when her mother knocked on her bedroom door.

'There's someone here to see you.'

Gray looked up in surprise. Aside from Chloe, she wasn't allowed guests. 'Who is it?'

Her mother gave her a mysterious look. 'I think you'd better come and see for yourself.'

Puzzled, Gray followed her down the hallway.

She thought it might be Julia. She was still in charge of Gray's security – in fact, ever since that night at the museum, her mother wouldn't trust anyone else.

But when she walked into the living room, it wasn't her bodyguard who stood waiting for her. It was Jake.

Speechless, Gray turned to her mother for an explanation.

'I've some things to do.' Her mother rested a hand lightly on Gray's shoulder before adding quietly, 'You need to leave in twenty minutes.'

Gray waited until she'd gone into her bedroom, before throwing herself at him. His body felt thin and wiry against hers. But also strong and warm. 'I can't believe you're here. I thought I wouldn't get to see you again.'

With her crushing him in a hug, he answered into her hair. 'Your mum set it all up. I think my dad's got her all wrong, you know?'

'How'd you get in?' she asked. 'What about the press? Your dad will lose it if he finds out.'

'I came in through the Foreign Office down the street, so the photographers wouldn't see me,' he said.

She pulled him over to the sofa and sat down next to him.

'I'm going to miss you so much,' she said, not for the first time.

'We'll stay in touch all the time,' Jake promised. 'And you'll come home for Christmas, right? I'll come down from Leeds to see you. That's in less than two months.'

It was true. But two months seemed to stretch out endlessly. Nearly sixty days, in a school surrounded by strangers.

The two of them were only friends, but she liked him more than that. Or she thought she did. Everything had happened so fast, and there'd been no chance to find out if there could be more to their relationship. Now, she'd never know. They'd be miles apart.

It felt as if the chance that they might have something together had passed quietly, while she wasn't looking. And now it was gone.

But it was too late to talk about that. So she told him about the packing, and not knowing what to bring. How the letter the headmistress had sent suggested bringing a 'formal gown' for a winter ball.

'And there was a whole page of rules. No leaving the grounds without permission. No going into the woods after dark?' She held up her hands. 'Where is this school anyway? Transylvania?'

Jake, who'd been listening quietly as she prattled on, captured her hands in his.

'I hate that you have to go,' he told her quietly. 'But I know without question you'll be fine. And I think it's the right thing to do.'

Just like that, Gray was crying.

Everything she'd bottled up, all the things she'd said about how she understood why this had to happen, and how it was the right decision – it was all lies.

'What's this?' he said, surprised. 'You want to go.'

'I know.' She swiped her tears away with the back of her hand. 'It's just, it feels like I'm leaving at the wrong time. Mum and I are finally getting along. My dad's back. And then there's you.'

'Gray, it's not safe here.' He smoothed the hair back from her face. 'You know that. You can't risk it.'

'I know.' She'd stopped crying now. She was holding it together. But she looked at him anxiously.

'You won't forget about me when I'm gone?' Shaking his head, he tried to answer but she spoke over him. 'People forget. And Jake, I'd hate it if you forgot.'

His gaze held hers. 'Who could forget you, Gray Langtry?'

He pulled her into a rough hug. And Gray tried not to think that this was goodbye.

Just after four o'clock that afternoon, a sleek, four-door government-issued car drove through a thick stretch of forest and arrived at a set of tall black gates, as the last of the day's light was fading from the sky.

In the gloomy shadows of tall pine trees, the car stopped. Gray sat in the passenger seat, staring into the shadows.

She'd said goodbye to her parents at Number 10, and slipped out through one of the side entrances two hours earlier. Nobody in the media was going to be informed about where she'd gone.

The entire journey had been conducted in absolute secrecy.

At the wheel, Julia stared at the gates, her hands gripping the wheel tightly.

She'd told Gray that she used to be a student here, but that was all she'd said. She hadn't mentioned that she'd left under a cloud. Or that she still saw this place in her dreams – and in her nightmares.

How could she explain all that to a girl she was supposed to protect?

Now, as she stared at the forbidding black bars, her stomach was so tense she thought she might be sick.

'How do we get in?' Gray asked. 'Is there a bell or something?'

'No,' Julia said. 'You wait. And if they want you in, they open it.' There was hint of resentment in her voice.

As if it heard her, the imposing gate shuddered and began to move, sliding back slowly, with a screech of metal.

'I guess they want us,' said Gray.

Julia didn't respond.

Raj had been right. She knew everything about this school. She knew its forests and smooth lawns, the little chapel hidden in the woods, and the spooky castle ruins at the top of a hill. She also knew that it had state of the art security.

But no one was safe now. Not even here. And she had one job – to protect Firefly.

She intended to do that by any means necessary.

Gray peered into the gloom as the gate settled into place with a clanging of metal.

'Right.' Julia shifted the car into gear. There'd been a strange nervousness to her throughout the journey. The closer they got to the school, the quieter she became. Her mood was contagious, and Gray found herself shivering as they drove onto a smooth gravel drive that curved through the dark forest. Her muscles were so tense the scar on her neck throbbed. A reminder of why she was here.

The car's headlights flashed across thick tree trunks, disappearing into the shadowed spaces between them. The place felt ancient – prehistoric. Cut off from the world.

Slowly, the car followed one last dark bend and a building appeared in front of them.

The rambling, four-storey Victorian mansion was backlit dramatically by the setting sun, which lost itself behind the high peaked roofs, glinting off black metal spires that jutted up as if trying to stab the sky. All the windows were aglow and for a moment, it gave the illusion that the school was alight. Flames flickering at the glass.

Gray blew out a breath. 'That's my *school*?'

They pulled up to the low front steps and cut the engine. Neither of them moved. They stared at the building. The only sound was the ticking of the engine as it cooled.

'Well, I guess we should get out.' Julia sounded nearly as uncertain as Gray felt.

When they opened the car doors, the cold air smelled of pine needles and wet grass. That in itself felt foreign to Gray, who instantly missed London's asphalt and exhaust.

The place felt strangely empty – as if they were the only people there. Their voices sounded too loud, and they compensated for this by talking in whispers as they unloaded the luggage.

They were moving the last bags when two figures appeared in the distance, racing across the grass towards them. Both were tall and dressed in black. They moved with almost sinuous athleticism, every step in sync.

Gray spotted them first. She didn't like the way they moved.

'Julia.' Her voice was taut. 'Someone's coming.'

Automatically, the bodyguard dropped the bag she held and stepped between Gray and the new arrivals.

As the runners neared, Gray saw that one was a man and the other a woman. Up close, they looked too old to be students, but young for teachers. Next to her, she noticed Julia stiffen.

The two stopped a short distance away and began to walk. Despite the exertion, they weren't breathless. They weren't sweating.

The woman said something to the man, who dropped back as the woman continued towards them. She had long, golden-brown hair and an oval face. Her eyes were the colour of a winter storm approaching.

Julia moved back to stand beside Gray, her hands limp at her side.

When the woman neared them, something passed between the two of them – a glint of recognition. And something else – something like distrust.

But then the woman turned to Gray, and gave a smile.

'You must be Gray.' Her voice was steady, assured. She looked absolutely fearless.

'My name's Allie Sheridan. I'm the acting headmistress.' She held out her hand. 'Welcome to Cimmeria Academy.'

An exclusive look at the
opening chapter of Book 2…

CODENAME
FIREFLY

ONE

It was late and Gray was running through the frozen dark. Around her the woods crowded in, thick and threatening, branches stretching out as if to grab her. The moon had disappeared behind the clouds some time ago, leaving her stumbling along a path she could barely see. Her fingers, clenched into fists, were numb. It had rained all day and now the December night was turning the water to ice.

The wind picked up, shaking the trees and sending a shower of frozen water from the sodden pine needles, sending ice down her spine.

With each strep she thought of the people who had brought her to this place. Her mother – the prime minister. Her father – the spy. And the men who'd tried to kill her – a shadowy group of traitors who wanted power at any cost.

Thinking of them made her furious. Hatred kept her warm.

It was the only way she was getting through this.

A jutting tree root lost in the dark caught her toe and she reeled forward, pinwheeling her arms until she caught her balance. Swearing under her breath, she slowed to a walk, her lungs burning.

She wanted to go home.

Not the prime minister's residence at Number 10 Downing Street where she'd lived in the months before she came here, but her home *before*. The south London flat she'd shared with her mother, before everything changed. If she closed her eyes, she could see its comfortable worn rugs and the long, navy sofa, cushions flattened into a cosy nest. Her little room on the top floor, with its view of tree tops, chimneys, and red brick houses.

The memory was so strong, it made her chest ache with longing and, for a fleeting instant, she could almost smell its toast and marmalade morning scent. Feel the warm sun flooding through the windows on a summer day—

A snapping sound jerked her from her lonely thoughts.

Her breath caught and she spun around, scanning the dark woods around her. Nothing stirred.

What had made that noise?

Maybe it's a fox or a badger or something, she reasoned. *They live in woods.*

But some primordial instinct much older than her made the fine hairs on the back of her neck rise. That part of her knew animals wouldn't make that sound. That sound had been made by a human.

The attack was coming.

Her heart began to race, fluttering erratically in her chest. Her thoughts grew muddy. She had to run. She had to run *now*.

Spinning around, she began stumbling back toward the main building, trying to remember everything she'd been taught. But her mind had gone blank. Her chest tightened until she could barely draw a breath.

Sweat stung her eyes. Without slowing, she glanced to the right and instantly regretted it. Something was moving in the bushes. A shadow shifting just out of sight, lost in the darkness.

Above the sound of her feet thumping unevenly on the path, and the *thudthudthud* of her heart, she thought she could hear hiss of branches moving and then sliding back into place.

She turned to look over her shoulder and instantly tripped over a fallen tree branch. This time, she went sprawling, landing hard. The rough earth scraped her hands and burned her knees, but she barely felt the pain as she scrambled back to her feet lurching forward unsteadily. Before she'd taken three steps, a figure clad all in black burst out of the shadows onto the path just behind her.

All the breath left Gray's lungs.

All dressed in black. A knife in his hand…

She froze. She felt as cold as the ground on which she stood. Unable to move.

"Leave me alone." The words came out as breath, lost on the breeze.

He advanced on her steadily, his features hidden behind a balaclava, his empty hands twitching at his sides.

No knife, she realised, distantly. But by then, it was too late to run. He was upon her.

The second his hands touched her she recovered her voice, screaming so hard her throat burned. Now she could fight, and her hands clawed at his head and shoulders, her feet drumming against his legs as he swung her into the air.

"Let me go! Let me go!"

"Jesus, Gray, will you calm down?" a male voice grumbled gruffly in her ear, as he set her back down.

Another black-clad body burst out of the trees and joined them.

"What's the matter?" The new person demanded, lifting the fabric covering her head and face. A shock of short blonde hair caught the moonlight and she saw her bodyguard, Julia Masterson looking at her with concern.

At the sight of her, Gray began to sob in earnest.

The man removed his headgear, and through her tears she saw the familiar brooding features of Carter West, the school's security expert. He observed her meltdown with a steady, concerned frown.

Julia pulled a water bottle from her pocket and handed it to her, resting a hand lightly on her shoulder. "It's all over. You're safe. Drink this."

Gray took a small sip. The water cooled her throat. She took another sip, and another. Slowly her breathing returned to normal.

"I'm sorry," she mumbled, looking down at the bottle in her hand. "I panicked again."

"Don't worry about it. It's a process. You'll get better at this." The bodyguard's voice was confident, but Gray was very aware that Carter had said nothing. He was always thoughtful and laconic, and yet she found herself resenting that he was here at all. His silence felt like judgement.

She wanted to shout: 'You don't know what it was like that night, when an assassin dragged me away from a crowded party and told me I was going to die! You didn't feel a knife slicing your skin! You have no idea why this is so hard.'

Julia, though, had been there. She'd fought the man off and saved Gray's life. She understood. She was just trying to help. But it wasn't working.

The three of them began walking down the wooded path toward the school, the air heavy with everything nobody was saying.

It still felt strange to Gray, being out in the country after years in London. She could hear no cars, no sirens, no trains rattling by. No sounds of civilisation at all. But, the woods didn't seem nearly as frightening now as they had a few minutes ago. It wasn't even that dark — the moon had reappeared and there were stars overhead.

It never feels quite so dark when you're not alone.

An icy breeze froze the sweat on the back of her neck. Shivering, she shoved her hands deeper into the pockets of her fleece and yanked the hood up around her face.

This was all pointless, anyway. When Julia came up with the idea to try to teach her self-defence techniques, Gray hadn't been very keen on the idea, especially after her bodyguard suggested doing the training at night.

The truth was, she was really fine as long as it wasn't dark, as long as the attacker wasn't male, as long as she knew what was coming.

So, she was basically useless, then. A victim waiting to happen.

Ahead of her, Julia and Carter were talking in hushed voices, their heads bent towards each other. Gray held her breath to hear them above the noise of the breeze through branches.

"She panics so fast, Jules," she heard Carter say softly. "Fear completely immobilises her."

The December wind swirled around, ruffling Gray's hood, and cutting off what Julia said next. She only caught the end of the sentence: "…she's traumatised. Give her time."

Gray dug her hands deeper into her pockets. She didn't feel traumatised. She felt like a failure.

She trudged along, lost in her thoughts until they emerged from the treeline and, suddenly, the huge, Victorian gothic school building appeared in front of them, glowing with light, like something out of a dream. Cimmeria was an imposing four-story structure with two sprawling wings. Rows of arched windows looked down on them below a roof that rose up into sharp peaks. At the highest point, tall chimneys thrust up at the sky like fists.

As she stared up at it, Julia dropped back to walk alongside her. "We'll try again tomorrow," she said, a perky note in her voice. "We'll stick to the training room. Maybe if you're not in the dark…"

"…I won't freak out?" Gray finished the sentence for her, morosely.

"You'll get there."

Julia was saying all the right things but, as they crossed the smooth green lawn and climbed the steps to the imposing front door with its ancient, elaborate locking system, Gray didn't feel any better.

Inside, the air was warm and dry. They walked along a worn stone floor beneath faded, antique tapestries and candleholders that stood four feet tall. Through another door and then they were in a long, wide hallway with oak panelled walls and oil paintings in gilded frames that had, from the very beginning, reminded Gray of London's Houses of Parliament.

When they reached a wide staircase that curved up beneath a glittering chandelier, Carter stopped. "Have a good night," he told them both. Giving Gray a direct look, he added with unexpected warmth, "Jules is right – it'll get better. Just keep falling up."

In her rare encounters with him, the school's handsome young security director had always been just a little distant and, for a moment Gray was so surprised she couldn't think of anything to say.

She managed, 'Thanks,' as he jogged away, lifting a hand in response.

NUMBER 10

Julia and Gray trudged up the elegant stairs, their movements watched by the painted eyes of men in elegant 19th century suits and women in fantastic dresses, draped in pearls.

At the landing, they passed three statues on low plinths in front of huge windows hidden behind velvet curtains, before turning into a second, simpler staircase, which led to a slim corridor lined on either side by identical doors, each painted plain white with a number in black. It was curfew, and the dorm was a hive of activity – girls running down the to the bathroom and showers, chattering non-stop. They were all too sophisticated by far to stare at Gray, but she felt their eyes against her back as they reached the door with the number 326 painted on it. She stepped aside, waiting as Julia opened the door and flipped on the light.

The bodyguard did a quick assessment of the room — and then walked back out again.

"Safe as houses," she told Gray, who attempted a wan smile, but failed.

Julia's face softened. "Get some sleep, Firefly," she said, gently. "Tomorrow will be better."

Firefly was Gray's codename with the Secret Service agents responsible for protecting the first family. Nobody used it here, except Julia. It had become a kind of nickname between them.

"You keep saying that," Gray said.

"Because it's true." Julia rested a warm hand on her shoulder for just a second. "I promise."

Gray wanted to accept this, but it was just so hard to believe when she'd had two weeks of bad days.

After the door closed and the bodyguard was gone, Gray let out a long breath. Maybe Julia was right and tomorrow would be different. But she doubted it. Today had been lonely. Tomorrow would be lonely. And the day after that.

Blinking back tears, she studied her reflection in the frameless mirror on the back of the door. She thought she looked ridiculous in the dark blue exercise gear with the still-unfamiliar Cimmeria Academy crest on the left chest. Her dark, wavy hair was escaping from the ponytail she'd pulled it into an hour ago, tendrils curling loose around her face. Her cheeks were bright red. Her dark blue eyes glistened with unhappiness.

"Pull yourself together," she told the image in the glass.

But the truth was, she didn't know how to do that.

Her phone vibrated and she pulled it from her pocket. Her best friend Chloe's name was on the screen.

She hit answer. Chloe's familiar face appeared, dark hair pulled back in a braid, beaming at her.

'There you are!' she said, with typical enthusiasm. 'I've been calling all night. I have to tell you what happened today. Tyler Bolino asked me to Aidan's Christmas party. Can you believe it? I didn't even know what to say. I mean he's gorgeous, obviously, but he's kind of boring and you know…'

She chatted on and Gray tried to relate. Aidan's parties were the events of the year back at her south London school. His dad was a nightclub owner and concert promoter, and he always made them incredible, renting out a hotel ballroom and decorating it into a winter wonderland.

There was no way she'd get to go, of course, now that she was here. There was no guarantee she'd go home for Christmas at all — her mother had been hazy on that point lately. Everyone was obsessed with security, security, security. Which made sense after everything that happened.

But still. Chloe's voice fizzed with enthusiasm, and Gray felt completely left behind.

Finally noticing her silence, Chloe stopped, and said, 'Hey, you're really quiet. Are you okay?'

Gray, biting back tears of unhappiness, said, 'Yes... I mean, no. Oh, I don't know.' She forced a laugh. 'I just miss you so much. And I hate that I can't be there.'

'I miss you, too,' Chloe said, sobering. 'Nothing is fun without you. And now I have to decide about Tyler Bolino by myself, all because of stupid terrorists chasing you away. It's hideous.'

Gray laughed through her tears. 'Go out with him, you idiot. He's cute. You'd be an adorable couple.'

'Yeah, but all he ever talks about is rugby.'

'So, don't talk to him. Wear him on your arm like a fancy bag.'

The easy banter they'd always had cheered her a little, and Gray kicked off her damp trainers and settled down on the bed, shaking off her hoodie and throwing it onto the floor.

Lifting a soft blue blanket off the footboard, she wrapped it around herself, creating a warm nest. The cold that had sunk into her bones outside began to fade at last.

At least for a while she could talk to her best friend and pretend she was home, and everything was fine. And Cimmeria was just a bad dream that would disappear in the morning.

ACKNOWLEDGEMENTS

This book would never have happened without a dedicated cadre of Night School fans who never stopped asking me to write Night School 6. I have received hundreds — if not thousands — of emails from around the world all asking the same question. I didn't feel that I could continue the Night School story I'd explored in the five books of that series. It felt complete. But the idea of what it was like to be the daughter of the prime minister kept coming back to me. A new story, with new characters, in that world. That, I realised, I could do. So thank you to everyone who has written to me over the years. I'm very grateful to each and every one of you for being there in my inbox, on Facebook, on Instagram and in my book club.

I also owe an incalculable debt to my editor, Karen Ball. We worked together on Night School, and are, at last, reunited by Number 10. She's absolutely one of the best in the business and I am so privileged to work with her. More thanks go as well to the brilliant editor Helen Grant, who proofread the manuscript and sorted out my commas. Helen is also an award-winning novelist, and her ghost stories are not to be missed!

Huge thanks also to the small but mighty team at my new publishing imprint, Moonflower Publishing, especially to the multi-talented Jasmine Aurora, who was responsible for the fabulous cover and the interior design of Number 10, as well as the new Night School redesign. I cannot imagine what we would do without her.

Thanks always to my amazing agent, Madeleine Milburn, who fights like a tiger to make sure the books I write get into your hands.

And, as always thanks to Jack Jewers. He is the first reader of every single book I write, and the first person I want to talk to when everything is great, and the first one to fix things when everything is terrible.

ABOUT THE AUTHOR

A former crime reporter and accidental civil servant, C.J. Daugherty began writing the Night School series while working as a communications consultant for the British government. The series was published by Little Brown in the UK, and went on to sell over a million and a half copies worldwide. A web series inspired by the books clocked up well over a million views. In 2020, the books were optioned for television. She later wrote The Echo Killing series, published by St Martin's Press, and co-wrote the fantasy series, The Secret Fire, with French author Carina Rosenfeld. Her books have been translated into 25 languages and been bestsellers in multiple countries. She lives with her husband, the BAFTA nominated filmmaker, Jack Jewers.

Follow C. J. DAUGHERTY on...

INSTAGRAM @cj_daugherty
YOUTUBE /nightschoolbook
TWITTER @cj_daugherty
FACEBOOK /CJauthor

Join her book club at...
www.christidaugherty.com

Christi●Daugherty

Allie Sheridan's life is falling apart.

She hates her school. Her brother has run away. And she's just been arrested. Again. This time, her parents are sending her away for a 'fresh start'. And yet, instead of hating boarding school, Allie is surprised to find she likes it. She's making friends. And there's Carter, a brooding loner with whom she feels an instant connection. But Cimmeria Academy is no ordinary school. Her classmates — and her teachers — are hiding something. And soon it becomes clear that this is a very dangerous place. And that nobody can be trusted.

Discover the million selling series that started it all.
All CJ's books are available in good book stores, or from
www.moonflowerbooks.co.uk